THE SNOWMAN & THE SCARECROW

(Another Dark Comedy for Grown-Ups)

Adrian Baldwin

Also by Adrian Baldwin

BARNACLE BRAT
STANLEY McCLOUD MUST DIE!

Dark Comedy Fiction

Books: Novels and Short Stories
for Grown-Ups

Welcome to my World

This one's for Harry, Keira and Jamie.

Acknowledgements and the usual Warning

Firstly, the warning: As it states on the cover, this is a novel aimed at *grown-ups*. The story is *not* for youngsters. Why? Because some of my characters use Adult Language; often foul, blasphemous, or sexually charged – on several occasions, *all three*. I didn't necessarily *want* them to but sometimes they insisted. That's characters for you! Some of them can be a right bunch of f***ers.

Okay, now I've got that out of the way, the acknowledgements:

I'd like to gratefully recognise the help of some very important members of my team: Harry Baldwin, who checked that teenage parlance and attitude were reasonably realistic and not just the 'down with the kids' ramblings of an old fart; and of course, Maggie Fitzpatrick-Reeves and Bronwen Burgess for their continued and indispensible assistance, wherever it was necessary, with grammar, spelling, punctuation, ideas, continuity, facts, logic, clarity and all that other good stuff where I goofed from time to time.

Oh, and Americans please note: the British English spelling of words has been used throughout.

And a final thanks need go to Denise Bentulan, who granted the author commercial license for her wonderful font: *Denne's Old Handwriting*. Check out her fonts at: douxiegirl.com

THE SNOWMAN & THE SCARECROW

(Another Dark Comedy for Grown-Ups)

'Never play to the gallery. Never work for other people. It's terribly dangerous for an artist to fulfil other people's expectations. They generally produce their worst work that way. And if you feel safe in the area you're working in, you're not working in the right area. Always go a little further into the water than you feel you can cope with. Go a little bit out of your depth. And when you don't feel that your feet are quite touching the bottom, you're just about in the right place to do something exciting.'

- David Bowie

PROLOGUE
Setting the Scene

Picture if you will a high panoramic view of timeless countryside, verdant and rolling, crisp and cold, under a sharp, bright winter sky. And as we glide, sailing as if cloud, we hear a voice, almost godlike; resonant, pervasive and wise; an utterance that somehow makes us feel it possesses knowledge of things that we do not.

'All over the world,' informs the voice, 'in rural villages and small towns off the beaten track, country folk have told tales for millennia of bygone heroes, enchantment and magic, local legends of the supernatural, strange events and mythological beings. Stories handed down through generations.'

The accent is difficult to pin down; somewhere between cool, gentle African-American, and calm, well-informed Brit; it is authoritative, reassuring and confident – with perhaps just a dash of swagger or flamboyance. If this were a film, it would surely have required a seasoned actor to narrate: Morgan Freeman or John Hurt perhaps; Alan Rickman, Sam Elliot or Samuel L. Jackson – maybe Christopher Walken or Geoffrey Rush. Imagine whoever you like, it's all good as they say, but for best results choose someone with absolute reliability, a mellow soothing tone and genuine gravitas. Actually, as we are in Wales, perhaps we could agree to settle on Sir Anthony Hopkins . . .

'And whatever the tale, good or bad, funny or sad,' continues the voice, 'it would normally find an enthusiastic audience, eager to hear more. Storytelling has a long tradition in the countryside.'

Field after field passes below: farming land; agricultural heaven – and we begin to descend, softly, by degrees.

'Of course, not all stories are spiritually edifying, sometimes they're simply tales of what's been happening in the neighbourhood, and to whom. Not stories at all. Not really – not in the true sense of the word – just gossip, hearsay and tittle-tattle, and, frankly, of little interest. No, what we desire are unforgettable urban myths, hypnotic works of fiction . . . ripping yarns.'

Moving lower, ancient countryside gently rising, the land draws us in towards its crops and gorse and stationary sheep then aims us in the direction of a small, backwater market town in the near distance. We soar over trees, low stone walls and yet more fields, one of which contains a handful of static caravans where, atop one of the parked homes, caw four crows – technically enough for a murder.

'Prepare to meet Joseph Edward Evans,' advises the narrator, 'son of Paul Evans, grandson of Wilfred Evans, and great-grandson of Percy Evans . . . or just Joe to his friends.'

Sweeping over the town we spot a small school and swoop down as if we were a wing-suited skydiver or stooping falcon. We skim over school grounds, breach swinging doors (the main building's entrance), shoulder-surf a corridor, turn a corner, fly around another, then exit a high open window before finally slowing to a stop on the far side of the playground. (It would have been quicker to simply travel here directly but never mind, the scenic route is always nice.) And here we hover, ghostlike, at a height of eight-to-ten feet, above a group of kids, teenagers mostly but only just; close enough to feel their edginess, catch a rolled eye and stifled yawn, sense their growing restlessness: a heightening frustration with the one doing all the talking.

'Joe is twelve,' speaks the voice, 'and like his grandfather and great-grandfather before him, Joe loves to tell stories.'

Cheeky-faced, a frizzy Fro of curly red hair and affable manner, Joe appears happy, healthy, if a tad overweight, and, though jocular by nature, sad to say, somewhat blind to rising waves of apathy. On and on he drones – something about a toad, a scorpion, and a river – addressing a crescent moon of his peers, oblivious, it seems, to their rapidly diminishing levels of attentiveness.

'But, despite Joe's charming nature,' continues the narrator, 'he'd never really grasped the true magic of storytelling. Try as he may, he just wasn't very good at it. Shall we listen for a moment?'

'So the frog said he would take the scorpion, on his back, over the river,' spouts Joe, 'but when he got halfway across, the scorpion *did* sting him. "But why?" asked the frog sinking.' Joe mimes an amphibious drowning. ' "Why did you do that? Now we'll both drown." "I couldn't help myself," said the scorpion. "It's my nature." '

To a chorus of disappointed grumbles the audience quickly dissolves and drifts away to classes. Joe is left shouting ineffective explanations at parting backs.

'Don't you get it? *His nature!*' Fleshy fingers find chunky hips. 'The scorpion couldn't help himself,' he calls. 'It's his nature!'

'Like I said, not very good at it.'

'But it's Aesop! Aesop's fables,' appeals Joe. 'Don't any of you read?'

'All that would soon change, though,' narrates the voice, 'and in a most sudden and spectacular way. I'll meet Joe in a little while. And you will meet me.'

CHAPTER 1

Let it Snow

The room has a strong snow theme: Raymond Briggs Snowman bedding; model AT-AT (snow-walking vehicle from The Empire Strikes Back) on the bedside table; snowscape pictures and posters; and the remaining wall space taken up by lines of shelves: one a display shelf for a multitude of snow-globes, the rest home to several rows of books:

All of *Lemony Snicket's A Series of Unfortunate Events* novels, every *Diary of a Wimpy Kid* book, Tolkien's *The Hobbit* and *Lord of the Rings*, Jack London's *The Call of the Wild*, and the *Percy Jackson* series, to name just a few.

Had you been here a few hours ago you would have found him with his nose buried in Stephen King's *The Eyes of the Dragon*.

He's not reading now.

Joe, currently sporting a brown dressing gown over blue-and-white striped pyjamas, is playing an MMO (Massive Multiplayer Online) computer war game. He's trying hard to be helpful to his teammates, offering directives or following instructions, but he keeps dying; his on-screen character suffering a variety of sudden demises: explosion, sniped from distance, machine-gunned or knifed at close-quarters, flattened by speeding Humvee, that kind of thing.

'Oh come on!' barks Joe as he's fragmented by a grenade. 'Again? Seriously?!'

'Boom!' squawks a thin, tinny voice.

'Never mind, Joe,' encourages another filtered voice through the background of laughter. 'We'll get you back at the next spawn point.'

'Joe? Joe, you there?' asks the discarded headset as the battle rages on around Joe's dismembered corpse, his mates still playing like pros despite being outnumbered by oncoming enemies.

'Shit, Joe, you've not fuckin' rage quit again, have you?' barks a third voice.

'Not having much luck, Joe?' This question posed by the grizzle-haired chap in the doorway. 'I did knock.'

'Nah, it's fine, Gramps, come in – stupid game anyway.'

Joe turns off the monitor and unplugs his headphones. He kicks off his Snowman slippers, shrugs off his dressing gown, jumps into bed and slips under the 'We're Flying Through The Air' quilt.

Joe's grandfather walks his white whiskers over to the bed, sits beside his grandson, and beams a smile as warm as his big old heart. Wilf may be late seventies, slightly bowlegged and missing a tooth or two, but he doesn't look a day over sixty-five. Not in Joe's eyes.

'Ready for a story?' asks Wilf.

A spirited nod from Joe.

'Okay, you shuffle.'

Wilf hands over a pack of cards and Joe shuffles awkwardly; for these are not the usual set of fifty-two – here there are at least a couple of hundred cards, maybe more.

'You sure you don't want to tell? It'd be good preparation.'

'No, you.'

Wilf tugs an imaginary cap. 'Well, alright, sir.'

Not the smoothest of shuffles but Joe's pink and portly fingers mix well enough. Only one card spills: it lands face up on the quilt. Queen of Spades? Seven of Diamonds? No, for these are not playing cards at all; these cards contain neither suits nor values Ace through King – indeed they bear no relationship to the traditional pack everyone is familiar with. These cards contain only words; mostly nouns but some verbs and adjectives – one word per card, and each unique.

In the case of the fallen card, the word is Pitchfork.

'Okay, let's take that as our first,' smiles Wilf. 'One last shuffle, Joe, then pick the other four; no looking, mind – one discard.'

'I know, I know,' frowns Joe playfully.

'Bit old for bedtime stories, isn't he?' huffs Paul staring at the living-room ceiling.

'He's twelve,' Sally reminds him.

'Exactly; he'll be thirteen in a few weeks – a teenager.'

'This from the man who still thinks it's okay to tell him what to wear.'

'Have you seen the latest clothes in his wardrobe?'

'Of course I have, who do you think bought them?'

'He'll be a laughing stock, if he isn't already.'

'Jeez, give it a rest, Paul,' chides Sally, a warm, pretty woman with large red specs and prominent prenatal bump. 'They all wear stuff like that now, you old fuddy-duddy.'

'What next? One of those weird side-cuts?'

'Maybe. Why not?'

'No, no, I'm not having it.'

Paul jumps off the sofa and paces the room.

Sally removes her glasses and stares at her husband. Paul Evans is a short, tubby man of forty-five with thinning hair forever volumised by hairdryer and/or product: spray, gel, mousse and wax – you name it; Paul uses it.

'I happen to think he'd look good with a side-cut,' adds Sally. 'And stop pacing; you know it does my head in.'

'No, no, no, it's all going too far. And I'm sorry, but I blame you. If you didn't—'

'Ooh,' winces Sally leaning forward on the sofa.

'What is it?'

'Probably just junior,' fibs Sally, a convenient white lie to shutdown her husband. Once Paul gets on a roll . . .

'Maybe we should call a doctor. That's the third today.'

'I'm fine. I'll take a fresh glass of water, though.'

'Sure. You just relax and I'll be right back.'

And with that Paul heads off to the kitchen.

'No hurry,' whispers Sally. She pops her glasses back on and returns to her book, a horror anthology of clown-based short stories. 'Relax,' she scoffs. 'Not sure how I'm meant to do that with Snappy McShortfuse always up and down.' She eyes her swollen tummy and nods as if she heard it speak. 'That's true,' she responds, patting him or her. 'And trust me; I would have a spliff if it wasn't for you, my precious little passenger.'

'– Coming over the horizon with his hair on fire,' relates Wilf patting his bald spot excitedly. 'And all the villagers followed behind him, a huge crowd of them; waving their pitchforks and shouting: "We know what you did! We know what you did!" And so that was the end of him.'

'Wow that was awesome.'

'Well, that's very kind.' Wilf collects the four word cards: CONSPIRACY, FIRE, AMBIGUOUS and PITCHFORK (currently face-up on the quilt) and returns them to the pack. 'But I'm sure you'd have come up with something far more interesting.'

'Not bloody likely, cobber,' quips Joe in his best Australian accent.

'Don't tell me . . . cockney,' teases Wilf.

'Was it that good?'

'Nailed it.'

'Yeah, right,' laments Joe.

'Better than Dick Van Dyke.'

'Who?'

'Mary Poppins.'

'Never read it.'

And with that, Joe is up on his knees; opening the blizzard-themed curtains to peek outside. But even as Wilf is placing the card deck on the bedside unit, Joe, disappointed, has already redrawn his curtains.

'Nothing?'

'Nope.'

'Never mind.'

Joe snatches up a snow-globe and shakes it violently.

Wilf had witnessed Joe's temper tantrums before: he takes after Paul, his dad; who certainly didn't get it from *his* dad – Wilf has always been the most patient of men. No, they could thank Wilf's wife, Joan, bless her, for any shortness in the fuse department. Lord, when she got one on her, you better watch out.

'What are you thinking about, Gramps?'

'I'm thinking you should stop being Mr Angry and put that down before you shake it to pieces.'

Wilf eases the globe from Joe and sets it on the bedside table.

'Do you think it will snow for us tomorrow, Gramps?'

Joe leans and peers into the globe at close quarters, his blinking, magnified eye looming large as it scrutinises the tiny snowman caught in a maelstrom of swirling snow.

'If we think about it hard enough, we can make anything happen. Haven't I always told you that? Now you settle down and I'll see you in the morning.'

Joe snuggles down, a cherub face lit by soft lamplight.

'Merry Christmas, Gramps.'

'Merry Christmas, Joe.'

Wilf kisses his grandson's forehead and reaches past the framed photo; a picture of himself pulling Joe (4) on a sled (both dressed in winter clothing: Joe in a bright red anorak, Wilf in a checked cap and matching scarf). He clicks off the lamp, pads across the darkened room, and gently closes the door as Joe whispers wishfully:

'Let it snow, let it snow, let it snow.'

In Mid Wales it usually does snow at Christmas; indeed, Joe had never known it not to, but he was smart enough to know it wasn't guaranteed.

'Let it snow, let it snow, let it snow,' he repeats quietly, the silvery snow of the snow-globe still to settle around the snowman.

A telescope lens, cracked and grubby, watches the jittery blue square of bedroom curtain turn dark, and from its lofty viewpoint it scopes left, down, and right, scouring the house windows for an illuminated room.

6

Downstairs, a man has brought a woman a drink. She (Sally) has him (Paul) set it on the coffee table then appears to send him off for something else.

The lens judders upon this scene for a moment before blurring upward, where it finds a girl on a sewing machine.

The girl is Lucy, Joe's sister. Lucy is sixteen, has wild, frizzy red hair, and a thing for fashion. She's currently dressed in a homemade 'Welsh Girls Rule' T-shirt under a fluffy candy-pink dressing gown — which she also made. Her head nods rhythmically to whatever is playing through the wires dangling from her ears as she turns a garment under the bobbing needle.

Glassing back to the ground floor, Paul, now kneeling by the coffee table, squirts foot moisturiser from a dispenser, spreads it over his fingers then rubs his wife's raised feet.

The lens, shaky but persistent, hooks to the shapely, arched feet as hairy hands work lotion into soles, the dorsal muscles, around ankles and heels, and between every toe . . .

How do you see it over there; slow and workmanlike — or intimate and sensual? Here, inside the telescope, the image sharpens, blurs, then quickly sharpens again; a sense of enthusiasm conveyed through a jerky lens and the eye of the beholder's keenness to remain zeroed in.

CHAPTER 2
Winter Wonderland

Joe's back garden is thick with snow and clunky-clanky noises ring out from the rickety old shed; a relic from World War II by the looks of it. A rusty nameplate reads WILF'S WORKSHOP. The shed roof, like the surrounding house roofs, holds several inches of snow.

'Here we are,' beams Wilf emerging from the shed with a large metal funnel, 'how about this?'

Joe offers a mittened thumbs-up and Wilf joins him by a large snowman, over six-foot and stout. The old man lifts his grandson, no mean feat, and Joe places the funnel on the snowman's head. After Joe is landed, Wilf takes a moment to straighten his aging spine, and the pair step back to admire their handiwork.

'Well done, Joe. That's finished him off nicely.'

Joe nods in agreement. 'He's cool.'

In addition to the funnel for a makeshift hat, the snowman has one of Paul's old rugby scarves tied around his neck and a pair of gardening gloves stuck on the ends of sticks for arms. He also has a pine cone nose, one and a half Oreo cookie eyes (the half eye a wink of sorts), a banana smile, and some of Lucy's buttons for . . . well, buttons.

'Is he leaning slightly?' asks Joe tilting his head.

'No, I don't think so.'

'I think he is.'

'Well, if he is, that's okay. It gives him character.'

'Agreed,' nods Joe. 'So, now we just need a name.'

Christmas Day morning had passed in the usual manner: the exchanging of presents, wrapping paper everywhere, hugs and Thank Yous and You're Welcomes. Joe received a Kindle Paperwhite and £100 worth of Amazon gift vouchers (redeemable for Kindle e-Books) from Wilf. Mum and Dad's present was a bike. Not the Mountain bike Joe had asked for, not the Mountain bike Paul had been instructed to buy – no, he'd unwrapped a Raleigh Chopper! Paul had always wanted one when he was a youngster but never did get one; which is why he'd thought Joe would *really* appreciate the surprise. After all, every kid and his dog ride a Mountain bike. On *this*, Joe would be special; different; stand out from the crowd – all the things Joe did *not* want. The Chopper would most likely never see the light of day, unless Paul took it for a spin. Not if it was up to Joe. Although he was too big for his old 'kiddie' bike, Joe vowed he'd be *walking* to school rather than ride this ancient article.

'But it's a classic,' Paul declared upon seeing Joe and Sally's faces drop. 'A fully refurbished Mark One . . . padded high-back seat, ape-hanger handle bars . . . it's retro chic.'

'Never mind, Joe,' comforted Sally. 'Your dad will take it back and get it changed.'

But Paul hadn't purchased the Chopper from the local bike shop, he'd bought it at a car boot sale; so that was that – and anyway, 'tis the season to be jolly, they could talk about bikes tomorrow. Christmas Day would not be spoiled by a 'wrong' bike. Indeed, other than his dad's usual gaffe, Joe was having a wonderful day: he'd already bought half a dozen e-Books for his new Kindle, he still had the snow to look forward to – the traditional building of a snowman – and we haven't even mentioned *Lucy's* present: a handmade backpack in the style of one her brother's favourite Star Wars characters. Now that was the kind of 'special' he didn't mind.

'Wow, check this out.' And Joe had modelled the backpack using the room as a catwalk.

'Ooh, that's nice, Joe,' Sally beamed.

'Honestly, Lucy, you're a genius on that machine of yours,' Wilf had added.

And after they'd played some traditional festive games, including the annual round of family Monopoly, the Evans' had tucked into a wonderful Christmas lunch; cooked by Sally, assisted by Lucy and Wilf, and served by Joe. Everyone enjoyed it immensely. This was followed by homemade eggnog (just a tiny glass for Sally after Paul had taken charge of adding the brandy and poured in far too much) and crackers and terrible jokes and Joe asking for seconds of pudding.

'Okay, so whose turn is it this time?' asks Wilf.

'Yours,' points Joe.

'Are you sure?'

Joe nods.

'Alright,' concedes Wilf.

They consider their snowman.

'How about . . . Mr Coney.'

'Love it.'

Joe breathes into his mittens, rubs them together.

'You know, because of the pine-cone nose and the funnel being kinda cone-shaped—'

'Yeah, yeah, I got that, Gramps,' smiles Joe.

'Or it could be Mr Winky,' suggests Wilf, referring to the snowman's one-eye-open one-eye-closed appearance; an effect enhanced by the clever addition of two short lengths of coloured string which lend a quizzical one eyebrow-up, one eyebrow-down demeanour.

'Oh, I love that too,' enthuses Joe. 'Coney or Winky?'

'Or . . .' suggests Wilf, 'we could combine the two.'

'Mr *Kinky*?' frowns Joe.

'Hmm, I was actually thinking Mr *Wonky*,' muses Wilf playfully, 'but—'

'No, no, I love it,' fizzes Joe.

'Then it's settled,' announces Wilf. 'Mr Wonky it is.'

'He has to be the tallest yet.'

'Easily,' agrees Wilf. 'The twelfth white Christmas Day in a row – not bad, eh?'

'See, I told you it would snow,' teases Joe.

'Why you—' laughs Wilf.

'Grrr,' grumbles Joe.

'Now what's the matter?'

'It's fallen off again!'

'Hey, what happened to not taking things too seriously?'

'I'm not.'

Wilf raises his eyebrows. 'We talked about this.'

'I know – *enjoy life* – it's just a bit annoying, that's all.'

'Is it though?' asks Wilf. 'We're full of festive pud; it's a lovely snowy day; we've got our Christmas snowman – and guess what time it is: it's time to—'

'Oh, this is ridiculous,' growls Joe as Mr Wonky's nose drops off again. 'It won't stay on!'

'Here, let me.' Wilf takes possession of the pine-cone.

'Ho, ho, ho!' chortles a voice.

Joe and Wilf turn to find Sally, materialised at the back door, head to foot in a Santa onesie and black rubber boots.

'I said: Ho, ho, ho,' repeats Mrs Claus in the deepest tone she can muster, rubbing her Santa belly, no padding required, 'and a *very* Merry Christmas. I hear someone needs a photo taken.'

'Yes,' smiles Wilf, 'we must keep our snowman collection going, eh, Joe? It might be unlucky to break the cycle.' He reunites Mr Wonky with his nose and this time it sticks.

'Okay, Mum, we're ready.'

'Good job I brought the camera, then,' Sally grins through her fluffy Santa beard. And from the sack tied to her belt she whips out a Polaroid camera.

'Positions, Joe,' urges Wilf.

Joe claps his hands, the joy of anticipation illuminating his face. He shuffles and stands at Mr Wonky's right. Wilf takes up position on the snowman's left.

'That's good,' smiles Sally. 'Just move in a little – okay, a bit more . . .'

'Another one for the album,' enthuses Joe.

'Now say Cheese,' Sally directs.

'Cheeeeeese,' grins Joe.

'*Jeez*,' grimaces Wilf.

'Wilf?' barks Sally lowering the camera. 'Are you okay? What's wrong?'

Clutching his chest, Wilf collapses into the snow.

Sally rushes forward, accidentally snapping a photo; it drops from the camera and lands face up, a small fuzzy grey square upon a vastness of glittering white.

'Wilf, speak to me! What is it, your heart? Oh, Wilf.'

Joe backs away in horror, mittens to face, not knowing what to do, deaf to mother's fraught call for an ambulance on her mobile; oblivious, he sees nothing beyond the all-encompassing vision of his treasured grandfather twitching in the snow – wheezing, gasping, and sweating despite the cold, the old man never looked older. Sally, breath misty and hurried, unties the knot of Wilf's scarf and opens his coat.

'Just rest, Wilf, an ambulance is on its way,' she soothes. 'Be here soon. Joe, go inside and fetch your dad.'

But for Joe, Time has frozen, he's stuck in a vortex, not hearing anymore; what with the confusion, dread and panic, his mind has jumped and he's now in his safe place: the Ice Cave, a cathedral-like rock cavern deep underground, the silent sanctuary his mind sometimes flees to when things are too much; big things, like when his missing babysitter turned up murdered (her head in Llandudno, her body in Aberystwyth), or small things, like that time at school when someone hid his towel and every piece of clothing whilst he showered after Swim Club – to Joe, equally traumatic events in their own way. And though he isn't aware that the switch from Real world to Safe world is sometimes involuntary, sometimes sought; it happens regardless – this matters not, for in his cave he is safe, at least for a while. Whether it proves to be a temporary ill-wind blowing beyond the mouth of the cave, or is, in fact, a long-lasting shit-storm; within, the boy has a chance to gather his thoughts, have a word with himself, to re-read the countless signs stuck to the rock walls; the words of his grandfather – advice he's imparted over the years: Keep On

Keeping On, Joe; Don't Let Things Get You Down, Lad; Bounce Back; Never Give Up; Seize the Day; Anything is Possible—

'Joe,' echoes a voice. '*Joe!*'

Joe becomes vaguely aware of a sound not unlike his mother.

'*Please*, Joe,' repeats Sally, soft but firm.

With a shake Joe is jerked from his ice cave.

'Come on, Joe, snap out of it. I need you to fetch your dad.'

But Joe's manner is that of a faulty wind-up toy, his distressed feet crunching back and forth, back and forth, trampling snow as he searches for a meaningful action, a valid idea, or just a word, any word, but finds not a one – he produces nothing but a noise, guttural and heartbreaking, almost primal.

'*Joe!* Go inside and fetch your dad. Do it *now*.'

Again the boy fails to move toward the house. Sally senses her son has already fallen back into his ice cave.

'Paul!' she yells. '*Paul!*'

And on that plaintive cry, not wishing to appear ghoulish, let us allow Wilf, Sally, and the pacing Joe, a little privacy; let's frame out the commotion and focus instead on the still developing Polaroid . . .

Closer, please.

Closer.

Note the blurry photograph keenly; watch as it continues to develop, slowly, quietly, unaffected by the pandemonium beyond its borders – the colours taking shape, the image deepening, its definition intensifying: a section of Mr Wonky's midriff, Wilf at an acute angle aimed for snow, and Joe's hand instinctively reaching down.

Owen, a mischievous lad with a square face and a prominent jaw, peeps over the fence . . .

Blue flashing lights strobe the houses in every direction; the ambulance moves away – and at the end of the cul-de-sac it turns on its siren.

As the emphatic blare races into the distance Owen signals then clambers over the fence. He's followed by Gary and Melvin, and they've come prepared: all three are armed with buckets and spades.

The boys circle Mr Wonky.

'Look at the state of that,' sneers Owen.

'What a joke, he looks like Melvin's gran made him.'

'Is that . . . a funnel?' asks Melvin.

'Meant to be a hat,' scoffs Gary.

13

'Wait, I think the votes are in,' announces Owen stopping in his tracks. 'Yes, they are,' he declares, one finger on a pretend earpiece. 'And they've been counted and verified . . .'

'And?' asks Gary.

'And the public have decided . . .'

Melvin vocalises a dramatic drum roll.

'It's Death!' decrees Owen.

Laughing maniacally, the boys demolish Mr Wonky with kicks and spades. Gary performs a flying two-footed drop kick to the body which dislodges Mr Wonky's head and sends it rolling to the ground.

'Down with this sort of thing!' chants Owen in an Irish accent. A cruel reference to Joe's known liking for Father Ted – Wilf's favourite sitcom.

'Yeah, death to lame snowmen!' hisses Gary.

Melvin drop-kicks the funnel over the fence, Gary stamps on the snowman's head, and Owen pisses on what's left of the body. In just a few minutes there is little trace of Mr Wonky – nothing beyond a snow 'stump' tainted with ugly streaks of yellow.

'Pissed on him!' boasts Owen.

'He got what he deserved,' asserts Gary.

But it doesn't end there. Now the boys begin clearing the garden to the fullest. Gary and Melvin dump bucket-load after bucket-load of snow over the fence as Owen checks the back door. Finding the door unlocked, Owen enters, and exits almost immediately with a large container of salt.

'Hey, look,' remarks Melvin; he's found the Polaroid.

Gary takes possession.

'Worst pic ever,' he decides.

Screwed into a ball the photo is tossed over the fence.

Sprinkling salt in all directions, Owen orders his troops to the kitchen, from where they quickly reappear with buckets of steaming water. They pour this way and that, before excitedly retracing their steps for more. The snow is disappearing fast and the bucket-runs are repeated until Owen has used up every speck of salt and the garden is fully returned, in a relatively short space of time, to green grass.

'Try building a snowman now, Joe,' spits Owen.

If you had an aerial view, say from a high-flying drone, you'd see snow everywhere but Joe's back garden.

When Joe returns from the hospital he is shocked to discover the snowman missing and the garden totally free of snow. He finds a pine-cone and a few buttons in the middle of the lawn, but the rest of his accessories, the funnel hat for example, like Mr Wonky himself, is nowhere to be seen.

Joe's first thought is a ridiculous one:

It's a small town, how far could he have got?

He immediately berates himself for thinking in such a silly and childlike way. Aloud he chides:

'Jeez, grow up, Joe; you'll be thirteen next month!'

Nevertheless, he still checks over the back fence to see if his snowman is out there. (Late evening now but a full moon and so much reflective snow produce an intensely bright vista.) But of course Mr Wonky is long gone. Joe's investigation does, however, confirm one thing: that the snow, as you already know, hasn't disappeared from anywhere except his back garden.

Totally weird, thinks Joe, sitting atop the wooden picnic table (normally situated outside the patio doors, relegated to the back fence in winter). Then he notices the back gate, off the catch, swing slightly open.

What the—?

Joe discovers four white postcards pinned to the gate's rear; handwritten, they read:

LARDY . . . SAD . . . WEIRD . . . and LOSER.

Three are torn up by the time Sally approaches from the house. Joe quickly folds and stuffs the last into a pocket.

'Well, this is strange,' observes Sally picking up Paul's old rugby scarf from the middle of a bush.

'Where did all the snow go?' asks Joe.

'It's a weird one alright.'

'And where's *Mr Wonky*?'

'It's a small town, he can't have gone far,' smiles Sally.

'Mum . . . what a stupid thing to say.'

'Sorry, Joe, just trying to—'

'How can you joke with Gramps lying in hospital?'

'Because I have a dark sense of humour, okay? Because that's how I cope with shit, okay? Trust me, I haven't forgotten.'

'Sorry, Mum.' Joe hugs his mother.

'It's fine. I'm sorry too.'

'Besides, he's not dead, right? And he *will* get better.'

'Of course he will; strong as an ox that one.'

They hug a little tighter then Sally has an idea:

'Hey, wanna rebuild Mr Wonky?'

'Make another?' brightens Joe. 'Can we do that?'

'Why not? It's still Christmas Day.'

'Yeah, it'd still count.'

'We can take a photo and show Gramps,' suggests Sally.

'Yay, he'd like that.' Joe's face drops. 'Except we haven't got any snow.'

'We can get snow from the road, there's plenty there; apart from our car and the ambulance no-one's been out.'

'Yeah, but knowing my luck, it'll probably melt or something before we get there.'

'Don't talk daft, there's tons of it – come on.'

Carrying buckets, Joe and Sally take the path around the side of the house and walk onto the driveway.

Hearing a loud vehicle approaching, they stop.

A snowplough gritter, its orange strobe lights flashing, passes on the road and a shower of rock salt lands near their boots. The driver waves then swings a deft one-eighty sweep and heads back down the cul-de-sac.

'That's a shame,' remarks Sally evenly.

Joe drops his bucket.

'They work on Christmas Day?' he grumbles.

Sally shrugs. 'Must do.'

The duo stare silently at the aftermath: every trace of snow obliterated from their road, the pavements heaped with wet, filthy slush. Only when the noisy vehicle has grown quiet and the strobing orange lights have finally disappeared, does Joe turn to his mother.

See, I told you, reads the message in his eyes. *With my luck—*

'Don't be silly. With the stuff left here (she indicates their small front garden), the shed roof, and the side of the drive, we'll still have enough.'

'Mr Wonky was big, Mum; *biiig* – the biggest yet.'

'And I still say it'll be plenty. Come on, you, shake a leg.'

And they move off back the way they came.

'If there isn't enough,' advances Joe. 'I suppose we could take it from a *neighbour's* garden.'

'Joe!' barks Sally. 'That's a great idea.'

As Joe compacts yet another load of snow into Mr Wonky's body, Sally shapes a massive snowball for his head. It's late now but not as cold as it had been.

'Wasn't,' repeats Joe.

'Was too.'

'Wasn't.'

'Was.'

'No, it wasn't,' he maintains.

'Course it was funny,' she contends.

'Mum!'

Sally gives her son a playful nudge.

'Go on, then,' challenges Joe. '*What* was funny about it?'

'The timing, silly; I mean what are the odds of a snowplough gritter just when you don't need one – and on Christmas Day of all days.'

Another nudge: still playful but a touch firmer this time – insistent. Joe says nothing.

'Go on, tell me that *wasn't* comical.'

'Hmm, okay . . . I guess it was kinda farcical.'

'See, I told you. Here help me lift his head.'

Once Mr Wonky's head is in place, the resurrection complete bar the adding of a few facial features and one or two sartorial whimsies, Joe steps back to assess.

'Not sure he looks as wonky as before,' he muses.

But Joe's train of thought is lost when Sally sprinkles snow in his Fro. He quickly scoops a handful of snow from the last bucket-load, shapes a tiny snowball and aims.

'Not in the stomach,' quips Sally turning away.

Joe's snowball hits her in the backside.

'Now, that was a good shot,' quips Sally.

'I could hardly miss,' teases Joe.

'Hey! What are you trying to say?' she protests playfully.

Joe laughs, then, despite protestations, Sally tickles him. He's super ticklish and it's as much an ordeal as it is fun.

'What are you two giggling about?'

Paul's at the kitchen door.

'Nothing you'd understand,' mutters Sally.

'Mum,' chastises Joe.

'What? Your dad has no sense of humour,' she whispers. 'It's a recognised scientific fact.'

'I know but—'

'Luckily, you take after me,' she adds a touch louder.

'Have you been at the eggnog?' asks Paul.

'Just ignore him. He knows I can't drink in my condition – more's the pity. What do you reckon?' she adds softly. 'Think if we're vewy vewy quiet he might go away?'

Joe smiles – he knows an Elmer Fudd impression when he hears one – but then he smells tobacco. 'Dad!'

'What?'

'Oh, Paul, are you smoking again?'

'Just one. After the day I've had—'

'After the day *you've* had!' barks Sally.

'After the day *we've all had*,' offers Paul.

'Well, keep it away from me,' Sally warns.

'I am.'

Sally fumes a moment, then turns and punches Mr Wonky in the face, drills the fist into his cheek, moulding a cheekbone with her knuckles, then she left-hooks the other cheek before again screwing her fist into the packed snow.

'Mum . . .'

'What, sweetie?' bristles Sally through gritted teeth.

'What are you doing?'

Sally thumps the snowman twice in his gut then knees him where his snowballs would be if he had any.

'Stop, please,' appeals Joe.

'No, Joe, let her work it out of her system,' advises Paul. 'Better him than me,' he mutters.

'Actually, Paul,' carps Sally, 'why don't you make yourself useful and fetch Wilf's camera; y'know, if it's not too much trouble.'

'No trouble,' replies Paul, smiling unconvincingly. 'Give me a minute,' he adds in a sarcastic tone, 'and I'll *fetch* it.'

'Couldn't you do it now?'

'I'm finishing this.'

'Fine, finish it then!'

Sally returns to punching Mr Wonky – *hard*.

'Mum,' petitions Joe. 'Mum!'

He pulls on Sally's arm, gains her attention, then sucks in his cheeks and wobbles his head, eyes bulging.

'What are you doing?' frowns Sally.

'Wonky's supposed to look like a jolly snowman,' contends Joe. 'Not an injured skeleton.'

'He's got a point,' nods Paul blowing a cloud of smoke.

'Joe, tell your father to shut up, or *so help me* –'

'We're going to show Gramps the photo,' Joe quickly tells his dad. 'We thought it might cheer him up.'

'*Cheer him up?*' scoffs Paul. 'He's had a bloody heart attack.'

'Yeah, I know,' rebuffs Joe sharply, 'but he doesn't like hospitals.'

'No-one does.' Paul drags on his cigarette. 'Why don't you just wait till he gets home?'

'Because it might have melted by then,' rasps Sally.

Joe spins to face her.

'I'm sorry, Joe,' explains Sally, 'but Gramps might not be home for a while.'

'If at all.'

'Paul!'

18

'Sorry, just saying,' retorts Paul. 'Keeping it real. We have to be prepared for the worst.'

'Jesus, what are you like?' snarls Sally. 'Come on, Joe; help me rebuild Mr Wonky's head – I seem to have messed up his face.'

Paul blows another plume of smoke. 'Do you need any more snow?' he asks in a conciliatory tone.

'No, you finish your fag, Paul. If we need more, we know where it is.'

'I'm done; I was just having a few blasts.'

Paul flicks the burning end from the cigarette and returns what's left to his packet.

'Right, well if you're done you can get the camera, then,' bids Sally. 'We're nearly ready, aren't we, Joe?'

'Is it still Christmas Day?' yawns Joe.

Sally checks the time on her mobile. 'For another fifteen minutes it is. Come on, let's get cracking.'

By the time Paul returns, the snowman is finished; Sally applying the final touches: Paul's rugby scarf and the funnel 'hat' – found dumped in the wheelie bin. She's also recreated Mr Wonky's face as per her son's instructions. Joe himself is fast asleep on the garden bench, a travel blanket from Wilf's Workshop laid over him.

'Is he done?' asks Paul.

'Who? Joe or Mr Wonky?'

'The snow—'

'Yes, he's done.' Sally tweaks the snowman's pine-cone nose. 'Where's the camera?'

Paul's reaction tells her he forgot.

'Useless,' she grunts. 'One thing, that's all you had to do.'

'Jesus, woman, calm down,' huffs Paul. 'I'll get it.' He turns to leave. 'I don't know why you encouraged him to rebuild the snowman anyway.'

'To take his mind off things, Paul,' snaps Sally.

Paul pauses at the back door. 'And did it help?'

'Well, I'm sure he hasn't forgotten that his granddad's in hospital, if that's what you mean,' states Sally pointedly. 'But I think it did help, actually. Their snowman's important to him.'

'Good, I'm glad – That's what I was checking – One camera coming up.'

'Wait,' calls Sally. 'Take Joe with you.'

'What; *carry* him?'

'Well, I can't do it, can I? I'm carrying number three, if you hadn't noticed. Pregnant *again* – thanks to you.'

19

'No, I mean, why not wake him and let him walk?' proposes Paul. 'You know I've got a bad back.'

'Jesus,' rasps Sally setting off. 'I'll carry him myself.'

'No, no, I'll do it,' carps Paul. 'I'll never hear the end of it otherwise.'

'Gently,' urges Sally as Joe is fork-lifted into Paul's arms.

'Sally, he's not a baby,' grunts Paul.

'Put him in bed. He can sleep in his clothes.'

'Okay if I take his shoes off, is it?'

'And leave his night-light on.'

'I know, I know.'

'Then come back with the camera.'

Paul stops. 'Hang on, where are you off?' he asks as Sally heads inside.

'I'm going to bed. It's been a long day.'

'So, you want *me* to take the photo?'

'Think you can manage that?' she asks over a shoulder.

'Oh, good one,' puffs Paul.

On the move again, the straining dad has a suggestion for the sleeping son: 'How about a cake- and pudding-free diet in the New Year, Joe?' wheezes Paul. 'Just a thought.'

'Only if you give up smoking,' mutters Joe in his sleep.

Paul pauses. 'Okay, that's just spooky,' he decides.

The Evans' living-room curtains open to a low winter sun and a Boxing Day morning washed out with rain. Sally is the first to notice Mr Wonky Mark II melted to a sad, icy grey stump in the middle of the lawn. Indeed, apart from the snowman's stubby base and shrunken head there isn't a scrap of snow to be seen anywhere: neighbour's roofs are now clear, as are the trees – even the surrounding hills are no longer the pretty Christmas card backdrop they were just last night.

Joe's voice from upstairs: 'Noooo!'

His feet thump across the ceiling and down the stairs.

'Have you seen?' he barks entering the room.

'Never mind, Joe.'

'That's *twice*.'

Joe's forehead thunks against the patio doors, his breath instantly misting the glass door.

'It never rains but it pours,' sighs Sally joining him.

The pair stare out:

Wilf's Workshop, previously a snow-capped frosty-windowed Santa's Grotto is now just a plain old wet corrugated metal shed with featureless grey walls and dripping eaves. But even worse, the combination of increased temperature and persistent rain has worn the snowman's head down to a grapefruit-sized ball of watery ice. At the present rate of precipitation Mr Wonky's *stumpy base* might last until mid-afternoon but his *shrinking noggin?* – An hour or two, tops.

'Is life always this hard, or is it just when you're a kid?'

'Always like this,' replies Sally in her best French accent.

Leon, the Professional may be a 15 certificate but Sally let Joe watch the film because he'd been asking to see it for ages. She doesn't think it's that bad, and well, he's nearly thirteen. They'd watched it together when Paul was away fishing. He wouldn't have approved but what he doesn't know can't hurt him. On this, Sally, Joe and Lucy are invariably united.

'What are you two talking about?' asks Paul.

He tightens his dressing gown and wipes sleep from an eye. Not at the same time, obviously.

'Mr Wonky's gone.'

'Oh, is that all?'

'Paul!' chides Sally.

'See, he doesn't care,' whines Joe.

'Of course he does. That's why he took the photo for you last night. Isn't it, Paul?'

'Did you, Dad?' Joe's been let down too many times before to count on one of his father's promises.

'Now before you lose it,' ventures Paul, 'let me explain—'

'Oh no,' groans Sally. 'Please tell me you didn't forget.'

'I knew it!' Joe buries his head in a sofa cushion. 'He always does this!'

'Bit dramatic,' frowns Paul.

'It was the *only* thing you had to do,' gripes Sally.

'Hey, it's not my fault there was no film in the camera. Someone must have used the last one.'

'So why didn't you put a new one in?'

'Everywhere's closed; it's Christmas – or have you forgotten?'

Sally marches to the cupboard, opens a door and points to several boxes of Polaroid film.

'Whoa, when did we get those?'

'Jesus, you are fucking useless,' moans Sally. 'Excuse my French, Lucy.'

'No problem.' Lucy, just entered, looks to the sofa where Joe remains curled up. 'What's with him?'

'Ask your father.'

'Jesus, it's just a snowman,' gripes Paul, 'it's not the end of the world. I'm more worried about my dad being in hospital, to be honest.'

Sally and Lucy roll their eyes, shake their heads sadly in unison, then sigh and pfft together. He's *always* playing the pity card but this is a new low even for him. Paul didn't even want Wilf moving in to begin with. Even though his dad had spent years unselfishly looking after Paul's Alzheimer's stricken mother in their one bedroom flat in Manchester. It was Sally who'd said he should see out however many years he had left in the countryside of Wales. They had a spare bedroom. He'd be able to spend more time with Joe, who he adored. Lucy, too, but he and Joe had always had a special bond.

'Hey, Joe.' Lucy nudges the sofa with a knee. 'Come on don't be like Dad.'

'Whaddaya mean?'

'He just played the pity card again.'

'Not true, Joe,' contests Paul. 'Don't listen to her.'

'Oh, so you won't mind if we visit him again later, then?' suggests Sally.

'What, today?' Paul grumbles.

'Are you for real?'

'No, I just mean – will they *have* visiting on Boxing Day?'

'Right, right, because they didn't admit him yesterday; what with it being Christmas Day. Oh, hang on a minute, they did, didn't they? Y'know, because *he'd had a fucking heart attack*.'

'Ok, fine. I just thought you wanted to visit your sister.'

'We can still do that; after we've been to the hospital – if that's alright with you?'

'Yep, great, whatever you like,' agrees Paul.

'Well then, good!'

Sally pauses, focuses on remaining calm. All this stress isn't good for her passenger.

'So, do you want your coffee now?' asks Paul.

Paul is the master of changing the subject. He also knows making Sally a cup of her favourite brew is the quickest and easiest way to slide back into her good books: his wife's a sucker for a frothy cappuccino. The question is actually: Want your one and only *real* coffee now? For, in her condition, Sally is limited to just one 'real' cup per day; all others must be decaf – doctor's orders.

'Yes . . . thank you,' breathes Sally. 'But make mine first.' By which she means: *Don't go stirring it with your sugary spoon again.* Paul takes three heaped spoonfuls in his cuppas; Sally is currently 'off' sugar and has come to hate even a trace of its nauseating sweetness.

'Sir, yes, sir,' quips Paul.

No-one laughs because he isn't funny. Not in content. Not in delivery. It's been that way forever.

With a shake of her head, Sally exits the room.

Lucy pokes Joe with a sofa cushion.

'So, what's up with you, little bro?'

Joe elevates a pointed finger, aims it at the back garden.

Lucy peers through the window.

'What? I don't see anything.'

'Exactly,' grumbles Joe.

From its elevated vantage point, the same cracked telescope lens is once again scanning the rear windows of the Evans' home. Its circular view drops briefly, inspects the insignificant lump of ice melting on the lawn, then quickly rises back to the house.

The man, now outside the back door, is having a crafty smoke.

The woman sitting at the kitchen table lifts a cup to her lips and blows.

The girl in the window appears to be talking to herself.

As the owner of the telescope continues to gaze down from Finger Hill, here's a little local geography to establish the surroundings:

Finger Hill (so called because it's shaped like a finger; well, duh) points north, towards the medieval market town of Llanidloes, with its chapels and pubs, shops, homes and school.

If we were to meet on the summit of Finger Hill (sometimes referred to as Scarecrow Hill) – on the first 'knuckle', so to speak – and survey the area, we wouldn't see the *centre* of Llanidloes – not clearly, anyway – due to the large copse of trees that covers the hill's 'fingernail'.

Turn though, and look: in the valley to the west, where scores of modern houses squat. Amongst them, the Evans' place.

And below, in the eastern lowland, sits Tall Trees Trailer Park and its twenty-odd static caravan homes. Do you see?

Then, over in the northwest: another hill, Bryn Crow (Bryn being the Welsh word for Hill), a patchwork of sprawling sloped fields dotted with grazing cattle and wandering sheep, and in the middle, roughly speaking, a large farmhouse replete with outbuildings and barns: the Jenkins' place.

And finally, completing this somewhat sketchy map: to our northeast, covered with bracken, brush and thickets – Poacher's Hill.

CHAPTER 3

Back to School

Mr Schneider, Joe's craggy-faced English teacher is fifties, balding, thin as a rake, and German.

'Are you sure you vant to do zis?' he asks Joe quietly.

Mr Schneider's Germanic-accented English is perfect, probably a damn sight better than a lot of Brits!

Joe nods and hands over five cards selected from the open Word Box; a simple yet elegant wooden box with a hinged lid containing hundreds of cards that stand in one long row, each behind the other; packed tight enough to hide their faces, but loose enough to allow for extraction. Size-wise, imagine an elongated shoe-box designed to accommodate a pair of clown shoes; and now picture it devoid of footwear and loaded instead with filing cards.

Joe waits, standing before the class, as Mr Schneider places the cards, face out, on the easel beside them; an easel that appears specifically designed for this exact purpose. Perhaps it was. The wood certainly matches that of the word box – walnut.

RIFLE says the first card.

'Rifle,' announces Mr Schneider. ARROGANCE and BALLOON follow, then SARDINES, the teacher confirming each word aloud. 'Und your final vurd is . . . King.'

Despite being a teacher of English in Britain for the last twenty-five years, there's that strong German accent again. (As you might expect, Mr Schneider also teaches German.)

'Okay, Joe, you have a few seconds to determine vich vurd to discard.'

As Joe reflects, classmates make various suggestions, each in favour of losing a different word, it seems.

'Quiet please, allow Joe to make his own selection,' insists Mr Schneider. 'Danke.'

'Balloon,' elects Joe. 'No, Sardines. Definitely Sardines.'

'Sardines it is.'

The teacher removes the rejected word card from the easel then steps behind the countdown clock on his desk. The timer is currently set at thirty seconds.

'Okay, ve all know ze rules. Joe, you have thirty seconds thinking time und zen you must begin your story.'

Someone mutters somewhere and a snigger ripples around the class; a dig at him or Joe, perhaps.

'Absolut ruhe, bitte!' bellows Mr Schneider.

(The class has heard the instruction enough times to know it means: *Silence, you little shits!* Something like that, anyway.)

Joe focuses intently on the cards. Important to use these precious few extra seconds before the 'official' allocated thirty begins. Make a connection between the words. Come up with an idea. Come up with *any* idea.

'Rifle, Arrogant, Balloon und King,' repeats Mr Schneider. 'Remember, you must include all four vurds,' he cautions Joe. 'Und your time starts . . . Now.'

Mr Schneider slaps the timer:

[00:30] changes to [00:29]

[00:28] . . .

[00:27] . . .

RIFLE. ARROGANCE. BALLOON. KING.

All attention falls on Joe as he studies the cards. He can feel their cynical, unhelpful laser beam eyes. Ignore them, ignore them. It only takes a few seconds – and he has thirty, well, twenty-five now – an idea will come. Yes, once the dots are joined, so to speak, a story will ping into his mind – and it'll be awesome; he'll show these—someone coughs; trying to put him off, no doubt. Probably Owen, the mean bastard – but Joe won't be distracted. Any second now . . .

[00:19] . . .

[00:18] . . .

[00:17] . . .

As the beats tick by, Joe mouths the words. Rifle, Arrogance, Balloon, King. Rifle, Arrogance, Balloon, King. *Jesus!* No, don't panic, don't panic! . . . Perspiration trickles down his forehead and rolls between his eyes. The would-be storyteller has taken on the appearance of the proverbial fish out of water – a fish that's been asked to forge a narrative link between Rifle, Arrogance, Balloon and King, and doesn't have a clue. Should he have kept Sardines? Joe asks himself. *Too late now*—Stop! Focus! Rifle, Arrogance, Balloon, King. Oh, why is he so bad at this when it matters? Surely there's something reasonably obvious there. Rifle, Arrogance, Balloon, King. He should be able to come up with *something*; he's definitely smarter than the rest of these dopes. But nope, he's got nothing; nothing yet, anyway – how long left?

[00:13] . . .

[00:12] . . .

[00:11] . . .

Rifle, Arrogance, Balloon, King. *Rifle, Arrogance, Balloon, King!* Something should be sparking by now. Maybe try the words in a different order? But his head feels like a swamp. And he's in there, or rather, on it, sitting on one of those flat-bottomed airboats, the propeller spinning but the rudder or accelerator or engine or whatever it is, stuck – and the alligators are circling. Joe's never fainted but he imagines this is what it must feel like when you're about to; that moment, a split second before you drop to the whirling ground. And on that thought his mind jumps back to Christmas and Wilf's collapse.

Aberystwyth hospital had been full of sights and smells Joe didn't care for: squeaky corridors; antiseptic whiffs; nurses on the move; chatting medical teams; Wilf's bed surrounded by drips and monitors, and other sick people in beds or on seats or shuffling around. He'd assumed Gramps would have his own room, they always seemed to in films and TV shows, but no, Wilf was on a ward.

The Evans' stayed late on Christmas Day (worst Christmas ever!) and as there were no specific visiting times, returned to the hospital on Boxing Day morning. At some point, a doctor updated Joe's parents; told them that Wilf remained 'in a stable condition' – not improved but no worse. Gramps was half asleep or woozy from medication, Joe wasn't sure which. The family lingered until lunch then left; they'd quickly felt in the way once patients were being fed or roused to that end. Besides, Wilf needed rest and recuperation. The doctor said that, too.

The afternoon was spent at Auntie Jean's house; Jean is Sally's sister. When they arrived, the twins, Amy and May, were upstairs breezing through Halo 4: the same game Joe had been playing so badly the other night. Was it Christmas Eve; only two nights ago? It felt like an eternity to Joe.

'You got this?' asked Amy. (Or it might have been May; Joe could never tell them apart.)

'Uh-huh,' nodded Joe.

'Great, isn't it?'

'Yeah.'

'We love it.'

'Bit surprised you're allowed to play it, though.'

'We're ten.'

'Nearly as old as you.'

'And anyway, it's not *that* violent.'

As the adults talked downstairs, amongst the festive decorations, Joe looked on as the twins, equally expert on their controllers, easily destroyed wave after wave of enemies. Ducking and diving in the midst of explosions and zipping tracer bullets, they utilised pistols, grenades, shotguns, assault weapons, laser cannons, rail guns and rocket launchers; switching back and forth between weapons like pros. Joe was envious of the girls' gaming skills but tried not to show it.

'You can play if you like.'

'No, no, I'm good,' replied Joe. 'I play enough at home.'

'We've not really got the hang of it yet,' said the girls in unison, their little hands intuitively manipulating the controller buttons; thumbs and fingers a blur, tap-tap-tapping at lightning pace.

'We only got it yesterday.'

'For Christmas.'

'Boom!'

'Oh, nice one, sis.'

'Whoa, you hear that?'

'Yeah, sniper; quick, down.'

The girls ducked behind a wall. Well, their characters did.

'Storm him?' asked May.

'Deffo,' replied Amy. 'No-one likes a camper.'

'Okay, ready?' prompted May. 'Three, two . . .'

Back in the classroom, the clock is down to [00:02].

Then [00:01] . . .

BZZZZZZZ, rings the timer.

'Okay, Joe,' cues Mr Schneider. 'Off you go.'

'Er, okay, so there was this, er, King . . . and he, er . . . this was back in The Dark Ages, by the way . . .'

As the class look on, amused and bewildered by Joe's faltering start, someone asks:

'Did they have balloons in the dark ages, sir?'

'Quiet!' barks Mr Schneider. 'No interruptions. Sorry, Joe, please continue.'

'And his jester . . . an arrogant little man . . . who danced with an inflated pig-bladder tied to a stick . . .'

'Ja, good,' encourages the teacher softly. 'Keep going.'

'No, not a stick, a rifle . . . and it wasn't in the dark ages . . . this happened in the 1800s when they *did* have rifles . . .'

Gary snorts and pulls the universally recognised *How dumb is he?* face.

Joe mutters a line about the king being tired of pig-bladders, mumbles something to do with the jester being in love with the queen, then, red-faced, flustered, and appearing out of breath, he

28

suddenly goes blank; yep, dried up good and proper – and he appears not in the least bit likely to recover.

Mr Schneider steps in to quell the growing sniggers.

'Never mind, Joe, never mind,' he soothes. 'Nice try. I zink you vur a little unlucky, ja? Some very tricky vurds zer. Come on, give him a hand, zat's it. You can't vin zem all.'

Pity applause accompanies Joe's walk of shame.

'Right, who is next to try?'

Mr Schneider reinserts Joe's cards into the box then moves a few sections around, a shuffle of sorts.

'Remember, practice makes perfect und Storytell finals come round quicker than you think,' he reminds the class.

Owen stands, takes a bow, and then, looking far too cocky, swaggers to the front.

'Let's hope ve can give you a bit more of a challenge zis time, eh, Owen,' smiles Mr Schneider.

The teacher steps aside and waves a hand at the box.

'If you'd like to pick your five vurds.'

Owen steps up and casually runs a finger along the top edges of the cards as if he hasn't a care in the world.

'Don't feel bad, Joe,' comforts Mr Schneider quietly as he passes Joe's desk. 'Ve all understand you had ze vurst Christmas imaginable.'

Joe is waiting outside the school gates, not far from Owen, Gary and Melvin, who hang around in a loose cluster. Glancing at Joe, they exchange remarks and giggle inanely.

'Never mind, Joe,' calls Owen.

'Could happen to anyone,' grins Gary.

'Yeah,' agrees Melvin. 'I'm useless at words, too.'

'I'm not *useless at words*, Melvin,' retorts Joe, 'I've just got things on my mind, okay?'

'And how is your granddad, Joe?' asks Owen.

Noticing the hint of a sneer, Joe gives Owen the stink-eye. 'Oh, piss off, Owen,' he hisses.

'Oooh, get you,' chorus the boys, raising invisible handbags to their chins in high camp mode.

'And for your information, just saying Piss off isn't necessarily having a hissy fit.'

'Yeah, you're right, Joe,' nods Owen. 'Sorry about that.'

'We was only playing,' explains Melvin with an empty-headed chuckle.

'We *were* only playing,' Joe points out.

'Exactly,' chortles Melvin.

Joe instantly feels cruel for correcting the big dope; it isn't his fault he—

'By the way, almost forgot: nice backpack, mate,' grins Gary, a reference to Lucy's handmade Christmas present: the backpack forged of fabric and filling; Master Yoda, in Jedi robe, riding Joe's back.

'Oh, thanks,' acknowledges Joe somewhat begrudgingly.

He shrugs the pack and the diminutive Jedi comes alive: his green, pointy-eared head snatching a peek over Joe's shoulder before quickly resettling; his stubby arms and legs (attached to the straps) maintaining their grip throughout.

'Who made it for you?' smirks Gary. 'Your momma?'

Before Joe can respond, his sister cycles through the gates; she's dressed in a modern-take on a Mao Tse-Tung outfit: homemade trousers, long jacket and beaded cap.

(Although sixth-formers do not have to wear school uniform, perhaps a Chinese Zhongshan tunic suit, traditionally considered 'male attire', isn't what the school had in mind as 'own clothes'. But as Lucy is studying Fashion she gets away with it. She's also taking A-levels in Business Studies, Music and Sociology.)

Lucy pulls up beside Joe and lets out a 'Hey, you.'

'Hey,' Joe replies flatly.

'You okay?'

'Yep.'

'Those idiots bothering you?'

'Nope.'

Lucy studies the boys for a moment.

'Want me to wait with you?'

'Oh yes, please,' grovels Joe mockingly. 'That'll make having to wait for Dad so much *less* embarrassing.'

Lucy raises an eyebrow. 'You could always—'

'I'm not riding an ancient Chopper, Luce. You saw it: big wheel, small wheel – the bike's not safe.'

Lucy nods as if she understands, pauses, then:

'But if you did—'

'I'm not riding an ancient Chopper.'

'Yeah, but if you—'

'*I'm not riding an ancient Chopper.*'

'Fine,' puffs Lucy. 'Have it your way.'

Owen, Gary and Melvin cackle and snicker.

Lucy turns to them. 'Do you lot want a beating?' she asks. 'And don't think I won't.'

'Hey Lucy, I thought you were studying *Fashion*,' quips Owen. 'Not *Fascism*.'

'It's Communism, you idiot.'

'What?'

'In China,' explains Lucy. 'It's a communist state.'

'But growing more capitalist by the day,' mutters Joe. Unlike Owen, Joe actually listens in classes.

'Big girly swot,' mocks Gary.

'Hey, less of the "girly",' protests Lucy.

'Oh yeah?' braves Owen. 'And what are you gonna do about it if we don't?'

With a loud war-cry, Lucy charges the obnoxious trio with her bike and the boys scatter, shouting back insults about her clothes as they flee.

'Perfect,' sighs Joe.

Maxine, Lucy's best friend and fellow sixth-former, cycles out: a stunning sight in her inky attire and layers of dark make-up; everything black apart from a streak of maroon in her long dark hair. Today she's wearing a military jacket over a charcoal crystal-organza skirt, a neck choker, over-knee socks and platform ankle boots adorned with batman insignias. Max likes to play around with a variety of Goth looks and it would be fair to say that Joe is – how shall we put it – a fan.

'Hi, Max,' he grins.

'Hello, bright eyes,' she winks. 'You know, you really should let me do something with those; a touch of guyliner and you'd have the girls queuing up.'

Maxine is studying Art, Psychology, Drama and English Literature. If they'd offered a course on Period make-up she'd have definitely signed up. Today hers is moody Seventies Punk. Like Lucy, Maxine is also into Fashion: she loves anything Victorian, Emo, Steampunk and regular Punk; everything to do with Vampires, skulls or bats – and, of course, Goth. She's as bad as Lucy for 'out-of-the-ordinary' outfits; mixing styles and time-frames, and flaunting the results. The friends always attract attention around town. Not all of it positive but they don't care.

'Nice bike, Max,' grins Joe.

'Still the same one, Joe,' smiles Maxine; extra pretty when she does. Joe remains focused on her even when Lucy returns, red in the face.

'There,' she puffs. 'They shouldn't bother you again for a while.'

'I can handle them, sis, thanks,' scoffs Joe. 'I've done judo, remember.'

Lucy rolls her eyes. It was Dad's idea. Joe only stuck it out for a couple of months. He's a thinker not a fighter.

'Judo,' echoes Maxine. 'Impressive. So, what belt are you?'

'Yellow,' beams Joe.

'Yellow, eh . . . is that good?'

'Put it this way, if I put a hold on you, you'd find it hard to shake me off.'

'Really?' laughs Maxine.

Joe nods eagerly, no doubt imagining that very scenario.

'O—kay,' drawls Lucy, awkwardly reminded of Joe's crush on her BFF. 'Right, Joe, do not wander off.'

'Yeah, yeah,' snips Joe. 'Jeez, I'm not a kid.'

As he continues to gaze at Max, now riding away with Lucy, Joe's mobile rings.

'Hello? . . . What? . . . No, I don't. And stop calling me!'

Joe disconnects the call with a growl.

The funnel-shaped entrance to Tall Trees Trailer Park has a bench on one side, a faded sign on the other. The lot, a small field ringed by several trees (none of which are especially tall) and a low wall, contains two dozen or so shabby, lime-green static caravans.

Puffing his cheeks, Joe drops his backpack on the bench and flops beside it. Eyes shut, his mind draws a carefree picture of Maxine on her Mountain bike and he beside her, also riding a Mountain bike; then their separate transports morph into a single Hells Angels style Harley-Davidson, him driving and Max holding on, her ringed fingers laced tightly around his muscular six-pack. He pictures the wrist and ankle tattoos she had planned for her 18th birthday, and thinks, not for the first time, about the *extra* tattoo Lucy had told him about: a Moth, Skull and Ram's Head theme, designed by Max herself – for under her boobs!

'Penny for them,' whispers a voice in his ear.

Joe's eyes pop open and he's startled to see, sitting beside him, a man: late-sixties to early-seventies and of scruffy appearance, borderline tramp and yet, somehow . . . 'of the stage'. Had Joe been making up a story, he might have used the phrase 'theatrical drifter' or 'unkempt thespian hobo' and he'd be spot on, for the man did indeed have the air of the proverbial trained actor reduced to the status of a bum; once-famous, now homeless – from his well-worn campfire boots to his foppish brown hat worn at a jaunty angle.

'Jeez, where did you come from?'

'Worry not, Joe, we come in peace,' bids the man. 'I just need to take the weight off my aching feet for a moment.'

The accent is grand and cultured but ambiguous; part Anglo-Saxon, part African or Jamaican perhaps? Joe isn't sure;

polyethnic, possibly. And that colour: a wonderful baked-in tan? – Perhaps from a lot of time spent outdoors, drifting and foraging, at one with the world. Or is his lustrous glow simply the gift of natural pigmentation?

The man removes his hat and places it on the bench.

Joe notes the dense, wiry hair; greying throughout his curly high top and frizzy beard; the strong pronounced jawline, broad nose, high cheekbones and deep set, brown eyes; and for all its lines and weathering, or perhaps because of them, Joe finds it a fine and noble face – he feels certain the man has a cool heritage, a fascinating past, and surely an amusing story or two to tell.

The man removes a worn boot and the grubby sock it contained then sets to rubbing an inflamed foot.

Joe's mobile rings and he answers it.

'Hello? . . . What? No, I told you before! – It wasn't you? Well, where are you all getting my number? What? Yes, I *am* sure. Now piss off and stop calling me!' Joe turns off his phone and pockets it. 'Sorry about that.'

The man shrugs. 'They call me Trevor, by the way.'

'Who does?'

'Friends, associates – people I have known.'

Trying not to be too obvious about it, Joe continues to study the newcomer's face.

'Do I know you from somewhere?' he asks at last. 'You seem familiar.'

Trevor looks the boy over.

'Perhaps you do,' he smiles. 'And I must say, Joe, it is most rewarding, to discover you here, waiting to greet me like this.'

'It's the least we could do,' quips Joe. 'I'm afraid you missed the musicians.'

Trevor feigns disappointment.

'They didn't sound very good to be honest. Good movers though; a marching band.' He cocks an ear. 'I can't hear them anymore; they're probably miles away by now.'

'That's quite the imagination you've got there, Joe.'

'It helps in this town, Trevor.'

Trevor guffaws, a deep, booming rattle. Joe thinks the laugh wonderful and can't help but warm to the stranger.

'I don't think I've ever met a Trevor before,' he muses.

'At least, not one like me, eh, Joe, I'll wager.'

At the risk of appearing rude, Joe again looks the man over. Despite the untidy and grungy, down-and-out vagrant appearance, Joe senses something much-travelled and wise about Trevor. He likes the voice too: articulate and engaging. Yes, an

33

educated man, Joe feels sure; well-read, well-spoken, and learned.

'Are you wondering how I knew your name?' poses Trevor.

With raised eyebrows, Joe points at the name inked on the top of his Yoda backpack. 'Good try,' he acknowledges.

'There is nothing either good or bad,' cites Trevor, 'but thinking makes it so.'

Joe's eyebrows drop; a frown now – he appears baffled.

''Tis a quote,' explains Trevor. 'From Shakespeare – You must know The Bard, surely? He was very big at one time.'

'Size matters not,' retorts Joe. 'Look at me. Judge me by my size, do you?'

It's Trevor's turn to appear puzzled.

''Tis a quote,' mimics Joe. 'From Star Wars. Oh but you *must* know Star Wars, surely? Yoda? Little guy, funny teeth.' Joe mimes funny teeth (screwed up face, parted lips) then holds up his backpack and makes Yoda's head bounce.

'Yoda – yes, of course,' nods Trevor. 'Though I'm more of a theatre person, to be honest.'

'I thought so. Are you part of a theatre troupe?'

'No. I used to be part of a repertory company, a small ensemble of fellow performers, but my performances tend toward the solitary these days. A one-man show, if you will.'

Trevor replaces his sock and the boot that goes with it.

'A travelling show?'

'In a manner of speaking,' booms Trevor. 'I go wherever I feel my magnificent presence will best be appreciated.'

Although overly theatrical, Joe recognises the tone as tongue-in-cheek rather than boastful. Could the thespian's distinctive skin colour be the result of a lifetime of vaudevillian make-up on the amateur stage? – Maybe not so much 'mixed-race' as 'mixed reviews'? Not that it matters one iota to Joe.

'So, is your magnificent presence staying in Llani?' he teases. 'Or is it just passing through?'

'That remains to be seen, dear boy. I'm not yet sure.'

'There are some cheap bed-and-breakfasts in town.'

'Is that so?'

Trevor ties the lace on his boot; the lace short from where it has snapped at both ends. Joe also notes the worn heel and an Oreo-sized hole in the sole. The hole reports a partial headline, stuffed as it is with newspaper inside.

'You're not . . . sleeping rough, are you?' asks Joe.

'Under a canopy of stars? No, I have a roof; a little ramshackle, perhaps, less than I'm used to, you understand but I dare say it will suffice – and rest assured, it is *not* a sheet of tarpaulin.'

'I could let you have a pound.' Joe roots a pocket. 'It's all I've got on me but—'

'Most kind, but I assure you, there is no need.'

Trevor now takes something from a pocket. A small object flashes silver as he passes it from hand to hand.

'You wouldn't have to pay it back or anything.'

'Thank you, dear boy, but I have already acquired a bed for the evening – and for the foreseeable future; at least, as far as I can tell at this moment in time.'

'Right, so, it's definitely not this bench, then?'

Trevor's laugh rumbles vibrantly.

'No. If you'd care to look yonder –'

They swivel their heads toward the shabby, grubby, disgustingly green caravans; each as crummy and miserable as the next.

'– That one there is my current abode. Like the colour? Somewhere between Lime and Puce, I'd hazard a guess. They don't make them like that anymore.'

'Just as well.'

'Oh, it may look gloomy on the outside,' shares Trevor, 'but I assure you the interior is *far* more lugubrious.'

Joe laughs, for his diction is rather remarkable (some might say annoyingly so) for a soon-to-be thirteen-year-old.

Lugubrious: Adjective. Synonyms: Dismal, Doleful, Dreary, Melancholy, Morose, Mournful, Sad, Sombre, Sorrowful, Woebegone, and Woeful – he knows them all. Joe is one of those so-called 'sad kids' who, when he isn't reading books by Sir Arthur Conan Doyle, Charles Dickens or Alexander Dumas, actually enjoys scouring a dictionary or thesaurus; even if Owen and Gary do take the piss when they 'catch' him in the library indulging his love of words. Not that they're in the library often.

Again, Trevor's mystery object passes from hand to hand, red and black as well as silver if Joe isn't mistaken; a toy of some kind, perhaps.

'Whatcha got there, Trev?' asks Joe.

'What, this?'

Trevor reveals a tiny robot, some ten centimetres high.

'I collect them,' he announces proudly. 'Meet Mr Atomic, smaller than most but all the more transportable for it.'

'Yeah, he's . . . cool.'

Trevor cups Mr Atomic in both hands then blows.

35

When he opens them, the robot has gone.

The old man and the young boy exchange a look.

Trevor cups his hands again.

He opens them and the robot is back.

'Ta-da!' sings Trevor.

But Joe seems unmoved.

'I'm a bit long in the tooth for magic tricks,' he sighs.

'*Long in the tooth*, eh? That's quite an *old* expression for someone so—'

'I'm thirteen,' retorts Joe.

'Thirteen, eh?'

'Well, nearly.'

'Fair enough; pay it no heed – 'tis just a silly hobby.'

Mr Atomic disappears once more, this time back into Trevor's pocket. 'But if you ask me,' hails the old man, 'I do not believe anyone is ever too old for magic; it never fails to impress the hell out of me. Especially *real* magic,' he winks.

'If you say so,' laughs Joe.

'I do say so.'

Joe mimics the trick: cups a hand. 'And like that . . .'

Joe blows on his fist, springs open his fingers.

'He's gone.'

Neither speaks for a couple of beats.

'Well, I suppose I really should be trotting along,' grunts Trevor rising.

'*The Usual Suspects*,' explains Joe. 'Kevin Spacey.'

'Ah Spacey, a fine actor. I met him once at a gala.' Trevor dusts off his gabardine trousers and resets his hat. 'So,' he sighs, 'time and tide waits for no man and all that.'

Joe fears he has upset his new acquaintance.

'I collect snow-globes,' he blurts, standing.

'Is that right?' Trevor fishes a silk hankie from a pocket and coughs into it.

'Yeah, I've got loads.' Joe shrugs on his backpack.

'How interesting,' Trevor remarks. 'I have a snow-globe back in the caravan. Would you like to see?'

'Er . . . No, that's okay. I'd better be getting home.'

'Okay, Joe. Well, nice to meet you. And if you change your mind, you know where I am.'

CHAPTER 4
Blow and Make a Wish

The turnout to Joe's birthday bash might best be described as pitiful, pathetic, or both; this despite Joe telling everyone at school, posting on Facebook, tweeting on Twitter, *and* advertising his party on a card in the newsagent's window.

And cruellest of all: Wilf was still in hospital.

Brian, the boy from next door, *he* came. Brian has a boss-eye, large lower face and no friends to speak of. Joe plays 'penalties' with him from time to time in Brian's garden. Fancies himself as a goalkeeper does Brian; has his own football gloves, plastic-frame goal and bags of enthusiasm – he just isn't very good – hopeless, in fact. Always dives the wrong way, even when Joe tips him off, and insists on playing in his glasses even though he has to find or reset them after every lunge.

Katie turned up, of course. Katie lives up the road. She's in Joe's class and has always been kind to him. Joe considers her a good friend. Katie hopes she'll be considered more than a friend by the time they leave school; she fully expects her ugly duckling looks to have swanned by then. Her mum had been just the same when *she* was young (Katie's seen photos) and now look at her, 'a stunner', as all her older brother's male friends will testify; so surely Katie will be pretty too – one day.

(Actually, Rhydian's mates – Rhydian being Katie's brother – sometimes rib him that his mum is a MILF – this usually in the privacy of Rhydian's room, unaware that Katie has a terrible habit of pressing an ear against his door. Katie once Googled the term, decided she didn't like its vulgar description, and assigned the acronym a *new* definition: *Mum Is Looking Fabulous!*)

Katie had arrived early and helped lay out the massive buffet Sally had amassed: sausage rolls, a variety of sandwiches, crisps, pork pies, quiche, a selection of cheeses; enough for a houseful. But by the time the cake appeared, it was clear that the four people currently present – Joe, Sally, Brian and Katie – would be it. Paul was out all day, he'd had to attend a large fallen tree blocking a B road into Cwmbelan (Joe's dad works for the Welsh Forestry Commission, and well, an emergency is an emergency), Lucy was away on a school trip for London Fashion Week, and Maxine had thanked Joe for the invitation but explained that she'd be in Cardiff at the time, spending a week with her dad. (Maxine's parents are separated and she lives with her mum.)

As Katie had been so helpful, filling party bags and blowing up balloons and the like, Sally agreed to let her carry in Joe's R2D2-shaped cake.

When Joe had blown out all thirteen candles, after a rousing chorus of 'Happy Birthday To You', he'd sneakily made *two* birthday wishes: one, that Wilf would get better soon – very soon – and that two, he, Joe, would improve at 'storyfying' (as Wilf called it), computer gaming, sports, diving and well, everything, really.

Yes, it was the saddest party ever.

But then came the phone call – from the hospital. The birthday boy was so excited: Wilf finally well enough to sit up in bed and unselfishly ask a nurse for a phone? Yes, to ring and wish his favourite grandson a Happy 13th Birthday! Finally: a light at the end of what had been a very long and extremely dark tunnel. Wilf would soon be coming home! The best birthday present ever? You betcha!

But no, it wasn't Gramps – it was a doctor – with news of Wilf's passing. A second massive heart attack had finally seen off the old man.

Bonnie scans the street as Clara scours a local newspaper.

'Can't say I'm surprised,' huffs Bonnie, 'all the inbreeding going on in that town.'

'A cesspit of swingers, I heard,' rasps Clara.

With the return of Bonnie from the window, the counter once again resumes its complement of two middle-aged spinsters; neither of whom attempts to hide the ugly, gossipy air floating around them. Not even when Gas & Graze (petrol station cum grocery store) is busy; which, as per usual, it currently isn't – unless you count Noah, hovering by the snacks stand, in a world of his own, gently bumping crumpet packs together close to his left ear.

'Now, you be careful with those, Noah,' warns Bonnie. 'You'll have to pay for anything you damage.'

Noah may have unruly hair and twitch occasionally but he's 'special', everyone says so – and totally harmless. Any holidaymaker who dares refer to him as the village idiot is given short shrift and sent on their way with a flea in their lughole. Noah gets by perfectly well, thank you. He might be pushing thirty and find falling leaves fascinating, but he has talents to astound visitors: his woodcarvings are highly prized and earn him a living wage throughout the season. In summer months you'll find Noah under the stilted market hall in the centre of town with his blocks of wood, wonky workbench, three-legged stool and set of whittling chisels.

'How's Bronwen, Noah?' asks Clara. Bronwen is Noah's half-sister and carer. He lives at her place, and she looks after his post office savings account.

'Good,' grins Noah, his angled head nodding.

Ping! – And in swings the door.

'Ta-da!' announces the customer.

'Oh hello, Trevor,' beams Clara. 'How are we today?'

'A wretched soul, bruised with adversity, we bid be quiet when we hear it cry; but were we burdened with like weight of pain, as much or more we should ourselves complain.'

'Wonderful,' froths Clara. She pauses a moment then asks: 'Whassat mean, then?'

'One mustn't grumble, must one?'

'Oh, very good,' fizzes Bonnie, handing Trevor a copy of *The Stage*.

'Any news about Hamlet?' asks Clara.

'No, still waiting, I'm afraid.'

'Noah!' clucks Bonnie. 'What *are* you doing?'

Noah is leaning against a tall fridge listening to the rhythm of its faulty stop-and-go buzzing. This makes Trevor smile.

Joe is on his bed, back to the wall, staring across the landing, through his open door, to his granddad's bedroom, full of his old possessions: all Wilf's books, the clothes in his wardrobe, the radio next to his bed. (Gramps used to like to listen to smooth jazz on low when he read.) Yes, a room crammed with so many things, but oh so empty.

Joe has been sitting like this for over an hour, totally unaware of the passing time, his unfocused eyes not really looking ahead at all, rather, looking back, replaying memories in random sequences: catch and throw in the park, time spent fishing by the river, snowman building, walks through the woods . . .

'Joe!' shouts Sally from downstairs. 'Are you alright?!'

No reply.

'Joe!'

'What?!'

'Are you alright?!'

'Yes!'

'Are you coming down for supper?!'

'In a minute!'

'Okay!' calls Sally.

Joe had been subconsciously fiddling with a snow-globe for however long it had been; he couldn't even recall picking it up. Scores to choose from and at some point he must have picked this particular one off the shelf. He studies it for the first time in a long time.

In the years Joe had been collecting snow-globes (which is as long as he can remember) he would always buy as many as he could find; at least, until his saved pocket money ran out. He'd buy them on family holidays, school trips, or days out with Gramps; though on these latter excursions, Wilf would *always* pay – he insisted on it. Joe also bagged any snow-globe that turned up in the town's charity shops, sometimes visiting all three as many as five or six times a week. (Bought so many, the various shop staff began saving them for him; often charging as little as twenty-pence per shaker.)

The one presently in his hand – a car pulling a white caravan – he'd bought in Cornwall. Must have been over three years ago now. Yes, summer 2009: they'd hired a 4-berth caravan for a fortnight, hitched it to their 4x4 and toured all the natural wonders of the Cornish coast: Perranporth, Penzance, Polperro, Mevagissey, Land's End – stayed at every place, a different view of the sea every two or three days. They took a boat trip out of Falmouth, had a jaunt to Tintagel Castle, enjoyed outings to St. Ives and The Eden Project; Hurlers Stone Circles and King Arthur's Great Halls. And on the way back, the touring Evans' called at Cheddar Gorge in Somerset; they explored huge caverns filled with stalactites and stalagmites and gained fascinating insights into our prehistoric ancestors. In the gift shop, Wilf bought Joe yet another snow-globe: a stone-age man sitting on a rock by a wood fire outside the mouth of a cave.

Fire and snow, Joe hears Wilf say. *Unusual in a shaker.*

Joe nods and glances to a middle shelf next to the window; four snow-globes in from the right – he knew exactly where.

Aw, happy times, Wilf's voice sighs.

Again, Joe nods.

Go on, give us a shake, prompts Wilf.

Joe peers into the 'saloon car towing a caravan' snow-globe (back in 2009 he hadn't been able to find a globe with a 4x4 but this one sufficed, it was close enough). He shakes, and the snow immediately swirls around within the domed scene: a twirling snowstorm circling the vehicles, individual flakes bumping on the outside of the caravan as if wishing to be let in. Joe watches for a minute, until all the artificial snow has settled in drifts against the miniature diorama.

You know, you should visit him if you want to, suggests Wilf insightfully.

'Who?'

Trevor, of course.

Joe eyes Wilf's photo. 'He's a bit . . . odd.'

Aren't we all, laughs Wilf.

'Hmm.'

Just go with your instinct, Joe.

'Maybe.'

In the meantime, why don't you have another go at the trick. Or should I say: the magic.

'I tried,' grumbles Joe. 'You know how that turned out.'

Well, I suggest you try again, Joe. Only this time, let go your conscious self and act on instinct.

Joe laughs. 'Are you channelling Obi-Wan now?'

Yes, I am, laughs Wilf. *Glad you noticed. But seriously, remember, you can do anything if you put your mind to it.*

Joe pauses then blurts: 'Okay.'

And he scans the room before selecting a 7cm-high plastic Star Wars figure: Wicket, an Ewok from the forest moon of Endor.

Good choice, commends Wilf. *That'll do nicely.*

Sitting back on the bed, Joe takes a deep breath then cups the bear-like figure in both hands and concentrates.

Stretch out with your feelings.

Joe focuses deeply, closes his eyes tight; so intense in his single-mindedness that he starts rocking, willing the Ewok to disappear.

Good, good, encourages Wilf.

Extreme concentration and silent determination; swaying back and forth – had Wilf actually been there in person he might have expected his grandson to burst into a Shamanic chant at any second.

'Come on, come on,' intones Joe.

Do it, Joe, do it. You can do it.

The would-be sorcerer's eyes pop open, wide and pink.

Excellent, Joe! Wilf praises. *Now open your eyes.*

'They *are* open, Gramps.'

Okay, so open your hands; look and check – what are you waiting for?

Joe regards his hands – unfurls them slowly – and finds nothing! Nothing but a plastic Star Wars figure! *Wicket*, with his stupid ripped hood and annoyingly hairy face!

41

Your eyes can deceive, warns Wilf. *Don't trust them.*

But Joe isn't listening anymore. He's already up off the bed and furiously set, as if to angrily hurl the stubbornly-still-present, bothersome little Wicket against the wall. In the end though, he switches position and gently flings the tiny Ewok onto the bedding. Wicket takes a small, soft bounce and finally disappears – into the little gap between the top of Joe's quilt and the bottom of his pillow.

Joe had stood near the entrance to Tall Trees Trailer Park for a long twenty-seven minutes before finally approaching.

The static caravan appeared to grow filthier with every step. A sane person would have turned back. But Joe wasn't for turning, he'd definitely made his mind up – of this he was reasonably certain.

All the same, by the time Joe was a bus-length away, the weathered and grubby, twenty-foot trailer had taken on an almost sinister appearance in February's dusky late-afternoon light and he'd stopped. He had stared at the dull brightness within, uncertain if the small gas lamps illuminating the inside magnified the caravan's creepy appearance or lent it a homely glow – it was a fine line between the two, he'd decided.

Now, after this long bout of indecisiveness, Yoda looks over Joe's shoulder.

Always with you it cannot be done, he sighs.

'Talking to a perfect stranger on a bench is one thing,' counters Joe. 'This is totally different.'

No! Not different! In your mind, only different.

'And if he turns out to be a homicidal axe-wielding child-murderer?'

Fear is the path to the dark side, reminds Yoda. *And, if once you start down the dark path, forever will it dominate your destiny; consume you it will, as it did—*

'Okay, seriously, enough with the film quotes already,' berates Joe. 'Besides, I'm *not* afraid.'

Yoda cocks his head: *Aren't you?*

'I'd say more . . . *apprehensive – hesitant.*'

Yoda huffs and rolls his eyes.

'But reluctant or not, *I have to try.*'

Bit dramatic, sniffs Yoda.

'What's dramatic about saying I have to try?'

No! Try not. Do. Or do not. There is no try.

'Again? Really?'

Last one; promise – you were saying.

'Er . . .'

Something about the trailer?

'Yeah – do you think it looks a bit, y'know – hazardous?'

Hazardous?

'Exactly,' affirms Joe. 'Unpredictable. Risky. Uncertain.'

Yoda shakes his head. *Always the words with this one.*

Remember what I said, Joe, reminds Wilf's voice. *Your eyes can deceive you. Don't trust them.*

'I know, Granddad, but—'

Joe stops; Trevor is definitely home. Or at least someone is. A shadow just cut across the dim luminosity inside the caravan. And again there, drifting back, floating like a spectre from one grungy window to another; their cruddy frames of muck-caked glass bookended with tatty curtains.

'Maybe this is a bad idea,' sighs Joe. 'Wilf?'

I said before and I'll say it again: Let go your conscious self and act on instinct. Tell him, Yoda.

Hmm. Difficult to see. Always in motion the future is.

'Shush,' hushes Joe gently. 'I need to decide for myself.'

Yes, quiet, Yoda, let the boy think.

But you just—Right, not another word will I say, puffs Yoda.

Joe looks around – he'd always assumed that all these trailers and caravans (he wasn't sure of the difference between trailer and caravan, if indeed there was one) were only populated in the summer by holidaymakers, but no, at least a quarter had signs of life: lights on, vehicles parked at the side, or in the case of the one next door to Trevor's, a woman cleaning the inside of her windows. Joe immediately recognises her as Becki and Chloe's mum.

Alison spots him and peers over, perhaps wondering what this suspicious boy is up to. *Does* he look suspicious? Joe asks himself. Hasn't she recognised him? Should he wave? Will she realise it's him if he does?

Joe waves.

Alison raises a hand but doesn't really wave back, just watches, as if curious.

Right, forget her; it's now or never, thinks Joe. And he attempts to tune in to his instincts as Wilf instructed.

Reluctant? – Yes. Afraid? – Maybe a little. Or perhaps it's just nerves, or excitement, or both – either feeling would be perfectly natural.

Okay, so, are we bailing out, abandoning this iffy venture and going home? – Definitely not. On then? – Yes!

Joe nods in agreement with himself; encouraged – he *has* to do this. He shrugs his Yoda backpack and sets off, up the steps and onto the porch, just a single stride from the caravan door – only a rush of heartbeats between him and the portal – and that's when he trips, lurches, and nose-dives into the scuzzy Welcome mat.

'*Man down!*' squawks Joe, an involuntary reaction to too many hours spent gaming on his computer.

Swiftly up again he dusts off his school trousers and growls at the jagged rip in the knee. Then, as he finally sets to knock on the door's frosted window, the door opens.

Trevor stands in the doorway, a face like he'd been expecting this visit for some time.

Joe can't help but notice Trevor's bare, wet feet. Knobbly, wrinkled and leathery, they are the extremities of someone who has clearly walked many miles, thinks Joe somewhat randomly.

Trevor sucks on a long, black cigarette-holder and the mauve-coloured cigarette stuck in the end burns crisply.

'How lovely to see you, Joe,' he grins exhaling a plume of smoke. 'Come in, do.'

With Joe in, Trevor looks around then closes the door.

As Trevor is quietly removing the TO LET sign from the window, Joe notices the shelved, almost-full, glass display cabinet and its housed collection: lots of miniatures, several medium-sized, and one larger robot.

'Nice little collection.'

'Brew?'

'Sorry?'

'I'm making tea. Would you like a cup?'

The boiling kettle clicks off.

'No, I'm good, thanks.'

'I have an Irn Bru in the refrigerator—'

'There's one missing,' notes Joe indicating a gap in a line of shelved medium-sized robots.

'But if the while I think on thee, dear friend,' recites Trevor, 'all losses are restored and sorrows end.'

'O—kay,' responds Joe.

'These aren't the droids you're looking for,' pipes up the larger robot.

'Wow, that one talks.'

'I never have the slightest idea what he's jabbering about but I'm afraid I can't find the Off Switch. Pay him no heed.'

'It's Star Wars. *A New Hope.*'

44

'Ah.' Trevor adopts his best thespian stance. 'That's no planet,' he delivers in his best Sir Alec Guinness voice. 'It's a space station.'

Joe laughs.

Pfft, scoffs Yoda. *Planet.*

'Something wrong, boy?' booms Trevor playfully. He sucks on his cigarette-holder and puffs out a smoky cloud.

'It's *moon*,' coughs Joe. 'Not *planet*.'

Not one to accept a fluffed line easily, Trevor frowns.

'Are you quite sure?'

'Yep, pretty sure,' smiles Joe. 'That's no moon,' he quotes. 'It's a space station.'

'Then I stand corrected,' bows Trevor.

Joe's mobile rings but he ignores it.

'Aren't you getting that?'

'Nah, I'm good.'

'But what if it's important?'

'It won't be.'

'All the same—'

'Fine,' huffs Joe impatiently.

He pulls the phone from his pocket.

'Hello?' Joe's tone is pessimistic and flat.

After listening a moment he abruptly ends the call.

'Yeah, I'm just going to leave it switched off. Sorry, do you mind if I open a window? It's very smoky in here.'

'By all means.' Trevor indicates the window next to the dining table. 'And please, make yourself comfortable. Best seats in the house.'

Joe notices a bowl of soapy water under the table. He sits on the 'free' side and Trevor sits opposite, sliding his feet back into the bowl as Joe opens the window.

'You know, those things are really bad for you. *And* me.'

'Yes, you're quite right, dear boy. It is a filthy habit. *Ziganov Colours*: strong Russian tobacco. Sadly, I am but a helpless slave to the pernicious weed. However, from this day hence, I vow never to smoke in your presence again.'

Trevor removes the brightly-coloured, gold foil filtered cigarette from the holder, stubs it out then leans back and deposits the ashtray on the kitchen counter behind him.

'Pernicious: good word.'

'Thank you, my boy. Oh, and I see you've discovered my shaker; the globe I believe I mentioned when first we met.'

'Well, yes, it was right here on the table.'

Joe shakes the small ornament.

'I thought you'd like it.'

'Who doesn't like a snow-globe?'

'Philistines,' suggests Trevor.

'Do you collect these, too?' Joe looks around for others.

'No, I just liked that one because of the robot. See.'

Joe peers inside.

'I would imagine snow is bad for robots,' he muses.

'Keep it,' offers Trevor. 'Add him to *your* collection.'

Joe glances at the old man then slowly places the shaker back on the table.

'Problem?'

'I'm not sure it would be a good idea.'

'But why ever not, dear boy? It is merely a gift; an offering to mark our newfound friendship.'

'I know, but I'm not even sure if I should really be here.'

'You're right, I should keep it.'

Trevor takes possession of the globe, shakes it, and then sets it to one side.

Joe eyes the shaker intently.

'Shame, though,' he laments. 'It is a nice one. And I haven't got a *robot* snow-globe.'

'What if we were to make a trade?' proposes Trevor. 'A noble exchange. Quid pro quo.'

'A swap?' replies Joe. 'I suppose. But I haven't really got anything on me.'

'You must have something. Boys always have something interesting in their pockets. How about we trade for whatever you have in there.'

Joe roots his pockets but finds only a piece of paper – and he knows what it is.

'Let me see.' Trevor sticks out a liver-spotted hand.

Joe obliges: he fishes out the note and surrenders it.

'*Loser*,' reads Trevor. 'So, have you lost something?'

'Lost something?' laughs Joe sadly. 'You could say that.'

Trevor folds the note. 'I imagine Loser is not referring to the loss of your grandfather, though.'

'Heard about that on the grapevine, did you?' sighs Joe.

After four folds Trevor cups his large hands around the small paper square.

'What are you doing?' Joe frowns. 'Another trick?'

'No, I'm doing what you should have done when you first found it.'

'But how do you—?'

Trevor throws his hands in the air and there's an eruption of tiny pieces of paper, hundreds of them; they burst out and rain down on Joe's shoulders and head.

'Ta-da!' exclaims Trevor.

Joe exhales loudly then sticks out his bottom lip and blows away bits of confetti caught in his Fro's fringe curls.

'Not impressed?'

Joe shakes his head gently; another sprinkle of teeny paper scraps flutters to the table.

'I don't believe in magic, Trevor. Not anymore.'

'Not even when the magic is clearly real?'

'I'm not a kid.'

'That's a shame,' sighs Trevor touching Joe's hand.

Joe withdraws his hand and stands.

'I think I should be going.'

Joe heads for the caravan park exit trailing an occasional piece of confetti. Trevor watches him go.

'Come back any time,' he calls.

Alison, noticing Joe's departure, rubbernecks behind her window.

Joe paces in front of the school, periodically hooking the top button of his shirt and blowing cold air down inside.

The man in the parked burger van leans on the counter watching intently, a curious, some might say creepy, look on his face.

Joe's pacing (and blowing) stops as Lucy and Max, wheeling their bikes beside them, exit through the gates. Lucy's in platform boots and a shortened red Sari pinched at the waist by a large yellow belt; a kind of East meets Westwood. She's also rocking a Bindi (forehead dot), jewelled nose ring, and, on the back of one hand, a red-and-blue henna tattoo: the iconic Aladdin Sane lightning bolt. Max's look today is perhaps best described as Bride of Dracula meets steampunk ass-kicker: buckled corset; short, ruffled black lace skirt over a ruched, crimson petticoat; ripped stockings under knee boots, that kind of thing – plus the usual bold make-up.

'Hi, Max,' beams Joe. 'You look amazing.'

'Aw, thanks,' smiles Maxine.

'And what am I?' quips Lucy. 'Chopped liver?'

'Nice bike,' Joe continues.

Maxine raises her eyebrows. 'Still the same one, Joe.'

'About time you got on yours,' suggests Lucy.

Joe ignores his sister's gibe and sticks to grinning at Max; he knows it's getting weird but just can't stop.

'Are you hot?' asks Maxine at last.

No, but you are, Joe almost blurts. 'Er, no, why?'

'Your face.'

'What about it?'

'It's all red,' remarks Lucy matter-of-factly.

'So's his belly!' calls an approaching voice.

Joe's heart slumps: Owen with Gary and Melvin in tow, cackling like simpletons.

'He belly-flopped in swimming,' crows Gary.

'From the high board,' guffaws Melvin.

'Ooh,' frowns Maxine sympathetically. 'Sounds painful.'

'Nah,' Joe bats away any concerns with a dismissive hand, 'it's fine,' he assures her.

'Fine?' snorts Owen. 'Well, it was better than our last football practice, Joe, I'll give you that much.'

'Yeah, why don't ya tell Maxine all about it,' goads Gary.

'I don't know why,' sneers Owen, 'but I *always* score when Joe's in goal.'

'Which is, like, every game,' adds Gary. 'Coz he can't play anywhere else.'

'Haven't you lot got homes to go to?' asks Lucy sharply.

But Owen isn't for home quite yet:

'Chill out, Luce,' smirks Gary, 'it's just laddish banter.'

'Is it, Gary?' seethes Lucy. 'Is it really?'

'Not everyone's into sports, Owen, you dickhead,' bristles Maxine.

'That's true,' acknowledges Owen. 'I mean to be fair, he *is* good at storytelling. Oh no, wait – he's not good at that either, is he?'

'Jeez, what is your problem?' Maxine wants to know.

'You wanna drop out of the Storytell comp, mate,' urges Gary, 'before you embarrass yourself anymore than you already have.'

'Right, piss off,' warns Lucy. Maxine holds Lucy's bike as she shoos the trio. 'Go on, do one, before I lose my shit.'

'We were going anyway,' bleats Gary backing up.

'Good. So, go.'

'And Joe's way smarter than any of you dumb-asses,' rasps Max. 'He'll slaughter you in Storytell, you just see if he doesn't.'

'Oh yeah,' splutters Melvin, 'well, for someone who read the dictionary – if he really did – how come he can't— y'know – how come he can't—' Melvin is unable to formulate his puerile thoughts into meaningful words and the sentence tapers away unfinished.

'Go on keep going,' orders Lucy arms wide, shepherding.

'I believe what Melvin's trying to say is, and correct me if I'm wrong here, Melvin.' Owen's retreating face bobs behind Lucy's head, from one shoulder to the other. 'How it sure is funny, that for someone who supposedly reads a lot of stories, he can't make one up!'

'Yeah, that was it,' grunts Melvin.

'Especially when,' another head bob, 'it's just so, what's the word,' another shoulder switch, 'so fucking easy!'

'Right, that's enough!' warns Lucy sternly.

'Alright, alright,' protests Owen as Joe's sister attempts to shove them beyond the van. 'We're getting burgers.'

'Fine, get your shit in a bun and piss off.'

'Yes, Miss,' mocks Gary after Lucy has headed back.

Owen can't resist one final taunt either:

'Hey, Joe, maybe you could steal a story from one of your books!' he hollers. 'We wouldn't tell anyone, would we, boys?'

'Yeah, maybe an Aesop's fucking Fable,' shouts Gary.

Melvin guffaws at that, though, in truth, he doesn't know why. No matter, he has a hotdog to look forward to.

'No need to cheat to beat you, Owen!' barks Joe at last.

'You okay? Lucy asks, returned.

'Yeah, why wouldn't I be?'

'Don't let that lot bother you.'

'They don't.'

'Good.' Lucy repossesses her bike. 'Right then, I'm off.'

'So, go then.'

Remounted Lucy cautions her brother:

'And don't wander off this time.'

Joe rolls his eyes as Lucy rides away.

'See you later!' she calls back.

'Bye, Luce!' exclaims Maxine, lifting a leg over the bike frame. 'If they give you any more trouble, Joe,' she nods at the boys, 'just let us know and we'll sort them out for you.'

'Er, martial arts; remember?'

Joe pantomimes a leg throw, or shoulder throw, or whatever that weird move he just performed was.

'Oh, that's right,' smiles Maxine, 'judo. I was forgetting.'

She winks and pedals off, Joe attentively scrutinising her departure up the road. *Poetry in motion*, he thinks; a cliché perhaps but so apt, he feels. He'd been having adolescent stirrings, wanton thoughts, about Max for a while now. Not that she'd ever be interested in being his girlfriend, not really; he was far too young for her – and what girl in her right mind would be interested in his uncool awkwardness and lardy arse. Still, he could look, he could imagine, he could fantasise. And it wasn't just Max's stunning face (those smoky eyes!), magnetic presence and bewitching manner he daydreamed about – it was more earthy than that: it was her girlish well-proportioned shape, her nimble trimness – in essence, *all* her curves.

Much to learn you still have, my young padawan, sniffs Yoda. *This is just the beginning*, he warns.

'Quiet, you.'

Attachment leads to jealousy, the shadow of—

'Hey Max!' Joe bellows.

'What?!' Maxine will disappear behind the burger van any second.

'Do you like magic?!'

Joe fails to hear Maxine's response, if indeed there was one. Instead, all he hears is Owen, Gary and Melvin. Clucking loudly they parrot: 'Do you like magic?' as if he'd just asked the most pathetic question ever.

CHAPTER 5

Storytelling

'I didn't forget,' insists Paul sternly. 'And I wasn't late. He just wasn't there.'

'Okay, okay,' groans Sally with impatience. 'I'm sure he's fine. He's probably just with friends.'

Sally, her bump far more prominent now, places the Turn And Face The Strange mug (one of a set bought by Lucy) on the table in front of Paul then leans back on the kitchen counter.

'Sugar in this?' checks Paul.

Sally rolls her eyes. 'Think I know how you take your tea, Paul. You should be the one making me a drink.'

'You don't have to make coconut water. Just pour it.'

'Still, it'd be nice if you actually offered for once.'

'Well, speak of the devil,' Paul interrupts.

Joe is passing the open door, carrying a box marked WILF'S THINGS through the hall.

'And where the hell have you been?'

'What do you care?'

'Hey! I won't be spoken to like that.'

Sally's demeanour sighs: Here we go again.

'So, where were you?' grills Paul.

'What? I was upstairs.' Joe stares intently. 'Okay?'

'I'm talking about after school,' barks Paul. 'And why was your phone switched off?'

Joe shrugs.

'Hasn't got a clue,' mutters Paul.

'Paul,' chides Sally.

'Well, look at him, carrying that box everywhere. What's that all about? It's morbid. Been months now, he should get over it. *I've* had to.'

'Jesus, Paul, it's been four months,' fumes Sally. '*Are* you over it?'

'And why is he wearing that silly backpack all the time?'

'Lucy made it for him,' objects Sally. 'And it's not silly.'

'Can I go now?' huffs Joe. 'This is heavy.'

'You do understand we had to clear Wilf's old room, right, love?' asks Sally softly. 'Make it up for the baby. You're okay with that?'

Joe gazes into the box for several heartbeats and eventually produces a small nod.

'Yep,' he sighs.
'We'll have to pull that shed down too at some point.' Paul
blows his tea. 'Before it *falls* down, rickety old thing.'
'What?!' barks Joe.
'Joe, it's becoming a hazard,' asserts Paul.
'No!' And with that Joe rushes away, the box's contents
rattling ahead of him.
'Where does he think he's going now?'
Paul indicates the kitchen clock.
'It's Friday, Paul,' chides Sally. 'No school in the morning. Let
him be.'

Inside *Wilf's Workshop*, between the junk, Chopper bike and
giant animal paw on a stick, sits Joe, cross-legged on the floor.
Speckles of dust flicker around the sooty bulb hanging from the
shed's ceiling. The dull light casts a tawny glow of barely-
perceptible warmth over Joe's head. He's sitting next to
Granddad's old trunk: an antique piece of luggage; something,
according to Wilf, an old buccaneer once owned. Probably just
Granddad storifying but it certainly has an ancient swashbuckling
sea-faring look to it – at least Joe has always thought so – with its
brass studs, leather straps and brass lock.
From the box of *Wilf's Things* Joe retrieves a framed photo, a
picture of Joe and Wilf wrapped in winter clothing and
surrounded by fir trees, smiling in the snow. After studying it for
a moment he stands it front and centre on the trunk.
Next out of the box, an award: a Storytell trophy won by Wilf
back in the day. Hard to imagine Wilf at school, young and in
uniform, but the trophy is testament to his attendance – as well
as his storytelling skills.
There are four trophies in the box, won in succession from
1947 to 1950, each engraved *Wilf Evans, Freestyle Storytell
Champion* followed by the year that particular trophy was won.
They are clearly based on the 'Oscar' statuettes handed out at the
Academy Awards: picture the same gold-coloured chap atop a
circular base, but open hands rather than holding a sword – as if
telling a story.
Joe sets the trophies in a row on the back of the trunk's lid.
Then a second framed photo is lifted from the box: an 'official'
snap taken at one of the award presentations: Wilf in blazer, cap
and sharp-creased trousers, smiling and waving all happy and
proud, yet modest at the same time.
Joe's thoughts drift to school caps and how relieved he is no-
one has to wear them anymore; they look so corny and old-

fashioned, not cool like baseball caps. It is at this point that the bulb fizzes briefly and a sharp pop puts the shed in complete darkness.

The sound of rummaging, not in Wilf's box but the drawers of his workbench: metal objects scrape against wood and each other, chisels, screwdrivers, tins of screws or nuts and bolts, drill bits, work gloves, string, wire . . . (Wilf had all the odds and ends you'd expect to find in any shed worthy of the name – and some you wouldn't).

The foraging falls silent then there's a click: a torch beam, brown it's so dull. Scarcely illuminating the interior, the weak shaft of light picks out floating dust particles, mere specks, too airy and lightweight to descend, as it throws ghostly shadows all around.

So much dust, thinks Joe. And what is dust? – Barely detectable fragments of plant pollen, textile fibres, animal hairs and human skin cells. Joe wonders what infinitesimally small percentage of this floating lint was once a part of Granddad – what amount of his DNA, a piece of this powdery cloud of microscopic snowflakes. A fleck catches the back of Joe's throat and his subsequent barking cough causes the sooty haze to rush and dance.

Once Joe has recovered and the dust has settled somewhat, Wilf's cap makes an appearance from the box. The headpiece is followed by its matching scarf and together with a couple of Wilf's favourite 'pulp' paperbacks, the items are laid gently on the trunk lid, the scarf made to snake softly between trophies and framed photos.

The torch beam stutters and dulls to less than useless.

'Seriously?' Joe sighs.

The scrape of a drawer, more rummaging, another drawer, yet another rummage, a rattle, then a final scrape before a match finally lights a stubby candle. Shadows warp and waver as Joe sets the candle gently in the middle of Wilf's possessions, careful to make sure there's no danger of scarf or cap catching fire.

Joe isn't religious but a feeling of spirituality suddenly washes over him. Perhaps it's the kneeling, the display: it has all the hallmarks of one of those small roadside shrines he saw dotted around when they took a trip to Ireland. He brought back a keepsake that he felt caught the holiday's flavour, even if it was a bit cliché: a snow-globe with a river-dancing leprechaun; four-leaf clover in one hand, pint of Guinness in the other.

Wilf had bought it for him. (It was the first summer after Joan had passed; Wilf came along after Sally insisted he needed a holiday. Joan, who was older than Wilf, had suffered a long time with dementia, and Wilf, despite arthritis, diabetes, and his own increasing age, had been her main carer.) And yet, in spite of all this, Wilf had always found time for Joe.

Joe pulls the leprechaun snow-globe from his pocket, shakes it, and adds it to the trunk's display.

It's a shame we couldn't find a Father Ted snow-globe like we'd wanted, Joe hears his granddad say.

'I don't think they make them, Gramps,' smiles Joe.

Father Jack was my *favourite. Arse! Drink! Girls!*

Joe laughs. Everyone loves Father Ted. And everyone loved Wilf. Look at him there in the photo, bless him, all fresh-faced and smiley, a young lad himself, clutching one of his storytelling prizes; the *actual* trophy – *all* his trophies – over sixty years later, now glinting in the candle light.

Joe gazes at the Storytell 'Oscars', marvels at how, relocated from the past, they flicker and glimmer before him – and his imagination flits; transports him to a different time and place . . .

The school hall is much the same as it ever was. No different to present day as far as Joe can tell – except that it's in black and white for some reason. The school teachers seem strange somehow, though; different, sterner, less friendly, more formal – strict, even.

The stuffy headmaster, a pigeon-chested galoot, calls up the young Wilf. Applause rings out as the boy approaches the stage, the audience made up of smartly uniformed school children, row upon row of them clapping politely. Joe pictures Wilf as he is in the award photo, thirteen probably, the same age Joe is now. (Joe would look exactly like him, if only he could lose a little weight.) Young Wilf climbs the three wooden steps at the side of the stage and walks the boards toward the musty, self-important headmaster.

'Well done, Wilfred.'

During the formal handshake and the handing over of the trophy there are several flashes as a suited photographer snaps the moment for posterity and the local newspaper. Young Wilf holds up the award for all to see and there's a resurgence of applause from the hall, cheers from a group of close friends, one or two jocular thumbs-down from the losers, and another round of camera flashes.

In the background, behind Wilf and the headmaster, on the old, familiar easel, are four word cards:

REFLECTION. JESTER. CROW. STREAM.

There's a long pause, after which, a familiar voice reminds:
Going to look at the other photographs, you were, hmm?
'Hmm?' wonders Joe absentmindedly.
Yoda prods Joe with his cane.
The other photographs, Yoda sighs.
'Oh, yes – the snowman album.'
Yoda nods at the box.
Put it in with Wilf's things, you did, hmm?
Joe reaches in and produces a white A4-sized photo album
with a picture of a snowman on the front. He rests it on his lap
and turns the cover. After a title page: The Snowman Chronicles, and
a blank page 2, each further white page contains a single glued-in
Polaroid above Joe's handwritten notes and doodles.

The first photograph, taken at the turn of the millennium, has
an annotation that reads:

Christmas Day 2000. Mr Zero, my first ever snowman. Granddad Wilf
(65), Joan (68), Mum (26), Lucy (4), Dad (31) and me (0). Not much snow
but enough for my inaugural snowman. The whole thing was Granddad's idea
but Lucy picked the name.

In the photo, the snowman is tiny, maybe a foot tall, as wee as
the baby held in Paul's arms. Sally and Lucy are holding hands
and Wilf is knelt beside the snowman, arms outstretched towards
Mr Zero as if he were a fantastic prize to be won on a Christmas
game show.

With each slow, deliberate page turn, the snowmen grow
larger and more fabulous, the family a year older.

Mr Nippy.

Mr Sparkles.

Mrs Freezy.

Noel.

Monsieur Shivers.

On some, Joe appears on Wilf's knee, in others at least one
person from the family is missing (perhaps taking the photo);
nonetheless, all the snaps capture a sense of joy.

In Joan's final appearance, with Mr Melt, she appears sick and
grey and lost. She had passed by the time Mr Abominable appeared
in the winter of 2007.

The pages continue to turn at a leisurely pace . . .

Mr Eight.

Little Miss Blizzard.

Brrrrronwen.

And the final Polaroid, dated Christmas 2011:

Mr Frosty.

Twelve photographs in total.

With the next turn, the page is blank; there's no photo for 2012 – no Joe, no Wilf, no family, no snow. And Mr Wonky is conspicuous by his absence.

Joe stares at the empty page for the longest time.

It is Yoda who eventually breaks the silence:

Train yourself to let go of everything you fear to lose.

'Fear to lose?' echoes Joe sadly. 'I've already lost that.'

Good point, sniffs Yoda. *Then something else you must.*

'What; Mr Wonky? – I never had *him* to start with.'

No! Yoda smacks Joe on the head with his cane.

The snow-globe, he barks.

'Huh?' Joe rubs his head.

The one in your pocket; no trace of it there must be.

Yoda taps Joe's pocket with the cane.

'Sorry, what are you asking me to do? Get rid of a snow-globe – are you mental?'

Yoda rolls his eyes. *Not rid of. Make it disappear. Vanish. Dematerialise.* He shakes his head, closes his eyes and sighs heavily. *Lose it,* he drawls dramatically.

'Oh okay, I get it,' Joe catches on. He fishes the snow-globe from his pocket; the one inhabited by a robot, gifted from Trevor in exchange for Joe's *'Loser'* note.

Maxine, impressed she'll be, hmm?

'Yeah, ya think?' smirks Joe.

Yoda nods. *Big time.*

Joe likes the idea of Max being dazzled; *he'd* thought she'd be fascinated, too. He shakes the globe, sets it on a palm then looks to Yoda.

'Right, let's give it a try.'

Try?! barks Yoda.

'I mean . . . *do*. Let's do it.'

Good. Yoda points his cane at the snow-globe. *So, do.*

'Where did you get the cane, by the way?' asks Joe.

Focus!

'Ow!'

Sorry about that. Hand slipped.

'Uh-huh.'

Yoda aims a sharp nod at the globe.

'Fine.' After rubbing his head, Joe takes a long deep breath and lets it out real slow. He closes his eyes, concentrates and centres himself, but then, whilst trying to clear his mind in order to attain ultimate zenness, he accidentally pictures Max, riding away on her bike, pedals rising and falling in slow motion; wheels turning – her tight little bum on the saddle—

56

Yoda whacks Joe with the cane.

Control, control, you must learn control.

'Ow! – and shush. I was just – gathering my thoughts.'

Younglings, sighs Yoda.

'Okay, I'm ready. Here we go.'

Finally, mutters Yoda.

'I need you to believe in me, Max,' practises Joe. 'Do you believe? *Really* believe? You do? Cool, watch carefully.'

Good, good, encourages Yoda.

Joe cups the snow-globe and closes his hands around it.

'Keep watching, Max; stay with me . . .'

Yoda closes his eyes and nods keenly.

'And now be amazed as I magically –'

Joe opens his hands:

The snow-globe is as present as it ever was.

Yoda's eyes blink open but as he moves to see, Joe swiftly and slyly re-cups his hands.

Come on, you can do it, urges Wilf's disembodied voice.

'Can I, Gramps?' sighs Joe.

If we think hard enough we can make anything *happen.*

Already know you that which you need, adds Yoda.

'Fine, one more try—I mean, go.'

One is all you'll need, Joe.

Use the Force, young padawan.

Joe shuts his eyes, squeezes them as tight as his hands, and growls, his whole body shaking with steely determination. This goes on for several seconds, then:

Yoda raises an expectant eyebrow.

'Yeah! You feel that?!' squeals Joe.

He opens his hands to reveal . . . a circular impression where the base has pressed into fleshy palm. The mark, though deep and pink, will shortly disappear – unlike the globe, which stubbornly remains in the physical realm.

'Oh, come on!'

Joe is up on his feet, angrily pacing within the confined space and looking for somewhere to throw the globe, preferably into something soft: he doesn't want to break it.

'I don't know what I'm doing!' he snarls. 'We're just wasting our time!'

Having not found anything soft enough to launch the globe into, Joe settles instead for harshly shoving it back into his pocket with a frustrated grunt. Yoda sighs.

Teach him I cannot. No patience the boy has.

He will learn patience, insists Wilf.

Much anger in him . . . Like his father.
Was I any different when—?
'Jeez, could you two knock it off?' gripes Joe.
Silence for a long beat then Yoda muses: *Hmm, so storm out of the shed now you must, yes?*
'Yep,' grunts Joe. And he does.

On the easel: COWBOY, SWAMP, STAR, and MONEY.
Owen is addressing his amused classmates, hardly able to finish his story for laughing. Only Joe and Mr Schneider appear unimpressed. The teacher was distracted several minutes ago by a group of girls on the sports field engaging in some early practice for the Morris dancing team's sheep-bladder tossing competition ahead of the upcoming summer Eisteddfod. Joe, stony-faced, is rolling the robot snow-globe in his hands as if it were a grenade.

'But the Marshal had passed out in the saloon,' snorts Owen. 'And the Sheriff *couldn't* follow,' he wraps up, 'because of what happened to his horse.'

All the students, apart from Joe, laugh hysterically. Owen bows, soaks up their applause and whistles. Joe shakes his head. Melvin, on his feet, congratulates Owen as he returns to his seat.

'Now *that's* how it's done, young Jedi,' winks Owen.

Joe's story had not gone well. At first the cards looked promising: MIRROR, DENIAL, OGRE, and TIME. But Joe's attempt to string them together in an interesting and amusing narrative had spluttered, stalled, and then fizzled out to a weak, baffling, and unfunny punch-line – a complete and utter fail.

As Owen bullishly attempts to stoke the now fading praise, Mr Schneider finally moves away from the window and its athletic distractions.

'Right, settle down, class,' he orders. 'Now remember, the chance to enter this year's competition closes at the end of this week. All entrants must declare themselves on the notice board by 4 p.m. Friday. Okay, so does anyone else want a practice run?'

The teacher studies the faces of his students.

'Hey, by the way,' asks Owen, 'what's with your Fro today, Joe? It's kinda . . .'

'My hair's kinda what, Owen? Frizzy? Bushy? Ginger?'

'Kinda Shit,' advises Owen.

Joe clutches his stomach mockingly. 'Oh, bravo, Owen,' he mocks. 'Insulting, insightful, and *so* inventive.'

'Well, it *is* shit.'

'Really? *Shit's* the best you can come up with? How about –' Joe shrugs, points at Melvin. '– You, pick a letter.'

58

'Er, D?'

'For D you could have had detestable or disagreeable, dreadful or dismal, deplorable—'

'Shut it, showoff.'

'Oh, touché.'

'Careful, Owen,' warns Gary. 'He might use his sumo on you.' And they start a chorus of: 'Sumo! Sumo!'

'Alright, that's enough.' Over Owen and Gary's laughter the teacher asks: '*Will* you be entering again this year, Joe?'

'What, after last year's fiasco?' snickers Gary.

'Oh, come on now,' pleads the teacher. 'We all know it's been a tough time for Joe recently.'

'It's always a tough time for some people,' quips Owen.

Gary laughs, cruel and loud, but the rest of the class are not amused and even Melvin looks sympathetic.

Exchanging a challenging look with Owen, Joe tests the weight of his snow-globe as if it really *were* a grenade he might roll under the clown's desk. A snow-bomb that will burst with a mighty bang under the terrified buffoon's arse, showering him and Gary with glitter and embarrassment and making them shit their pants (whilst leaving the rest of the class unharmed and highly entertained).

Joe nods absentmindedly and smiles to himself.

'What *is* that?' sneers Owen.

'Brought one of your toys in?' mocks Gary.

'Joe, over here, dear boy,' calls Trevor. 'Join us, do.'

Trevor is seated at the back of The Cliché Café, installed in a booth, holding court; those around him clearly enthralled by whichever anecdote he's been recounting.

'Make room, make room,' bids Trevor, and those sitting opposite, Mrs Spencer the old woman from the charity shop, and Ben, a middle-aged clerk in the town's only bank, scoot their bums along the green vinyl bench seat. The young woman beside Trevor is Polish dental assistant slash receptionist Marta. Joe knows them all to be Jehovah's Witnesses; he's seen all three at his front door on various occasions. Paul always sends them packing; tells them he's not interested in religion – theirs or anyone else's.

'What *is* that?' asks Joe at the table.

'A Saville Row Smoking Jacket, dear boy – the finest.'

Once upon a time, a dapper smoking jacket it may have been, *the finest* even, but today, the quilted burgundy over-garment is faded, worn, riddled with holes and absurdly out of place.

Where does he think he is? Joe wonders. In a stately home, by a roaring fireplace, packing a pipe with tobacco; like Sherlock Holmes in Sir Arthur Conan Doyle's famous detective stories?

'Pure velvet. Feel that quality. I wore this in our touring production of Noel Coward's *Present Laughter*. I played the lead, Garry Essendine. And I was magnificent.'

Trevor catches the attention of a server.

'A treat for my guest: a milk-shake, or Knickerbocker Glory, or whatever it is the kids are into these days.'

Then, to Joe: 'Please, sit.'

Joe considers the offer. His last memory of Trevor was the old man touching his hand. Was that just a normal physical expression of a genuine human emotion – or was it 'inappropriate behaviour'? No, on reflection, Joe would *not* call the contact *inappropriate*. And besides, this is a public place, lots of customers, it should be fine.

He squeezes onto the bench seat next to Marta and is happy to do so. Close proximity to a pretty blonde who, as it turns out, smells divine – what's not to like?

'Just a half-pounder with large fries and an ice-cream sundae to follow, thanks, Jess,' he tells the server. 'Oh, and a diet coke. No, make it a regular.'

The full name on her badge is Jessica but Joe knows her well and frequents The Cliché Café regularly – and why wouldn't he? The diner has a Never-judge-a-book-by-its-cover corner where a host of paperbacks are available for any customer to read for free.

(The books are also available to buy for a modest charge if you find one you like. Or spend £10 and take home any title for free.)

'One Ignorance-is-bliss burger, a Chip-off-the-old-block fries, an Everything-in-moderation coke, and a What-doesn't-kill-you-makes-you-stronger sundae coming up,' affirms Jessica before spinning on a heel and disappearing.

'So, who's Garry Essendine?' asks Joe, secretly enjoying the weight of Marta's thigh against his own.

Trevor is suddenly on his feet, hamming it up as Garry Essendine: 'I don't care whether they've put a swimming bath in my dressing room, and a squash court and a Steinway Grand,' he recites. 'I will not play a light French comedy to an auditorium that looks like a Gothic edition of Wembley Stadium.'

Trevor's dining companions clap politely and gently stamp their feet. The old actor takes his bows as if it were an opening night debut. Although Joe doesn't recognise the play, if indeed that's what it is (he doubts the others know either), he feels compelled to join in with the applause.

'Ah, my public still love me. Thank you, thank you. You really are too kind.'

The server walks over and stands by their table.

'You're quite right, Jessica,' apologises Trevor profusely. 'We should keep the noise down. This is a respectable establishment. Any more noise,' – he points at the door – 'and out we'll go.'

'No, I was just bringing Joe his Everything-in-moderation coke,' sniffs Jess. 'There you go, Joe.'

'Still, we were making rather a commotion, for which we wholeheartedly ask forgiveness – it shan't happen again.'

Jessica shrugs. 'Can I get anybody anything else?'

'No, we're fine,' agree Trevor's companions, sipping the last of their tea as Jessica collects Trevor's empty plate.

'That was delicious, my dear – and thoroughly deserving of a pudding. What do you have? Enthral me with your sweet delights.'

'We have An-apple-doesn't-fall-far-from-the-tree pie, You-are-what-you-eat lemon meringue, There's-no-time-like-the-present sherry trifle, At-least-I've-got-my-health—'

'Ooh yes, the sherry trifle – thank you.'

'One No-time-like-the-present coming right up.'

And with that Jessica returns to the counter.

'Well, that was a close one,' whispers Trevor conspiratorially.

'What was?' asks Mrs Spencer.

'About the noise.'

'Oh, I don't think she was bothered,' smiles Marta.

'All the same, perhaps it would be best if you were to leave,' encourages Trevor.

'Us?' asks Ben. 'But I really don't think—'

'The clapping, the whistling, the stamping of feet,' interrupts Trevor. 'We must consider our fellow diners must we not? Besides, I have a rather compelling matter I'd like to discuss with Master Joe in private.'

'You do?' asks Joe with regret. He could happily listen to Marta's Polish accent all day – and then there's her leg, still pressing against his own, after all this time!

'If you wouldn't mind,' asserts Trevor to the group.

'In private, eh?' frowns Mrs Spencer.

'Exactly,' confirms Trevor.

The companions look to each other a little taken aback.

Fine, we'll leave you to it, they agree wordlessly at last.

'You're too kind,' praises Trevor.

Ben and Mrs Spencer rise, and Joe moves too, reluctantly allowing the lovely Marta to escape.

61

'Oh, and would you mind settling the bill on your way out?' petitions Trevor. 'I appear to have forgotten my wallet. Perhaps a third each would be most fair.'

Ben, Marta and Mrs Spencer amble to the counter muttering to each other. It's Ben who asks for the bill.

'The next one's on me!' calls Trevor. 'Lovely people,' he tells Joe, now seated opposite. 'But fans can be somewhat tiresome on occasion.'

'Fans?' parrots Joe.

'Ah, here's dessert – and your burger.' Trevor pushes aside a folded copy of The Stage and Jess tables their order.

Joe dives right in and Trevor tries a spoonful of trifle.

'Mmm, you can *so* taste the sherry,' purrs Trevor. 'Want a taste?'

Joe shakes his head and speaks around a mouthful of fries and burger: 'Watching my weight.'

'Nonsense, you look fine.'

'I was kidding,' attempts Joe, accidentally spitting out a piece of partially chewed burger.

'Kids are far too worried about their bodies these days; their self-image.' He laughs and booms: 'Let it all hang out I say and the devil take the hindmost!'

Jessica frowns at that, not quite sure what he means, this new guy about town. Llanidloes had known its share of eccentrics over the years, some of them transients, many of them locals, but Mr Smoking Jacket here was still relatively unfamiliar and the server hadn't quite worked out how she felt about him; not yet.

Jessica turns to Joe and raises an eyebrow.

'You okay?'

'I'm fine,' he assures her continuing to tuck in.

'We'll call you if we require anything else,' adds Trevor.

'Right, well if you need me,' Jessica's piercing blue eyes switch to Trevor, 'I'll be just over there.'

'Thank you, Jessica,' replies Trevor. 'And *mmm*, this is simply delicious.'

'I'll let the management know you're happy,' advises Jessica flatly before walking away.

'More than happy,' froths Trevor. '*Ecstatic!*'

Another spoonful of trifle disappears.

'Mmm, this really is so good,' he moans softly. 'Sure you won't try?'

The spoon, laden with custard, jelly and cream, is held out close to Joe's mouth. As tempting as it looks, Joe remains resolute; he shakes his curly-mopped head and pops in another batch of fries.

'Fine,' smiles Trevor. 'Your loss.'

And he continues to noisily finish off the trifle, heaped spoonful by heaped spoonful, until finally, the glass is empty bar a few colourful streaks of red, yellow and white.

He sighs, sits back rubbing his tummy and belches.

'Oops, pardon.'

He wipes his moustache and beard with a paper napkin.

'Now, what can I do you for?'

'Excuse me?'

'Just a corny old expression, dear boy. I mean, of course: *What can I do – for you?*'

'*You* called *me* over, Trevor. You said you had "a rather compelling matter you wished to discuss".'

'No, no, that was just an excuse.'

'An excuse?'

'To be rid of those three.' Trevor nods his head toward the door. 'Lovely people but honestly, I'm sure they'd have had me reciting Shakespeare until closing time if you hadn't come along to rescue me.'

'Is that so?'

'Indeed it is, and as much as I enjoy my art, I am *not* a performing monkey.'

'If you say so,' mutters Joe.

'But enough about me,' laughs Trevor, 'isn't there something *you* wish to ask me?'

'No.'

'No?'

'Not really.'

'Then fine, there's nothing more to be—'

'Yes, okay,' blurts Joe. 'Can you show me the trick again?'

'The trick?'

'I mean . . . *the magic.*'

'Of course, dear boy, I thought you'd never ask.'

Trevor roots a pocket and produces a black-and-silver robot no bigger than your thumb.

'Will Mr Sparky here suffice?'

'Sure.'

The robot is passed to Joe.

'Then be so kind as to place Mr Sparky in my hand.'

Trevor pulls back his sleeve and holds out an open palm.

Joe places the robot in Trevor's sizable paw.

63

'Watch closely, mind. At no time must you avert your eyes from Mr Sparky or my hands.'

Joe's eyes narrow with concentrated focus. He *will* uncover how this illusion is performed.

Trevor slowly folds his fingers around the robot then cups the fist with his other hand.

'Now, to ensure everything is above board and bona fide, you must squeeze my hands as tight as you can.'

Joe hesitates.

'I need you to trust me, Joe.'

After a long beat, Joe acquiesces and clasps Trevor's hands within his own.

Trevor nods approvingly.

Here and there, turns a head or two – people tuning in.

'Good,' he breathes. 'And of course, there is one other thing.'

Joe's eyebrows rise quizzically.

'You need to *believe* in magic.'

'Okay, yes, I believe.'

'I mean *really* believe, Joe.'

Joe nods. 'I do.'

Not entirely convinced, Trevor closes his eyes.

'There, did you feel that? He's gone.' Trevor smiles broadly. 'Now, would you like me to bring him back?'

Joe frowns and sighs.

'Just kidding,' winks Trevor. He nods at their still gripped hands hovering above the table. 'Look.'

Joe disengages in the manner a fortune-teller might release a crystal ball after a long reading.

And little by little Trevor opens his meaty paws . . .

No Mr Sparky! Trevor's hands are completely empty. Both are rotated, fingers spread apart, thus proving that the robot isn't taped to the back of a hand or secreted between fingers.

'That's good,' nods Joe casually (even though he is, in fact, *extremely* impressed). 'So, where is it?'

Trevor's face registers disappointment in the boy's continued scepticism.

'Come on, Trevor, it has to be somewhere. Things don't just disappear.'

Trevor's frown deepens.

'I'm not a child, Trevor. I know it's not *Ooooh, magic*.'

Trevor sighs. 'Very well, perhaps this will convince you.' He extends a flattened palm. 'Keep watching.'

Joe watches the hand . . .

Nothing.

'So—?'

'Shush,' hushes Trevor.

Joe shakes his head but continues to observe – still nothing. But then, yes! There *is* something; something slowly materialising; an object, before his very eyes – Mr Sparky, reappearing as if from nothing, as if from nowhere.

Joe, open-mouthed, lost for words for once, touches the robot, checking it's really there. He shakes his head.

'And . . . he's back in the room. That is *sooo* freaky.'

Joe takes Mr Sparky and taps him on the table, testing his solidity perhaps.

'Yeah, that's perfect,' froths Joe. 'You have to show me how you do it. I want to do it exactly like that.'

'Then why don't you?' suggests Trevor rubbing his temples.

'Do it now.'

'But how? I don't know how.'

'You just need to believe, Joe. *Really* believe. – Only then can true magic happen.'

'Show me,' petitions Joe.

'Here.' Trevor shapes Joe's hand, fleshy palm up, places Mr Sparky in the centre, closes Joe's fingers around the robot and moulds his other hand so it cups the fist. Trevor then squeezes the resultant robot-fist-hand combo.

'Now, will it away, Joe,' urges Trevor before removing his own mighty paws.

Joe, intense concentration on his face, holds his locked hands in place; they shake a little from the pressure.

Trevor nods, spurring Joe on.

After a long beat, Joe's eyes widen. 'I can't feel it.'

'It'll come to you, keep trying.'

'No, I mean I can't feel *it*. I can't feel *anything*. I think it's gone.'

'Might just be the pressure making your hand go numb.'

'Nope, pretty sure I've cracked it, Trev,' beams Joe.

'I may have misheard you there. Did you just say: *Trev?*'

Joe nods enthusiastically.

'Well, I guess there's only one way to find out – *boy*.'

After a knowing smirk and a suitably suspenseful delay, Joe springs open his hands with a celebratory 'Ta-da!'

And there's Mr Sparky, twinkling in all his shiny black-and-silver magnificence.

'That's because you didn't believe, Joe,' sighs Trevor. 'You *have* to believe.'

CHAPTER 6
Rudolph the Red-Nosed Undies

The man in the burger van leans over the counter conspiratorially. 'So, can I get you anything else?' he asks of the schoolgirl who just cadged a cigarette from him, the one with the permanent trout-pout and affected manner. 'I mean, besides a free smoke – a hotdog or something?'

He winks at her sour-faced non-smoking friend.

Jade believes the burger man is being crude and doesn't appreciate it. Bad enough hearing filth from certain boys in their school – one might even expect it from immature teenagers – but so much worse from a guy in what, his thirties, forties? – Hard to tell with the full beard.

'You'll cop it if a teacher catches you, Megs,' warns Jade. Her head swivels, scanning for staff.

Megan blows smoke at her friend. 'Chill out, Jade.'

'Yeah, chill out, Jade,' parrots Liam.

Jade rounds on burger man, certain now that her initial instinct was correct: there's something not right about him.

'And you shouldn't be looking at girls our age.'

'Who's looking at you?' asks Liam, immediately wishing he hadn't been so confrontational. People, especially females, remember contentious conversations.

'Don't suppose you've got any gum on ya, do ya?' asks Megan; presumably to replace the piece she's been chewing noisily since approaching the van with free fags in mind.

Gum, fags? carps the mummified head in the van's fridge. *She'll be asking for a free burger next.*

Although Liam could respect Megan's moxie, the duck lips and affected manner were painful to look at. Then there was Jade: all cold, snippy and fish-eyed. No, he didn't like either of these two very much.

I don't know which one's worse, whines Joel's head.

Jade, definitely. At least, that's Liam's gut feeling on the matter. He'd always hated stuck-up individuals; snotty smarty-pants who act all condescending and superior. For that reason, if nothing else, he thought she deserved to lose her smug, supercilious head.

Yes, kill her, urges Joel. *Kill them both! That'll take us to a hundred. We'll have hit the century! Not exactly Shipman but still.*

True, the Head Honcho is currently on ninety-eight according to police records, and these two would make the accredited murder count an official one hundred, but Liam's beginning to regret bringing the van to the school. Yes, he'd accidentally 'promised' Joel a non-adult murder – the so-called deal he'd foolishly agreed to back in Manchester – but here, outside the school's main entrance – well, it was just too high profile.

Bullshit, rasps Joel. *We're hiding in plain view.*

Bollocks, contends Liam internally.

Grab 'em! Grab 'em both. Do it now! No-one's looking.

No, there's no way, insists Liam inwardly. Not here, not now; not both of them – too many people about. If we're going to snatch a kid we have to do it on the quiet.

What do you mean, if?

Fine – *when.*

'So, can I keep these?' blinks Megan exhaling a cloud.

Liam had killed college-aged kids before, of course (as had Joel, when he was alive) but an actual non-adult of the juvenile variety would be different. If he were to be caught, prison would be a nightmare. This had been a long-held concern. Ninety-eight, ninety-nine, a hundred adults, *young* adults, even; that would be fine – but just one victim even a smidgen under sixteen and—

That was the deal, Liam!

Christ, would his dead brother ever get off his back about the fucking deal! He'd been keeping a low profile since arriving in Llanidloes in 2011 and there probably wasn't a single day when Joel hadn't nagged him about it.

'Come on, let's go,' urges Jade. 'He's not even listening.'

'Sure,' Megan sighs. She tosses back the burger man's cigarette packet, minus the two she's taken; the one she's drawing on now and the one she's cheekily stuck behind one of her pierced ears.

Jade hooks arms and leads her unruly friend away.

'Don't know how you can smoke those things.'

'Jeez, Jade, give it a rest, it's just a ciggie,' grumbles Megan. 'If he's daft enough to give them away.'

'I think he was after a bit more than just a smoke.'

'Fuck, Jade, you're so crude sometimes,' teases Megan.

'And you're a foul-mouthed mother-flipper,' nudges Jade.

'Go on, say motherfucker, it won't kill you.'

'I will not.'

'Cocksucker!' bellows Megan.

'Megs, quit it,' barks Jade.

'Tits, arse, fanny!' shouts Megan into the air for anyone to hear. 'Cunt!'

Jade's jaw drops. 'OMG! You are unbelievable.'

'They're just words, Jade. They won't kill you.'

'*Your mum* will kill you if she hears you saying that.'

'He was nice looking though, wasn't he?'

'Who? Creepy burger guy?'

'Aw, don't call him that.'

'Ew, it'd be like being hit on by your dad.'

'Ew.'

'Exactly,' snorts Jade. 'Seedy fucker.'

Megan laughs. 'Finally,' she grins. 'That's my girl.'

'Glad you're happy, now keep walking.'

Just as well, thinks Liam as the duo continue to distance themselves from the van. Even if it were practical, there was too much of a connection. Someone had surely seen him talking to the girls. Then both go missing after school? No, if he was to snatch a child, it would have to be on its own. No-one around to play hero, to try and muscle in and save—Shit, do they have CCTV cameras on schools here? Liam knew they did back in Manchester; hell, they had them on everything back there.

Narrowing his eyes he scans along the building's eaves.

Don't see any, remarks Joel's voice.

'Some of those fuckers can be tiny,' Liam reminds his brother's head. 'No, it's too risky. Coming here was a stupid idea.'

And with that he decides they'll fall back to maintaining a low profile, return to the 'lay-by plan' – a quiet out-of-town country lane and lie in wait for a solo backpacker or cyclist – until the situation is foolproof: the right time, the right place, zero witnesses and the perfect victim.

[The murderous lay-by plan had been unavoidably knocked on the head for a while: a large group of menacing Irish travellers had forced a 'trade' of the *original* burger van for a rusty VW Camper rolled off a trailer. Liam lived in the VW for a time after first arriving in Wales, which was handy, but when he later had the opportunity, just a couple of months ago, he swapped it back for a near identical burger van he'd spotted on a used vehicle lot in Newtown.]

Maybe you're right, concedes Joel. *Shame though, because that blobby, red-haired kid over there looks like he'd make a great ninety-nine.*

'Which kid?'

The one talking to himself; and are they – judo moves?

'Excuse me, do you have *permission*?' squeaks a voice.

'Permission?' sneers Liam.

'Yes, permission to trade,' clarifies the little bald-headed fella below the counter,

'And who the fuck, are you?' Shit, thinks Liam, so much for maintaining a low profile.

'Mr Smallwood,' states baldy puffing out his chest. 'I'm the headmaster of this establishment.'

'You're the head?'

'That's right.'

'The head?'

'Yes.'

Oh, we could definitely do a sign on that! laughs Joel.

As you may be aware, Liam and Joel, aka the Head Honcho, always left their victims' heads in one place, limbed torsos in another, both in plain view but usually many miles apart. The serial killers' other usual 'signature' was a cardboard sign bearing a so-called humorous message. Who could forget the body posed in a passport photo booth – the gruesome scene recorded on a strip of neck-and-shoulders photos in the dispensing slot – the Honcho's sign left hanging around the torso's stubby neck; it bore the message: HOW DO I LOOK? I CAN'T SEE A THING WITHOUT MY GLASSES.

That guy was a teacher too, coincidentally. So many murders and yet the police always pooh-poohed them being the evil exertions of two men working in tandem. Only after Liam killed Joel with an axe during an argument about Liam's level of intelligence, did this actually become true. Then, with the Honcho down to one pair of hands, Liam began leaving heads and torsos together; this meant less labour, less travelling, a reduced risk of being caught, and it provided him a whole new opportunity for dark humour. Sick-but-funny, Liam called it; like that tall bloke (six-foot prior to decapitation) he crammed into the Postman Pat coin-op ride and made it look as though he'd 'run over his own head' – the sign read—

'I say; excuse me,' pesters Smallwood. 'I said you're supposed to have a trading license from the council's Environmental Health Department.'

'Yeah, yeah, I've got one,' grunts Liam.

'Then can I see it, please. Where is it? It's supposed to be displayed.'

'Sorry, mate, but I'm packing up.'

Liam reaches for the shutter handle.

'Right, well, if you come back I'll need to see that license. Or I'm afraid I will be forced to report you.'

'Report me, eh?'

'That's right.'

Kill him! screams Joel's rotten head from the under the counter. *Pull him in and club him, no-one's looking.*

'Yeah, no worries,' sneers Liam with a sniff. 'Trade's crap here anyway.' And with that, Liam snaps down the shutter, closing off the serving window and any possibility of further discussion.

Good, thinks Smallwood. He doesn't want his students eating fatty processed foods of unknown origin. That stuff, he's always telling them, can kill you.

Little did he know.

Retired farmer Don rattles his rickety rust-bucket of a Land Rover over a corrugated strip of frozen mud and pulls up outside one of the farm's many storage buildings. A pack of farm dogs, a mix of kelpies and huntaways, announce the arrival, barking loudly at Don's ancient (and also retired) border collie, Jed.

Don stopped working several years ago – he'll be eighty-four in a few days – but hardly a day goes by when he doesn't visit the farm (he now lives in a little cottage just up the lane with wife Carol) or go out and about tending to smaller tasks, such as reattaching a loose wire to a fence post or oiling a squeaky gate.

After a slow extrication from the Land Rover, Don aims a sour expression at the dogs. 'Gwor, shoo!' he orders.

The ancient collie isn't bothered about the new dogs; he remains unmoved, sitting bolt upright on the passenger seat, milky eyes staring blankly through the muddy windscreen. Jed loves being in the Land Rover, it had become his home many moons ago; he sleeps in there – he's sleeping more and more these days, hardly ever being called upon to do any proper work.

Not anymore.

'Go on, shoo!' the old farmer repeats; and this time the dogs bolt, in the direction of the milking shed. Then, following a string of frustrating attempts to close the vehicle's slack door, Don, with ruddy cheeks (partly from a long life outdoors, partly from bottled beer) turns his gaze to the nearest barn.

Sam, who has been the head of the family-owned farm, running it with his own sons Mark and Robbie since Don stepped down, is repairing the engine of a large tractor. In and out the barn, Mark and Robbie ferry large sacks of animal feed, shouldering them from tractor-trailer to a corner of the building.

Don ambles over, relocating his frowzy beanie hat and grubby petrol-green overalls.

'Here, let me help you with those,' he tells Robbie.

Robbie and Mark both look to Sam for guidance.

'Dad, you're retired now,' Sam reminds the old man, not for the first time. 'Stop worrying. We can manage just fine.'

'I know you can, son, but I can still lend a hand. I'm sure Dawn would appreciate that. Wouldn't you, Dawn?'

Dawn, Sam's wife, has just emerged from the barn. 'You really don't need to bother,' she tells Don breezily whilst easily sliding the next feed sack to the edge of the trailer. 'They're very heavy.'

Don laughs. 'Listen, dear, I've been shifting far heavier loads than this since before you were born.'

Dawn glances to Sam whose expression suggests: Just let him help if he really wants to.

'It's no bother,' sniffs Don.

'Well, okay, if you're sure.' With consummate ease, Dawn smoothly slips a broad shoulder under the sack of feed and hoists it off the long trailer, straightening her knees in the process, loaded up ready to go.

'If there's one thing I can still do,' insists Don stepping forward and emulating her actions, 'it's—'

As Don takes the weight there's a sudden ratchet-like sound loud enough for everyone to hear; something has cracked or torn at the base of Don's back.

Sam and Dawn help keep Don upright; supporting him under his unexpectedly sweaty armpits, as Mark and Robbie quickly divest the old man of his burden. Then Sam and Dawn awkwardly escort Don the ten yards or so to the piggery's low stone wall and sit him down.

'I'll just rest here for a minute,' puffs Don immediately looking to stretch out horizontally on top of the rough, uneven stones.

'Will you be okay?' frowns Sam helping his dad lie back.

'Course, son,' he groans. 'Right as rain in a minute.'

'Do you want us to call Carol?' asks Dawn.

'No, no, I'll be fine,' Don assures her. 'You carry on. You've got the farm to run.'

Trevor pours another large sherry, teeters gently to the caravan table, and plants himself opposite Joe.

After a long, silent beat, Joe muses, 'So it's definitely not a trick. And it's not hypnosis.'

'Hypnosis?' slurs Trevor, merrily scoffing. 'Pfft.' Tipsy eyes fixing on Joe, as best they can, Trevor wiggles his fingers in the air like a hypnotist. 'Woooooh,' he intones as if portraying the proverbial spooky ghost.

'Which means,' continues Joe, 'that you can show me.'

Trevor arches an eyebrow. 'Show you?'

'Show me how. How to—'

'How to what?' blinks Trevor. 'Perform a trick? A sleight of hand? How to—'

'Believe,' Joe interrupts. 'How to believe.'

'I can't show you how to believe, Joe.' Trevor quaffs his sherry in one go. 'Either you do, or you don't.'

Joe considers this. He studies Mr Sparky, turning the small robot over in his pudgy hands.

'What do you think,' asks Trevor hoisting his empty glass, 'room for one more before supper?'

Joe studies Trevor's face. He'd seen that expression before: on his mum's face when she came home after one of her rare girls' nights out. Actually, no, his mum usually looked merry and light-hearted – Trevor appears gloomy and serious.

'What does Mr Sparky say?' asks Trevor.

Joe stands the little robot on the table, facing Trevor.

'He says you've probably had enough.'

'Does he indeed?' Trevor places the glass over the robot. 'Now what does he say?'

'He says I should be going.'

'But the evening is young and . . .' Trevor appears to lose his trail of thought. 'Young and . . .'

'Not like you to forget a—'

'I don't know where I'm going from here,' blurts Trevor rising dramatically to his feet, 'but I promise it won't be boring. Do you know who said that?'

'Dunno. Shakespeare—?'

An unsteady Trevor slumps back onto his seat. 'Nope. David Bowie. Ha, see! I'm hipper than you are.'

'You should speak to my sister. She's a big fan.'

'No, no, stay, dear boy,' slurs Trevor. 'And Mr Sparky's quite right: I feel sure I have reached my limit. Anymore and I fear I should be compelled to lie down for an hour.'

Joe stands. 'No, I really should be going.'

'Very well, but answer me one question before you depart.'

'Okay, if I can.'

'Mr Sparky there – he isn't the only reason you came here this evening, is he?'

Joe frowns. 'Er, yes, he is.'

Trevor studies his visitor for a moment.

'Oh very well,' he sighs. And with that he removes the glass dome imprisoning Mr Sparky. 'Let's do it, then.'

'You'll show me?' blurts Joe. Excited, he sits down again. 'You'll show me exactly how it's done. I mean, for real.'

'Indeed, sir,' hiccups Trevor. 'For real.'

He places the little robot in the palm of Joe's right hand.

'Now squeeze. Good. And cup your other hand around.'

Joe cups his left hand around his right. 'Like this, yes?'

Trevor nods. 'Exactly so.' He reaches across, squeezes Joe's hands in his own. 'And now . . .'

Joe looks across, a tad uncomfortable.

'Stay focused, boy.'

'Okay . . .' replies Joe shakily.

'You *must* trust me for this to work.'

Joe nods that he understands.

'Good. Now concentrate – concentrate and believe.'

Joe becomes intent, focused. He breathes in and out, in and out, slow and even.

'That's it, good, good. Keep believing. Make it happen.'

If you think about it hard enough, echoes Wilf's voice, *you can make anything happen. Anything.*

Joe takes a deep breath and screws his eyes tight shut; he begins shaking with the sheer effort – perspiration trickles down his furrowed brow. Trevor wills him on.

'Yes, Joe, push.'

'Grrrrrrr!' growls Joe and an image springs into his mind. One of the many times that he's been constipated and had to—

'Focus!' snaps Trevor.

'Sorry,' puffs Joe. And he returns to his deliberations, grunting and groaning.

'That's it, my boy, go on.'

Joe's eyes pop open.

Trevor nods, then disengages in the manner a healer might after laying hands upon a sufferer and relieving them of a sickness. Joe looks to his hands. He removes the left and opens the fingers of his right. No Mr Sparky! Joe's hands are one-hundred percent robot-free.

'Oh my God, where is it?' asks Joe genuinely shocked.

'You did it, Joe,' Trevor assures him. 'You did it.'

'I did?' checks Joe.

'I did!' he announces proudly.

'I DID!'

Well done, Joe, congratulates Wilf's voice. *I told you, you could do it.*

'Now watch,' points Trevor. 'Wait. Keep looking. Do not allow your eyes to wander.'

Joe stares, as directed, at his open, empty hands.

'Stray not your gaze.'

Joe's eyes remain locked.

Still nothing; Mr Sparky has well and truly—No, wait, what's this? A nebulous shape; unclear at first, but then slowly appearing, as it did in the café. Yes, a robot shape, there it is; flimsy, dubious, shaky but increasingly less so, gaining density in waves of atoms it seems – until at last it is tangibly solid. Joe is ecstatic but then quickly troubled.

'What is it? – I did say it could only disappear for a moment.'

'No, it's not that,' gasps Joe, 'it's the head banging.'

'Ah, the price of success, dear boy. And that was for such a little thing.'

'A little thing?'

Trevor presents the tiny robot within finger and thumb.

'Anything more and your head might explode. Boom!'

Joe laughs. Trevor laughs too. Then both suddenly stop.

'Oh dear,' groans Trevor. 'One sherry too many, I fear. Why didn't you stop me?'

Joe doesn't reply, he looks like he's about to pass out.

'Are you quite alright, dear boy? Here am I, complaining of a tipple too far when you must have a head like thunder.'

Trevor moves seats to comfort Joe.

'Better now?' asks Trevor outside the caravan.

'Yes, I'm okay.' Joe rubs a temple. 'I think so anyway.'

'Good, good. You'll be fine.'

They say goodbye and Joe sets off. He's no more than a trailer length from Alison's twitching curtains when Trevor hails him.

Joe stops, turns. 'What?'

'Are you sure you won't tell me the other reason why you visited this evening?' calls Trevor.

'Huh?' replies Joe loudly. 'What other reason?'

'The one besides Mr Sparky.'

Joe shrugs, shakes his head.

'Never mind, it'll come to you.'

'Oh and Trevor!'

'Yes?'

'I still think it might be a trick!'

Trevor's face registers disappointment.

The cracked lens surveils the house: closed curtains, blinds down, and barely a light on; as if the place is in lockdown. It had been this way for over an hour, with nothing of interest to see the whole time.

Don sighs, collapses the telescope, tosses it onto the dashboard and thinks about driving home. He'd had several beers but doesn't see that as a problem; country police rarely patrol local lanes. No, the only reason he doesn't immediately turn the ignition is apathy, plain and simple. He just can't be bothered. So he stays. There's always a thin chance he'll see something of interest if he sticks it out a while longer.

With the house still in darkness (apart from a small lamp illuminating Joe's curtains) and a heavy lethargy weighting his old bones, Don swivels his inebriated head.

To the left of the Land Rover: fir trees.

To the right: fir trees.

Indeed, all around, except for the hard track road and the small clearings in front and behind: fir trees. Finger Hill is covered in them. Trees currently alive with a multitude of Carrion Crows, big, bold and noisy, as they always are when returning to their roost for the evening; quickly filling every bough and branch, clicking and cawing to their neighbours.

The farmer and his aged dog pay them no heed. Jed has settled down to sleep on the passenger seat and Don is considering the scarecrow that stands in the clearing to one side of the Land Rover.

'Jack' has an old leather football for a head, with cut-out facial features, much like a Halloween pumpkin – only fossilised. A ripped and dirty red cagoule hangs over washed-out Hessian sackcloth trousers; each roughly-stitched leg still bearing sections of faded green lettering left over from the brand name of the original feed supplier. The scarecrow's arms, such as they are, are tied, crucifix style, to the long handle of a rusty scythe which in turn is secured horizontally, by baling-twine, to the vertical stand.

Don transported Jack here over two decades ago when the daily running of the farm was handed over to Sam, Don's son. One of the first decisions Sam took was to replace the 'old-fashioned' scarecrow with a newfangled machine that emits high-frequency ultrasonic sounds to drive birds away from freshly broadcast seeds.

'Did I do right, Jack?' hiccups Don. 'Or should I have set you alight? *They* wanted to. *Happy* to. Thrown on gasoline and ready to burn. Was it a mistake? Should I have allowed it? Reduced you to ashes and – hic – left you in your field?'

He sucks down another gulp of Theakston's Old Peculier (the petrol station had run out of Old Speckled Hen).

Had you had enough, Jack? Don wonders for the umpteenth time. For years he'd drunkenly posed the question: Should I have

76

let you go? Destroyed you? Would it have been a kindness? By bringing Jack here had he condemned the old scarecrow to forever—?

Jed yelps, legs kicking, no doubt chasing a bitch or rounding up a sheep in his sleep.

'Go on, Jed, good dog,' encourages Don. 'Nice to dream you're young again.' Then the farmer, as he so often does, revisits the subject of Jack . . .

Don's father had built Jack when he, Don, was just a lad. Don had always thought the scarecrow terrifying. He often felt watched by him. The eerie figure disturbed the boy greatly and that feeling never really went away. Not even when Don was older and wiser. (Not that he was ever that brainy; land-smart, yes, but not scholarly. He was educated at home: an education that consisted almost entirely of learning how to farm.) Then, when the time came to replace the longstanding prop with modern technology, Don suddenly had an awful feeling that something dreadful would befall the farm if Jack were destroyed. And though the old farmer, unlike most of his counterparts, had never been superstitious, he panicked and shifted the scarecrow in his Land Rover to this new out-of-the-way spot. He regretted it now but felt stuck with the result of his actions. Not that he would ever tell Jack that.

'To you and me, eh, Jack?' Don raises his beer bottle. 'And to old times.'

Jack's cut-out eyes stare back, silent, hollow and grim. Don had faced the scarecrow outward many times, spun him to overlook the trees on the 'nail' of Finger Hill, but whether turned back by wind or wildlife, it always seemed to Don that Jack had insisted on a view of his own choosing; usually the houses below, the farm up on Bryn Crow, or Don himself, who the ungrateful Jack blamed, the farmer felt, for his useless seclusion.

'Don't blame me,' blurts Don, ready, as always, for the inevitable argument. 'It's not my fault you're an old fossil!'

Don sucks on his beer.

A cold gust flaps the ripped cagoule, agitates straws sticking out of the holes in Jack's sackcloth trousers and flutters the hardy weeds that had long ago rooted into the top of his head, making the sunken-football face appear to shake out a defiant *Says you!*

Don wipes dribble from his chin.

'And don't think I haven't seen you looking down there.'

He taps the neck of the bottle against the steering wheel.

The scarecrow stares back.

'Oh, shut up, it was *you* who suggested we—'

77

Don raises beer to lips but stops short.

'No, not *me*, Jack – *you*! You're the filthy old has-been! Carol may think I've got the urges of a horny old goat,' slurs Don, 'but she doesn't know what *you're* like!'

Don senses he might have gone too far as he grows increasingly aware of Jack staring at him. And not for the first time: it was undeniable that over the years Jack had progressively adopted a negative, sinister vibe toward him – more dark and creepy with each passing season – of this he was sure; standing there silently watching him and his doings; doings which Don considered to be *harmless*, not lewd and salacious at all. Bloody Jack! And anyway, what did *he* know about it? He was just a stupid, rotten scarecrow. Not flesh and blood like farmers.

'What do you say, Jed; no harm in looking, eh?'

The collie twitches in his sleep, perhaps at the sound of his name.

'And that's a fine show of gratitude from someone rescued from a near hellfire,' Don reminds Jed for Jack's benefit. 'It was Sam who said scarecrows had become, how did he put it? – Archaic. Not me. *I saved him.*'

The last of the bottle is quaffed and with a loud clink he dumps the empty into the pile in the passenger footwell.

Jed opens an eye.

'Sorry, old boy. Go back to sleep.'

Jed falls almost instantly back to sleep and the farmer contemplates the house below – until a carrion crow lands on Jack's head and eyeballs him.

Caw-caw-caw-caw!

'You can shut up too,' the farmer tells the black-eyed corvid.

Caw-caw-caw-caw!

'What?' barks Don. 'Ah, you don't know what you're talking about.'

Caw-caw-caw-caw!

'Hey! If I'd been a minute later, he'd have burned to ash. Wouldn't that have been worse, Jack, than standing there?'

The bird shits on Jack's shoulder and launches itself, flapping wide wings before disappearing into a tree top.

'Right, bollocks to this,' huffs Don. He climbs out, staggers over to the scarecrow, wipes the shat-upon shoulder with a crusty old hankie, turns Jack's face away, back towards the trees, then returns to the Land Rover.

After several attempts to close the door Don gives up.

He checks that Jack hasn't immediately spun around again – he hasn't – and so, no longer suffering the scarecrow's accusatory gaze, the farmer reverts to spying on the Evans' house with the telescope.

'*Definitely* no harm in looking,' he retells his dozing dog.

Time passes with a whole lot of nothing noteworthy, just Jed snoring and Don absentmindedly slow-scraping the steering wheel with his pocketknife. A final beer, he decides then he really must be getting back.

He leans to the side and reaches down for an Old Peculier but finds only empties; they clink together as his hand agitates the jumble of bottles.

Following a deep, protracted sigh, Don slowly tips the rest of the way over, until his head rests on Jed's warm body – a sort of dog pillow – and there he stays.

Hardly a minute later, at the bottom of the hill, Sally sneaks out the back of the house, closes the door quietly behind her, and lights up a thin cigarette.

Had Don still been spying, the telescope would not have been able to determine that Sally's cigarette is in fact a long-long-long-awaited spliff (well over nine months) but it would surely – had the farmer not passed out – have spotted the boy sneaking in some time later. He climbs onto the sun-lounge extension, crosses its roof and slips in through a bedroom window.

The farmer's mobile rings in the Land Rover's glove-box.

After a short while the unanswered phone rings off.

Don and Jed remain fast asleep, snoring like saws.

Like the farmer and his dog, Paul is also creating a horrible noise.

Sally nudges him. 'Wake up,' she orders.

The guttural blare continues: like a whale in great pain.

'Paul, wake up.'

Another nudge and he wakes with a grunt.

'Hm? What?' Paul looks around the room, sluggishly regaining his bearings. 'Dreamt I was swimming.'

'Drowning more like.'

'What time is it?'

'I think I heard something. Go and check on Joe.'

'Was it Emily?'

Sally rechecks the baby-monitor speaker; its light blinks green.

'No, she's fast.'

Paul sighs, head sinking back into his pillow.

'Paul,' barks Sally.

'In a minute.'

☆ ★ ☆

79

Joe is down to his reindeer underpants when the main bedroom light comes on.

'It wasn't me!' he blurts, startled.

'Nice pants,' teases Lucy.

Still squinting, Joe's hands quickly drop from his nipples to cartooned crotch as Lucy, in a Sixties 'Twiggy' nightshirt, gently closes the door.

'Sister's room, down the hall,' advises Joe. 'No need to knock, apparently.'

'Okay, Rudolf,' mocks Lucy brushing past. 'Don't wet yourself.'

She steps over to the bed and pulls back Joe's Snowman duvet, revealing pillows strategically placed to convince casual observers that he's in there and asleep. Aiming narrowed eyes over a shoulder Lucy shakes her head, then sits on his desk and settles into a look which affirms: *We need to talk.*

'Make yourself comfy.'

'You're late,' scolds Lucy. 'You didn't go to see Trevor again, did you?'

Joe takes his pyjamas out of a drawer.

'Joe?'

No reply.

'Joe, answer me.'

'I did the trick.'

'What trick?'

'That thing I told you about.'

'Oh, that.'

'Do you think I should show Max?'

Lucy rolls her eyes, shakes her head scornfully.

'Sure, why not,' she sighs.

'Actually, it makes my head hurt – a lot – so, I might not.'

'Your head? Joe, what are you—? You're worrying me.'

'There's nothing to worry about,' Joe assures her.

He indicates she should avert her eyes.

'I mean it's not like you really know this . . . Trevor, is it?'

'I know he likes plays and poetry and books – so, he can't be all bad, can he?'

'As long as that's all he likes.'

'Lucy.'

Again Joe gestures for her to turn her head.

Lucy just closes her eyes. '*Well* . . .'

'Well, what?'

'Word is – he's a bit . . .'

'What? – Theatrical? – Affected?'

Lucy shakes her head.

'Camp? – Pompous?'

'Great word: pompous.'

'Thanks. You can open your eyes now.'

'And there's nothing wrong with camp; no-one's saying that,' insists Lucy. 'No, I mean, you know,' she widens her eyes, 'a bit – scout master.'

'Nice. And, by the way, that wasn't *our* scout master. That was some bloke over in Llandinam or Trefeglwys or somewhere.'

'Fine.'

'And I never went to more than the first session because I hated the silly uniforms. Dad and his bright ideas.'

'I said, Fine.'

'It wasn't because of some dodgy scout master.'

'Jesus, Joe, I said, Fine.'

'Not everyone's a—'

'Okay, okay. I just hope you know what you're doing, that's all.'

'I do know what I'm doing,' Joe assures her. He climbs in bed and adds with less certainty: 'Pretty sure I know what I'm doing.'

'I'm just saying it all sounds a bit shady to me. And if Dad finds out – well, you know what he's like.'

'How's he going to find out? He's always at work. And when he *is* at home, he spends all his precious time faffing with his hair.'

Joe clowns around, performing an impression of their dad spraying and teasing his hair into place. They both get the giggles, the infectious nature of which spurs them on to even louder chuckling.

'Shush,' urges Joe, though *his* chuckles are loudest. He throws a pillow at his sister which she deftly catches and holds to her face in a hopeless attempt to stifle an unladylike guffawing. They're still giggling inanely when their mum bursts in.

'What's going on in here?' Sally wants to know. 'Do you want to wake Emily? Come on, it's school in the morning.'

'It's Lucy, Mum,' pleads Joe. 'I told her to go.'

'Lucy, let Joe sleep.'

Lucy stands, open-mouthed, not quite believing her ears. As Sally unnecessarily shuts the curtains tighter together, Lucy whacks Joe with the pillow.

'Oh, that's nice,' gripes Joe.

'Come on, Lucy, bed,' insists Sally. 'And give Joe his pillow back.'

Lucy throws the pillow at Joe.

'Thank you,' trills Joe in a tone that suggests he'd been asking for a while.

After turning out the light, Sally exits, pushing Lucy ahead.

81

Joe turns on his bedside lamp, shakes the robot snow-globe and sets it under the light. As he studies the whirling flurry of snow, Lucy sticks her head round the door.

'You be careful,' she reminds him.

Joe smiles and gives a thumbs-up.

The door closes.

CHAPTER 7
Challenge Accepted

Katie approaches Joe in the school canteen.

'Mind if I join you?' she smiles.

'Sure,' grunts Joe, not taking his eyes off Owen, who's currently selecting his lunch.

'How could a girl resist,' mutters Katie taking a seat.

'Sorry,' thaws Joe. 'Please, be my guest.'

'That's better,' grins Katie.

She pops the lid on her plastic lunchbox. 'So, what did you think of his latest?'

'Who? Owen?'

'Of course, Owen.'

Joe shrugs. 'It had all the elements, I suppose; a beginning, middle and end.'

Katie stabs a straw into a small carton of juice and has a quick drink. 'Is that it?'

Joe frowns. 'I dunno – it was alright, I guess.'

'Just alright?'

Again, Joe shrugs.

'I thought it was good.'

'Really?' challenges Joe.

'Just good,' backtracks Katie a little. 'Not great.'

'The class loved it.'

'What do they know?'

'That they didn't like mine.'

'Oh, Joe,' sighs Katie.

'What?' Joe finally gives Katie his full attention.

'You're just not very good at telling a story.'

Joe has no words.

Katie bites off the end of a carrot stick and chews.

'Don't give me that face,' she tells him.

'I can't believe—'

'I'm sorry but it's true. And on a technical point: *Trolls* live under bridges.'

'But *Ogre* came up,' counters Joe. 'And they're basically the same thing.'

'Are they, though?'

'Similar. As far as that lot know, anyway – bunch of philistines.'

'And that's another thing: you should stop using words like philistine. To other kids our age it just sounds pretentious.'

'But it's a good word.'

'Know your audience.'

'I see,' huffs Joe, 'any other complaints while we're at it?'

'You really want to know? Seems to me that most boys—'

'I can handle it,' Joe assures her. 'Come on, out with it.'

After a long suck on her straw Katie launches into:

'Sometimes your presentation tends to be rushed, other times you seem hesitant, either of which is unsettling for an audience; if you look uncomfortable telling your story, we'll surely feel uncomfortable hearing it, and no-one wants to feel awkward when they're listening to a story; there are often glaring holes in your narratives, too.'

'Don't hold back will you?'

'I hadn't finished,' smiles Katie, a slender finger pushing back her glasses. 'Sometimes you mumble; your comedic timing is often off; and suddenly or randomly backtracking to fill narrative holes: that's a definite no-no.'

'But apart from that?'

'Apart from that, you often lose your thread, sidetrack, or over complicate.' Katie noisily sucks the dregs from her carton. 'Keep it simple.'

'Thanks,' sniffs Joe.

'Sorry but you asked.'

A long silent beat is broken by Owen:

'Check out the lovebirds,' he mocks.

'Oh, hello, Owen; didn't see you there,' baits Joe. 'And with Gary and Melvin in tow – who'd have thought.'

Owen ignores Joe's sarcasm and instead addresses Katie: 'So, you two; another lunch together – how many times is that this week?'

'Well, let's see,' offers Joe. 'It's Thursday, so I reckon –'

'Problem?' asks Katie.

'No, no, I'm just trying to get my head round it,' Owen frowns. 'So, do you actually *like* him?' he asks, exaggerating a tone of incredulity. 'I mean *like-like*?'

'Yes,' answers Katie plainly.

'Seriously?' scoffs Gary.

'Why wouldn't I?'

'Where do we start?' sneers Owen. 'I mean, what about the hair for starters? Wouldn't you say it was a bit –?'

'Really, Owen – his hair again?'

84

'No, let him finish,' Joe tells Katie. 'This should be interesting. Which adjective do you think he'll choose today? Billowy? Unkempt? Girly?'

'I'm gonna go with pubic or like a cat's fur-ball.'

'Good ones, Katie.'

'Thanks.'

'A bit shit,' smirks Gary.

'Really, that's the best you can come up with?' scoffs Joe. 'Not wiry, frizzy or woolly – just *shit*? And that's the same shit *he* said.'

'Now, *that's* shit,' mocks Katie.

'Shut it, you,' warns Gary.

'Oh, touché,' retorts Katie.

'Touché,' snorts Melvin.

'Dafuq is *touché*?' hisses Gary. 'Who even says that?'

'We do,' smiles Katie. And she and Joe nod to each other – smugly, like Laurel and Hardy.

'Seriously?' asks Owen. 'That's what you're attracted to?'

'As I said – perhaps you weren't listening – why wouldn't I? He's kind, funny, smart—'

'Handsome?' tries Joe.

But Owen and his mates are no longer listening; they're walking away.

'He's also polite!' barks Katie. 'God,' she seethes quietly to Joe, 'I loathe those . . . those . . .'

'Philistines?'

'Cretins.'

'*Excellent* word.'

'Thanks.'

Two tables down, the boys, now seated, whisper loudly and with great vulgarity about embarrassing relationships and supposed illicit fumblings.

'You *have* to beat him,' fumes Katie.

'Well, I am a Yellow Belt but three of them might be tricky even for me.'

'No, you dolt – the Storytell competition.'

'Okay, but how? We've already highlighted the various reasons why I probably won't.'

'I dunno.' muses Katie. 'Maybe Trevor could help.'

Joe's frown relays his thoughts: *You think?*

'He's an actor, isn't he? That's a type of storytelling.'

'True,' ruminates Joe. 'But Lucy said stay away.'

'And what does your gut tell you?'

Joe's eyes widen. 'That's what Gramps used to say.'

'Yeah? And what's the answer?'

Trevor, standing by the boiling kettle, picks up a teabag and cups it in his hands. When he opens them the teabag has gone. He re-cups, opens, re-cups and opens; but the teabag does not return. A furrowed brow aimed at the floor scans for the missing teabag – until there comes a gentle, almost apologetic knock.

The caravan door opens to an upturned face: Joe's puppy eyes look up, his face contrite and rueful.

'The wanderer doth return,' announces Trevor.

'Yep. Back again.'

'And how is the head?'

Joe absentmindedly rubs a temple. 'It's okay.'

'Glad to hear it, dear boy, glad to hear it,' smiles Trevor. 'So, did you forget something?' He swivels his head for a brief examination of the caravan's interior.

When he looks back Joe is staring at him.

'I need your help.'

Trevor's eyebrows arch. 'Pray tell, what kind of—?'

'To storytell.'

Trevor nods, smiles, and nods again. 'Thank you, Joe.'

Joe frowns. 'For?'

'For that's what I'd been hoping to hear.'

Trevor takes a step back and swings an extended hand.

'Please, enter stage left.'

By the time he'd finished telling Trevor about Owen's glowing successes in storytelling practice, his own fails and ultimate flop in last year's Storytell final, Joe's untouched tea had gone cold.

Trevor's final image was of a lost soul standing before an easel bearing the words: TREACLE, LOST, ARCHITECT, and INERTIA; the timer at zero; the boy frozen and humiliated; his family out in the awkwardly hushed audience unable to help (shouting encouragement such as 'You got this, Joe!' or 'You can do it, buddy!' would have been counterproductive; might as well have yelled 'Relax for Christ's sake!'); and a sympathetic teacher finally stepping in to end the torture.

'That's terrible,' sympathises Trevor.

'Oh that's not all,' explains Joe. 'After I'd conceded defeat and shuffled head down back to my seat, I heard Gary and Melvin burst out laughing in the audience.'

'Truly awful.'

'Then Owen was up next. They had to give him a minute to compose himself because his eyes were watering; you know, from his struggle to contain his amusement after all the hilarity. Oh, but not to worry, he still won by a landslide. I still don't know how he did it. His words looked really tricky; much trickier than mine, anyway. Maybe I just have to admit it: this dolt, this idiot, this buffoon, is better than me at storytelling.'

'I'm sure that can't be true.'

'Everyone is.'

'Now you're just exaggerating.'

'Well, tell me what I'm doing wrong because I sure as shit can't figure out what's happening.'

Joe thumps the table in frustration.

'Stage-fright, as with any manner of public speaking, can be a nerve-wracking ordeal. I remember when I first played the Dane—'

Trevor's about to get all theatrical until Joe's eyes widen.

'Yes, well, enough about me. Let us return to you.'

'I don't suffer from stage-fright, Trevor. I *like* being the centre of attention.'

'Marvellous. We can cross that off our list of potential problems then. Oh, but you haven't touched your tea.'

'I don't really drink tea.'

Trevor transports Joe's cup to the sink, pours the tea away, and stands, looking out of the window.

After a long pause Joe asks:

'So, any idea what you think it might be?'

'Be not afraid, Joe, for we're going to attack this one step at a time.' Trevor turns energetically. 'It won't be easy. Nothing is. You'll need to apply yourself. Be committed, hard-working. A neophyte must be like a sponge. Are you able to fully dedicate yourself to a cause?'

Joe nods enthusiastically.

'So, you can teach me?'

'Of course, I'm an actor. But tell me, Joe, why do you want to win this Storytell competition? Is it to be like your grandfather? – For self-fulfilment? – Or is it to simply defeat those beastly boys?'

'I won't lie; I'd love to shut the Beastie Boys up for once.'

'So, it's revenge then?'

'Not really; I just want to win – to show everyone, including myself, that I can actually tell a story and have people enjoy it.'

'Excellent.' Trevor retrieves a hankie from a trouser pocket and coughs into it.

'Are you alright?'

Trevor bats away Joe's concern and sits back at the table, opposite his guest. 'Something went down the wrong way,' he explains. 'Please, continue.'

'Okay.' Joe thinks for a moment. 'I mean I've read books; *lots* of books – heard countless stories. I've even read the Oxford English dictionary.'

'Is that so?'

'And Roget's Thesaurus.'

'What a strange boy you are.'

'I just can't *tell* stories. Not really good ones. Not like Grandpa Wilf used to.'

'He sounds like a fascinating character. Tell me about him, I'm keen to know more. Did he ever act? Did he crack the boards?'

'No, he was a forest worker; until he retired.'

'Trees, eh?' Trevor quips: 'I've worked with a few wooden actors in my time.'

'Trees, fencing, drainage; the Forestry Commission does all kinds of stuff. My dad works for them too.'

'And do you intend to follow in their footsteps?'

Joe shrugs.

'Was he a tall man, your grandfather? Perhaps I'm wrong but I picture him lofty in stature.'

'I can show you.'

Joe pulls the photo album from his Yoda backpack.

'Photographs,' froths Trevor. 'How delicious.'

Joe turns the album to face Trevor and flips a few pages.

'Snowmen; how adorable. Do they have names?'

'That's Miss Blizzard.'

'Snow-*persons*, I should say.'

'We made eyelashes out of plastic straws,' smiles Joe. 'Topped her off in Mum's only hat.'

'An Ascot chapeau I presume; unusual, yet so very de rigeur.'

'And that's Gramps.' Joe proudly points to one of several pictures in which his grandfather appears.

'Grandpa Wilf,' nods Trevor approvingly. 'He seems charming; so sad that I never met him. He sounds like a fascinating individual.'

'You'd have liked him. Everyone did. He'd have liked you, too.'

'Ah, clearly a man of impeccable taste.'

'He liked colourful characters. I know he'd have enjoyed knowing a great actor like yourself.'

'Oh, dear boy, you say all the right things.'

Trevor's hand lightly touches the back of Joe's for a short, silent beat, then Joe's hand moves to turn the page and point at the final photo.

'And that's Mr Frosty. He was built when I was eleven.'

Page 15 is blank.

'I haven't got Mr Wonky – the last one.'

'Yes, most unfortunate. It would appear we both have an incomplete collection.'

Trevor turns his head, as does Joe, to look at the empty space in Trevor's robot cabinet.

'So it's agreed?' checks Joe. 'You'll help me.'

'We'll see what we can do,' smiles Trevor. 'But if I am to tutor you in how to produce, stage, present, emote, execute and perform, so that you can bring down the house, I shall expect, as I said, total commitment and your full acquiescence – nothing less.'

'It's a deal.'

'Then this calls for another sherry.'

Trevor returns with a near empty bottle and two glasses.

'Only a small one for you – a snifter as it were – with which to seal our very own *entente cordial*.'

'I feel like Luke Skywalker, about to start Jedi training.'

'Except that this isn't science fiction, Joe. This is real. Not make believe.'

'What; like theatre?' quips Joe.

'Trevor, I didn't mean anything bad,' explains Joe outside the caravan. 'I just meant that theatre—'

'Hurry now, child, you must make haste.' Trevor looks up and addresses an invisible gallery: 'The firmament already commences its change to deepest amethyst. Return tomorrow and prepare for love's labour. For now, I must rest my weary head and bid you a fond adieu.'

Trevor closes the caravan door as if it were part of a dramatic scene in a play.

After a beat the door re-opens.

'Come tomorrow after school.'

The door closes again.

'Hear that, Yoda?' asks Joe over a shoulder. 'I'm going into training.'

He fires up an imaginary lightsaber with a 'Tsshwww.'

But finish what you have begun, will you, hmm?

Yoda is forced to hang on as Joe runs off, zigging left and zagging right.

'Vrooo! Vrooo! Vrooo!' He swings at a squad of stormtroopers, slays them in seconds.

'Vrooo! Vrooo! Vrooo!' He swipes at a series of calor-gas containers, slicing through hissing connector hoses and canister bodies alike.

At the entrance to the park, Joe turns and studies the explosions and burning caravans. He nods at a job well done then douses the lightsaber:

'Pssshhww.'

Panting loudly, Joe climbs in through his open bedroom window. He slips and falls head first into the dark room.

Downstairs, Joe's parents, a gap between them on the sofa, stare blankly at a television screen, not really watching. The film is a saddening bore.

Sally looks up.

'Sounds like he's fallen out of bed again.'

She throws out a hand that catches Paul on the bicep.

Paul fails to reply.

'Paul,' badgers Sally. 'Go check on him.'

'Oh, he'll be fine,' grunts Paul. 'He's a big boy now.'

After climbing into bed, Joe watched YouTube clips of Eminem's 8 Mile rap battles on his phone, rapped along to lyrics he'd heard so many times he knew them by heart. He sang about how you shouldn't ever try to judge him, dude, because you didn't know what the fuck he'd been through. But he knew something about you: You went to Cranbrook and that's a private school. 'What's the matter, dog, are you embarrassed?' Joe asked an imaginary crowd. How could the guy be a gangster? His real name was Clarence. And Clarence lived at home with both his parents, and more, Clarence's parents had a real good marriage. The guy didn't want to battle; he was shook – because apparently there's no such thing as a halfway crook!

Joe was word perfect, no mess ups, and his timing was spot on; and shortly afterwards he fell asleep, quietly snoring on his back, comfortable and content.

And now, about an hour after dropping off, Joe is dreaming of winning the Storytell competition:

His cards are MAGIC, TROPHY, BELIEF and CHAMPION.

On stage, clapped and whistled by fellow contestants and a capacity crowd, Joe humbly takes his bows. He hears Owen telling those around him that Joe's victorious story was: 'So much better than my shit.'

As Joe soaks up the adoration and a standing ovation, with Gary and Melvin applauding louder than anybody, he looks to Maxine, who has modelled her hands into the shape of a heart.

After strapping Emily into the baby seat in the back, Sally moves to open the driver door but is startled by Don.

'Don!' squawks Sally. 'Goodness, don't do that. You gave me the fright of my life.' She laughs tensely.

'Sorry.'

'No, no, it's fine; always nice to see you, Don. You just— you always seem to appear from nowhere.' Like a creepy old weirdo, she thinks, not for the first time.

'Just wanted to surprise you.'

'Well, you certainly did that.'

Sally opens her door. 'Right, well, I really must be getting along – things to do and all that jazz.'

Don reveals a bunch of flowers he'd been hiding behind his back. He smiles inanely, the dried mud on his overalls pressing gently against the driver door.

'Oh, uh, they're nice.' Sally squeezes into the car.

'I could have picked wild ones but I didn't. These are bought specially – from the petrol station.'

'Are they for Carol?' asks Sally through the narrow gap. 'Is it her birthday? I'm sure she'll love those.'

'Most expensive ones they had.'

'Well, give her my love, won't you. Mind fingers.'

Sally closes the door, points to her watch, waves, and then drives away. Don hardly moves, not even when the wheels roll dangerously close to running over his grubby work boot toes.

Sally watches Don grow small in her rear-view mirror as the ancient farmer stands, statue-like, holding the flowers.

'I mean when you're past it, you're past it, aren't you,' gases Clara.

'True,' agrees Bonnie. 'Mind you, he seems to be the only one who doesn't realise—'

The ping of the door and the entrance of Don's ruddy mug stops Bonnie in her tracks. Clara takes over:

'Hello, Don, we were just talking about you.'

'Why doesn't that surprise me,' mutters Don aimed for the beer section.

'How's the back now?'

'Back?' calls Don as if puzzled.

'We heard you'd slipped a disc or something.'

'No, no, I'm fine.'

'Still spending time up on the Finger, Don?'

No reply. If it wasn't for the clink-clink of glass bottles there would surely be an awkward silence.

'Did Carol like the flowers?'

No response.

Don eventually emerges from the alcohol section and approaches the counter with packs of Old Speckled Hen.

'We sell Thermacare Heat-Wraps if you'd like some,' smiles Bonnie. 'You know, for backs and things.'

'Just the beers, thank you.'

'Still, can't be easy,' bids Clara over-egging a supportive tone, 'watching the family run the farm without you.'

'Not when you were the big cheese for— goodness how long was it?' asks Bonnie.

'I'm fine, I tell you.' Don slaps a twenty onto the counter.

Ping!

'Your change!' calls Clara to Don's back. But he's already exiting the door, almost colliding with a man on his way in.

'No, after you,' sneers Liam stopping abruptly.

'Pump Number Two, is it?' asks Clara.

'I guess,' shrugs Liam. There *are* two pumps but how the fuck is he supposed to know which one is which?

Bonnie casts a beady eye over the van, brightly illuminated under the petrol station's canopy lights:

'How's the burger business, then?'

They, whoever they may be, say that the Welsh have only *one* business – and that's *your* business. The Mancunian was starting to think it might be true.

'Doing okay. Ticking over.'

'Not sold enough hotdogs to move out of those dreadful caravans yet though, eh?' Clara swivels her head, looks up the road, to the entrance of Tall Trees Trailer Park.

'You two don't miss much, do you?'

'Just being neighbourly, Craig,' smiles Bonnie. (Since his move to Llanidloes, Liam had adopted the name Craig. And Craig has a Liverpudlian accent – when Liam can remember.)

Liam pulls out a fold of notes.

'And your usual smokes?' asks Clara.

'Sure, why not,' replies 'Craig', Scouse as you like.

Bonnie selects two packs of Marlboro, hands them over.

'Okay for cable ties and duct tape?' asks Clara.

'Excuse me?'

'Last time you were in, you bought cable ties and duct tape,' reminds Bonnie.

'Did I?'

'Yes, don't you remember? You said you had some repairs to do in the caravan.'

'Oh yeah, that's right.'

'And he bought a sheet of plastic,' Clara reminds Bonnie. 'Leaky roof, wasn't it?'

'You know, you really should get on to Griff Edwards,' advises Bonnie. 'It's *his* trailer park; *he* should be doing any repairs.'

'It's sorted now, thanks.'

'We could mention it next time we see him.'

'Like I say, it's all good.'

'Not that he'd be quick to fix anything.'

'Too busy messing with that barmaid in The Red Lion.'

'They're both married,' Bonnie tells Liam.

'What a carry on,' agrees Clara. 'It's a disgrace.'

'It's a disgrace the condition of some of his caravans, I know that,' carps Bonnie.

'It'll do for now,' Liam assures them.

'If we had a word,' suggests Clara, 'he might move you into one of his better ones.'

'Yes, some are worse than others,' agrees Bonnie. 'Sounds like you got—'

'Never noticed that before,' Liam interrupts, eyeing a closed-circuit television camera up in a corner.

'It's new,' explains Clara.

'Oh yeah?'

'But don't worry you're not on Crimewatch,' quips Bonnie.

'Between you and us,' Clara leans forward and whispers conspiratorially: 'it's a dummy.'

'Keep it to yourself though, eh,' winks Bonnie.

'Don't want someone coming in and shotgunning us for the takings.'

'They'd be very disappointed,' laughs Bonnie rattling the open till drawer as if to underline her point.

'Doesn't worry you, then?' asks Liam. 'Someone coming in and robbing you? Or worse.'

'Worse? You mean like molesting us?'

'Jesus, no,' affirms Liam.

He meant murder you, joins in Joel's disembodied voice. *Then do the nasty with your dead headless torsos.*

'Not at all,' continues Liam. 'I wasn't suggesting—'

'Chance would be a fine thing,' blurts Clara.

This immediately has the pair cackling like witches.

Christ, they're annoying as fuck!

93

His brother's head may be in the van but Liam hears Joel as clearly as if he were standing next to him at the counter, axe at the ready; an axe much like the one Liam had swiftly and energetically planted into his neck that time. Still, he wouldn't think about that right now.

So, what do you think?

Yep, annoying as fuck, agrees Liam silently.

Okay, let's do it!

No, we stick to the plan, insists Liam.

But that's the hundred, right there.

'No, I said!' blurts Liam. He scans the women – still snickering like witches – and is thankful his outburst went unnoticed – at least, he's pretty sure it did.

'Oh, just ignore us,' laughs Bonnie. 'We're only teasing.'

'I'm sure no-one would ever rob us,' smiles Clara.

'Yes, we're too nice,' agrees Bonnie.

'Even though some people *do* call us Bonnie and Clyde,' complains Clara.

'At least they do when they think we're not listening,' adds Bonnie.

'But we don't miss much.'

'Yes, we know everyone in this town – *and* what they've been up to.'

'And then some.'

'Seems everyone knows everyone here,' sniffs Liam.

'Indeed they do, and word soon gets round.'

'Yep, you can't get away with much around here.'

'Locals have to think of their reputations.'

And what if it wasn't a local that walked in and shotgunned you, ya daft cunts?!

Liam rephrases the question: 'But what if it was someone just passing through?' he asks. 'A stranger, just in for say, petrol or smokes, and they decided to, y'know . . .'

He mimes shotgunning Bonnie: 'Choom!' Racks in another shell: 'Ker-Kck.' Mimes shotgunning Clara: 'Choom! – A barrel for each of you. What then?'

Clara aims her eyes at the CCTV camera.

'I thought you said it was a dummy,' frowns Liam.

'Yes,' winks Bonnie, 'but they don't know that, do they?'

'Ah,' nods Liam.

And people say we're fucking mental.

94

Outside, under the bright canopy lights of Gas & Graze, Liam's eyes widen and he stops dead in his tracks. That unshaven, scruffy fella he's seen wandering around town is paying close attention to the burger van.

'Hey, get away from there!' calls Liam, absentmindedly slipping back into his native Manchester accent. 'What do you think you're doing, mate?'

'Sticker,' intones Noah, eyes only inches from a set of colourful decals advertising the van's meaty products.

(One decal, for a Chilli-Dog, is slightly unstuck, its corner sticking out.)

'Sticker,' repeats Noah flicking it gently with a fingertip.

'What are you, some kind of mentalist? Go on, piss off.'

Noah turns to face the antagonistic tone.

'Sticker,' he explains.

'Yeah, yeah, sticker to you, too.'

Liam looks around warily and with good reason:

'Mumhfhh!' pleads a weak, muffled voice inside the van.

'Mumhfhh!' parrots Noah excitedly clapping hands.

Liam spots Clara and Bonnie tuning in at the window. He sends them a friendly *It's fine* wave. Then he softens his voice, adopts what appears to be an understanding stance, and squeezes Noah's shoulder firmly.

'Mind if I give you some advice?' smiles Liam. 'You want to clean yourself up a bit, mate. Maybe do some laundry. Even try having a bath. You can never have too many baths.' Liam becomes distant for a moment but finally snaps out of it: 'Now, go on,' he urges in an exaggerated friendly tone, 'get out of here.'

Liam turns and signals a thumbs-up to Clara and Bonnie who nod and return the gesture.

'Seriously, fuck off,' he whispers with a soft but insistent push.

'But mumhfhh!' complains Noah.

'You're hearing things, mate,' warns Liam. 'Now jog on.'

'Mumhfhh!' pleads the shaky, stifled voice in the van.

'Ahh!' points Noah eagerly. 'Mumhfhh!'

This guy, pantomimes Liam to Clara and Bonnie, laying a hand on where his own heart would be if he had one.

'Love him,' he mouths.

Then he climbs in, waves a smiley goodbye at the ladies, rolls the burger van off the petrol station forecourt and drives away. A final and barely-audible hoarse 'Mumhfhh!' disappears with the van, past the trailer park entrance, and on, into the night.

'Mumhfhh,' whimpers Noah, a feeble echo of what he'd heard.

CHAPTER 8

Let the Training Begin

'So, where do we start?' asks Joe.

'Why don't you tell me a story,' suggests Trevor. 'It could be one of your grandfather's; or a story you've read – anything at all.'

Joe ponders as Trevor imbibes wine from a glass.

'Any will do,' smiles Trevor. 'Remember, the story itself doesn't really matter.'

'It doesn't?'

'Not at this stage. It's about how you tell it.'

As Joe ponders some more, Trevor drains his glass, reaches back blindly for the unfinished bottle, finds it and pours another, smiling as he does so.

'You must be able to think of one,' he says softly at last.

'Of course,' huffs Joe. 'I can think of lots.'

'Splendid. Let's hear one.'

'You've probably heard them all before.'

'Remember, Joe, there are no *new* stories, *not really*; only variations of old ones.'

'Is that true?'

'It is.'

'Huh,' replies Joe. 'Okay.'

'Now . . . Action.'

Joe sits forward, clears his throat, cracks his fingers as if preparing to play piano, then leans forward on the caravan table.

'This is a story about Zak, a man who became obsessed with an amusement arcade claw-machine, you know, where you try to grab the prize with a three-pronged claw.'

Trevor nods. 'I am familiar with such apparatus.'

'Anyway, so this guy, this Zak, he spots this creepy little toy clown in there, its sinister face pressed against the glass of the cabinet, and for some reason he becomes totally preoccupied with snagging it. It's like he's consumed by the clown or something and must own it. But all his subsequent attempts at grabbing the toy end up costing him all his money – it's like two quid a go or something.'

'Try not to keep saying "something" or "it's like",' advises Trevor gently.

'And yeah, so, he ends up spending all his time at the arcade, often arguing with the manager that the machine is rigged; accusing him of deliberately setting its claws to Weak. And when

97

Zak isn't there, he's panicking that somebody else will step in and swipe the prize – *his* prize. It's a *seaside* arcade, by the way. And not only does he end up losing all his savings over this weird plastic clown, he loses his girlfriend and his job and his flat and he becomes homeless—'

'Slow down, Joe. You're rushing.'

But Joe isn't for slowing. 'Did I mention that he wasn't on summer holiday?' he asks. 'He lives there, in the town – before he became homeless, of course.'

'Is that important?'

'Yeah, no, kinda, dammit.'

'Never mind, please continue.'

'Yeah, so – he finds a two-pound coin on the pier and rather than spend it on food, a hotdog or something, he decides to have one last try.'

Joe pauses, takes a breath; perhaps finally taking Trevor's advice – or maybe because he's lost his thread.

'And does he win?' prompts Trevor wishing to be helpful.

'I'm coming to it,' frowns Joe. 'Where was I? Oh yeah – so Zak is sleeping rough in a shop doorway – I've got to get this bit right.'

Trevor nods appreciatively.

'And he wakes up in the morning . . .'

Trevor smiles expectantly but Joe falls quiet.

Trevor nods encouragement. 'Yes?'

'He wakes up in the morning,' reprises Joe, 'and . . .'

Trevor stops smiling, waits a moment then asks:

'Have you forgotten?'

'No,' Joe sighs. 'It's just that when I try to tell other people I sometimes mess up, like now, get things jumbled, in the wrong place, or I forget bits, or just tell it wrong.'

He growls and elbows his backpack; a furious dig, enough to make Yoda wheeze.

'It's fine,' Trevor assures him.

'Oh, who am I kidding? I'll never win the Storytell.'

Joe punches the backpack, lifts it up and slams it back down, shakes it and whacks it again, Yoda's head snapping this way and that – a rage flare which dampens as swiftly as it boiled over and leaves Joe suffering a look of disappointment on Yoda's face.

'Do you wish to throw in the towel?'

'No,' bristles Joe.

'Quitters never prosper,' lectures Trevor.

'I'm not a quitter. Not unless the situation's *completely* hopeless.'

'You said "Whatever it takes", remember?'

'Yes, and I'm here, aren't I?'

'You know your trouble – you're too uptight.'

'You'd be uptight if you had my life,' mutters Joe.

'But you're just a child.'

'I am not a child.'

'Well, we could debate the point but can we at least agree that you shouldn't be so uptight? Not at your age.'

Joe sits back, arms folded.

'Plenty of time for umbrage later: life is meant to be fun – a pleasure. Is not our very existence the wonder of all wonders?'

'Yeah, yeah, we are stardust and all that.'

'Such old-fashioned defensive scepticism with you; I know the transition of a boy to a young fellow can be laden with troubles and concerns but more than anything you should celebrate the joys and beauty of your youth.'

'Well, I don't know about beauty.'

Joe curls his lip and describes a self-deprecating circle in front of his face with an index finger.

Trevor raises bushy eyebrows.

'I suppose I could be more cheerful,' softens Joe. 'It's just been hard, you know, with—'

'Joe,' Trevor's tone is tender and reassuring, 'wouldn't Wilf want you to be happy?'

Joe nods slowly.

'Then seize the day, my lad. Seize the day.'

'Carpe diem?' brightens Joe.

'Exactly,' laughs Trevor.

'Okay. So, what would you suggest?'

'You just need to learn how to relax, my boy, that's all.'

Trevor stands, moves behind Joe and lays hands on his shoulders. 'That's it, just sit back and relax,' he soothes. He massages Joe's collar bone and kneads the base of his neck. 'Oh dear boy, you're so taut; do try and loosen up.'

Despite the upbeat nature of their chat Joe is unsure about the touching. It does feel nice, in a physical sense, but he's never been a touchy-feely kind of person. Then again, it's just shoulders – mostly. Is this wrong? Maybe he *does* worry too much. Mum's always saying how much she'd like a massage – *needs* a massage. Perhaps he should indeed relax as Trevor advises. *Chill out*, as Dad (hopelessly attempting to sound cool) is forever saying.

'Loosen up,' urges Trevor. 'Don't be so tense.'

Yeah, it's fine, Joe tells himself. Some people are just more tactile than others. And it's not like Trevor has ever overstepped the mark – still, best to get back on track.

'So . . . the story?'

'Yes, the story,' echoes Trevor. 'Don't think about *how* to tell it – just *feel* it. Allow it to happen, like you did with the robot. Remember how you felt then. You allowed yourself to believe. Go with those feelings. Upon any battlefield, they are your allies. Trust in them. Release your subconscious, let *it* do the work. It will light the way. You need only follow.'

'My subconscious?'

'Yes. That's the part of the mind that performs all the spontaneous creative work. It's the conscious mind that ignites one's worries and stems the flow.'

Joe shrugs. 'Don't feel like I'm worried.'

'You are!' booms Trevor. 'Trust me, I know.'

He digs strong fingers into Joe's shoulders, works them, ratchets up his already considerable grip.

'Okay, relaxed now,' winces Joe. 'Fully serene.'

'You sure?'

'Yep.'

'Excellent.' Trevor moves back to his seat. ''Tis the fear of forgetting our lines,' he advises dramatically, 'that makes us forget our lines.'

'So, basically – just go with the flow?'

'Exactly,' smiles Trevor. 'Don't try so hard. And no more temper tantrums.'

'Yeah, sorry about that – sometimes I just—'

'And there endeth the first lesson,' Trevor interrupts.

'Already?'

'Don't worry, there's homework.'

'There is?'

Out of the caravan, Joe awaits an explanation.

'The claw-machine story,' starts Trevor.

'Uh-huh.'

'I want you to tell it to a friend.'

'A friend?'

'A friend, stranger, anyone you like.'

Trevor closes the door and calls from inside:

'Oh, and try narrating your life.'

Joe thinks on this a moment then turns and walks away.

'Not all the time, obviously!' calls Trevor.

Joe stops, turns back.

The door opens and Trevor's head sticks out.

'Just sometimes; parts of your day-to-day deeds as they happen – as if it were a story.'

Joe's frown perfectly demonstrates his puzzlement.

'Preparation,' explains Trevor. 'Start now if you like.'

Again the door closes.

Joe quickly takes up the challenge:

'The ancient malcontent slammed the door in the face of the handsome young hero: a brave warrior with fortitude of heart and sincerity of soul.'

How do you like that, Trev? Joe thinks pointedly, before continuing his recital in a style that might best be described as 'audio-book' narration:

'Our protagonist thought the slamming of the portal uncouth and disrespectful but shrugged it off as mere eccentricity or just plain weirdness; the creaky curmudgeon was, after all, an old fart. And with that, the hero turned, shrugged his one-of-a-kind backpack then ambled away in manly fashion, leaving the dingy caravan behind and the decrepit coot alone with his rudeness.'

'Good start!' hails Trevor, unseen.

'Thanks!' Joe calls back.

'More gusto, though; by all means keep it dramatic – but also fun and playful.'

'Dramatic *and* playful? Isn't that a contradiction?'

'It's about finding the right balance.'

'Er . . . okay.'

'And not so much of the "old fart" next time.'

Paul makes a final check of his hair in the hall mirror; he needs to be sure nothing has moved out of place since the application of *Mr Spiff's 'Primp & Preen' Styling Mousse* in the bathroom just five minutes earlier.

'Where is he?' he asks impatiently.

Sally shrugs. 'I'm sure he'll be down in a—'

'Joe!' calls Paul up the stairs.

'Don't yell; you'll frighten Emily.'

'Doesn't he know the time?' Paul swings open the front door. 'If he's not out in one minute, I'm going without him.'

'And if you're late to pick him up again,' warns Sally, 'I'll cut your balls off—Oh, here he is.'

Joe trots down.

'All ready, love?'

'Yep.'

'Got everything you need?'

'Yep.'

'Let's go!' shouts Paul from the driveway.

Sally hugs Joe – a really tight bear hug.

'Okay, Mum,' wheezes Joe. 'Ease up on the death-lock.'

'Ooo, he's still my big cuddle-bunny.'

'Sheesh, Mum, what's up with you? You haven't called me that since I was a kid.'

'*Since I was a kid*,' scoffs Sally. 'What are you like?'

From outside: an impatient horn blast.

Joe exits and Sally leans against the door, watching him go.

'Make sure he wears his seat belt!' she calls.

Not even halfway and Paul's eyes are rolling.

'But the scarecrow had other ideas,' gases Joe. 'He'd had his fill of the Beastie Boys using him for target practice. And so, when they next climbed the hill with their air-rifles and buckets of stones, Mr Sackhead was waiting for them. He'd already dug three ruffian-sized holes—'

'I said knock it off, Joe,' grunts Paul.

'Philistine,' mutters Joe.

'And why would they carry buckets of stones up a hill? It doesn't make sense. Just fill them at the top.'

'It's a comedy.'

'Well, it's not making me laugh.'

'That's because you have no sense of humour,' snips Joe.

Other than Paul double-checking that Joe remembered his lunchbox, neither speak for the rest of the journey. And when Paul finally drops Joe at school, he again asks:

'Now, you're sure you've got your lunch?'

'Yes, Dad, I do have my lunch,' drones Joe. 'Just go, will you?'

Megan and Jade are leaning against the gate, talking; although she's hiding it, Joe can smell Megan's cigarette.

'Right, see you later. And don't wander off this time.'

Joe looks to the girls who smile in an empathetic way.

'You got that? Wait here – *right here*.'

'Jeez, just go, Dad, please.'

Joe sighs with relief as Paul finally drives off but then spots Gary and Melvin smirking at him.

'Now what?' Joe asks resignedly.

He looks to where they are gawking: his feet.

'That's not good,' mutters Joe quietly.

He's wearing his fluffy Snowman slippers.

'Man, they is the gayest slippers I have ever seen,' cackles Gary. Gary thinks he's from the 'hood' – better known as the picturesque village of Cwmbelan.

'They *are* the gayest slippers,' corrects Joe. 'Check your grammar.'

The lads walk towards the school entrance laughing the whole way and Joe follows, padding along in his slippers.

Damn, why couldn't it be a PE day? At least then he'd have his trainers with him.

'Could today have got off to a worse start?' Joe sighs. 'Oh no, hold that thought.' He's spotted Owen ahead, in the corridor, inside the main entrance. He's talking to Gary and Melvin and all three are looking his way – at his feet. Nigela Lewis and Lily Morgan are there too.

Joe shuffles forward and stops beside them.

'Go on, get it over with.'

'Hey, Joe, those are a bit special,' Owen smirks.

Feeling for Joe, Nigela gestures for Owen to leave it.

'No, no, I just want to know: are they for . . .' Owen switches to high-pitched singing: '*walking in the air.*'

'Yes. Yes they are,' nods Joe. 'They're for walking in the air. They're for,' he sticks out a slipper, stretches his arms as if flying, and switches to even higher pitched singing: '*floating in the moonlit sky.*'

Everyone but Owen laughs; he clearly feels the joke is being turned back on him. Nigela smiles warmly but Owen no longer finds it funny; until he spots the headmaster staring right at them – in Joe's blind spot.

'*The people far below,*' continues Joe, still in soprano voice, '*are sleeping as we fl—*'

'Joseph Edward Jones!' barks Mr Smallwood. 'What on earth have you got on your feet, lad?!'

'Oh, busted,' snorts Owen.

'Sir?' asks Joe in the headmaster's office.

'I said take them off, lad.'

Mr Smallwood has opened a large storage locker full of old school items: a cap, blazer, photos, sporting trophies, and a worn leather football.

'Yes,' he enthuses, 'I *thought* I still had these beauties.'

He turns, holding out a pair of ancient shoes, two sizes too big for Joe, and several decades too square.

Mr Smallwood jiggles the shoes: thick-soled brothel creepers with suede uppers. Joe doesn't know much about shoes but feels these have an 'orthopaedic' look.

'No need to thank me,' grins the headmaster, head shining brightly under the office's dazzling strip light.

Mr Smallwood, as well as being short (barely an inch taller than Joe) and bald (apart from a fluffy sprout of hair over each jug ear), also has a beak nose, large glasses and a thin moustache.

'Perfect,' mumbles Joe reluctantly accepting the antiquated footwear.

'You can pad them with tissue paper if necessary.' Mr Smallwood closes the locker. 'Drop them off at the end of the day.' He claps his hands rapidly. 'Now off you pop to your first lesson. Go on, scoot.'

Katie's waiting in the corridor outside the Science room with the rest of the class. 'Think I preferred the slippers,' she quips.

'Yeah, good one,' laughs Joe. 'I couldn't walk in the air with these, that's for sure.'

Katie laughs, until the Beastie Boys crash their chat.

'Think I preferred the slippers,' quips Owen.

'I've already said that,' remarks Katie.

'Oh yeah?' he sneers.

Katie nods. Owen looks at Joe. Joe nods.

'Have you got a different one?' Joe asks Owen.

Owen can't think of an alternative put down and it shows. Gary elbows him and prompts:

'Tell him about the café.'

'Oh yeah, the café,' chuckles Owen.

Joe shrugs. 'What about it?'

'We heard someone saw you two in there all cosy like.'

Katie's about to ask: *So what?* But Joe's already in denial mode. 'I don't see how,' he frowns.

'No?' smirks Gary.

'They must have made a mistake,' asserts Joe.

Katie stares, unhappy with Joe's rebuttal – and so quick with it too. She marches off.

'Katie!' calls Joe. He aims a thumb. 'It's Science next!'

But Katie keeps walking.

'She'll realise in a minute,' Joe assures the others.

'Yeah, she obviously made a mistake,' scoffs Owen as Katie disappears around a corner.

'Sorry I'm late, Miss.'

'That's fine, Katie,' puffs Miss Thompson running laps around her desk. 'We've only just started.'

Joe indicates the empty chair beside him, where Katie usually sits but Katie makes a show of looking around, apparently assessing alternatives. She shrugs then heads for her usual seat.

'You're not still mad at me, are you?' whispers Joe.

'A girl doesn't like to be denied, Joe,' she mutters, sitting. 'Why didn't you just say "Yes, we were together, actually, what's it to you?" We are friends, you know. At least, I thought we were.'

'Sorry.'

'Are you ashamed of me or something?'

'No, no, I just hate gossips. It's none of their business.'

'It doesn't bother me, Joe. Does it bother you?'

'Again, sorry.'

'We're thirteen, Joe; and just mates, that's all. It's not like we're an old married couple or something. But to deny even being with me—'

In the awkward pause that follows, Joe has an idea.

'I'm seeing Trevor again later. Would you like to come?'

Katie makes Joe wait but eventually she replies:

'I'll think about it.'

Some students are giggling: Miss Thompson, late fifties, is still rushing in circles around her desk. In desperate need of a serious wardrobe update, her long, flowing clothes flap around comically.

'Come on, come on,' Miss Thompson urges. 'What am I?'

'Madder than a box of frogs?' Joe asides to Katie.

'Completely hat-stand,' agrees Katie softening.

'Come on,' pants the teacher. 'My desk's the sun, so . . . ?'

'Hey, an eclipse!' shouts Owen as she passes between his braying head and the centre of the solar system: her desk.

'Yes, very good, Owen,' cheers Miss Thompson. '*So* . . . ?'

'The Earth, Miss,' Katie sighs.

'Well done, Katie, excellent.' Still jogging, Miss Thompson makes a fist and circles it around her head. 'Now, what's this?'

'Just a minute!' barks Mr Smallwood from the other side of the closed door; this in answer to Joe's knock.

Joe looks up the corridor as he waits.

'Enter!' calls the headmaster at last.

Joe opens the door to find Mr Smallwood standing by his locker, making a big thing of polishing the old leather football. Mrs Kennedy, the music teacher, is hovering by the desk. She looks jittery, ruffled, and red around the gills.

Joe sniffs the air. There's a strange musty smell in the office and it's not Mr Smallwood's old ball.

'Yes, Joe, what is it?' asks the headmaster impatiently. He turns to Mrs Kennedy. 'Thank you, Grace, we'll pick up where we left off—about those exam papers—later.'

Joe and the teacher catch eyes as she exits at pace.

'Well?' asks Mr Smallwood.

Joe holds out the headmaster's shoes.

'Oh, yes, just leave them there. In fact, no, keep them; the way you boys shoot up you'll no doubt grow into them soon enough.'

'But—' Joe starts to protest.

'No, no, I insist.' Mr Smallwood ushers Joe to the door. 'Look after them, Joe, and they should see you right through to sixth-form. I assume you will be staying on?'

After dumping Mr Smallwood's shoes in one of the school's bins, Joe sets to waiting outside the main gate.

Why wait? Yoda asks. *Just go.*

'I have to stick around; at least, for a *few* minutes.'

But come, he won't, blinks Yoda. *Why bother?*

Joe looks up and down the road.

'Just so I can say I did,' he shrugs.

And not because you're hoping to bump into Max, hm?

'Hey, here's a good one—'

Heard it.

'I haven't told you what it is yet.'

Yoda rolls his eyes. *Pretty sure am I.*

'What app do Jedi use to view PDF files?'

Adobe Wan Kenobi.

'Oh, you *have* heard it.'

Foolish boy.

'Quiet,' shushes Joe, spotting his sister pushing her cycle through the gates. Today Lucy is in a blue 1960s cat-suit with matching headband and platform boots from the 70s.

'Talking to yourself again?' she teases.

'No.'

'Hmm. He wasn't talking to you, was he, Yoda?'

Yoda shakes his head.

'Oh, Joe!' barks Lucy spotting her brother's bare feet. 'Where are your shoes?'

'It's either this or the slippers,' he explains flatly.

Lucy gestures that she's not even going to ask.

'Right, well you'll have to wait for Dad; you can't walk home like that.'

'I'll give him ten more minutes,' states Joe defiantly. 'But then I *am* walking.'

'Oh, Joe.'

'Luce, I'm not a child.'

'Well, you can't walk in your socks.'

'Got my slippers,' he reminds her.

Gary, Owen and Melvin snicker at Joe's feet.

'Yeah, that's right, keep moving,' warns Lucy.

The lads look back speaking covertly; defiance in their eyes but they keep walking.

'There they go,' calls Lucy. 'The three stooges!'

Joe sighs, shakes his head. 'And why are *you* still here?'

'I'm not,' replies Lucy mounting her bike. 'I'm off.'

'Okay, great,' grins Joe. 'Want me to give Maxine a message when she comes out?'

Lucy laughs. 'She won't be coming out, Joe.'

'Oh; why not?' Joe's disappointment is obvious.

'She's in Swansea, something to do with her course.'

Lucy places a foot on the uppermost pedal.

'Now, you *wait*; I don't think Dad will forget again – not after Mum's warning.'

'Yeah, right,' scoffs Joe as he watches his sister ride off.

'See you later!' she calls.

'Not if I see you first.' Joe swivels his head, addresses Yoda over a shoulder. 'You reckon that's been ten minutes?'

Say more like fifteen, I would, winks Yoda. *Hmm?*

Trevor leans over the caravan porch handrail, eyeing Joe's fluffy slippers as they approach then stop at the bottom of the steps.

'Goodness, you really do love snowmen, don't you?'

Joe studies the slippers a moment. He looks up with an expression that's part smile, part grimace.

'Considering how comfortable they are indoors, they're surprisingly *un*comfortable on long walks outside.'

'I would imagine that's true.'

Trevor straightens up, studies the sky, takes in a long, deep breath and lets it out through his upturned nose.

'And yet here you are.'

Joe rubs a foot.

'Are you still annoyed about the old fart remark?'

'Not at all; what a dull place is Life without humour and bouts of friendly ribbing.' Trevor drops intense eyes to Joe. 'I trust the quip was meant without malice or disrespect.'

'Oh God, yes, I would never—'

Trevor thumps the porch handrail and thunders:

'For if you did—'

'No, no,' protests Joe.

'Relax, boy, I'm just messing with you,' grins Trevor. 'See, what I did? I made you believe – it's all in the delivery.'

'Yep. Good one.'

'Too kind, too kind,' bows Trevor.

Joe mugs a comically scornful face and claps playfully.

'Thank you, ladies and gentlemen, I'm here all week.'

After Joe's impish derision has dried up Trevor asks:

'So, have you been practising your narrations?'

'Yes.'

'And what about your delivery?'

'My delivery?'

'The conveyance – the rendition – the presentation.'

'Yeah, I know what it means, Trevor. I'm just not sure—'

'I asked for drama – theatre – passion.'

'Well, I'm obviously not at your level but—'

'It would doubtless benefit your storytelling.'

'Okay,' nods Joe. 'I'll work on it.'

'Why don't you come in,' suggests Trevor. 'I have an idea that might prove helpful.'

'O Romeo, Romeo, wherefore art thou, Romeo?'

Joe steps out from behind the caravan's petition curtain and Trevor, sitting at the table, looks him up and down; from Joe's Elizabethan court shoes and bright blue leggings to his foppish hat with side feather.

'A twirl please, Romeo.'

Joe's outfit creaks as he turns. Excessively padded tunic with elaborate trimmings over a white puffy shirt and satin trunk hose: large pantaloons that resemble a pair of inflated shorts which balloon out from the waist and taper in around the upper thigh.

'And this will help how?'

'Trust me, it will – objects focus the mind.'

'Tights?'

'Props.'

'If you say so,' sighs Joe. 'And can I just check that I definitely don't look like an escaped lunatic?'

'More like a young Olivier or Gielgud.'

Trevor raises a glass of sherry.

'Shame you haven't got a skull.'

'Deny thy father and refuse thy name,' recites Trevor as Romeo playfully strikes several dramatic poses.

'You *haven't* got a skull, have you?' checks Joe. 'I couldn't see one in the chest.'

'Alas no.'

Joe takes this as his cue:

'Alas poor Yorick, I knew him well.'

'I knew him, Horatio,' corrects Trevor. 'A fellow of infinite jest, of most excellent fancy—'

'Whoa, whoa, I thought this was about me.'

'And indeed it is but one can hardly sit idly by as the great Bard is misquoted.'

Joe gestures for Trevor to get back on track.

'Patience, Romeo, patience. Now, did you retell the claw-grab story as I asked?'

Joe's nod sways the hat's tall white feather.

Trevor appears doubtful.

'To friends or strangers?'

'Both.'

'Both, eh?'

'Uh-huh.'

'And how did that go?'

'Good.'

'Show me.'

'Well,' hesitates Joe, 'I fleshed out Granddad's original story – you know, added to it, made it even more interesting.'

Trevor frowns. 'Just get on with it.'

'Okay, so I started with Brighton Pier and how it's over 520 metres long. Then I said . . .' Joe switches to recital mode: 'At the heart of its high-stilted Victorian boardwalk, sits Aladdin's Arcade, where Zak had been losing to a myriad of one-arm bandits, pinball machines and various slots for the last few hours.'

'Stop, stop, stop.'

'What?' Joe gripes. 'That was word for word.'

'But that's how you told it?'

'Yes, fun and relaxed, like you said. Why, what's wrong?'

Trevor sighs. 'Maybe it's a tad *too* relaxed.'

'Really?'

'Yes, I regret to say, it sounded a little on the bland side; rather vanilla – somewhat bald.'

'Bald?'

Trevor pours a fresh glass of sherry. 'I blame myself, I should have been clearer. When I said relaxed, I really meant your state of mind, not the actual storytelling.'

As Trevor knocks back his drink, Joe notices, on the table, an old theatre programme featuring a young man with a familiar face on the cover.

'Is this you?' asks Joe picking up the programme.

'Ah yes, *Measure For Measure*. I was Lucio, a young Nobleman who falls foul of a deceitful judge and is sentenced to death. And I was splendid, dear boy, splendid. 'O pretty Isabella, I am pale at mine heart to see thine eyes so red. Thou must be patient. I am fain—'

'Er, hello.'

'Oh, yes; back to you.'

Trevor indicates that Joe should return to the part of the caravan designated as the 'stage' area.

Joe obliges.

'So – what am I doing?'

'Put yourself in the story. Become the Hero. Act it out. Lose yourself in the part.'

'So, I should be Zak?' balks Joe. 'But he's in his twenties, has a job and a girlfriend, both of which he loses. No-one would believe it was me—'

'Okay, maybe not; although it might have lent the story greater feeling, made it more convincing, more real, personal.'

'I could try a different story, one in first-person.'

'Yes, good, I'd like to hear that,' nods Trevor. 'And let us have gestures and voices, accents and projection. Remember, it's all about the delivery.'

'Delivery – gotcha.'

'Yes, for you Joe, I'm certain: storytelling should be like acting. Imagine you are part of the Royal Shakespeare Company, a player performing at the jewel that is The Globe Theatre, in front of a huge, adoring crowd.'

'I like the sound of that.'

'Excellent. You are a man after my own heart.'

'I mean there's a nervous excitement, obviously, but yeah, I definitely love the attention of a really big crowd.'

'You're absolutely certain?'

'Er, I think I'd know.'

'Because stage-fright is perfectly normal and we can work on techniques to combat that fear.'

'No, trust me, I love seeing all those fascinated faces hanging on my every word.'

'Yes, well, although I'd be reluctant to admit it in public, I myself fully understand the attractions of attaining the full attention of one's audience—'

'Lending me their ears, so to speak,' continues Joe.

'Oh, good one – a touch of the Bard.'

'Welcoming me; taking notice – appreciating, even *adoring* me.'

Trevor nods enthusiastically.

Joe's face drops. 'Until they turn hostile.'

'Hostile?'

'No-one wants a crowd of people to see them fail.'

'You won't fail.'

'And then they laugh – and not in a good way.'

Joe appears to grow anxious at the thought of that.

'Then imagine the theatre is empty, my boy; absolutely no audience.' Trevor shudders at the very idea. 'And no need for the limelight, for this is just a one-to-one rehearsal, with me, your director, far off in the back row.'

'Okay, I can do that.'

'Excellent. Now, give me your best performance. I want Burton, Redgrave, Finney. I want to be dazzled.'

'So – the claw-grab story again?'

Trevor shakes his head.

'How about one of yours?' he suggests.

'Mine?' laughs Joe. 'Mine aren't very good.'

'How about one of the stories you made up in your school Storytell contest.'

'Like I said, they're not very good.'

'They can't be that bad.'

'Why do you think I've never won the competition?' Joe adjusts his hat. 'No, I'm going to do another Gramp's one.'

'Very well,' sighs Trevor, 'one step at a time, I suppose. But a *new* story, please.'

'I thought there weren't any *new* stories,' Joe teases.

'New to me, of course, you cheeky rapscallion,' retorts Trevor. 'One *I* haven't heard before – if you can.'

Joe clears his throat unnecessarily.

'Take it from the top. And remember, project. I'm right at the back of the theatre.'

Joe adopts what he believes to be a performance-ready position, but then seems lost for his opening line.

'In your own time, dear boy.'

Joe takes in a deep breath, lets it out through his nose then starts: 'It all started on a hot summer morning.'

'Good. There are those who say never start with weather but I say that's poppycock. Now continue. But louder.'

'The farm was quiet,' booms Joe.

'Better.'

'Only a feisty rooster noticed as I approached, limping unsteadily along the track; so tired and stooped that my hands actually dragged through the dust.'

'More passion.'

'Almost immediately I noticed the hen house and my belly rumbled. I didn't hesitate: the lock was child's play, I crept inside, stole four eggs and ate them raw, right there and then.'

Outside, Alison is walking her pet Labrador.
'Good boy,' she praises quietly. Benji has stopped by Trevor's caravan. Not that Alison is an eavesdropper, you understand, it's just that the dog happens to have paused for a sniff around this particular porch and she's giving him a minute, like you do.

Edging nearer the porch, Alison catches Joe's voice; something about 'an enraged cock' but the words aren't clear. Leaning over she aims narrowed eyes, glittering with suspicion, at Trevor's door.

'So, there I was, running up the hill,' recounts Joe. 'And though the rough bracken slowed me, I pushed on, scrambling over the rocky terrain as fast as I could. My little legs ached but there was no time to stop; I knew the farm workers weren't far behind – I heard them shouting, an angry mob chasing after me.'

Trevor is captivated as Joe acts out his story.
'Their baying calls spurred me on but I was tiring. And when I reached a barbed wire fence I thought I was done for – until I spotted the stile.'

Looking fearful, Joe pretends to climb over the stile.
'As I climbed over something hit me on the shoulder; a large stone, I think. I was so scared by now that my teeth were chattering. And glancing back I saw the farm hands had grown closer – they were gaining on me.'

'Good, Joe. Good.'
'I pushed on; felt that if I could just reach the trees I'd be safe.'

Trevor bites his lip.
'I heard dogs, three or four of them, barking and snarling. Another glance and I saw the vicious brutes frothing at the mouth and straining their leashes. Thank goodness they hadn't been turned loose – so far. They looked angrier than the men; men armed with pitchforks and spades and sharp pointed sticks; waving them violently as they rushed towards me. One of them had what looked like a bundle of knotted ropes – a net!'

Trevor wrings his hands.
'Another stone whizzed past my head and I was almost done. The trees were just there – right there – but they were at my heels. Then I tripped over a rock and was suddenly down on the ground. I tried to clamber back to my feet but again stumbled, this time ending up in a shallow gulley staring up at the cloudless

June sky. And as I lay there, egg on my lips and the sun beating down, the angry farm workers gathered around me in a tightening circle. A man in a rounded hat – the foreman, I think – leaned over, so close to my narrowed eyes and puffing cheeks that I could smell tobacco on his breath. And in an East London accent he sneered: "We gotcha now, you thievin' little monkey." '

(Here Joe had adopted a Victorian cockney twang for the man in the hat and he would continue in that vein for the other characters, dropping his aitches and that.)

'But the man beside him said: "E ain't no monkey, e's an ape." "Yeah, chimps is apes, stoopid." "E must've escaped from that travellin' circus I 'eard wuz over in Ammersmith." "Yeah, I seen posters." "Blimey, he musta walked over ten blinkin miles." "Is there a reward?" asked the man in the hat. "Nah, don't fink so." "Well then, I don't fink we need worry ourselves about—" No, no, no, this won't help me.'

'Wait, what?' Trevor had been about to applaud.

But Joe is no longer lost in the story, his face has changed, his engrossment turned to anguish, an unhappiness bordering on distress. He sits and removes the foppish hat.

'It won't help me,' bleats Joe. 'We don't know the story we're going to tell before we get there. It's improvised. We have to make it up on the spot; it's not prepared beforehand.'

'But I was just about to cheer: Bravo, dear boy, bravo, marvellous. Not the best story I've ever heard but for sheer performance that was a presentation worthy of—'

'None of it's going to help. Not this reciting-with-feeling rubbish. I have to actually ad-lib – spontaneously. We don't know the story in advance.'

'We'll get to that later,' soothes Trevor. 'But for now it's good practice.'

'Is it?' asks Joe pointedly.

'Our doubts are traitors, and make us lose the good we oft might win, by fearing to attempt.'

'See,' fumes Joe, 'reciting again. You didn't *create* that. See the difference? If you'd just come up with that, right now, I might be impressed. But you didn't, you just remembered it, and then said it. It's not the same. Not the same at all!'

'Losing your temper won't—'

'I have to invent it!' snaps Joe. 'Which bit of that do you not understand? I haven't got time for this . . . crap!' The hat spins, aimed for the sink. 'And this.' There's a dull thud as he slaps the padded trunk hose. 'Or this.' A button is snapped from the tunic.

'Hey, come on now.'

113

☆ ★ ☆

Joe storms out through the trailer's door and down the porch steps, almost knocking Alison over in a flamboyant swoosh of Elizabethan clothing.

'Everything alright, Joe?' asks Alison.

'He thinks dressing me up in tights and telling me to relax will solve all my problems. Well, it won't work!'

Having briefly stopped, he now storms off across the caravan park, Benji barking at the hatless Romeo's fat, satiny shorts as they squeak sharply with every stride.

CHAPTER 9
Wherefore Art Thou?

Romeo has retreated to the familiar safety of Wilf's Workshop. He sits in silence by the workbench before Granddad's possessions, everything arranged on the trunk lid as if a shrine, an effect greatly enhanced by the framed photos and an array of flickering church candles.

The stars are out tonight: they wink and shimmer overhead; magical lights beaming down from far out in space; the celestial canopy a speckled inky backdrop to the network of overhanging branches where leaves rustle gently, instigated by soft night breezes. A high drifting cloud uncovers a serious moon that casts silver light over the shed. The shadow of a lone crow, alighting high in a neighbouring tree, stretches across the roof. Feathers are preened. Calls are made. A circling bat chases invisible insects. And far beyond, inconsequential to the nocturnal wildlife and imperceptible to the human eye, Time slowly wheels its astronomical scenery.

Back inside, undetected by the stars, Romeo remains reflective, lost in thought. Close by, an owl hoots, and through the cobwebbed window, above the tree tops, a distant aeroplane tracks high across the sky, winking lights at the heavens. After a while, perhaps an hour later, maybe two, a fox pads by outside. The soft sounds of its paws pass unnoticed but as happenstance would have it; this is the moment when Joe catches sight of a door, slightly ajar, under the workbench.

Was it ajar when he came in? He couldn't say.

A hand reaches out over the backpack and Yoda partially opens a tired eye, like a sleepy cat might do, as Joe carefully creaks back the open door. Then a solitary candle floats, unhurried, inside the black hole, where its gentle glow softly illuminates a second trunk; not quite as large as the 'shrine' trunk but still a good size.

A mile away, as the crow flies, Trevor is seated at the caravan table, a parade of robots before him, glass of sherry close by, dust cloth in hand. He points at Mr Radar, next in line for a polish.

'And you, my good fellow, were acquired from Bolton flea market. Do you remember?'

He raises a toast, drinks, sleeves his beard then refills his glass from a near-empty bottle.

'It was a Saturday,' slurs Trevor. 'Rain outside, a jostle of coats and umbrellas in the market hall; acutely crowded as I recall, yet I spotted you from a distance; blue despite the dust. The tag asked a shilling but the ragamuffin was a tanner short and said so; then the perky stall-holder offered the boy a kindness and knocked off the sixpence. "In light of your bent aerial," he said.'

Trevor barks abruptly, hard and loud. He whips out a hankie and hacks into it. When the coughing fit is over, the hankie is folded and stuffed back into the pocket from whence it came.

'Whereas you, Mr Sparks,' continues Trevor undeterred, 'were discovered at a car boot sale in sunny Scarborough.' He prods the little wind-up tin toy: a silver, square-headed cyborg with block feet. '*Yes, that's right,*' he sighs, 'you *did* have a weapon.' – The retort is mechanical, as if he's heard this complaint many times. 'I know, I know, and a jet-pack.' Trevor raises his glass. 'No, sadly,' – he looks around – 'I still haven't—'

From the corner of an eye Trevor notices Becki and Chloe in their pyjamas, waving to him from the adjacent caravan. He smiles and waves back. The younger girl has a question: *How many robots do you have?* she signs. Chloe, nine, a year younger than her sister, is both hearing-impaired and non-verbal.

Trevor signs back: *A whole caravan full!*

Chloe laughs silently; signing it thusly: hands extended with index fingers and thumbs forming an L shape pointed at her cheeks, the fingers then describing upward spirals.

Trevor draws the girls' attention to the metallic wind-chime hanging outside their window. They look, he closes his eyes and concentrates . . . and after a suspenseful delay the chimes knock together and play a tuneful lullaby.

Although only Becki *technically* 'hears' the jingling melody, Chloe, senses the vibrations and is excited to witness the chimes' mysterious movements. Encouraged by Becki, Chloe signs a follow-up question but Alison appears with the girls' suppers.

Chloe hides her hands.

Becki nudges her sister and mouths: *This is your fault.* For their mum, peering through the window, has spotted her neighbour: sherry in one hand, toy robot in the other, and grinning like a simpleton, the cigarette-holder (bright pink cigarette smoking in the end) clenched in his teeth. She quickly tables the cereal bowls and snaps the curtains shut.

Joe slides the trunk out of the cupboard and closes the door. He clicks the trunk's catches. They're locked but a quick search of the workbench drawers and he has a key.

116

Unlocked and opened, the trunk reveals its contents.

First out, an adult-sized outfit: a furry, white, yeti-like onesie. Joe recognises it and smiles accordingly. Next up, a spiralling horn; the type you would expect to find on a unicorn if they existed. And finally, after a few immaterial odds and ends, a pair of large, hairy feet (on the ends of extendable poles); feet consistent with those an abominable snowman might walk upon should they also exist.

Recognise them? asks Wilf's filtered voice.

Joe jumps and almost knocks a candle off the trunk.

'Jeez, you startled me, Granddad.'

Oh, sorry, Joe, laughs Wilf. Seated beside his grandson, he appears as a spectral, translucent blue, sparkly-with-static hologram – much like those in Star Wars films.

Always the unexpected, one should expect, advises Yoda lazily, before falling back to sleep.

After resetting the disturbed candle, Joe turns to Wilf.

'Maybe cough first next time,' he suggests.

Why?

'Er, hello, naked flames everywhere.'

Wilf laughs. *Yes, I like what you've done with the place.*

'Thanks.' Joe places hand on heart, testing its rapidity.

Is it still going?

'For now,' laughs Joe, immediately feeling guilty for making light of such matters after what happened to Wilf.

The old man slips a phantasmal arm around Joe's shoulder and administers a grandfatherly squeeze.

Sorry, I will try to remember to cough next time. Hey, are those my trophies?

Joe elbows a playful nudge. 'You know they are.'

I'm surprised you had room for them all, Wilf teases.

'It *was* a bit of a squeeze but I managed in the end,' quips Joe.

They laugh then sit in quiet contemplation; one dressed as a hatless Romeo, the other in the hospital gown he died in.

'I expect you're curious about the outfit,' asks Joe at last.

No, replies Wilf softly. *I was still thinking about my trophies,* he teases.

'Alright, Gramps, don't rub it in.'

Wilf chuckles quietly. *Don't worry, Joe, you'll have one of your own soon enough.*

'Pfft,' puffs Joe. 'I wouldn't hold your breath. Oh, sorry.'

It's fine, laughs Wilf. *But do me a favour.*

'What?'

A hospital gown, really?

'Sorry— I— It was just how I saw you last.'
I know, but come on.
'Bit draughty, is it?' kids Joe.
It is a bit, frowns Wilf. *But at least I don't look like a second-rate pirate.*
'Hey!'
Wilf laughs. *I know what* would *look good: the suit I wore to your mum and dad's wedding; you remember the photos.*
'Or we could just go for this . . .'
Wilf studies his new image: a matching Romeo outfit.
Well, we do look a bit silly, but at least I have a hat to keep my head warm. Wilf blows his hat's feather comically. This as Yoda's snoring rises from faint to wheezy.
'Sorry, Gramps, just messing – is . . . this better?'
Much, confirms Wilf, now realised in a form replicating the time he and Joe built their last snowman.
'It's what you were wearing when—'
Joe chokes on the words.
I know, soothes Wilf. Again he extends a phantasmic arm around Joe, tenders a familiar hug. *You okay? You're shaking.*
'Yeah,' sighs Joe, though he clearly isn't.
Actually, that reminds me; I wanted to give you this.
Wilf raises a flat palm and Joe's caravan snow-globe materialises instantly – solid, not holographic.
'Where did you find that?' barks Joe excitedly. He takes the shaker and mulls it over; surely it's real, the density and coldness confirm as much.
Hmm, thought he'd lost it, he did, stretches Yoda, woken by Joe's outburst.
Sometimes what we think we've lost, offers Wilf, *was actually with us the whole time; close at hand – we just didn't realise.*
Yoda's head bobs in agreement.
'That's beautiful,' sighs Joe.
Of course, sometimes they are actually lost—
'See, no, you've spoilt it now.'
Don't listen to me, laughs Wilf. *Because this,* he waves a hand over the shrine, *all this – isn't about* me.
'It isn't?'
No, this is about you, *Joe – this is* your *story.*
Wilf's grandson nods slowly. He shakes the globe and watches the snow storm around the miniature caravan. Joe feels he's beginning to understand: this *is* about him – it is indeed *his* story.
Flakes are still swirling when he asks:
'But should my story – include Trevor?'

Hmm, to be with Trevor, wonders Yoda.

Or not to be with Trevor? adds Wilf.

'That is the question,' answer the three in unison. They laugh heartily. Then a follow-up question narrows Wilf's holographic eyes: *What does your gut tell you?* he asks.

Listen to it, you should, nods Yoda sagely.

Trevor hears a knock as he's returning Mr Signal, Mr Radar and Mr Sparks, polished to a shine, back to their places in the display cabinet. He opens the caravan door to find Joe with Romeo's bundled clothes held up as a peace offering.

'Thought you might want these back,' grins Joe.

Trevor smiles warmly and ten minutes later they're sitting in silence, staring at each other across the table.

Joe appears to be trying to formulate an idea.

Mr Bucket-Head (a five inch tall robot; two of those inches an elongated metallic head) stands between them.

'Just make something up,' suggests Trevor at last. 'About anything. Anything at all. And kindly refrain from telling me: "Oh, my stories are rubbish" again or—'

'I didn't say *rubbish*, I said—'

'Whatever. *I* will decide if a tale is of merit or not.'

'Fine,' huffs Joe.

'Now proceed, sir,' compels Trevor in his best American Wild West accent. He leans back, arms folded.

Several beats pass with a cavalcade of facial movements: displays of brain-racking interlaced with hope, then despair, then hope, then despair again. There is a start, a false start, but after that, nothing; no words – none.

'Anything?' asks Trevor.

'Oh, this is hopeless!' groans Joe. 'I'm completely blank.'

A fist thumps the table making Mr Bucket-Head jump.

Trevor seizes the robot, lest the boy suddenly decide to manifest growing frustration into object throwing.

'Sorry,' fumes Joe.

'It's fine,' soothes Trevor.

Joe grips the table and growls – actually growls.

'Don't give up so soon,' urges Trevor.

'I'm not, but what can I do if nothing comes? Do you know what it's like, trying to think of something, and just having an empty head?'

'Even I, an experienced actor,' booms Trevor grandly, 'have been known to dry on stage and forget my words from time to time. Not often, you understand, but occasionally.'

'I haven't really got an empty head,' softens Joe. 'There are lots of things in there; I just can't seem to get all the different bits into any kind of sensible order. I get lost, and the harder I try, the more I lose my way.'

'Remember what I said,' encourages Trevor, 'you just need to relax—'

'I am relaxed!' barks Joe.

'Okay, good.'

'I can, I do, sort of think of something. But when I try to shape the idea into words – into a story – out loud – it kinda becomes muddy. Things get jumbled up, they're in the wrong place, or I forget bits, or I just tell it wrong. Oh, who am I kidding? I'll never win this competition.'

'Let's try something,' suggests Trevor placing Mr Bucket-Head before Joe. 'Alright now, remembering to remain calm, think about Mr Bucket-Head.'

'Mr Bucket-Head?'

'Yes. Focus on him – for inspiration – and simply allow words and thoughts to come to you.'

Trevor's hands mix the air, demonstrating how such thoughts and words might mysteriously arrive.

'That's his name? Mr Bucket-Head?'

'Don't worry about the name; that is incidental. Just zero in on him, concentrate – and stay relaxed.'

'He's a bit dusty.'

'Yes, he's the last to be polished. Use that if you like.'

Joe nods. He sits forward and stares at the robot.

'That's it,' encourages Trevor. 'Don't search for a fully formed story, don't push, just see what comes to you – a single word – *two* words – a sentence.'

Joe's eyes drill down, unblinking.

'Good, good, that's it. Build up a few words inside, a feeling, just a start – and a yarn will assuredly follow.'

Joe remains focused.

'A pocket-sized tale,' prompts Trevor. 'We're not looking for War and Peace here; only a beginning, middle and end.'

Joe breathes through his nose, slowly, in and out.

'Start with the introduction; still relaxed, still calm – let it come to you. Allow that beginning to take shape in your mind. Don't search for it. It will come if you let it. That's it. Good. Let it form. See the path opening up before you. It's a journey of which you need find only the first step; your genesis – the rest will naturally fall into place.'

After a moment of silence Joe's eyes widen.

'Yes, you have it. You have it, don't you?'

Joe nods.

'Excellent. Now, prepare to take that first step. The path will instinctively lead you to the middle, and then on to the end. Take us on the journey with you. Okay – and deliver your opening line.'

Joe's face contorts; he's lost whatever he had.

'It's fine, don't worry, take your time – don't push, it's still there; just let it keep coming— No, Joe, don't panic, relax, relax.'

Joe blows a raspberry.

Frustrated, he stares angrily outside.

Trevor sighs. 'You're acting like a baby.'

'I am a baby; a big baby.'

'No, you're not, so don't act like one. Listen to me, Joe, you just need to stay calm, that's all. You panicked because it seems like a big deal, but it isn't and you'll master it.'

'Yeah, Panickin' Skywalker, that's me.'

'Perhaps if we played some of your favourite music?' muses Trevor. 'Would that help?'

'Yes, or maybe a glass of sherry, dear boy,' booms Joe, a comic impression of Trevor. 'Hey, I know; I could nip back and nick some of Mum's weed. I know where she hides it.'

Trevor smiles wryly. 'Well, we certainly need something to help you chill out. That's the right expression, isn't it?'

Joe rolls his eyes.

'For once you master that, believe me, the rest is easy.'

'Easy?!' blurts Joe. 'If you think it's so easy, why don't you tell one? I've not heard anything from you. Oh, quotes, yes; from Shakespeare, bloody Shakespeare, but nothing of yours. Not a single story. Let's hear one from you.'

He looks around, grabs a milk carton from the counter and plonks it in front of Trevor.

'There, use that for inspiration.'

Joe sits back, defiant, arms locked around his chest.

'Go on, take that first step.'

He nods at the milk.

'In your own time, Trevor. No rush.'

This is a nice neighbourhood; semi-detached houses on a sunny day – the Fifties or Sixties judging by the various fashions and hairstyles populating the area.

'When I was a boy, a little younger than you are now,' narrates Trevor, 'I had a friend. His name was Robert. Robbie to his friends: myself and skinny Nigel.'

A boy, presumably Robert, aged twelve or thirteen, stands with his dad, outside their home, admiring a shiny green two-door saloon. The buckets, patch of wet avenue and the vehicle's gleaming paintwork, speak of a proud car wash, wax and polish.

'Mr Thompson, Robert's father, had just bought his first ever car: a brand new Morris Minor. He was so delighted with it – as was Robert – that rather than park it on his drive, he proudly parked it on the tree-lined road so all their neighbours could also enjoy its elegant magnificence. Fresh from the factory and in pristine condition it was a feast for the eyes – a thing of beauty. At least it was, until early the next morning.'

We cut to Robert wheeling his bike along the side of the house. 'Robbie,' Trevor continues, 'was always up early for his paper-round.; the newsagent demanded *all* paperboys report to his shop by six-forty-five at the very latest. He was just about to mount the bike when he heard a thud and the sound of breaking glass.'

Robert drops his bike and stares at the electric milk-float: the vehicle's *extremely* close to the Morris. As he hurries down the drive, the float reverses jerkily then races away – if fifteen miles an hour can be classed as racing.

'Hey!' shouts Robert.

The milkman looks back but far from stopping, the milk-float drives off.

Robert runs to the back of the car: the saloon is dented and scratched, a tail-light broken, its glass on the road.

Angry, Robert can do nothing but watch the float turn a corner and disappear.

'But early the next day, *we were ready*: Robbie, myself, and skinny Nigel, avenging amigos, seeking retribution for the Thompson family's seriously wounded Morris Minor.'

Robert meets a young Trevor and skinny Nigel, all three of a similar age, on the corner of Cherry Tree Avenue and Hawthorne Road. It's early; low light and a dawn chorus.

'Robbie had filled us in on what had happened. We were as enraged and unhappy as he was. With the car forced to spend time in the Morris garage, our promised trip to the Forest of Dean had to be cancelled. It felt like an attack on all of us. So, do you know what we did?'

The three boys confiscate empty milk bottles from a variety of doorsteps, creeping in and creeping out, intent on avoiding a telltale clink.

'Back then, milk was delivered in glass bottles to just about every house in the nation, and with every delivery the empties collected – except on this day. Because on this day, on this early

122

morning, we seized every empty milk bottle from every doorstep on Flighty Fred's round – well, almost every one.'

The boys are chased from a garden by a growling, but thankfully chained, Alsatian. No matter, though; from a long series of steps, porches and doorways, they *are* successful – bottles in ones, twos, threes – and on occasion, four – all liberated from front doors and disappeared.

'Why?' asks Joe's voice. 'What did you do with them all? Aren't you just making less work for him? What's the point of that?'

The boys have taken up a hiding place with a good vantage point, up on a hill behind the houses. And here comes the gentle click and whirr of electric motor as the float advances piecemeal up Bromley Close – stop and move, stop and move – until it reaches the very end of the long cul-de-sac, where Fred disembarks for the umpteenth but final call – just these last houses and he'd be done for the day. A day made far shorter than usual by the surprising but welcome lack of empties to collect.

'Ah well,' replies Trevor to Joe's question, 'here's the clever bit: we knew which was the very last house on Fred's milk-round.'

The milkman slowly opens the gate but takes not a step; he simply stands, unmoving, eyes agog.

'We put *every* empty bottle right there. And there must have been over a thousand of them.'

Hundreds and hundreds of empty one-pint bottles surround the doorstep of 47 Bromley Close. Fred swivels his head, scanning in all directions, but the boys, squirming with laughter, remain well-hidden. The acutely disgruntled milkman has no option other than to transport the empties – in his skinny wire-carrier, six empties at a time. And on just the second trip, so angry is Fred, and so distracted (who could have done such a thing?) that he accidentally drops one at the side of the float. And squatting to collect shards of broken glass from the road, he looks back in anger at the ocean of bottles still to be collected.

'I love it!' barks Joe voice.

'But never mind,' reflects the narrator. 'Only what, another nine hundred and eighty-eight left to collect?'

Trevor knocks back a sherry and plunks the empty glass on the table with a satisfied exhalation: 'Ahh.'

'But just a minute,' carps Joe.

'What?'

'That's real. It's not the same as *making up* a story.'

'Who says it's real?' counters Trevor wiping his beard. 'Believable perhaps, but maybe that's because I made it so.'

Joe's eyes narrow. 'You just made that up?' he queries. 'It wasn't real?'

'Parts may be real. Parts may be made up. Remember, you can mix truth with fiction. Some of the best stories are often based on partial truths. Maybe that's what I did.'

A dramatic pause then Trevor pours another sherry.

'Or did I?' he winks.

Joe nods. He understands – sort of.

Joe, panting heavily, climbs onto the wood pile at the side of the house. From here he makes his way to his bedroom via the garage roof – an alternate route to the sun-lounge extension in order to avoid any risk of a surprise appearance by mother sneaking out for an evening spliff.

'Having scaled the lethal cliff face,' puffs Joe, 'the Hero pressed on; a stealthy shadow weaving through the subterranean tunnels of Castle Dark.'

On unsteady feet, mini torch in hand, Joe approaches his open bedroom window.

'The secret entrance lay just ahead but first he'd have to blow the reinforced steel door. That's what the C4 was for.'

Joe's homework: not to simply *narrate* his activities, but to use Life, his exertions and experiences, his trials and tribulations, as inspiration for flash fiction.

'Whenever you can,' Trevor had advised. 'It'll be good preparation. Just work with whatever comes to you as you go about your routines and adventures. Do it on the fly, Joe; go with the flow.' And with that Trevor had closed his caravan door with a dramatic flourish.

So here's Joe teetering across the garage roof tiles about as sure-footed as a baby elephant in hobnail boots, but in his mind, a trained assassin, an expert at infiltration, sabotage and guerrilla warfare – and now he's planting high-explosives.

Crouched and head covered, he imagines a loud, controlled detonation. 'Boom!' narrates Joe. 'Then, swiftly pushing on through the strong smell of cordite, and smoke that would have choked a lesser man, the master ninja slips through the opening, catlike and unseen—'

At this point, Joe slips and falls head first into the dark room with a mighty crash.

Below, on the sofa in the living-room, Joe's parents look up from their Friday night film.

Then they look to each other, no words needed.

CHAPTER 10
A Midsummer Night's Dream

Paul's car, a forest-green Nissan 4x4, drives along the main road, in the shadow of the tip of Finger Hill, with Joe's face pressed to the passenger window.

'Dad!' squawks Joe. He grabs the back of the driver's seat. 'The scarecrow just shouted for help! He said the farmer caught him trespassing and as a punishment tied him to a pole and stuffed his clothes with straw to make it look like—'

'I said knock it off, Joe,' bleats Paul. 'You've been talking nonsense all morning. You can't even see him from here.'

'Why are we going this way?' asks Joe as Paul misses the turning for town. 'This isn't the way to school.'

Moments later the car passes Gas & Graze and pulls into Tall Trees Trailer Park.

'Why are we stopping here?' grills Joe anxiously. 'You don't usually stop here.'

'We're picking up Mrs Beal.'

Joe's face registers a lack of enthusiasm for this change of plan. Of all the places to throw an unscheduled detour! The car stops outside the caravan before Trevor's and Paul blasts the horn. As if on cue, Trevor lurches from his door, coordinates a theatrical bow – perhaps to Joe – and staggers over to the trailer's gas canisters, intent it seems on swapping old for new.

'He's been at the sherry early,' mutters Joe.

'Come again?' asks Paul sharply.

'I said: Mrs Beal invented the Curly Wurly?'

'What are you talking about?'

'Not only that: she was one of the earliest torch bearers for the Olympics. The first ever, in fact; at the Amsterdam games in 1928. She won silver in the women's high diving.'

'Joe, give it a rest!' barks Paul. 'Jesus, what is she doing in there? Come on, come on,' he blares, giving it more horn.

Joe relocates from the back to the front passenger seat.

'What are you doing?' asks Paul impatiently.

'Getting in the front with you,' replies Joe. 'Mrs Beal can go in the back.'

Finally opening her door, ice-cream haired Mrs Beal, eighties, possibly nineties, waves a slow hand. Everything about Mrs Beal is slow: coming down steps, walking toward the car, stopping to unwrap what Joe assumes must be a Werther's Original.

Paul checks his hair in the rear-view mirror then sets to drumming fingers on the steering wheel.

'Today would be good,' he mutters.

Eventually, Mrs Beal arrives – at the *driver* door. She pulls on the handle.

'No, no, in the back, Mrs B. *I'm* driving.'

Mrs Beal moves around the front of the car.

'Now where's she going?'

After completing her detour, the old lady arrives at the front passenger door and tries the handle.

'What's she doing?' Joe frowns.

'Jump out,' sighs Paul.

'What?'

'Just jump out. It'll be easier.'

'No, Dad.'

'Yes, Joe,' insists Paul. 'Now, please, or we'll be here all day.'

Under protest and muttering Joe clambers out and relocates into the back. 'Right jump in, Mrs Beal,' advises Paul loudly. 'Or climb in the back with Joe if you'd prefer.'

'No, Dad! If she does I'm getting back in the front.'

'I just want to go, Joe,' barks Paul. 'Christ, why did I agree to this?'

'Why did you?'

'Because I promised your mum.'

After much sighing and shaking of heads within the vehicle, Mrs Beal finally sticks her swirly mop of hair inside and snuffles: 'Good morning.'

'Morning, Mrs Beal,' acknowledges Paul. 'Say good morning, Joe; where's your manners?'

'Morning,' huffs Joe.

'Climb in, Mrs B,' urges Paul. 'We don't want you to be late for your appointment with the doctor.'

A considerable backside reverses in, followed by a single wrinkly stocking leg into the footwell, but then Mrs Beal has a sudden concern.

'Wait, did I lock my door?' she asks no-one in particular.

'Yes, I saw you lock it,' Paul advises.

'Hmm . . . best check,' grunts Mrs Beal setting off.

'With luck I'll miss Physics,' brightens Joe.

'You're not going to be late!' brays Paul.

'You sure about that?' laughs Joe.

They watch as Mrs Beal shambles beyond the car, back towards her caravan.

'Let's just hope she can remember why she's seeing the doctor when she gets there,' gripes Paul.

Joe laughs and moves closer to the back of Paul's seat.

'That might just be one of the funniest things you've ever said,' he tells his dad, who's instinctively leaned forward to protect his hair.

'I have my moments.'

Paul checks his watch.

'She'll probably get there and go back inside,' offers Joe. 'Forget we're even here.'

'Well, if she does, we're leaving,' fumes Paul without a trace of humour. 'And I'm not joking.'

'Oh this is taking forever,' complains Mrs Beal. 'Can't you go any faster? I could walk quicker.'

'Yeah, right,' snickers Joe quietly.

Mrs Beal angles herself to face the backseat.

'Haven't you got a bike?' she asks.

'He has, but he's never really got the hang of riding.'

Paul puts eyes on Joe via the rear-view mirror.

'Isn't that right, Joe?'

This touches a nerve and Joe's narrowed eyes glare back. This as the car drives past a lay-by occupied by a high-visibility police patrol car and a burger van: a pair of uniformed officers at the open hatch.

'There you go, officers – a hotdog for each of you.'

Liam hands the dog with onions to the female, the one without to the male.

'Ketchup and mustard's right there. Help yourselves.'

Police Constable Billy Mills, twenty-five, takes a small bite as Sergeant Nerys Hughes, thirty-six and heavily pregnant, squirts a thick line of yellow and then a thick line of red on hers.

'How's business?' asks PC Mills.

'Think I've picked the quietest lay-by in Powys.'

And for good reason, quips Joel's head.

'They're all pretty quiet,' advises Billy. 'Not like where you're from I'll bet. What is that, a Manchester accent?'

'Er, Crewe.'

'Oh, not far off,' grins Billy.

'It does sound like Manchester, though,' adds Nerys around a mouthful of sausage.

'Yeah, I get that a lot.' Damn, why hadn't he used the Scouse accent? Or Scottish – or anything other than Manc!

Liam smiles and changes the subject: 'You keeping busy?'

'What round here?' sniffs Billy Mills.

'We're only on patrol to get us out of the station for an hour,' confides Nerys. 'Isn't that right, Constable?'

'Nothing ever happens round here,' complains the PC forlornly. 'Haven't got to use my Taser once.'

'Really; then it's true – about Wales having the lowest crime rate in the UK?'

'Yep,' sighs Billy Mills. 'Afraid so.'

'Actually, I'll take a second dog,' directs Nerys shoving the last of the first into already bulging cheeks. 'Extra onions this time.'

Owen, Gary, Melvin and several others watch Joe exit the Nissan 4x4 outside the school gates.

'I won't be late.' Paul dips his head close to Mrs Beal's sunken boobs. 'But if I am, don't wander off this time.'

'What's up with your mum, Joe?' quips Owen.

'Oh yeah?' counters Joe already preparing his best witty retort – his sarcastic peers will be laughing on the other side of their faces in a second. But nothing comes – absolutely zilch. And then the moment has already passed; he's taken too long – he tried, clearly, but came up empty.

Joe blows a loud raspberry then marches off, towards school, away from the sarcastic applause and inflated, derisive guffaws.

'Wait for me!' reminds Paul loudly.

'No, I'm walking!' bellows Joe.

'I said wait and I mean wait!'

When Joe exits school, through the same gates he'd entered over seven tedious hours earlier, Paul, of course, isn't there. But someone is. Trevor.

'Come, Joe, we shall go to town.'

'I'm supposed to wait for my dad.'

'Whereupon I shall purchase for you,' continues Trevor regardless, 'the finest ice cream sundae money can buy.'

'It's a deal,' agrees Joe.

'Splendid. See, I knew you'd say that.'

'You did not,' scoffs Joe.

'*Exactly* that.'

'Yeah, right.'

With great showmanship, Trevor whips a crumpled piece of paper from a pocket, unfolds it and shows it to Joe.

IT'S A DEAL states the note.

128

'Hmm,' Joe frowns, sceptical. 'You've probably got a different one in each pocket.'

Trevor holds opens his coat. 'Search me, officer, if you don't believe me,' he retorts theatrically.

And this is when Alison, holding hands with Becki and Chloe, exits through the school gates.

'No, it's all good,' declines Joe. 'I believe you.'

'Everything alright, Joe?' asks Alison.

'Fine, Mrs Thomas.'

'You're sure?'

'Yep.'

'Well, okay,' concedes a doubtful Alison – and blazing a mistrustful look at Trevor she ushers her daughters away.

And so, with the Thomas' exiting stage right, Alison casting a series of wary glances over a shoulder, the old man and his young companion finally move off, in the opposite direction, toward Llanidloes town centre.

'Hey, Joe, what's up with your dad?' bellows a voice.

'You've already done that joke, Owen!' Joe calls back.

'He looks like a tramp!'

'Whatever!'

'Loser!'

This gains the middle finger – from Trevor.

'Was that street enough?' asks Trevor. 'Did I perform the gesture in the correct manner?'

'Spot on,' confirms Joe.

In The Cliché Café, between scoops of Life-is-too-short knickerbocker glory, Joe updates Trevor on his flash fiction pieces: ninjas, scarecrows, and Mrs Beal at the Olympics.

'Sounds like you've been having fun,' smiles Trevor.

'Yeah, once you get the hang of it, it's just like rapping.'

'Oh, so you rap as well?'

'Not very well but I've been practising.'

'Excellent. Can you freestyle?'

'Er, it's coming along.'

'Because that could be most helpful; freestyling is a highly creative skill – improvised and spontaneous, much like your Storytell competitions. Have you ever had a rap battle, Joe? Because if you can do that—'

'This is such a surprise,' Joe interrupts. 'I had no idea you were a fan of rap.'

'Well, not all of it but I do rather enjoy a blast of Eminem from time to time.'

'Seriously?'

'Have you listened to his lyrics; I mean *really* listened?'

'Well, duh.'

'There's something almost Shakespearian about them, don't you think?'

Joe's brow furrows. 'Can't say I've ever—'

To underline the claim, Trevor delivers his opening line in the dramatic style of a Macbeth or Richard III:

'Look, if Joe had one shot,' he paraphrases theatrically, 'or one opportunity, to seize everything he ever wanted in one moment, would he capture, or just let it slip?'

'Yo, that's awesome,' laughs Joe. 'You *do* know Eminem.' In an attempt to be super cool he snaps his fingers, hurting them in the process.

'I met him once.'

'Really?'

'At a fete.'

'Wow!'

'Pretty sure it was him.'

'Oh, okay.'

'What was that line?' wonders Trevor. 'Ah, yes.' And he continues in the same overly-thespian style as before. The old actor speaks of Joe's palms being sweaty, knees weak and arms heavy; how there's vomit on his sweater already, his mom's spaghetti.

Joe takes up the proverbial baton: 'I'm nervous,' he raps, 'but on the surface I look calm and ready.'

Trevor pulls a face at that but Joe doesn't stop:

'To drop bombs!' he booms.

'But Joe keeps on forgetting the story he was about to lay down,' adds Trevor, old hands jabbing beats to the flow.

'The whole crowd goes so loud. I open my mouth but the words won't come out.'

'Joe's choking but how? Everybody's joking now. The clock runs out, time's up, over, blaow!'

'I snap back to reality, oh there goes gravity.'

Trevor mugs a sad face. 'So there goes Joe, he choked.'

'I'm so mad, but I won't give up that easy. No!'

'Good for you,' laughs Trevor.

'Yeah,' crows Joe, fired up. 'Success is my only option, failure's not. Cause this Storytell may be the only opportunity I got.'

'That's the spirit, Joe.'

Joe mimics firing off Uzis: 'Braap-braap! Braap-braap!'

Smiling, Trevor nods. 'Okay, you can stop now.'

'Too much?'

'A little bit.'

'Fair enough.' Joe blows on the Uzis and shoves them into invisible holsters.

'But why don't you make one up for me, right now,' prompts Trevor.

'A rap?'

'No, silly, a story.'

'Oh, okay,' agrees Joe. 'But first I want to tell you about my great-grandfather Jack.'

Trevor rolls his eyes and shakes his head.

'No listen, I'm not stalling, Jack was a lighthouse keeper – back when they were all manned, not automatic like they are now – and he told me a super-scary story.'

'Fine,' Trevor sighs. 'I really wanted to hear one of *your* stories, not Great-grandpa Jack's, but okay, carry on, perhaps it'll be interesting.'

'Oh it is, trust me.'

'Then pray continue,' smiles Trevor.

'Picture the scene,' directs Joe softly. 'An offshore lighthouse, far out to sea, late at night . . .'

'Amidst the dark, agitated ocean,' Joe's words have become a voice-over on a movie; a movie featuring an offshore lighthouse, far out to sea, late at night, 'storm-driven waves smash against the small island of jagged rocks, relentlessly forced to crash and churn, below the high tower. As the turning signal beams out its warning over a furious sea into the cold night sky beyond, froth and spray flash spumes high enough to catch and dance in the light.'

Trevor and Joe are seated at an old table in the keepers' rest room inside the lighthouse. Trevor is enthralled; he looks around. The drum-shaped room is packed with nautical items: nets, floats, ships-in-bottles, driftwood, knotted rope, lobster pots. And sitting at the other side of the table is Jack, a salty, whiskery old sea dog with a face forged and tanned by sea air, weather and rum.

'I like him already,' whispers Trevor.

'Shush,' nudges Joe. He turns to Jack. 'Tell him, Pops.'

'A long time ago,' begins Jack, a Cornishman judging by his accent, 'before the lighthouse was built, on a night such as this, when the wind was howling, and the sea was raging, a ship was blown off course into these very waters. Try as they might the brave crew couldn't control her. Within minutes they were thrown against the rock. Smashed to a thousand pieces they were.'

131

Trevor's eyes widen. The storm rages outside. The light bulb flickers. Rain lashes against the tiny, circular window.

'Many good men were lost that night,' continues Jack. 'Only one survived. And somehow, no-one knows how, not even he: the sailor managed to swim over to this very rock. Marooned though he was, all through the storm, despite losing a leg, and an eye, he clung to the rock for dear life. He was determined the sea wouldn't take him that night.'

The storm outside grows louder; thunderous. Trevor is captivated.

'But he survived. And it's said that for weeks afterwards there were many sightings of a dark figure sitting alone on the rock – the lonesome form of Jake Whistler, pleading to be rescued. But no-one ever dared approach. Scared they were, scared they might suffer the same misfortune and also become marooned.'

'What became of him?' asks Trevor.

'Suddenly, the sightings stopped and he was never seen again,' explains Jack. 'But legend has it that old Jake vowed to return and take revenge for being so cruelly abandoned and left to rot. Even today, during the worst storms, if you listen very carefully, you can still hear old Jake – whistling.'

The wind whistles around the tower.

'Goodness, how awful, the poor man,' consoles Trevor. He turns to Joe: 'How come you never told me you had a great-grandfather who was a lighthouse keeper, Joe?'

Joe pauses. 'I don't,' he smiles.

Trevor faces Jack, now lighting a pipe, and frowns.

'But—'

'I never did,' winks Joe. 'I just made him up.'

He stands, drops his spoon (as a swaggering rapper drops the mic) and it clatters into the empty sundae glass.

'Or did I?' grins Joe.

Then he departs the café with hardly a backward glance.

With a wry smile, Trevor applauds quietly.

'Bravo, Joe,' he acknowledges. 'Bravo. Very good.'

That night, as Trevor sits in his caravan, partaking of sherry and reading an old theatre programme (a play from the Fifties: *The Boy with the Bowed Legs*), Joe turns off his lamp and settles down with a smug smile on his face.

And soon he is dreaming yet another dream about winning the storytelling competition.

Actually, he's already won. Joe is onstage in the school hall, bowing, being applauded by the crowd. His fellow contestants are also clapping; even Owen, who's clapping and whistling the loudest of all.

'So much better than mine!' he calls.

Joe soaks up the adoration: a full-house standing ovation. He sees Gary and Melvin applauding wildly; Max punching the air repeatedly, blowing a kiss and mouthing, I love you; Sally and Paul hugging each other; Lucy filming the event for posterity on her mobile; and Wilf, he's there too, two thumbs in the air and Yoda on his shoulders.

Behind Joe, on the easel, are four word cards:

FAITH, PROPHECY, BATTLE, and WINNER.

Everything is so real and believable and authentic; apart from Mr Smallwood – his little bald noggin appears to have been replaced by a massive moose-head.

The next day Joe approaches the notice board outside the school library wearing a fierce, determined look and adds his name to the list of Storytell Competition entrants.

'You are joking, right?' asks Owen over Joe's shoulder.

'What's up, Owen?' counters Joe loftily. 'Scared?'

Owen laughs hysterically. As do Gary and Melvin. Are they never apart?

'You will be,' adds Joe.

Other kids arrive. 'Really, it's official?' asks one of them. 'You've actually put your name down?'

'Yeah, why wouldn't he?' snarls Katie. 'He knows more words than all of you lot put together.'

'Bollocks, he does,' challenges Gary.

'Oh yeah? Well, Joe's read the dictionary; all of it. Most of you haven't read anything – unless it's something with pictures in.'

'Whole dictionary, my arse,' sneers Owen.

'Go on, then, test him,' challenges Katie. 'I dare you.'

Joe tries to ease Katie off her soapbox but she's not for coming down.

'What's up, Owen? Frightened he'll humiliate you?'

'Who, Jabba?' scoffs Owen. 'Yeah, right.'

'Anyway,' Joe frowns, 'we haven't got a dictionary so—'

Katie produces a dictionary from her bag and raises it for everyone to see.

'It's lucky for you I was here,' she smiles.

'Yep,' nods Joe.

'Right, give it here,' snaps Owen. 'We'll soon settle this.'

The book is snatched, a page turned to at random; a finger hovers over the words then stabs into the lexicon.

'Gregarious,' he sneers.

Joe looks to Katie. All this is her fault. How many is he expected to know? How many successful answers will Owen deem necessary to concede defeat and piss off. He can't possibly remember the definitions of all the words in the dictionary. He's bound to have forgotten some; *some?* – Loads! But luckily for Joe, Gregarious is one he does know.

'Gregarious; adjective; of a person: to enjoy the company of others, sociable. Of an animal: to herd together, seeking safety in numbers. Of plants: to grow—'

'Here, I'll find one.'

Gary commandeers the dictionary from Owen.

Katie laughs. 'This should be fun,' she tells Joe.

Gary flicks a few pages then tracks a finger down the words.

'Hyper-bowl,' he grins.

'What?' Joe asks, puzzled.

'Hyper-bowl,' beams Gary smugly. 'What's up, Jabba, don't you know it?'

Titters in amongst the circle of kids, now swollen to around a dozen; wide-eyed spectators glued to the show.

'Do you mean hyperbole?' asks Joe straight-faced.

Gary checks the page.

'It says hyper-*bowl*,' he asserts.

'Yes, it may look like hyper-bowl but it's actually pronounced hyperbole,' explains Joe. 'High-per-ber-lee.'

'Who gives a fuck,' snarls Gary. 'What does it mean?'

'Hyperbole; noun: exaggerated statements or claims not meant to be taken seriously.'

'Pah, that was too easy,' scoffs Katie. 'Even I knew that. Give him a hard one.'

'Alright, Katie,' appeals Joe.

'What? I'm just trying to help.'

Owen snatches the dictionary from Gary and shoves it into Katie's hands.

'Okay, so he knows a few words,' Owen gripes. 'Swallowed the dictionary when he was still in nappies; so what? Storytell isn't about knowing a few useless words.'

'Yeah, remember what happened last year,' sneers Gary.

Joe is onstage in the school hall. The word cards on the easel are TREACLE, LOST, ARCHITECT, and INERTIA. The timer is at zero. Joe is frozen, lost, choked; and the silence that greets his non-performance is deafening.

Stage right, Owen is hardly able to contain his amusement: a huge belly laugh that builds and builds and threatens to erupt. But laughing before the *You've Failed, Get Off!* klaxon sounds can be grounds for dismissal (Unsporting Conduct) so he must hold it in – for the moment.

Out in the audience, Sally and Lucy look on with pained expressions, unable to help. They are surrounded by a sea of twitchy faces, lip-biting and sympathetic glances. Nearby, Katie watches through laced fingers. Elsewhere, other kids and fellow parents film proceedings on their mobiles. Are they recording a Tragedy or a Comedy? Well, that would depend on one's point of view.

After an extremely long painful beat, ended by the klaxon of doom, Joe concedes defeat and shuffles off, head down and humiliated, back to his seat under a smattering of polite applause. Owen, eyes watering, can finally explode into laughter – and does so. For this, Owen receives a reprimand from the MC, Mr Schneider.

(As Owen's outburst is *after* the klaxon, not *before*, he is not dismissed; a *yellow* card rather than a *red*.)

'Can't believe you choked again,' snorts Owen as Joe retakes his seat.

Bereft of a witty retort, Joe ignores the gibe, choosing instead, to contemptuously rock on his chair, head down, eyes locked to his feet.

'What a loser,' mutters Owen.

Then he rises to take his turn onstage.

'What have I done?' bleats Joe. 'I've put myself up again. What was I thinking?'

'But you had to put your name down,' soothes Trevor. 'Didn't you say if you missed the entry deadline it was, and I believe I'm quoting you correctly, Game over?'

'Yep, and I did well in the café, you have to give me that.'

'All the same, you are not ready.'

'No, no, but we still have weeks.'

'Weeks,' scoffs Trevor.

'I *really* want to win this year. It's enough time, isn't it?'

'Learning how to perform under pressure can take—'

Trevor winces from a sharp pain and shifts on the seat.

'You okay?'

Trevor bats away Joe's concern.

'You *are* making progress, I suppose.'

'Okay, good.'

'You have proved your skills in the intimate arena of my little theatre, no doubt; and your one-to-one in the coffee bar was indeed impressive – but are you ready for a full-house audience?'

'What do you mean? Of course, I am.'

'Could it be that you *do* suffer from stage-fright?'

'No, I told you. I love being the centre of attention.'

'You know, just a sprinkle of humility wouldn't necessarily be such a bad thing.'

'It's after they turn hostile,' Joe reminds him sharply. 'That's when I forget my shit.'

'No, you forget your shit *before* they turn. It's the very forgetting of your shit that turns them.'

'Okay; I can see that – so?'

'So, what does that leave us?' wonders Trevor. 'The fear of failure . . .'

'Yes, I have to remember to relax.'

'Or, as far as the Storytell is concerned, perhaps it's the cards themselves.'

'Yes, exactly!' sings Joe. 'We have to work on the cards.'

'Very well, then.' Trevor stands, gingerly, steps slowly to the door, and lets in the evening. 'Come back tomorrow and we shall.'

'I can't believe we haven't done the cards yet,' mumbles Joe on the move.

He stops on the porch. 'Why *haven't* we done the cards yet?'

'Because you weren't ready, but perhaps now, you are.' Trevor flinches and drops a hand to his side. 'Now if you'll excuse me I need my rest.'

'So, tomorrow?'

'Goodnight, Joe.'

'Night, Trevor.'

Joe calls through the closed door:

'Let me know if you need anything.'

CHAPTER 11

Mr Cromarty & Mr Mumbles

Don clinks packs of Old Peculier and Old Speckled Hen onto the counter of Gas & Graze then pays for seven litres of diesel and the beers.

'Hey, is it true that somebody was seen on the back of one of your cows, Don?' Clara dings open the till.

'Dunno what you're talking about,' mutters Don.

'No, no, it was a sheep, I heard.' – This from Bonnie tidying the magazine rack.

'You shouldn't listen to gossip,' advises Don firmly.

'No smoke without fire, Don,' contends Clara.

Don pings the door. 'And if you two can't tell fact from fiction, it might be best to avoid gossip and rumours.'

He exits, climbs into the Land Rover, and after four noisy attempts to close the door and two to start the engine, he splutters away.

'Yeah, it's true,' asserts Bonnie.

'Definitely true,' confirms Clara.

'And you've definitely checked the shower?' asks Billy Mills.

The octogenarian at the police station counter, hardly able to look the constable in the face thanks to a frozen neck, manages a painful nod.

'Alright then, Mrs Howe,' smiles the constable, 'we'll keep our eyes open and let you know if anything turns up.'

'His name is—'

'Answers to the name of Mr Cromarty; yes, I've made a note of that. I remember him from last time.'

'Do I get a Crime Report Number?'

'Well, we don't know a crime's actually been committed yet, Mrs Howe. Leave it with us and we'll get back to you.'

'Mr Cromarty,' repeats Mrs Howe. 'Kidnapped.'

'Yep, it's all down on this piece of paper.'

'Probably kids,' grouches Mrs Howe. 'Come on, Pugsley.'

'We'll ask around,' smiles Billy.

Mrs Howe nods, pauses a moment, then drags her overweight pug outside; lifts him onto her mobility scooter then tootles off, brolly up, into the rainy morning.

With a hefty sigh Billy crosses to one of the two desks at the back of the room. A smaller police station you will not find.

Picture a tiny two-roomed bungalow with just enough space out front for the station's single squad car.

'Garden gnome missing again?'

Sergeant Nerys is sitting, feet up, puzzle book in hand.

'How did you guess?'

'Did she check her bath? That's where he was last time.'

'Daft old bat. Who gives a garden gnome a bath?'

'He's not *any* garden gnome, Billy. He's Mr Cromarty.'

Billy flops heavily onto the spare chair.

'Nothing ever happens round here, Nerys.'

'Sergeant Nerys,' reminds Nerys playfully. 'And *nothing ever happens*? Er, – she points at the in-tray – 'two reports just this month – even without the gnome.'

Billy makes a face. 'Just for once, I'd like something serious.'

'What's up, a lost dog and knickers missing from a washing line not enough for you?'

'No, it's not,' huffs Billy.

'Honestly,' chides Nerys, 'wishing a crime wave on us just because you're bored. Now file that bad boy and start thinking about what we can have for lunch.'

Billy dumps the report into the in-tray.

'Not much chance of *her* dog getting lost, is there?'

'Pugsley?' Nerys thinks a moment. 'He could roll down a hill – end up in a ditch.'

Billy frowns. 'How would he get up there?'

Nerys shrugs. 'She could carry him.'

'What, on her mobility scooter?'

The two sit silently for a long beat.

'Go on, give us a clue,' prompts Billy at last.

'It's Sudoku, Billy – not a crossword.'

Billy scans the little office. Nothing he hasn't seen a thousand times before. He picks up the County Times, a local newspaper for local people, and flicks to page five.

'I see the Honcho has struck again.'

At one time, the Head Honcho's impressive death rate was front page news; now, with the murders slowed to a trickle, the headlines are reserved for more on-trend reports, even if this latest victim did boost the count to 99. Maybe the killer would be banner-heading-worthy again once he hit the 100 mark.

Today's front page news:

COLOUR PHOTOCOPIER FOR LIBRARY?

(Previous weeks' copies of Powys County's most popular newspaper featured such unforgettable headlines as: Out-of-date pasty sold to young mum; Scarf found in bookshop; Man gets finger stuck in plant pot; and Mysterious dent in Short Bridge Street's new litter bin.)

'Yeah, I heard that on the radio.' Nerys scratches the back of her head with the pen. 'Ninety-nine; can you believe it? Bloody Honcho; he better not show up on our patch. Where was it again?'

'Brecon Beacons National Park,' reads Billy, 'in a tree.'

'*In* a tree?'

'A *fallen* tree, an old rotted one, inside its hollow log; the torso lying at one end, head poking out the other − as if he had a really long neck.'

Nerys shakes her head. 'What a sicko.'

'Like a cartoon.'

'Yeah, yeah, I get the picture. What did the sign say? No, on second thoughts, don't tell me. I don't want to know. Those things freak me out.'

Billy walks over to the wall map and studies it.

'Travelling salesman wasn't he?' asks Nerys. 'Terrible.'

'Hmm,' Billy muses. 'That is one big park.'

'Nothing gets past you, does it, Constable?'

Billy ignores the gibe. 'But only forty-odd miles from here. He's getting closer.'

'Maybe he's on holiday,' sniffs Nerys. 'I imagine even serial killers need a break.'

Billy's eyes suddenly sparkle with excitement.

'God, wouldn't it be amazing if he was round here somewhere − and we were the ones who caught him.'

'Yeah, dream on, Constable Mills. Now get the kettle filled. It's time for elevenses.'

It's certainly a lot cooler, concedes Joel's satiny skull.

'Yeah, well, it had to be done,' advises Liam. 'People were starting to think our meat was off.'

Bit draughty, though.

'Better than stinky,' mutters Liam.

What?

'Nothing, shush; someone's coming.'

'Is this your dog?' calls an approaching girl, a grubby, skinny terrier in her arms.

With no other vehicles currently in the lay-by, Liam reckons she must have arrived here on foot, probably from one of the houses beyond the field.

'I just found him in a ditch up there, near that tree. He looks half-starved, poor thing.'

139

Sounds like a kid, notes Joel's skull. *She on her own?* he asks, his interest stirred.

Liam leans over the burger van's counter as if to gain a better look at the dog but really to scrutinise, potentially, the Honcho's one-hundredth victim at closer quarters.

Wiry, thin but strong (but nowhere near strong enough), possibly a fast runner (although definitely not fast enough), a screamer most likely (female victims usually attempt to shriek for help; fat lot of good that'll do this one, though, unless her black-hearted killer's timing is completely thrown by a random passing vehicle).

The dog growls; a weak, low growl, but instinctive and plucky – if any living creature can sense a savage twisted-fuck when they meet one, an animal can.

'Do you think he's lost?' The girl strokes the dog's matted hair. 'He hasn't got a collar.'

Liam shrugs. 'Aren't you a bit young to be out on your own, wandering along a dual carriageway?'

'No,' retorts the girl frowning and curling her lip.

'Fair enough,' laughs Liam. 'Feisty; I like it.' He raps a spatula (burger-flipper) rhythmically against the metal counter, all friendly like. 'So, you just out for a walk, or do you make a thing of searching for stray animals?'

'I was picking flowers.' The girl nods at a bunch of pink and white wildflowers gripped in a hand under the dog's backside.

'Very pretty,' smiles Liam. 'Bet they smell nice.'

'They're for my nan, she's not well.'

'Oh, I'm sorry to hear that.'

Liam! bleats Joel's voice. *Ask her how old she is.*

'So, how old is your nan?'

'Eighty-two.'

Not her fucking nan, you idiot!

Liam knees Joel's skull.

'Do not call me an idiot,' he growls under his breath.

'What?' asks the girl after a noisy motorbike has passed.

'I said: won't she be worried about you, out on your own? I mean, what are you: thirteen, fourteen?'

'Fifteen,' retorts the girl. 'Very nearly.'

Yep, she'll do, decrees Joel.

'Oops, one sec,' requests Liam after letting the spatula fall accidentally-on-purpose; and he crouches to face Joel's skull, on the shelf below the counter.

Country girls, mocks Joel's fleshless head. *They don't know what real danger is*, he laughs. *Grab her quick.*

'So this one?' rasps Liam. 'And then you'll definitely shut the fuck up about the whole killing a kid thing?'

Joel's skull would surely grin if it could. *That's the deal*, agrees the voice in Liam's head.

Liam purses his lips and nods.

'Who are you talking to?' grills the girl.

Liam resurfaces, friendly-faced, the mask of affability.

'My brother.'

The girl pulls a face. 'I can't hear him.'

'That's because Joel's a midget. You ever see a midget?'

Don't tell her I'm a midget! I'm as tall as you!

'Used to be,' mocks Liam in a low voice.

Apart from those times you teetered around in Auntie Ruby's high heels—

'Don't listen to him,' Liam tells the girl. 'It's not true.'

The girl pulls a face. 'There's no-one under there.'

'You sure about that?'

'Okay,' she challenges, 'what did he say?'

Liam pauses, as if considering sharing a confidence; and to let a noisy timber truck pass by – which will take a while because the ridiculously long vehicle's hauling two separate clawed-flatbeds, both piled high with stripped logs.

'He wants to know your name?' asks Liam quietly once the lorry has moved farther down the road.

'Kelly.'

'Hi, Kelly; pleased to meet you. I'm Craig.'

He leans nearer and waves Kelly in; because what he's about to tell her is just between them.

Had you been in that heavily-laden logging truck, you would have needed to be paying a whole lot of attention to your wing-mirror at just the right second to spot the girl in the distant lay-by being uprooted by her hair and dragged over the counter before the burger van's serving hatch shutter slammed down with an unheard thump and there was nothing left behind but dog hairs and a handful of wildflowers.

Trevor appears with an ornate wooden box. He sits at the table, places the box on the seat beside him and flips the carved lid.

'The words?' asks Joe from the other side of the table.

Trevor nods and transfers several stacks to the table. The decorative cards, slightly larger than standard-sized playing cards, are followed by a small egg-timer and a stubby easel, large enough to display up to five words.

'Can I have a look?' asks Joe.

141

'By all means, familiarise yourself.'

Trevor pushes a couple of decks across the table.

Joe studies the runic pattern on the back of the musty, Victorian-era cards a moment then turns one at random: FROG.

Another card is turned: PROTEST. Then TREE, JUMBLED, ANVIL, WILD and PREPARE. A quick scan through more cards reveals a host of nouns and a sprinkling of verbs and adjectives: MELTED. PAIN. OLD-FASHIONED. GATE. PLACID. MOON. PREDICT. FIRE. ALIGN.

'These are just like the ones at school,' beams Joe. 'Bit smaller but that's okay. They're nice. I like them.'

'Glad you approve, dear boy. Now, make sure they're all face down and mix them up – it's time to choose.'

Joe spreads the decks across the table, swirls them around, muddling and jumbling and rearranging the cards.

'Okay, good,' smiles Trevor. 'Happy?'

Joe nods then quickly selects two cards.

'Whoa, whoa, not so fast there.'

Joe is confused and it shows.

'You need to slow down, take your time. It's all part of preparing to take that wonderful journey – one's first step.'

Joe rolls his eyes.

'Joe,' chides Trevor.

'Sorry.'

'Let your mind become clear. Try to sense the cards that call out to you. Those are the ones you should choose.'

'Like feeling the Force?'

'If you like.'

'Okay,' blinks Joe.

He sits forward and stares at the cards, pressing on his temples and breathing slow as he concentrates.

With Joe mentally focusing, Trevor sets up the easel: the legs are a bit tricky, not quite doing what they're meant to, but after a few noisy attempts it appears to be stable.

'Trevor,' chides Joe.

'Sorry, it's done now.'

Joe returns to using the Force to choose his cards – or rather, allowing the cards to choose him.

As he waits, Trevor notices that it's growing dark outside and snaps the curtains shut.

'Trevor!' barks Joe.

Trevor holds up his hands. 'Okay, okay, I'm done.'

After a shake of the head, Joe extends his hands over the cards and keeps them there, hovering.

'Good,' encourages Trevor softly. 'Take your time.'

Joe picks one and then two – those he feels drawn to – and three and four. Keeping them face-down, he passes the cards to Trevor who places them on the easel, their fancy black-and-gold backs on show.

'Did you have a good feeling about these?'

'I think so.'

'Alright – are you ready?'

'Yep,' nods Joe.

Trevor turns the cards, one after the other, unhurriedly resetting them on the easel, word-out.

The words are: TROUBLE. SNAILS. ZANY. CARPENTER.

'What do you think?' he asks at last, taking possession of the egg-timer.

'They're crap,' whines Joe. How's anyone supposed to create a story from that terrible selection?'

'Would you prefer Bloomsbury rules: pick five, reject one?'

(This, as opposed to Kensington rules where one of four initial cards is irreversibly rejected in favour of a then fifth drawn card. Or Lexington rules where four cards are drawn and *no* substitutions are allowed. There are several official variations. Check out the many box sets available. Make a great Christmas present if you're stuck for ideas.)

'Fine,' huffs Joe. He draws a further card and turns it over.

SALT.

'That's worse than the others,' he gripes.

'So, keep these four?' checks Trevor.

Joe shrugs and pouts but in the end nods begrudgingly.

'Okay and what if we forget about the timer for now? Worry about that later.' Trevor places the egg-timer back in the box and flips the lid. 'Take as long as you need.'

'There's a time limit in the competition,' grumbles Joe. 'Thirty measly seconds!'

'Trust me, thirty seconds will be more than adequate once you've honed your skills,' counsels Trevor. 'We'll get to that later; when you are more proficient.'

'Later?' snaps Joe. 'The first round is this week. – This week! If I don't make it through that—'

'Fine, would you prefer the timer?'

'No,' growls Joe. 'Now please, just let me think.'

Whiny, Petulant, Short-tempered and Callow come to Trevor's mind but no matter, he hushes as Joe focuses on his actual words.

TROUBLE. SNAILS. ZANY. CARPENTER.

Trevor remains silent and studies his student. He nods slowly, willing Joe on before switching his gaze to the easel.

Unblinking, Joe continues to eyeball the cards. He glares at each word, mouthing them silently in turn: Trouble; Snails; Zany; Carpenter; Trouble; Snails; Zany; Carpenter; Trouble; Snails; Zany; Carpenter . . .

Trevor flicks his gaze back to Joe.

'Still nothing?' he asks quietly at last.

Joe fails to reply.

'Take heart,' encourages Trevor kindly. 'I'm sure you can make a story from these if you just—'

'Argh!' growls Joe.

'Are you getting *anything* at all?' asks Trevor softly.

'No, I'm not, Trevor!' barks Joe. 'Not a damned thing.'

'Never mind,' soothes Trevor. 'Let's call that a warm up.' He returns the four cards to the table and mixes them in with the rest. 'Go on, have another go,' he adds at last.

Though fuming and reluctant, his heart not in it, Joe refocuses on the wide puddle of face-down cards.

'Relax,' implores Trevor. 'It just takes a little practice.'

Joe quickly picks four, hands them over and sits back.

'These four?' checks Trevor. 'Are you sure these are—?'

Joe folds his arms. 'Yes,' he hisses impatiently.

Trevor places the cards on the easel, an elegant parade of fancy backs. 'You ready?' he asks.

Joe hits the table. 'Yes, Trevor, jeez,' he rasps. 'Let's see.'

Trevor turns the cards and again resets them on the easel, word-out. The words are:

DUMMY. BUTTON. TASK. POSSESSION.

Trevor spies Joe's reddening face.

'Would you like to change one?'

'Yes. No. Wait. No.'

The sound of Joe's breathing intensifies.

'Okay, just stay calm,' advises Trevor. 'Don't say anything for a moment, and eventually, when you're ready, try and make a start.'

Time passes with much blinking and staring.

'Not too late to pick a fifth if you—'

'Wait, wait,' brightens Joe, 'I've got something.'

'Excellent,' smiles Trevor.

'Right . . . so . . . Picture a busy car boot sale, and a man wandering near a table strewn with costume jewellery, knick-knacks, owl ornaments – and a ventriloquist dummy.'

'I say, you there!' calls the dummy to the passing man.

The young man stops, looks around incredulous and then points, questioningly, at himself. *Me?*

'Yes, you; I am in need of assistance!'

The dummy is dressed in a dark suit with tie, waistcoat and green carnation, under a chic hat. A dandy gentleman of bygone times; the man is reminded somewhat of Oscar Wilde, one of his favourite writers.

'Wait, a ventriloquist dummy that talks on its own?' asks the man stepping nearer. 'I've never seen that before. What does he have, a pull-string in the back?'

'Oh, he doesn't talk,' replies the old codger behind the table, one half of an elderly couple whose stall this is.

'Are you sure?' asks the man, confused.

'Well, not unless *you* do the talking,' sniffs the old biddy.

The man looks the dummy over. 'Why are you selling him?'

'Because he's creepy,' whispers the biddy.

'She doesn't like him,' explains the codger. 'But I still reckon he's worth twenty quid.'

'So, what are you doing with him in the first place?'

'Found it in the attic,' advises the codger. 'He must have been there for years – looks Victorian to me. I call him Mr Mumbles.'

'Yep, that's a . . . good ventriloquist dummy's name.'

The codger waves him in, as if to share a confidence.

'Sometimes I imagine I can hear him – muttering.'

'Nonsense,' barks the old biddy elbowing her husband. 'His hearing is worse than mine.'

'You're not thinking of buying that, are you?' asks a young woman appearing at the table.

'I'm thinking about it. How much did you say, a fiver?'

'Fifteen's the least I'll take.'

'How does a tenner sound?'

'It's a deal.'

The men shake hands and the women roll their eyes.

'What the hell did you get that creepy thing for?' asks the woman in the car on the way home.

'I dunno, it spoke to me.'

'What?'

'In a manner of speaking. Look good in my man-cave.'

'Pfft, you and your man-cave.'

'Hey, what are you doing with that?' barks the man later, in his man-cave, snatching back his phone.

'Nothing.'

'You were scrolling,' fumes the man.

'I assure you, sir, that I am completely unfamiliar with such devices. I am, after all, a mere mannequin.'

'A mere pickpocket more like,' mutters the man.

'I can resist everything except temptation,' the dummy grins. 'As I believe someone once said.'

The man studies Mr Mumbles at close quarters.

'Are you sure you don't have batteries or something?'

'Quite sure.'

'Voice activation?'

'Never heard of it.'

'Hmm.'

'So, who's Gwynth?' asks the dummy.

'Come again?'

'Gwynth.'

The man shrugs. 'Never heard of her.'

'And yet she appears to have sent you a plethora of extremely interesting messages – *and photos.*'

'Wait, you can talk, read, *and* hack Facebook messages?'

'I hardly think that's the issue at hand, Gordon . . . or should I call you Sweet Cheeks.'

Gordon chews his lip and grows red in the neck.

'I must say I'm a little surprised. You have a beautiful wife. I believe the term punching-above-your-weight applies in this case. And yet it's Debbie who you get to—'

'What do you want?'

'I have a task for you,' grins the dummy. 'Do it and I'll be free.'

'Free to do what?'

'That's no concern of yours. Do me this kindness and I will swear not only to never tell your wife, but also to leave.'

'Leave?' Gordon frowns. 'You can walk?'

'Not very well, as it happens, until I get going, but what difference does that make to you?'

Gordon makes no reply.

Mr Mumbles rolls his eyes, aims his gaze upstairs.

'Or, I could just speak to your—'

'Fine,' laughs Gordon, making light of the situation. 'What do you want me to do?'

'Press my belly button.'

'Come again?'

'My navel, push it.'

'That's what I thought you said.'

The dummy unbuttons his waistcoat, with less awkwardness than you might reasonably anticipate from wooden fingers, and lifts his shirt.

'Do you see?'

'Nope.' Gordon leans in and squints. 'But then I wouldn't really expect to find a belly button on a—'

'Yes, I was concerned this might happen,' sighs Mr Mumbles. 'You'll have to undo my trousers.'

'Excuse me?'

'Belt and fly: too tricky for my stiff fingers, I'm afraid.'

The dummy waits, shirt held aloft.

Gordon fails to move.

'Or we could just call . . . *Gemma!*'

Gordon jumps into action and opens the dummy's pants; both belt and fly – which feels totally weird and not a little seedy. Then he stands there staring at the small button navel, not unlike half a walnut case.

'Do you see?'

'Uh-huh.'

'Now, press it.'

'Press it?'

'Did I stutter? Yes, press it.'

Gordon hesitates but finally pokes the little, wooden belly button. There follows an internal, mechanical click and a whirr, then out pops a printed card from the dummy's mouth.

'Take-thith,' lisps the dummy, speaking around the card.

Gordon takes the card.

'What does it say?'

'Push a pregnant woman into a puddle,' Gordon reads.

'Not so bad.'

'Not so bad?! I can't do that.'

'Easier than what I had to do,' mutters Mr Mumbles.

'What did you have to do?'

'Doesn't matter; now, go, straight away, find a woman in the family way and push her over.'

'There's no way.'

'Gemma!'

They argue back and forth for a minute but eventually Sweet Cheeks is forced to agree. He is gone for well over five hours but on his return, Gordon, all hot and flustered, acknowledges that he has indeed performed the task he was set: the despicable act of pushing an expectant mother into a puddle.

'How did it go?'

'How do you think it went? Do you know how hard it is to find a puddle at this time of year? – A puddle in the vicinity of a pregnant woman? Hard work, mate, hard bloody work.'

'Yes, you look rather hot and bothered.'

147

'I was chased! – Quite rightly. I was lucky to escape with my life. Jesus, what was I thinking? I should have just told Gemma about Debbie and taken the consequences.'

'And yet you chose the task.'

'What can I say? I'm a bad man – a terrible man.'

'Oh well, the task is done now.'

'True,' concedes Gordon. 'So, at least I'll be free of you.'

'Indeed.'

'So, go on, then – leave.'

Mr Mumbles' eyes widen. 'There is one final thing.'

Gordon's eyes narrow. 'Oh yeah?' he asks suspiciously.

'First, you must burn the ticket.'

'And that's it?'

'That's it. Burn the ticket and we will both be free; you of me – and me of this dreadful' – he looks around – 'place.'

'You don't like my man-cave?'

'I do not, sir. Not in the least. No offence.'

'None taken, I'm sure,' replies Gordon. 'So, it just remains to burn this?'

'Exactly.'

'Fine.' Gordon fishes a lighter from a pocket and the ticket is set alight. It burns for a moment then Puff! – The ticket combusts in a flash of magnesium-bright light, leaving behind a thick cloud of acrid smoke. Gordon coughs until the smoke clears then barks: 'What the fuck!' – *For he is now the wooden dummy!* – And Mr Mumbles is in possession of his flesh and bones.

Just then, Gemma walks in.

'Gemma! Gemma! Thank God!'

'She can't hear you,' Mr Mumbles informs Gordon the dummy.

'Wait, what?'

'Don't ask me to explain. I think it's a guy thing.'

'Are you coming or are you spending the rest of the evening with that thing?'

'Coming, my beloved.'

'My beloved?' smiles Gemma approvingly. 'I'm not sure why you're talking all weird, Gordon; but I love it. Keep it up and I know someone who might just get lucky later.'

Mr Mumbles points, playfully, at himself. 'Me?'

Gemma flickers her eyelashes and nods flirtatiously.

'Well, it's not every day you turn thirty.'

'Gemma, for Christ's sake, I'm right here; it's me – Gordon!'

Mr Mumbles takes a step nearer to Gemma; he staggers but she catches him.

'Oh, hello, looks like someone's been having a few celebration beers without me,' chides Gemma playfully. 'I hope you can still, you know,' she winks, 'manage.'

'I shall do my best, my turtledove.'

Gemma nods favourably at that. 'And as it's your birthday,' she whispers in his ear, 'we can do that special thing you like.'

'Sounds wonderful,' grins Mr Mumbles.

'Might even wear that racy little black thing you got me.'

'Lead the way, sugar tits.'

'Nope, not so keen on that one.'

'Noted.'

The light switch clicks off, throwing the man-cave into darkness, and they exit, Gemma giggling like a newlywed. But in the dark, Gordon the dummy continues to shout for Gemma; throughout the whole evening, in fact – and ironically, he can all too clearly hear his wife, calling out *his* name, over and over and over again.

Joe sits back, basks in his perceived success.

'Very good,' nods Trevor. 'Excellent, in fact.'

'Thank you, thank you.'

'A little more risqué than I might have anticipated but yes, most entertaining.'

'Risqué?' huffs Joe. 'Don't be such a fuddy-duddy.'

'Fuddy-duddy?' parrots Trevor. 'Rest assured, boy, I am a man of the world.'

'If you say so.'

'I just wasn't expecting the uh, rather bawdy ending.'

'Always good to have a surprise ending, though, right?'

'Well, quite, but don't get too cocky,' warns Trevor. 'It was one time, and that could be down, I think it's fair to say, to a touch of luck.'

'Luck?' scoffs Joe.

'They were – how shall I put this – *favourable* words.'

'Yes, because I picked them, remember?' Joe's hands stir the air. 'Like you suggested.'

'Okay good; then do it again.'

'Nah, it's fine, I've got it. I know I've got it.'

Trevor's frown narrows his eyes.

'Joe, it was only the once; you need to repeat the process – and keep repeating it – until it becomes second-nature. Rinse and repeat, rinse and repeat; think of it as rehearsals – I remember one time, funny story—'

'Seriously, Trevor, I'm telling you, I've got it.'

'And you did need twenty minutes thinking time.'

'I said: I've got it!'

Trevor sighs. 'You know you sound – from what you've told me – just like your father.'

'I'm nothing like him!'

'Anger and arrogance are useless frames of mind.'

'Oh yeah, well you're useless!' hisses Joe. 'You're just annoyed because I picked it up so fast. Probably quicker than you ever did.'

'Joe,' pleads Trevor, but Joe is already up, away, out of the caravan and marching for the trailer park exit.

'Come back!' calls Trevor appearing on the porch. 'Don't be a party-pooper; no-one likes a stubborn sourpuss!'

Alison, halfway through smoking a cigarette outside her caravan, watches the commotion with shaking head.

'Joe!' shouts Trevor. 'Yes, you did well, but you need more practice! Return on the morrow and I'll show you how *I* do it!'

'No, stay away, Joe!' hollers Alison. 'That pervy old fart's not to be trusted!'

But Joe doesn't hear; Alison's words are drowned out by the passing burger van, its wheels noisy on the hard, rutted ground harshly illuminated by its headlights.

The vehicle turns and parks up outside a caravan on the other side of the track, opposite Trevor's caravan. Liam kills the engine and lights, jumps out, and heads up the porch steps.

'Hi, Craig!' waves Alison eagerly switching attention.

Liam ducks his head to acknowledge Alison's presence then lets himself into the trailer.

Alison licks her lips, sucks long and hard on her cigarette, exhales slowly.

'Now you, young man,' she drools, 'are welcome to munch on my burger anytime.'

'Who you talking to, Mum?' asks Becki through the window.

'No-one, sweetheart, go back to bed; I'll be there in a minute.'

Alison keeps an eye on Craig's silhouette behind the curtains as he knocks back a bottle; beer she presumes.

'Cheers, don't mind if I do,' purrs Alison as if she's just been invited over.

'You coming, Mum?'

'Yes,' chides Alison. '*In a minute.*'

CHAPTER 12
Lost in my Circle

'Okay, as you know,' Mr Schneider informs Joe and his classmates, 'the deadline to compete in this year's Storytell competition has now passed.'

A mixed reaction from the class: cheers, clapping, shrugs of indifference, playful boos.

'Ja, ja, give yourselves a round of applause, why not.'

When the noise settles, the teacher indicates six names on the whiteboard behind him.

'I was particularly pleased to learn that *six* students from this class put their names down as entrants this year. Joe, I'm very happy to see you decided to have another go.'

Hoots of derision from Gary and Melvin. Owen throws Joe a look that mocks: *What were you thinking?*

'But as you know,' continues Mr Schneider, 'there can only be twelve finalists –'

'How many from the other classes, sir?' asks Katie.

'Quite a lot,' acknowledges Mr Schneider. The amount had surprised him. 'I believe rumours of a cash prize have fuelled the numbers this year.'

'But it is true, though, sir, innit?' asks Neil. 'Like, about the prize money, I mean.'

Mr Schneider rolls his eyes at the use of this British informal contraction.

'No, Neil, it is not, I'm sorry to tell you.'

'Oh, well count me out then, sir,' grunts Neil.

'Fine,' sighs Mr Schneider. He turns to the whiteboard and strikes a line through Neil's name. 'And then there were five.' He twists back to the class. 'But now we need to see how many of you can make it through und with luck become part of the finals. Und that means the first elimination round. So, I'm sure you'll all be overjoyed to hear that we'll be doing it right now.'

Grumbles from the class.

'Come on, settle down please; I'll be doing the same for my other English classes. Katie, Chester, Michael, would you mind bringing up the easel, words und timer, please.'

As those deputised fetch the requested paraphernalia, the muttering continues. Katie keenly takes charge of the box of words and countdown timer, leaving the reluctant Chester and

Michael to awkwardly transport the easel from the back of the room to the front.

'A shortlist of eight will be drawn up then there will be a second elimination round, just like last year; from which four students will be dropped – or rather, become substitutes, should any finalist drop out at the last minute.'

Katie places the word box on Mr Schneider's desk, helpfully opens the lid and sets the timer to one side.

'Leaving just four lucky souls, who will have the great honour of appearing in the grand final, live on stage, in the assembly hall.' He steps aside as the boys finally arrive with the easel. 'As this is an elimination round, Kensington rules will apply: draw five, turn four; use the sub if required. So: Ryan, Jasmine, Laura, Owen, Joe; who'd like to go first?'

Jasmine sticks her hand up.

'Yes, Jasmine, please come up. Katie, perhaps you'd like to stay und operate the clock?'

'Happy to,' beams Katie.

The Cliché Café is busy today. Trevor weaves through locals collecting smiles and hellos and sits at the noshery's only free table, under a poster that reads: 'Why not try one of our The-grass-is-always-greener-on-the-other-side salads?' over a photo of what appears to be a standard cheese salad.

The faces of Mr Schneider's students let us know that Jasmine failed to fully entertain with her selected words:

LOOPHOLE. TORNADO. SAWDUST. PENGUIN.

She had included all four, sort of, but no, not a great job of storytelling if we're being honest.

'Well done, Jasmine,' encourages the teacher. 'Give her a round of applause, please. Tricky words there.'

Jasmine takes the walk of shame and slumps into her chair. 'I shouldn't have changed *Bridge*,' she tells a friend. 'What was I meant do with *Penguin*?'

The friend shrugs. 'I know, right?'

'No, don't be disheartened, Jaz, it was a valiant effort.'

Mr Schneider collects Jasmine's cards from the easel and hands them to Katie who files them back in the box.

'Right, who's next?' asks Mr Schneider.

Owen stands. Joe stands too.

'No, I'll go next,' insists Joe assuredly. 'Let *him* follow *me* – if he can.'

Jeers from the class; they know a challenge when they hear one – and check Joe out, getting cocky all of a sudden.

'Do you mind, Owen?' asks the teacher.

'Be my guest,' snorts Owen retaking his seat.

As Joe moves forward the class applauds politely, no-one quite sure what to expect. Once behind Mr Schneider's desk, he studies the box for a moment before levitating both hands over the tops of the cards.

'What's he doing, sir?' laughs Gary.

'Some kind of Jedi mind-trick,' speculates Owen.

Mr Schneider gestures for respectful quiet. There persists a couple of titters but Joe isn't fazed. Confidently, he picks his first card, and then a second.

Trevor, encouraged by fellow customers, stands and clears his throat, preparation for a *serious* performance.

'I have of late, but wherefore I know not, lost all my mirth,' states Trevor dramatically. 'Forgone all custom of exercises, and indeed it goes so heavily with my disposition that this goodly frame, the earth, seems to me a sterile promontory.'

With a self-assured smile, Joe hands over his five chosen cards to Mr Schneider, who places them on the easel, the words concealed.

'Ready?' asks Mr Schneider.

'Yep,' smiles a puffed-up Joe.

'Okay.' The teacher turns the first four cards in quick succession, reading each aloud: '*Spoon. Pimple.* Alright, simmer down, people. *Handbag.* Und finally: *Sailor.*'

Joe swallows hard and the colour drains from his cheeks, perhaps not so smug now. He glances out, to a sea of faces that stare back.

'Want to change one, Joe?' asks the teacher.

No reply.

'Joe, do you wish to—?'

'Nah, it should be fine,' peacocks Joe at last; no doubt attempting to hide his growing concern.

'Are you sure?'

'Come on, sir,' intones Owen. 'Don't keep us waiting.'

'Very well.' The teacher nods to Katie and she raises a hand; suspends it above the button of the countdown timer. 'Then start the timer, please, Katie.'

'No, wait!' barks Joe. 'I'll change *Pimple.*'

'No problem.' Mr Schneider takes down Pimple and replaces it with Joe's alternate word card.

Katie flinches, Joe sighs, and another round of sniggers is met with 'Settle down, settle down,' from the teacher.

Joe asks for water and is allowed back to his desk to retrieve the bottle from his Yoda backpack. After a long glug, the bottle is repacked and Joe returns to the front.

'Ready now?' asks the teacher.

'As ready as I'll ever be.'

'*Alright, let's hear it!*' announces Mr Schneider, making a show of pointing at Katie.

'Okay,' declares Katie flatly. 'Here we go.' But rather than *go* she pauses to allow Joe a few precious extra seconds' thinking time. 'Your thinking time . . . starts . . .' Her hand descends at a snail's pace but eventually has no other option but to press the timer button. '. . . Now.'

The clock's [00:30] changes to [00:29] then [00:28] . . .

Joe scrutinises the cards displayed on the easel.

SPOON. HANDBAG. SAILOR. LAVATORY.

He mouths the words, his face a blank.

The timer ticks down, the seconds passing almost in slow motion, yet fast, too – *too fast.*

[00:15] . . . [00:14] . . . [00:13] . . .

The entire Cliché Café populace, both customers and staff – with the exception of Noah who, in a world of his own, is jiggling a sugar sachet by his ear – listens intently to Trevor.

'In action, how like an angel!' he recites. 'In apprehension, how like a god! The beauty of the world! The paragon of animals! And yet, to me, what is this quintessence of dust?'

[00:09] . . . [00:08] . . . [00:07] . . .

Motionless and pink-faced Joe stares at the class: a multitude of transfixed mugs decked in roughly equal amounts of empathy, sympathy, pity and amusement.

[00:05] . . . [00:04] . . . [00:03] . . .

Owen and Gary look to each other, sharing the moment with cruel pleasure.

And the timer hits zero.

'Man delights not me,' concludes Trevor. 'No, nor woman neither, though by your smiling you seem to say so.'

As one, the café's masses applaud with passion and enthusiasm; a few actually stand, and at least two people whistle. Several continue to film on their mobiles.

'Bravo, bravo!' calls a voice from the back.

154

'Extraordinary!' cheers someone.

Trevor bows and bows again, milking it for all it's worth.

This goes on for some time.

'But the police wouldn't believe him,' Joe winds up, 'and that's the *real* reason he missed his ship.'

Silence from the class. No response from the teacher. Everyone seems dumbfounded.

'Because of the mix-up,' explains Joe. 'In the toilets.'

A sigh and a groan then a loud outbreak of what had been, up to now, *stifled* titters.

'Is that it?' scoffs Owen.

'Not bad, Joe, not bad,' applauds Mr Schneider at last. 'Come on; show some love, people, it was a good try.'

'Good try, sir?' parrots Melvin. 'It stunk.'

'Did he even mention the spoon?' challenges Gary.

'I never see either of you two getting up here,' rebukes the teacher. 'So stow it, boys, please.'

Katie quietly removes the SPOON, LAVATORY, HANDBAG and SAILOR cards, and returns them unceremoniously to the box as Joe traipses back to his seat.

'Now, who's next?' pumps Mr Schneider moving on swiftly. 'Ryan? Laura?'

Owen rises to his feet. Melvin claps like a lunatic. Gary whistles. One or two non-partisans applaud hesitantly.

Joe sulks.

Llani's only squad car is parked in Tall Trees Trailer Park.

Billy Mills sighs and checks the time as Nerys munches her way through a packet of crisps, slow and noisy. The chomp-chomp-chomp vexes the constable and it shows. Eventually, though, the crisps run out and his sergeant then sets to sucking her teeth.

'So, Powys has the *lowest* crime rate in the country –'

'Uh-huh,' agrees Nerys.

'But you *always* wear your gun. Even though you've never had to fire it; that's right, isn't it? You've never drawn it? Not for real.'

'Uh-huh.' Nerys picks at a tooth.

PC Mills rechecks the time.

After a long beat Nerys asks him to put his window up. Billy doesn't seem keen.

'I'm cold,' chides Nerys.

Under protest he closes the two inch gap at the top of his window. After another long beat Billy asks:

155

'So, why do you always bring it along?'

'What?'

'The gun.'

'You *know* why. Same reason you get to bring the Taser.'

The constable swivels his head to face the sergeant and furrows his brow. 'In case we need it?'

'Bingo.'

'You know they should be locked in the boot, right?'

'I won't tell if you don't.'

Nerys checks her teeth in the rear-view mirror.

'Do you want to lock yours in the boot?'

Billy taps the Taser attached to his utility vest.

'Nah, I'm good.'

An extra long beat is filled with yet more waiting.

Billy whistles gently through his teeth.

Nerys slurps on a bottle of coconut water.

Eventually, Billy has another question:

'So, how come you have a gun and I only get a Taser?'

The sergeant swivels her head to face the constable and raises her eyebrows.

'Because I failed the competency test?' suggests Billy.

'Got it in one. We'll make a detective of you yet.'

Billy sticks out his lower lip and wobbles his noggin.

'Whereas you're a qualified Firearms Officer,' he mocks in a childish voice.

Nerys nudges the constable. 'Heads up, here's he.'

Trevor approaches his caravan trailing smoke from the bright yellow cigarette at the end of his cigarette-holder. He climbs the porch steps and lets himself in.

Walter 'Wacky' Benson, BA (Hons) Natural History, is fifty-six but looks much older. He's into brown corduroy, elbow patches and has a more-salt-than-pepper goatee.

For today's lesson he's asked four reluctant volunteers, all male, to lie on his desk, face down, in layers, if you can picture such a thing. Gary, the least happy of the four, is at the bottom, Robert above him, then Brian, and a chunky kid called Russell on top, pinning the other three down.

The rest of the class look on, relieved they weren't conscripted for today's lesson and amused at the scene before them. Wacky's lectures are often as wild as the scraggly mop of grey hair atop his skittle-shaped head.

Mr Benson's trousers swoosh as he wanders between the students' desks.

'So,' he asks, 'how are you feeling down there, Gary?'

'Crushed, sir,' complains Gary.

'Aha!' exclaims Mr Benson turning on a heel. 'That's exactly how coal feels.'

The bewildered class exchange looks. Some laugh, some groan. Katie turns to Joe, rolls her eyes and makes a face.

'Right, stop laughing, please, and turn your books to the section on fossil fuels. That's *fossil* fuels. Page sixty.'

The students flick through books with little enthusiasm. A knock on the door and Mr Schneider sticks his head in.

'A moment, if I may, Mr Benson.'

'By all means.'

Mr Benson gestures for his colleague to enter.

'You handle this, Billy. I'm feeling a bit washed out.'

'Okay, excellent,' beams the constable.

'I'll jump in I have to.'

'I'm sure that won't be necessary,' smiles Billy smugly.

After a short beat Nerys suggests: 'Well, knock then.'

'I thought you'd already knocked.'

'I did, but he hasn't answered, and we know he's in, so knock again.'

PC Mills raps on the door. 'Police!'

'Don't shout *Police*, it's not a raid.'

Nerys winces; she grips the porch rail with one hand and rubs her swollen tummy with the other.

'You okay?' asks the constable.

'Yep, knock again,' instructs Nerys.

But there's no need, Trevor has opened the door.

'Sorry about that, I was indisposed.'

Billy narrows his eyes. *What does that even mean?*

'In the loo,' explains Trevor.

'Mr la Touche?' asks Billy.

'*De* la Touche,' corrects Trevor. 'But yes, I am he.'

'Mr *Trevor* de la Touche?'

'One and the same.'

'I believe you previously spoke with our colleagues.'

'Er, yes, that is correct.'

'Right, so, this is a follow-up call, Mr la Touche.'

'Well then, come in, do. And, please, call me Trevor.'

Inside, Billy sniffs the air and screws his face.

'Oh yes, sorry about that.' Trevor opens a window and after a few tries – 'Sorry, faulty catch,' – manages to close the toilet door.

Billy clears his throat. 'You not well either?' he asks.

Trevor notices Nerys leaning on the kitchen counter.

'Oh dear, are you quite alright, Sergeant?'

He indicates a seat at the table.

'Please do take a seat – if you'd *like* to sit, that is.'

'Not sure I'd fit in there in my present state,' jests Nerys.

'Yep, she's a proper porker at the moment,' laughs Billy. He's the only one who does.

'I'll be fine,' Nerys informs Trevor. 'But thanks.'

Trevor fetches a glass of water.

Billy has been scanning the interior:

'Quite the collection of toys you have there,' he notes.

'Yes, well, I wouldn't call them *toys* exactly.'

'What would you call them?'

'Robots.'

Billy shrugs. *Toys, robots, it's all the same to him.*

'Collected them since I was knee-high to a grasshopper.'

Billy frowns. *Knee-high to a grasshopper?* Another expression he's never heard before.

'Sorry, most remiss of me. Would *you* like a seat, Constable?' Trevor removes the talking robot from the table, where he'd been undergoing a polish.

'No, I'm good,' reports Billy remaining near the door.

Trevor transports the robot to his place in the cabinet.

'Why the space?' asks eagle-eyed Nerys. She might not be at her best but she seldom misses a trick.

'Oh, one's missing,' Trevor informs her.

'Why not just shuffle them along?' suggests Billy. 'You wouldn't notice then.'

Trevor nods but says nothing.

The slightly awkward silence that follows is broken by the robot: '*Quiet please,*' he drones. '*I – am – analysing.*'

'Just ignore him. His off-switch is broken.'

'Take the batteries out,' shrugs Billy.

'I already did,' replies Trevor.

'What?' Billy frowns.

'And now I hope you'll excuse me if *I* sit down.'

Trevor takes a seat at the table.

'My knees,' he groans, 'aren't what they used to be.'

'Constable,' prompts Nerys, face set to: *Get on with it.*

'So, well done, Joe, Owen und Laura,' beams Mr Schneider.

Hearty compliments and a patter of applause buzz the room.

'*Joe*, sir?' scoffs Owen.

'Yes, Owen, you heard me correctly.'

'But *Joe*, sir?' echoes Owen.

'Yes, Owen; from this class: yourself, Laura und Joe. You three have made it through to the last eight. I'm not sure I could be any clearer. The next elimination round will be on Friday. Remember four unlucky individuals will be dropped – though two will become stand-ins – so bring your A-game if you'd like to progress to the staged finals. Now, if you have any more questions, see me later; I've interrupted Mr Benson's lesson long enough. Thank you, Walter.'

'Not at all, Heinrich,' nods the head of Natural History.

Mr Schneider departs without any comment regarding the four boys stacked on the teacher's desk.

'Okay,' claps Mr Benson, 'have you all turned your books to the section on fossil fuels?'

Pages flick back and forth, then, from the bottom layer of 'coal', a strained voice pipes up . . . 'Sir?'

'Page sixty, Gary,' reminds Mr Benson. 'Page sixty.'

When Sergeant Hughes and Constable Mills descend Trevor's steps, Alison is waiting to intercept them.

'Afternoon, Nerys,' she pounces.

'*Sergeant*, when I'm on duty, Alison,' winks Nerys.

Alison makes a face then nods at Trevor's caravan.

'Everything okay, *Sergeant* Hughes?'

'No, it's not, actually,' she snaps, turning on Billy: 'For your information, Constable Mills, I'm not sick, I'm pregnant. And if you ever compare me to a porker again, I'll take that Taser and—'

Another twinge has Nerys wincing. She moves to lean against the caravan.

'It's probably just wind again,' mutters Mills.

'Shut it, you,' rasps Nerys.

'I'm not kidding, it's terrible in the squad car,' Billy informs Alison. 'Have to keep the window down.'

Alison makes a tutting noise, pushes the constable out of the way and steps over to Nerys, now bent double.

'Do you want to come in mine and sit down for a minute?' she asks putting an arm around the sergeant.

'No, no, I'll be fine in a second,' Nerys assures her. Then, to Billy, she prompts: 'Ask her about Kelly.'

'Kelly Owens?' asks Alison. 'Yes, I heard she wasn't in school yesterday. Why, what's happened? Is she alright?'

'Went out picking wildflowers on Saturday afternoon according to her nan,' explains PC Mills. 'She didn't come home. We've checked all her friends and classmates but nothing so far.'

Nerys unbends, blowing hard. 'Have *you* seen her?'

'No,' replies Alison. 'Here, you don't suspect *him*, do you?' She jabs a thumb at Trevor's caravan.

'What? No,' insists Nerys. 'She'll turn up.'

'No-one ever goes missing for long around here.' The constable sounds almost disappointed.

'So, what *are* you seeing him for?' Alison wants to know. 'Are you sure it's not to do with Kelly? Go on, you can tell me. I won't tell a soul.'

'I could tell you,' puffs Nerys bowing again. 'But then I'd have to shoot you.'

'But it's definitely nothing to do with Kelly?' Now Alison sounds disappointed.

'All I can tell you –' Nerys straightens up slowly, her discomfort passing, '– is that it was another matter entirely.'

'Is it to do with Joe Evans?'

'No. Why, do you—?'

'Missing dog,' blurts PC Mills.

'Billy!' scolds Nerys.

'What? It's not a secret, is it? Besides, if he expects us to find him.'

'But he hasn't got a dog,' frowns Alison.

'No, because he's missing,' Nerys reminds her.

Alison shakes a screwed face. 'He's *never* had a dog.'

'You sure?' checks Billy.

'Well, I've never seen him with one.'

'Right,' purrs Billy. With narrowed eyes, he scrutinises Trevor's caravan. This 'investigation' just cranked up a level: from Routine, to Curious. Subconsciously fingering his Taser he directs Alison to keep her eyes open.

'Oh I will, don't worry,' she replies, keen to the point of gleeful.

Liam peeks out through a small gap in the drawn curtains.

'Keep – fucking – quiet,' he warns, low but menacing.

Behind him, on the caravan floor, sits Kelly, tightly bound at the ankles, hands behind her back. She's gagged too, mouth bloody and drooling; eyes agog and watering profusely – tears and slobber staining her top, a T-shirt already damp from cold sweats. And in her lap, the skinny terrier, shaking and whimpering weakly.

From a shelf above Kelly's head Joel's skull looks down.

They're making too much noise! it screams. *For fuck's sake, Liam, shut them up!*

160

Liam turns sharply to Kelly. 'Keep that fucking mutt quiet,' he threatens under his breath. 'Or so help me –'

The claw-hammer in Liam's clenched fist rises into view.

Kelly rattles her head vigorously. A refusal, fear, a plea – or a *How the fuck am I supposed to do that, you sick fuck?!*

'Why the fuck did I let you keep him?' seethes Liam back at the window. 'I'm fucking allergic to dogs.'

And, as if on cue, a sneeze blasts the curtains.

Both officers had started walking in the direction of Liam's caravan, to where their squad car is parked; now, the male copper looks over.

Liam ducks.

Again he threatens his captive with the hammer, raises it over his shoulder. The dog whines – perhaps from its own fear, perhaps sensing the girl's terror intensifying – for Kelly is rocking back and forth, trembling wildly, her heels now beating on the thin linoleum. This drumming, and her sobs, though muffled by the spun tea-towel gag, is a commotion that could easily alert the uniforms outside.

Bash her head in quick! And the dog's!

'No,' snarls Liam at Joel's skull. 'It'd be too noisy.'

Remaining crouched he stows the hammer and creeps towards Kelly and the dog, hands outstretched.

The hostage snivels and shakes, wide eyes pleading for mercy but the grey, wolf-like eyes, unblinking, stalking, glide ever nearer. Kidnapped – bound – *strangled!?* If only she can get whoever it is outside making her captor nervous to hear her cries.

'Mumhfhhh!' she wails bravely.

The terrier whines, low and pitiful.

Liam inches closer, his meaty paws reaching for Kelly's crimson neck.

She turns her face away. 'Mumhfhhhhh!'

A noise outside; Liam jumps forward and covers Kelly's mouth with a grasping hand – then, with an ear cocked towards the sound, he listens.

A car door closes.

Then a second door closes.

And now an engine starts.

Liam slinks back to the curtains and through the gap, watches the police squad car drive away.

Then he spies the woman across the way – the one that's always waving at him: she's eyeballing the caravan. But not *his* – that weird theatrical guy's caravan; number seven.

CHAPTER 13

Spreading Rumours

Alison has been updating the Gas & Graze staff.

'I always knew something was off there,' fumes Bonnie.

Clara nods in agreement.

'Oh, look out,' warns Alison. 'Speak of the devil.'

Trevor approaches the counter with a smile for all.

'Good afternoon, ladies,' he beams. 'How are we today?'

Alison blows her nose. Bonnie folds her arms. Clara looks outside. No-one speaks. The silence is stony, arctic and persistent; an audience lost directly upon the entrance.

In the end, Trevor picks up a chocolate bar and raises an eyebrow for the price.

'Fifty pence,' states Clara flatly.

'Still no news about Hamlet, I'm afraid,' tries Trevor.

Nothing beyond awkward unresponsiveness.

'Thought I might have heard something by now,' he persists in a friendly tone.

But the secrecy of guarded tongues holds firm. It's as if Trevor were a court jester found wanting before a displeased queen and her ladies-in-waiting, unquestionably a heartbeat away from an *Off with his head*, such is the royal mood today.

'Right,' yields Trevor after paying. 'Well . . . *Parting is such sweet sorrow, that I shall say good night till it be morrow.*'

Still nothing; the absence of sound is thunderous.

A modest bow then Trevor reverses, a stage actor backing away before the curtain falls. But no applause here, no flowers thrown from the gallery; only gloomy hush and soft steps to the exit – whereupon a resounding *ping* spikes the stillness and he slips away into the morning.

'I still don't see why he can't go to school on his bike like other kids,' grumbles Paul in the hallway.

'Well, maybe if you'd ever bothered to teach him to ride one properly,' moans Sally from the bottom of the stairs.

'Oh, not this again – *please.*'

Sally's referring to this:

Joe aged six, in the park, on a small bike. Paul inside the car, parked outside the railings, smoking a cigarette.

Joe waves.

Paul tilts his head back in acknowledgment and shouts:

'Is your helmet fastened?'

'What?'

'Is your helmet fastened?!'

Little Joe indicates he can't hear because of the helmet.

'Just go,' urges Paul. 'It's grass, you'll be fine.'

'Okay!'

Joe tightly grips the handlebars, checks his dad is still watching then gingerly places one foot on a pedal, preparation for his first ever ride without trainer wheels. But after he's moved off, made that slow, wobbly start, Paul becomes distracted by Noah, who is also in the park: running around under trees, transfixed by noisy, fallen leaves that swirl and rustle in a shifting breeze.

Paul has always insisted that he *was* there to catch Joe when he fell off his bike even if it's not how his son remembers it.

'Another promise you didn't deliver on,' gripes Sally. 'You're all talk.' She adopts a mocking face for her cruel impression of Paul: '*Oh,* I'll *take him to the park.*'

'I took him to the park, *loads of times,*' retorts Paul angrily. 'Is it my fault he never picked it up like other kids?'

'*Twice.* Twice you took him. And it's not his fault you wouldn't get out of the car.'

'I got out of the car.'

'Too windy for your precious hair, was it?'

'I got out of the car! He just has no sense of balance that's all. And that's not my fault!'

'Oh no, it's never your fault.'

'The boy's not right. He's hardly said two words to me all year.'

'Well, are you surprised?'

'What's that supposed to mean?'

'You really want two words? Okay, I've got two words for you— Oh, hi, Joe,' smiles Sally; she's spotted Joe, in his school uniform, halfway down the stairs.

'I *can* ride a bike,' insists Joe, not for the first time. 'I just choose not to.' And he heads straight out through the open front door and onto the driveway.

'What the,' starts Paul, until Sally widens her eyes. 'I mean,' he continues, 'who the hell chooses not to—'

'I choose to *walk!*' shouts Joe. 'I *like* walking!'

'Just go,' urges Sally. 'Just go and give your son a lift to school. Is that too much to ask? It's on your bloody way!'

'I am doing,' barks Paul. '*And* picking him up, if he's there – which most of the time, by the way, *he isn't!*'

164

Don's back on Finger Hill gazing out over Bryn Crow's fields. Mid-afternoon and his son and grandsons are rounding up sheep for a dip: Mark and Robbie on quad-bikes; Sam, out of his Land Rover, whistling instructions to circling dogs, a young, well-trained pack of five.

'Doesn't seem like five minutes since *we* were doing that, eh, Jed?' slurs the farmer. 'And now look at us. Me in my eighties and you—Jesus, how old are you now? What is it, seven years for one dog year?'

Don sighs and takes a long swig from the bottle in his meaty paw. Jed's ancient eyes watch his counterparts working the slope of the hill opposite; a whirl of darting legs and pointed attentions.

'I mean, what use are we now? Fixing a hole in a fence here and there, straightening the odd post, putting out the occasional bucket of feed. But other than that what are we good for?'

Jed makes no reply. He never does. Despite Don waffling on like this for months – *years*.

'That's right, the knacker's yard,' snaps the farmer. 'Look at that,' he grumbles, spotting a sick sheep wandering near the Land Rover. 'That's us that is.'

Jed gazes at the limping, coughing sheep.

'Well, I suppose that's one job we *can* still take care of.'

Don climbs out, collects an empty 'decoy' bucket from the back and approaches the sickly sheep, now heading his way because it believes it's about to be fed a rare treat: something other than grass. Then, before the ewe can shout: 'What the fuck!' Don has grabbed the animal and expertly flipped it onto its back, her head at Don's stomach.

'Right, I suppose I'd better put you out of your misery.'

He seizes the sheep's head, raises its jaw, exposing its neck, and taps each pocket, but his knife is missing.

After walking the sheep to the back of the Land Rover, he pushes the animal to the ground, keeping it gripped between his boots, and grabs a spade which he raises high, two-handed, over a shoulder.

'Sorry, old girl,' mumbles Don with no real feeling. And he slams the spade down. The loud *thwack* of metal colliding with sheep skull sends a couple of crows flapping towards nearby trees.

Clank! Thwunk! – Don throws the spade and dead sheep in the back of the Land Rover and closes up the tailgate. Jed's glassy eyes are on the farmer when he climbs back in.

'What?' snipes Don.

Jed blinks.

165

'Don't look at me like that. She's just a dumb animal. You've seen enough dead sheep in your time.'

Jed makes a gruff noise in his throat.

'Oh yeah, well at least *she's* out of it.'

Jed tilts his head.

'Oh shut up, what do you know? You're spent too.'

Jed gulps.

'What do you say? Should I slit your throat and then take care of myself?'

Jed lies down.

'Least I could if I knew where my knife was,' slurs Don.

Time passes. Jed yawns, long and loud.

'Do you know what? Fuck this for a game of soldiers.' Don climbs out but turns and sticks his head back inside. 'I'm gonna do me,' he vents, 'then I'm coming back for you.'

Jed, ball-licking on hold, looks up.

'Actually no, I'll do us at the same time.'

Don climbs back in and after a rummage in the glove-box comes up with a roll of duct tape which he shows to Jed. If a dog can be said to frown, Jed does exactly that.

Don slams the door, which fails to close, walks to the rear and bends over the tailgate. He searches amongst the old tools and polythene sheets and finds a length of hose.

Squatting now, the farmer sticks one end of the hose into the exhaust and secures it with several wraps of black tape. Then he steps to the driver door and offers the hose up to the gap at the top of the open window. Except it won't reach, it's not long enough by several inches.

Back inside the Land Rover, Don slumps into his seat, sits silently, not moving, and stares blankly through the muddy windscreen at nothing in particular.

Jed barks: a single woof.

'Yes, okay, it was too short – happy now?'

Jed cocks his head.

Don sighs. 'I can't even do that right.'

Jed whines softly. Don rolls his eyes then swivels his ruddy face towards the dog.

'And what would you suggest?' he asks.

'No, slow down, take your time; it's all part of preparing to take the journey, that first step. Let your mind be clear.'

'I know,' huffs Joe. 'You said that last time.'

'Try to *feel* the cards that draw you towards them,' advises Trevor. 'Those are the ones you should choose.

166

'And that's where I said, *Like the Force*,' mutters Joe.

Trevor, setting up the easel, watches as Joe hovers his hands, slowly, deliberately, over the cards.

'Good,' praises Trevor.

Joe picks a card he feels drawn to. And then another.

'That's it. Not too fast.'

A third card is selected, a fourth, and then a fifth.

'Excellent. Now pass them over, face down.'

'I know,' mumbles Joe.

He passes over the chosen cards and Trevor places them on the easel, their fancy backs facing out.

'Bloomsbury or Kensington rules?' asks Trevor.

'Kensington.'

'Very well; remember, once I turn the four cards,' informs Trevor, 'you can reject one, should you so wish. Once rejected, I'll turn the fifth card then you'll have thirty seconds thinking time, after which you should begin.'

Joe rolls his eyes.

'You must include all four final words in your story.'

'I know the rules, Trevor.'

'Okay, good,' smiles Trevor. 'Just relax, breathe slowly, clear your mind, and we'll begin.'

Joe takes a deep breath then lets it out through his nose.

'Ready?' asks Trevor.

'Ready,' nods Joe.

The first card is turned. HOG. 'Hog' announces Trevor. The next card is WELL. 'Well,' he states.

For a moment Joe wants to say, *I can read, Trevor*, but that would be churlish. After all, this is exactly how it's done for real – in competition.

'Goblin,' states Trevor turning the GOBLIN card on the easel, 'and Princess.' The fourth card is indeed PRINCESS.

Joe studies the cards: HOG. WELL. GOBLIN. PRINCESS.

'Great words,' Trevor beams. 'You picked well. No pun intended – four nouns; or two nouns, one verb, and one adjective, if you prefer.'

After a moment Joe asks: 'Aren't you going to ask?'

'Oh yes, forgive me, dear boy. Would you like to change one of these for your substitute?'

'No, I don't think I will.'

'A wise decision,' nods Trevor.

A long beat passes.

'The timer, Trevor,' reminds Joe. 'You're supposed to—'

'Yes, yes, apologies,' flaps Trevor. 'Here we go.'

Trevor turns the prop hourglass.

Joe gazes at the cards.

The sand slips away.

Joe continues to stare at the cards.

He bites his lip.

'Just keep calm,' encourages Trevor.

Joe thinks, attempts to construct, create . . .

'Stay relaxed—'

'Shhhh,' hisses Joe.

Trevor falls silent and raises hands apologetically.

Joe is still studying the words when the sand runs out.

He nods.

'I'm going to do this one in third person present tense.'

Trevor sticks up a thumb.

'Picture the scene: a cold autumn night; a goblin walks through a tiny village. All the residents are fast asleep. As he passes the town well, he hears a weak cry for help.'

Joe's voice is strangely captivating: it exports us to a hill and creepy village full of crooked, wooden houses and dark moon shadows. Here a knock-kneed goblin, no more than four-foot tall, walks through the twisted streets whistling softly to himself. The goblin's swinging lantern casts a jittery, golden glow all around and spawns a long black shadow that walks beside him. The shadow kicks out and a stone skips along the bumpy street; raising a line of dust before it disappears into a small bale of hay stacked against a lichen-clad stone wall.

As the goblin passes through what appears to be a 'town square' of sorts, a roughly oval space with a drinking well at its centre, he suddenly stops.

He looks around, certain he heard something.

Beyond the low-roofed dwellings lies a ring of tall trees, the village built in a handmade clearing. A crow, hidden by night, calls out and receives a distant caw in reply.

'Down here. Down here.'

The goblin turns but sees nothing and no-one.

'Down here. Please help me.'

The goblin realises the wee voice that cried out is calling from within the well.

Holding his lantern over the hole, he peers down.

'Are you there? Can you hear me?'

And as his eyes adjust, he sees, at the base, a bedraggled princess clinging to what appears to be a dead, bloated hog.

'Help, I've fallen down this well and can't get out,' explains the princess. 'Save me, please. If it hadn't been for this dead, bloated hog I would *surely* be dead already.'

The narrator speaks and it is Joe's voice:

The goblin spoke a different language to the princess but he immediately understood her plight and what she must be asking. He looks all around, searching for a rope, anything useful, but there is only a small pail.

Picking up the pail, the goblin spots a hole in its bottom.

He thinks about calling for help, continues Joe's voice-over. *But he knew this village and he knew the locals. There's a reason why he passed through at night.*

They hated goblins here.

Dwarfs too, but especially goblins.

Then he remembers the stream at the bottom of the hill and has an idea.

'Kegeth ur,' the goblin calls down to the princess. 'Kàlrastere-rerirtan rilar istdub. Mirererermibvöt kul rost kal.' (A rough translation would be: Hold on. Don't be scared. I'll get you out.)

'Please hurry,' urges the princess. 'I don't know how much longer I can stay afloat.'

And with that, the goblin runs down the hill as fast as his tiny legs will carry him.

At the stream he fills the pail and, covering the hole with one hand, runs back. Returned to the well, he pours in the water. The Princess shrieks.

All through the night, the goblin kept up the pace, his little heart pounding in his chest. Bucket after bucket, on and on, into the dawn hours . . . and slowly . . .

Time after time, many, many times, the goblin runs back and forth to the stream. After each descent he fills the pail and covering the hole, runs back; where, at the well, he pours in the water and the princess shrieks.

Inch by inch and foot by precious foot the princess, still clinging to the floating pig, edges ever nearer to safety. But then, just as rescue seems within reach . . .

With dawn now broken the goblin empties his pail into the well surely for the final time. Again the princess shrieks. Then a hand grabs the goblin and spins him round.

'Look!' barks an ugly child. 'He's drowning the princess!'

'We hate goblins,' hisses a particularly nasty-looking villager. 'And dwarfs. But especially goblins!'

'Ingstëb, Mir räd ostuk zòlug ekast mot!' protests the goblin, which means: No, I was trying to save her!

169

But the villagers didn't understand. Like the princess, they didn't speak Goblin.

As a rope, brought by someone, is lowered down the well, the villagers gather tightly around the goblin and beat him with knobbly sticks.

By the time the princess is helped out, the goblin is a lumpy, blood-splattered mess – and quite dead.

The crowd step back as, dishevelled and sad, the princess kneels by the goblin's unmoving body. She closes his eyelids and kisses him on the forehead. The townsfolk now drift away silently, some realising they'd goofed, others unsure but still making themselves scarce. Even the instigators, Ugly and Nasty – who remain adamant that they did the right thing (*all* goblins are evil, everyone knows that) – elbow each other then quietly back off.

'You idiots!' wails the princess. 'What did you do?'

'He was a goblin, Your Highness,' blinks the ugly child.

'You can't take chances with their kind,' adds Nasty.

Then we too withdraw: floating into the air, above the closing doors and straw rooftops of the deserted village, leaving behind the shrinking, tearful princess, now totally alone with the diminishing, lifeless, spreadeagled goblin.

Later, many locals became sick. Some died. They convinced themselves the goblin had placed a curse on the well and so moved away in search of a new place, leaving behind the homes they'd lived in for hundreds of years.

The village fades to black as we pass through a dark cloud. Then the darkness slowly disperses and we gradually find ourselves back in Trevor's caravan.

'So,' muses Trevor, 'they never realised a rotten pig carcass was poisoning their well.'

'The same pig that helped save a princess,' smiles Joe. 'There's a kind of irony in that, don't you think?'

'Indeed,' nods Trevor. 'That was excellent, Joe; first rate. I can see you're going to have nothing to worry about.'

Paul is bending the ear of uninterested pet shop assistant Dean, a twenty-something stick insect with a face like the moon, thanks to serious bouts of boyhood acne.

'And so I said, "That's him up there now; why can't he use a door like normal people?" and then I said, I dunno, something like: "He's *always* out these days." And so she pipes up: "Perhaps if you'd got him that dog he wanted for his birthday." And I said: "He's not having a dog." And she says: "Why not?" So I say: "We can't afford one right now, Sally." So she says: 'No but you can still afford your fags though, can't you!" – I like the odd one now and then, where's the harm in that? – And I said: "You know how much it costs for a pedigree?" Only she says: "He doesn't need a pedigree, a mongrel would be fine." So I said: "No, absolutely not; not around the baby, Sal." And she tells me I'm being ridiculous. So I told her: "And anyway, he *can't* have a dog." And she says: "Why not?" So I say: "Because I'm allergic, that's why." And she says: "Since when? First I've heard." And, anyway, to cut a long story short, I said I'd come in if she promised to shut up banging on about it. So, yeah, I'm here.'

'So, you'd like to see some animals?' sniffs Dean.

'That's why I'm here,' huffs Paul.

'Wanna start with dogs?'

'What did I just say?'

Dean shrugs.

'About being allergic? Were you even listening? By the way, what is that smell?'

Dean sniffs. 'Pet shop,' he replies. 'This way please.'

Paul follows the assistant to a bank of bird cages where he points at a multi-coloured parrot or parakeet or something, he isn't sure. Paul knows plenty of *wild* birds but not pet ones.

'This is a—' starts Dean.

'Too squawky,' interrupts Paul. 'What else you got?'

'These are all the birds.'

Dean scratches his head and a tumble of dandruff, if it is dandruff, falls onto the shoulder of his blue jumper.

'*Besides* birds.'

'We got snakes and fish.'

'Have you got a chinchilla? I think I'd like a chinchilla. I even like the word: *chin-chilla*. Come on, say it with me. *Chin-chilla*.'

'Chinchilla?'

'No, sounds better when I say it: *chinchilla*. Hear the difference?'

Dean frowns.

'What is a chinchilla anyway?'

'It's a South American rodent,' advises Dean.

'A rodent?' echoes Paul. 'That's a terrible suggestion. Any other bright ideas?'

As Mr Schneider thanks the last eight of Year 10's Storytell contest for attending the pre-final elimination round on their lunch-break, Joe recalls a short conversation he'd had last night with Trevor, upon leaving the caravan.

171

'Now go home and get some sleep,' Trevor had said. 'And be ready for that elimination round.'

'What if I get crappy words, though?' asked Joe.

'You won't get crappy words,' insisted Trevor.

'But what if I do?'

'Then make the most of them,' smiled Trevor. 'Now scoot, you need rest if you're to be on top of your game.'

Then they'd hugged and Joe had set off, with, unbeknownst to him, someone watching his departure with suspicion: Alison, from her caravan.

'Are you with us, Joe?' asks Mr Schneider, interrupting Joe's reverie. '*Joe*, I said are you—ah, thank you; welcome back. Yes, so congratulations on making the final eight, everybody. Yes, yes, give yourselves a round of applause, why not.'

The teacher runs through their names:

'Okay, so – Owen Roberts, Joe Evans, Nigela Lewis, Lily Morgan, Clifford Griffiths, Megan Rees, Joanne Price, und Eric Collins – now we need to see which four of you have what it takes to make it through to the staged finals.'

The eight students look to each other.

'Which means another elimination round – und I'm sure you'll all be overjoyed to hear we'll be doing it . . . *right now*.'

Again, the students look to each other.

'Katie here has again very kindly offered to assist with the word box and timer.'

Mocking teacher's-pet noises are playfully batted away by Katie.

'Like I had a choice,' quips Mr Schneider.

'I can turn the cards as well if you like,' laughs Katie, indicating the nearness of the easel to the word box, both set up at the front of the classroom.

'Sure, why not,' agrees the teacher. 'Alright then, so . . . who would like to go first?'

Megan sticks her hand up.

'Yes, Megan, please come up.'

Five minutes later and the unspoken consensus in the room is that Megan blew it big time.

COLD, GYMNAST, WOLF and TRUST (she'd picked PERFUME, but under the Kensington rules they were playing to, had exchanged it for TRUST). Megan had incorporated all the words but her story failed to entertain, and more importantly, made little sense to anyone – including Megan who clearly lost her way at least twice.

'Okay – well done, Megan,' encourages the teacher. 'Give her a round of applause, please. Tricky words there.'

As her counterparts puzzle further on the confusing, disjointed and frankly, surreal narrative, a truculent Megan plods back to her chair and parks her defiant arse.

'Should of stuck with Perfume,' she mutters to herself.

(Yes, despite her on-going education, Megan actually says 'should of' and not 'should've' or 'should have'.)

'No, no, don't be discouraged, Megan, it was uh . . . a plucky attempt.'

Katie collects Megan's cards from the easel and files them back in the box.

'Right, who's next?' he asks. 'Yes, Eric.'

Eric lopes up to polite applause, quickly picks five random cards, and though he's not supposed to, takes a quick peek. Jeers and hoots of derision from the crowd and Eric's wishing he hadn't; not because he cheated but because he clearly isn't happy with his choices. So much so, that the teacher has to prise the cards from Eric's grip.

Mr Schneider hands the cards to Katie and the words are placed on the easel, backs out.

'Ready?' asks the teacher.

Eric sighs and nods. Katie turns the first four cards.

An apoplectic Eric stares at his selection, glances at the sea of faces staring back, then returns to the words.

REVENGE. CONFIDENCE. AIRTIGHT. FORGERY.

'Okay, do you want to play your substitute?' asks Mr Schneider after a brief wait.

'Yes.'

'Alright, which one do you wish to change?'

'Confidence.'

Katie removes CONFIDENCE and turns over . . .

TRIANGLE.

Groans and sympathetic sharp intakes of breath from the students abound.

'Okay, Eric; so, lots there to play around with – und your thinking times starts . . . now!'

Schneider nods his head at Katie and she immediately slaps the timer with gusto. She's never liked Eric much.

Eric stares blankly at the words then the class. He bites his lip and beads of sweat appear on his furrowed brow. An eternity later and in no time at all, the timer hits zero.

Eric's glassy eyes roam blankly across the faces staring his way. He's got nothing. Eric is empty. He's choked.

'Anything?' prompts the teacher kindly.

'Er . . .'

'Anything at all?'

Eric shakes his head.

'Never mind, it happens,' soothes Mr Schneider. 'The cards can be cruel.'

He waves a hand for Eric to return to his seat, which he does, and the cards are collected by the ever dutiful Katie.

'Okay, who's next?'

Owen stands. Joe stands too.

'Perhaps we should flip a coin,' suggests the teacher.

'No, let him go,' offers Owen. 'I can't wait to hear this. His last story was hilarious.' He turns to Joe: 'About a toilet, wasn't it?'

'You'll be laughing on the other side of your face in a minute,' asserts Joe.

'What does that even mean?' scoffs Owen.

'It's not my fault. I got *Lavatory*, remember.'

'Did you?' Owen shrugs. 'I just remember it was crap.'

Mutters from the students; they recognise trash talk when they hear it.

'Owen, sit down. Joe, this way please.'

As Joe moves to the word box, the room applauds politely. Katie steps back allowing Joe space to make his selection. Again, despite a snort of derision from Owen, Joe levitates both hands over the tops of the cards as if he were performing Reiki or warming hands over an open brazier.

There are mumbles and puzzled looks from the students not in Joe's English class: Nigela, Lily, Clifford, Megan, Joanne, Eric.

The teacher gestures for respectful quiet.

'What's he doing?' laughs Eric. 'A Jedi mind-trick?'

There are one or two sniggers at this, until Mr Schneider informs Eric that someone made that joke already.

Regardless, Joe picks four cards.

'And your substitute?'

'No need,' brags Joe handing the cards to Katie.

'Really?' checks Mr Schneider.

'You sure?' whispers Katie.

Joe is adamant.

'Well, okay then.' The teacher bids Katie proceed and with the cards placed on the easel, he readdresses Joe:

'Alright, Joe, ready to see your words?'

Joe appears more than ready: primed, pumped, keen to destroy Owen – but there's a knock on the door.

'Ah, yes, I nearly forgot,' declares Mr Schneider checking his watch. 'We have a few foreign exchange students joining us. Come in, please, do.'

Several foreign exchange students enter: older kids. These are quickly followed by three young adults, mid to late twenties.

'Plus some trainee teachers,' explains Mr Schneider.

Four older, smartly dressed adults also enter.

'Und a few members of the school governing body. Oh, und Mr Johnson, a Teaching Assessment Officer. But don't worry, kids, he's not here to test *you*,' laughs Mr Schneider. 'He's actually monitoring *me*.'

As if choreographed, the exchange students drift to the back as trainee teachers, assessment officer and governors shuffle down and around until they line the side walls.

'Right, I think that's everybody,' announces Mr Schneider after scanning the new faces.

Joe can't believe it; the classroom is now brimming. A show-off at heart, he *loves* an audience, but this: so many unexpected strangers, so many pairs of unforeseen eyes, all aimed at him, and in such a small space? Why, it's creepy and just plain weird.

'A very big Llanidloes High School welcome to each of you,' continues Mr Schneider. 'You've timed it perfectly as it happens because Joe here is just about to tell us a story. Aren't you, Joe? – Joe? – *Joe?*'

A ball of screwed up paper strikes Joe in the face.

'Hey, less of that,' chides Mr Schneider.

'Sorry,' apologises one of the governors, an ex-teacher. 'We used to be able to do that in my day.'

'Yes, well, not anymore, Mr Wells.'

Mr Wells nods sheepishly. 'Sorry, Joe. I'm looking forward to hearing your story.'

'Right, time to turn your cards, Joe. Here we go.'

On the teacher's nod, Katie turns the cards. They are:

ROCK. WHISTLE. FROTH. SIGNAL.

'Oh, and just so everyone knows,' explains Mr Schneider addressing the newcomers, 'we are playing *Kensington* rules.' He turns to Joe. 'So, would you like to change one? It's not too late.'

'No, I'm good,' confirms Joe assuredly. A wry smile has broken out on his face.

'Okay, then,' nods Mr Schneider. 'Rock, Whistle, Froth, Signal. Und your thinking time . . . starts now!'

He taps the air with a finger and Katie slaps the timer.

'Let's storytell!' booms Mr Schneider theatrically.

Well, check Joe out: he isn't at all fazed by Mr Schneider's cheesy new catchphrase (which he suspects was entirely for the unfamiliar audience's benefit), he is suddenly swaggering and cocksure; nodding his head rhythmically to a hushed beat, as if about to start a rap-battle. He is now Eminem. He's in the basement club: the Shelter, 8 Mile, downtown Detroit – in the 313 – and he's about to make the contemptible Owen kiss his white ass; metaphorically speaking, of course.

'Picture the scene,' showboats Joe confidently. 'An offshore lighthouse, far out to sea, late at night . . .'

'Threesomes, foursomes, I wouldn't put any number past her,' blathers Bonnie.

'Disgusting,' agrees Clara. 'I don't even like touching *Fred's* – let alone three or four of them.'

'I know. I'm the same.'

'And where does she put them all?'

After nodding along, having joined the conversation mid-flow – not necessarily agreeing but endlessly fascinated by the grapevine even if it is only hearsay – Alison is keen to know if the ladies have heard anything more on her current favourite scandal.

Bonnie and Clara's reports on Trevor are delivered with relish; the pair happy to share what they've heard – along with a few suppositions of their own. Alison is all ears until—

Ping! chimes the Gas & Graze door.

Paul passes the stalled rumour-mongers, approaches the cooler cabinet, takes out a large sausage roll then transports it – the roll, not the cabinet – to the counter.

Paul looks the women over . . . chattering magpies fallen quiet. Clara cleans her glasses (appears somehow startled without them); Bonnie is making strange wet noises with her tongue, as if she has an itch on the inside of her cheek; and Alison has relocated to the other side of the postcard rack, where she is less conspicuous but still within earshot.

No-one has spoken a word since Paul's entrance.

'What were you lot gossiping about then?' he challenges.

'Wouldn't you like to know,' mutters Bonnie to Clara.

'Not really,' sniffs Paul. 'I don't listen to idle tittle-tattle.'

'Not even when it's about people you know?' tests Clara.

'*Especially* when it—wait, what?'

Alison blows her nose. Bonnie folds her arms.

'Well, go on,' insists Paul. 'You have to tell me now.'

CHAPTER 14
Look Back in Anger

Joe is on his bed, quietly reading a book – until his dad storms in, all pink and flustered.

'Sit down,' rasps Paul. 'I want a word with you.'

'I am sitting down,' frowns Joe. 'And doesn't *anyone* knock around here?'

'What's all this I hear about you dressing up like a clown for some drunken old tramp in a caravan?'

'*What?!*' bleats Sally, fresh from a shower and exiting the bathroom. She crosses the landing, tightening her bath robe and enters the room. 'What's this?' she glowers.

Joe sighs, rolls his eyes. 'Where's Lucy? Maybe she'd like to—'

'*Well, my lad,*' presses Paul. '*Answer the question.*'

'It wasn't a clown,' Joe contends.

'Bleeding Romeo, I heard.'

'Where did you hear that?' questions Joe.

Paul turns to his wife. 'What's wrong with him, Sally?'

'There's nothing wrong with him,' insists Sally. 'Tell us it isn't true, Joe.'

'It was to help me with my storytelling,' Joe explains.

'Jesus,' hisses Sally.

'What?'

'So, who is he?' Sally wants to know. 'And why is this the first I'm hearing about it?'

'He's a hobo,' sneers Paul mockingly. 'A bloody vagrant.'

'Oh, Joe,' sighs Sally.

'He's not a hobo, he's a retired stage actor; he used to be famous – Trevor de la—'

'I don't give a flying fuck what he says his name is—'

'Paul!'

'You're never to see him again. Do you hear me?'

'Bollocks.'

'Hey, don't you dare talk to your father like that.'

'I've a good mind to go round there—'

'And he's coming to the competition.'

'No, he isn't!'

'I need him there!' barks Joe.

'Need him there,' scoffs Paul. 'You don't even know if you've made it to the finals.'

'Paul!'

'That's right, Dad, I don't.' Joe rises and squares up to his father. 'But at least Trevor believes in me. And he's a better man than you'll ever be!'

'Joe!'

'Oh, that's nice, isn't it? Have you heard this?'

'Yes, he gets more like you every day.'

'What's that supposed to mean?'

'Honestly, you're as bad as each other. I can't take much more of this fucking squabbling. That's right, I'm swearing now! You two have brought me to this!'

Sally storms out growling, almost in tears.

'Are you done?' asks Joe pointedly. 'Or is there something else you want to have a dig about?'

'Unbelievable.'

'*You're* unbelievable.'

'Maybe, Joe, but I'm a grown-up and I know about stuff that you clearly don't understand.'

'Pfft.'

Paul shakes his head. 'You know you might not be as smart as you like to think you are.'

'Smarter than you,' scoffs Joe. 'What have you ever done, apart from cut down trees and win a few stupid diving trophies?'

'We don't just cut down trees, defends Paul, 'we plant new ones and tend to the—'

'Whatever, Dad,' sneers Joe.

'And it wasn't only diving –'

'Just go, Dad.' Joe disengages and sits back on the bed.

'Now you listen to me.'

'No, I won't; I'm thirteen – I'm not a kid anymore. Now get out of my room and leave me alone!'

'Fine, I'm going, but mark my words, my lad,' warns Paul. 'I don't want you seeing this . . . weirdo again.'

'Get out!'

'Do you hear me? You're not to see him again.'

'Just go, will you!' yells Joe. He rolls over, drives his face into the pillow. 'Get ooοout!' he screeches, the words feather-muffled.

Paul exits and slams the door.

'Arghhhh!' screams Joe.

The next day at school and the notice-board is attracting attention. Mr Schneider has just pinned up the names of the four Storytell finalists: JOE EVANS, CLIFFORD GRIFFITHS, LILY MORGAN, and OWEN ROBERTS. Substitutes: COLIN DRISCOLL and NIGELA LEWIS.

Joe and Katie are at the front of a gradually swelling throng. After checking, they look to each other.

'You don't even know if you've made it,' mocks Joe, repeating his father's words.

Katie laughs. 'Well, you do now,' she tells him.

'Don't look so disappointed, Colin,' offers Mr Schneider. 'If a finalist can't make it for any reason, we'll be looking to you or Nigela to jump in.'

'Well, you won't be dropping out,' whispers Katie in Joe's ear. 'Your dad will have to eat his words.'

'Looking forward to it, Joe?' asks Mr Schneider.

'Yep.'

'Really?' asks Mr Schneider. 'So, try telling your face.'

'What?'

'You could look happier about it. Why the long face?'

Joe shrugs.

'Well, glückwünsche, anyway.'

'Right; thanks, sir.'

'Pretty sure I've heard that lighthouse story before, sir,' interjects Colin, a weasel-faced boy with a short neck. 'Isn't that, like, cheating?' He puts the stink-eye on Joe.

'Hmm.' Mr Schneider considers the question for a moment. 'Nothing in the rules about retelling an old story as far as I know, Colin; I mean, who could legislate against such a thing?'

'Sir?'

'Well, for starters, what are the chances of the exact words that you need coming up?' The teacher pauses. 'No,' he decides, 'I'm pretty sure that if such a thing were to happen it would not be a breach of Storytell regulations.'

But Colin continues to regard Joe with disdain.

'Now, if you'll excuse me, I have a class to prepare.' And with that Mr Schneider heads off up the corridor. 'See you on Saturday, Joe,' he calls back. 'Und again: glückwünsche!'

Lucy and Max are in Lucy's bedroom. Lucy is dressed in another of her own designs: a full on New Romantic fusion of Adam Ant, Madonna, and Boy George. Max's style today might best be described as Carnival Goth: tightly-buttoned, waist-clinching red corset/bodice; long black gloves; knee-length skirt; stockings and chunky boots; topped off with an ornate headpiece: a crow feather fascinator. Both girls are tipsy.

'No,' sighs Lucy, 'I'm not happy with it.'

'You look good,' Max assures her.

'Nah, I'm going to change.'

'Okay, but—'

'Right after we've had another drink,' giggles Lucy.

'Don't mind if I do,' titters Max accepting a beer Lucy removes from the secret stash under her bed.

The girls clink bottles and knock them back.

'Shit, who's that?' asks Max. 'Is that your dad?'

Lucy listens. 'Nope,' she concludes, 'just Joe.'

'How can you tell?'

'The sound of his feet,' explains Lucy. 'Hey, Joe!'

'What?' Joe calls from the bathroom.

'Come here,' calls Max.

After a moment, the door opens and Joe sticks his head inside.

'Close the door,' instructs Lucy, waving him in.

Joe steps inside and closes the door.

'We hear *congratz* are in order,' smiles Max.

'Yeah, well done, little bro; bet you're made up.'

Joe's smile falls somewhere between bashful and proud.

'Hey, we should do something to celebrate,' poses Max.

'Like what?' Lucy asks. 'I know,' she replies to her own question. 'He can have a beer.' An arm reaches under the bed. 'But tell Dad and I'll kill you myself.'

Joe accepts the offered bottle and takes a swig. 'Yeah, it's nice,' he coughs, one eye squinting.

Max laughs. 'Wait, is that your first ever beer?'

'No.'

The girls giggle and Joe feels slightly awkward but it's definitely worth it to be so close to Max, who looks amazing – and she seems to be studying him intently.

'Come here, sexy, let's do something with those eyes.'

'Max, no,' remonstrates Lucy.

'Relax, Luce; it's fine.'

'Yeah, Luce, relax; it's fine,' parrots Joe.

'Well, don't blame me if it kicks off again,' warns Lucy.

Max roots in her bag, comes up with eyeliner then approaches Joe. 'Now, hold still,' she tells him.

Max pulls down a lower lid, applies the liquid eyeliner pen to the eyelid's rim then paints the top edge and lower part of the lid. She then smears the black before moving onto Joe's other eye.

Lucy plays Eminem's 'Lose Yourself' on her phone.

'Oh, tune,' enthuses Joe, making a gun sign. 'Love this track.' He tries to nod his head to the beat but Max grips his jaw tightly.

'Look,' sings Lucy, 'if you had one shot, or one opportunity, to seize everything you ever wanted, in one moment, would you capture it, or just let it slip?'

Max steps back and admires her work.

'Awesome,' she beams.

Lucy whistles. 'Wow, check out Emo Joe.'

'Yeah?' asks Joe.

'*Yeah,*' confirms Max.

'But *you're* a *Goth*, not an Emo.'

'It has been said.'

'So, what's the difference?' asks Joe, disappointed not to be the same as Max.

'I thought you'd know that, Joe,' teases Lucy. 'What, with you being such a smarty pants.'

'Yeah, I meant to Google it but –'

'A Goth is when you hate the world.'

'And an Emo?'

'An Emo is when the world hates you.'

Joe thinks for a beat then quips: 'I'll drink to that.'

Max laughs, grabs Joe's jaw and plants a big kiss on his lips. Once Joe recovers from the shock, uproots himself, so to speak, he raises his bottle; as do the girls – then all three down another mouthful.

'Now, what else can we do?' grins Max mischievously.

Joe smiles and wonders what she has in mind.

Meanwhile, in the back garden, Paul is trying hard to sound down with the kids: Owen, Gary, and Melvin. He's invited them over for a little manly sports practice with Joe. Paul's even donned a Welsh rugby shirt for the occasion. The lads haven't bothered.

Owen, Gary, and Melvin couldn't believe their luck: parental permission to rough up a pompous classmate? They'd never had the chance before; Joe always seemed to have some lame excuse or other for escaping rugby lessons: headache, stomach cramps, someone stole my shorts.

'Props for coming over, guys,' fizzes Paul. 'Joe's really stoked about getting back into the old rough and tumble. You can dig that, right?'

The boys seem confused but Paul carries on regardless.

'Yeah, he's been bugging me for like forever to fix up a heavy training session with his mates; lots of tackling and shit, yeah?'

Paul laughs awkwardly.

The boys appear surprised to be called 'mates'.

'Nice one,' nods Paul enthusiastically.

Melvin pats the rugby ball under his arm, impatient to crack on with the sanctioned bloodshed.

Owen spreads his hands: gestures an impatient *Are we doing this or what?*

Gary stretches and yawns.

'Cool, no probs; you kick on with your warm ups – and I'll go grab the man, yeah? Sweet.'

Paul points towards the back door, grins broadly then departs with an unnatural clipped gait. He appears to have turned into Alan Partridge.

The boys frown at each other. As if they have any intention of doing warm ups. And Mr Evans is just as weird as his creepy kid!

'Milk bottles?' echoes Lucy. 'What a waste of time. Boys are so silly. How long ago was that?'

'I told you,' sighs Joe, 'when he was a boy, so fifty or sixty years ago.'

'Cool,' grins Max. 'I love the Fifties and Sixties.'

'Me too,' enthuses Joe, 'all those old black and white films and cool songs and . . . films and that.'

Lucy shakes her head. Her brother's crush on Max is too painful to watch.

'So, tell us more about Trevor,' urges Max.

'He's nice,' confides Joe. 'Not like Dad. He's helped me with my stories. We take turns. Before his milk bottle story I did one about a robot; just made it up on the spot – it was awesome.'

'Tell us,' encourages Max.

'What?'

'Yeah, tell it now,' urges Lucy.

'Er . . .'

'Unless you're bullshitting,' states Lucy matter-of-factly.

Joe's stern look to Lucy is emphasized by the eyeliner.

Lucy laughs. 'Look at him being all stern,' she teases.

'No, make up a *new* one,' decides Max. 'Right now.'

'About what?'

'I dunno . . . about your outfit.'

'Yeah,' echoes Lucy. 'Do that.'

Perhaps this would be a good time to point out Joe's current accoutrements and paraphernalia; you see, while you were away, the girls dressed him in what might best be described as Steampunk meets Victorian Gothic: black buttoned waistcoat over a white shirt with rolled-up sleeves; crossed-belts and buckles; zips and chains and bits of brass all over the place; dark military style greatcoat; vampiric platform boots with skull designs; bold rings on his fingers – oh, and a dandy cane! (Yes, that's right; Lucy's wardrobe is a set designer's dream, a veritable treasure trove of props and garb.)

Joe considers his costume. 'So . . .' he dithers.

'Who are you?' prompts Max. 'What do you do?'

'Well,' Joe starts, 'I'm Edward Jacob Garrett, obviously, and I work as a vampire and zombie hunter.'

'Who for?' giggles Max.

'For the London Metropolitan Anti-Undead Force of course.'

'Wait,' interjects Lucy. 'I have the perfect finishing touch.'

A stunted top-hat appears from Lucy's wardrobe and is planted on Joe's head. The hat has spiky eye-goggles wrapped around it, crow feathers and an Ace of Spades card in the hatband; and as a finishing flourish, a brass key and spent bullet cartridge stuck to the brim.

'My apologies, Edward,' smiles Lucy, 'do pray, continue.'

'Well, it all started when I first joined the L.M.U.A.F. as a trainee constable back in 1888—'

Tat-tat-tat-tat: a knock on the door.

'Lucy,' asks Paul's voice. 'Is Joe in there with you?'

Joe shakes his head and waves his hands.

'No,' states Lucy.

But Paul enters anyway.

'I know when you're lying, Lucy,' he tells her.

'Pfft,' scoffs Lucy.

Paul sniffs the air.

'Have you been drinking?' he wants to know.

'No.'

'I knew it.' Paul points at Joe. 'And what the hell is that!'

'What? This?' Max puts an arm around Joe. 'Lots of boys wear make-up these days,' she assures him.

'Joe's discovering his Emo side,' giggles Lucy.

'He bloody isn't. I forbid it.'

'Forbid it,' snorts Joe. 'Yeah, right, Dad.'

Paul's eyes narrow. 'Have you been drinking as well?'

'What if I have? There's no law against it, is there?'

'I think kids *can* drink at home,' offers Max. 'Unless they're under five.'

'What?' Paul barks. 'That can't be true.'

'Think it is,' nods Lucy.

'Well, not in my house they can't,' rules Paul.

He spots the near empty beer bottle Joe's hiding behind his back and snatches it away with unnecessary gusto.

'Partypooper,' hiccups Joe.

183

'And how about tidying your room, Lucy? This place looks like a bombsite. Seriously, how do you find *anything* in this mess?'

Lucy's room is basically a sewing machine surrounded by an ocean of clothing, raw material, and accessories; there's a bed under there somewhere, and by the door: a dressing table, its mirror currently edged in pictures relating to fashions from various Eastern cultures; Algerian belly-dancer, Manchu sing-song girl, Arabian Bedouin, Iranian folk dancer, etc.

Lucy is unwavering. 'I like it like this.'

'And last but not least,' continues Paul, 'why is he dressed like some kind of weird nun?'

'We're just having a laugh, Mr Evans,' Max assures Paul.

'Yeah, lighten up, Pop,' adds Lucy. 'You look like you're about to combust.'

'Pop!' laughs Joe. The girls laugh too.

'Lighten up?!' carps Paul. 'Now listen to me all of you –'

But Max grabs a two-horned naval hat (the bicorne type favoured by the French upstart, Napoleon Bonaparte) and plonks it down hard on Paul's head.

'Watch the hair,' grumbles Paul.

Max adjusts the hat, tilts it to a jauntier angle.

'I said watch the hair,' gripes Paul.

'Oh yes, that's just the job,' slurs Max. She reverses to admire the costumed menfolk but bumps into Lucy and the pair fall backwards onto the bed, giggling inanely.

'Right, come here, you!'

Paul grabs Joe and drags him out.

'I'll deal with you later,' he informs Lucy over a shoulder.

'No, I forbid it,' laughs Max.

'No, *I* forbid it,' titters Lucy.

'No, *I* forbid it,' chortles Max.

'No, *I* forbid it,' guffaws Lucy.

Back at the caravan, Trevor leafs through Joe's Snowman album. Joe had accidentally left it behind on his last visit.

Mr Zero. Mr Nippy. Mrs Sparkles. Mr Freezy. Noel. Monsieur Shivers. Mr Melt. Mr Abominable. Mr Eight. Little Miss Blizzard. Brrrronwen.

Trevor coughs strenuously, finishes his sherry then turns to the last *inscribed* page. At the top, in Joe's handwriting, it says: Christmas 2012. Other than its heading the page is empty; no photo.

The previous page has a snap of Joe and his grandfather with the last recorded snowman, Mr Frosty. Underneath, Joe has written: Me (12), Gramps, and Mr Frosty.

Trevor touches the empty page thoughtfully, the page where the photo of Mr Wonky should be. Then he looks to his own collection, also just one short of completion.

Paul leads Joe by the arm, out through the kitchen door and into the back garden.

'Right, let's play some rugby!' rasps Paul angrily.

Owen, Gary and Melvin, currently attempting to force the padlock on the shed door, quickly and surreptitiously relocate to the middle of the lawn where they join the incoming Paul and Edward Jacob Garrett.

'Check out the gear,' laughs Gary. 'Who are you meant to be: Dracula's sister?'

'No.'

'Are you drunk?' asks Melvin.

'Bit tipsy maybe.'

'Are you wearing make-up?' questions Owen.

'Little bit.'

'Look, it doesn't matter,' bristles Paul. 'None of this, whatever *this* is, matters. We're here for sports practice. You, Marvin –'

'Melvin.'

'I want you to run with the ball, and Joe, I want you to tackle him, *hard.*'

'What?'

'Tackle him.'

'I'm not doing that.'

'Oh, this should be *fun*,' froths Gary tossing the ball to Melvin.

'Yes, you are,' insists Paul. Just grab him by the knees as he runs past and—'

'Paul!' yells an angry voice. It's Sally at the kitchen door. She glares at Paul. 'What the hell are you doing?!'

'Sports practice.'

'*Sports practice?* Since when! And why's he dressed like that?'

'Hey, it was Joe's idea.'

'Actually, it was Max's,' grins Joe.

'So, if he wants to dress funny . . .'

'If he wants to dress funny, what: you have to embarrass him in front of this lot?'

'He needs toughening up, Sally.'

'No, he doesn't,' fumes Sally. 'Don't talk stupid.'

'Toughening up, that's what he needs. Not all this childish sulking and moping around.'

'I wasn't moping,' retorts Joe. 'And actually,' he breaks from Paul's grip, 'I was having *fun* until you came along.' And with that

185

he heads for the house – but drunkenly trips on his cane, stumbles, and lands face down on the grass.

This causes the boys to laugh hysterically.

'Face plant,' jeers Gary.

'Go on, you lot, clear off,' warns Sally.

'Hey, come on, Sal; don't talk to his friends like that.'

'*Friends?* Shows what you know. This lot aren't his friends. Not even close. They can't *stand* Joe. Do you hear what I'm saying? They hate our son.'

'Hate's a bit strong, isn't it?' Paul strides over to Joe. 'Come on, Joe, up.'

Joe rises onto all fours then vomits on Paul's shoes.

'Jesus!' gripes Paul. 'Now look,' he informs Sally.

'Oh, just get in the house the pair of you!'

'Right!' barks Paul and he cranes to offer his prostrate son a hand. 'Come on, lad, let's be having you.'

'Pussy-whipped or what?' Owen asks his mates.

'Oi, you, less of that,' bleats Paul.

'Dunno who's the biggest bitch,' laughs Gary, 'him or Joe.'

'Hey!' barks Paul.

'I thought I told you lot to clear off,' squawks Sally.

She grabs the broom, which happens to be leaning against the back wall, and charges.

'Go on, piss off!' she shrieks.

Paul and Joe watch as the boys flee through the back gate. When Sally returns Paul hooks a hand under one of his son's elbows but Joe shakes the arm free from his dad's grasp with a 'Leave me alone!' He picks himself up and heads inside, unsteadily.

'What's *wrong* with him, Sal?' asks Paul.

Sally glares at her husband.

'*You*, that's what wrong with him.'

'What do you mean?'

Sally rolls her eyes. 'Oh, just piss off, Paul.'

Then she heads inside leaving Paul to wonder how any of this is *his* fault.

The burger van pulls into an empty lay-by on a quiet road just outside Rhayader and slows to a stop. The driver's door opens and a skinny Cairn Terrier is forcibly ejected onto the sloping grassy verge. After a scramble of legs the dog turns and snarls.

'Shut it, you,' warns Liam. 'Just be glad I didn't wring your neck or tie you in a sack and throw you in The Severn.'

The terrier growls disapproval then yaps several times.

'Yeah, yeah, noisy little shit,' mocks Liam lighting a cigarette. 'Hey,' he smirks after puffing a cloud of smoke, 'sorry I couldn't drop you nearer to where Kelly found your sorry little arse but if it helps, Llani is back that way.' Liam aims a thumb up the road. 'Only about twelve miles,' he grins. 'See ya!'

And he drives away, leaving the terrier to fend for itself.

Alone in the lay-by, not a vehicle in sight, the dog looks each way, up and down the leafy country road, as if gaining his bearings and wondering which direction to take.

Edward Jacob Garrett bashes his pillow with the cane.

Hmm, it is angry you are.

'You – don't – say,' intones Joe to the beat of the cane. 'What gave it away?'

And a little drunk too, I think, notes Yoda. *Hmm, yes?*

'What's wrong with him, Sal?' mocks Joe. 'Oh, nothing a little sports practice won't put right. With his *friends. Friends!* Pah!'

Joe strikes his Snowman quilt with great force.

Yes, good this is, use that anger.

Joe turns to face Yoda, beating on hold for the moment.

'I thought you said *anger* leads to the dark side?'

No, I said fear *is the path to the dark side*, insists Yoda.

'But fear leads to anger?'

Yes, frowns Yoda. *Confusing, it is.*

'Thanks,' slurs Joe. 'Great help.'

Joe returns to caning the bedding and it goes on for a while. Finally, he slumps onto his bed, exhausted.

Finished, have you? asks Yoda. *Good.* And he tosses the snowman snow-globe to Joe.

'What's this for?'

Me want to see.

'See what?'

You do the disappearing trick.

'But why? You saw me. I did it in Trevor's caravan. You were there.'

Again do it, instructs Yoda. *This time on your own.*

Joe narrows his eyes. 'On my own?'

If you can, challenges Yoda. *Hmm?*

'Wait,' blinks Joe. 'Are you saying—? You don't think—?'

Yoda raises quizzical eyebrows.

'So, what – *you* don't believe in me now?'

Not a question of what I do not *believe, it is, hmm? More a question of what I do— No, wait, got that wrong, I have. It is a question of what* you *believe.*

'Huh?'

Oh, just shut up and do it.

'Okay – okay – good,' nods Joe prickled. 'Let's do this!'

Staring intensely at Yoda, he shakes the little globe until the snow swirls around the resident snowman – then he cups his hands around it.

Yoda looks on.

Brow furrowed, Joe scrunches his eyes and focuses all his energy, all his thoughts, concentrating hard . . .

Yoda, pursed lips and squinting, nods, willing Joe on.

A silent moment passes then Joe's eyes blink open and he opens his cupped hands, slowly, to reveal: the small snow-globe and its trapped snowman amidst the slowly settling snowstorm.

Yoda sighs, his face registering disappointment.

Frustrated, cheeks aflame, Joe growls to himself.

And here's Paul – again, entering without knocking.

Not moving his head, Joe looks up; the rolled irises almost lost under narrowing lids; the whites of his eyes on show – the whites all the whiter for the dark of the surrounding eyeliner. He exhales deeply through his nose but remains menacingly still.

'Joe, listen –'

'Get out,' states Joe flatly.

'Okay, I'm going, but one thing –'

'What?'

'Think on this: if Trevor really can make things appear from nowhere, how come he hasn't got that robot? – The missing one.'

'How do you know about that?' asks Joe sharply.

'Lucy told me.'

'When?'

'Does it matter? How come he hasn't got it? Why hasn't he just made it appear?'

Joe pauses, thinks; the question may have hit home.

'See, I'm right, aren't I? Go on, tell me I'm wrong.'

'Leave,' insists Joe. 'Leave now.'

'Okay but remember what I said: I don't want you seeing this Trevor again. Do you hear me?'

'Why can't you leave me alone?' yells Joe.

'Right, I'm going, but not because you told me to, but because I've said what I came to say.'

'Just get out, will you! Go!'

Paul nods, gestures *I've said what I came to say,* then leaves, closing the door quietly behind him.

Joe studies the snow-globe for a long beat – then throws it at the door.

CHAPTER 15
And it's a Hard Rain

Edward Jacob Garrett has escaped to the serene calm of the shed. He sits in quiet contemplation by his granddad's workbench, elbows on knees, chin on palms, gazing longingly at Wilf's possessions – the framed photo, flickering candles and glinting Storytell trophies – still arranged on the shrine-like trunk.

To Joe's left side, sits Wilf's shimmering hologram, blue and semi-transparent. To Joe's right, backpack Yoda, using the Force to levitate Joe's caravan snow-globe.

Wilf leans back and coughs to gain Yoda's attention.

Nothing.

A louder cough and the snow-globe falls to the ground. Scowling, Yoda swivels to face Wilf. They regard each other over Joe's arched back. Wilf aims a nod at Joe.

So, what's up with him now? Wilf asks.

Yoda's eyes roll. *Hmm, unsure I am; his father, I think.*

Oh dear, what's he been up to now?

Acting like a dick.

No change there then, laughs Wilf.

Not pleased about the guy-liner I think he was, hmm?

Well, I suppose it is a bit – girly, whispers Wilf.

Kids today, tuts Yoda quietly.

'I can hear you both you know,' chides Joe.

But I was just the same when I was a boy, admits Wilf.

You wore mascara?

No, I mean I was confused.

Always confused he is, sighs Yoda. *Whatever it is that troubles him*, he advises, *go with his instinct, he should.*

Yes, agrees Wilf, *always go with your gut.*

'My gut's confused,' answers Joe.

After a long silent beat, Yoda closes his eyes, stretches out a hand, and returns to levitating the snow-globe. Wilf turns toward the window and the sound of distant, rumbling thunder.

On the horizon, lightning flashes illuminate the hills.

A storm approaches, hmm?

Wilf nods, and in less than a minute the garden darkens as it falls under the rolling shadow of a large black cloud.

The snow-globe floats irritatingly close to Joe's face.

'Could you not do that?' rasps Joe.

He attempts to swipe the globe from Yoda's control but the Jedi master is too quick: he uses the Force to throw it, over Joe's head, to Wilf, who catches it and tosses it straight back. Joe turns this way and that, endeavouring to take possession of the globe. The game of piggy-in-the-middle continues for several passes; until Wilf misses his catch and the snow-globe clatters off the dusty bike resting against the shed wall. There follows a silent pause in which Joe stares long and hard at the Chopper.

Is he thinking what I think he's thinking? Wilf asks.

I think so, nods Yoda. *But see Trevor again, his father has warned he cannot.*

Oh well, better not, then, winks Wilf.

Besides, upon us the storm is, hmm?

Yoda gazes skyward and bang on cue, thunder claps overhead.

Yes, it's a terrible idea, agrees Wilf.

Soaked, he'd be, Yoda concurs.

It's a long way.

Hmm, a long way most certainly it is.

'Not if I took the short-cut,' counters Joe.

As Joe continues to stare at the Chopper, Wilf and Yoda furtively bump fists behind his back.

Joe pushes the Chopper uphill, along the uneven, winding track that will, when he eventually reaches the top, cross over the lower knuckle of Finger Hill.

Hmm, this rain I do not like, blinks a wet-faced Yoda.

'Almost at the top,' puffs Joe ploughing on, the steampunk outfit now soaked from the driving rain.

So much for the short-cut, gripes Yoda.

'You think we'd be drier if I'd ridden *around* the hill?'

Ridden? Yoda echoes. *Not yet have I seen you ride.*

'Quiet, you; I can't ride until I get to the top.'

Joe pushes on.

Over on Bryn Crow, northwest of here, a tractor driven by Don's son, lights blinking in the rain, works up and down the hill's south-eastern slope, cutting back the bracken one swath at a time.

Upon the Finger's upper knuckle, the scarecrow leans at a keen angle, slanted and ruffled by a sweep of wind; the better it seems to observe the Land Rover.

Don's muddy boots disturb the empty beer bottles and withered flowers in the footwell; a toe nudges, a heel drags, both actions unseen – for the farmer's mind is on Alison, who he watches through the telescope as his free callused hand gropes the meat and potatoes inside his unzipped grubby trousers. Eighties and still hornier than a ram in mating season; it would be impressive if it wasn't so sad.

As for the unsuspecting Alison, she is behind the large, rain-dappled rear window of her caravan, gazing over at the closed curtains of Liam's caravan.

Had Don not been glued to the telescope and so intent on self-gratification, he might have caught sight of a young lad riding past, unsteadily, in the rear-view mirror.

Jed noticed the boy, for he preferred to look away when his master was fiddling with himself.

Despite Joel's relentless nagging, Liam is yet to kill Kelly.

Remember our deal, Liam! reminds Joel's skull.

'Jesus, I haven't forgotten about our fucking deal,' rasps Liam.

On the sofa, bound and gagged; alive but abjectly dejected and utterly defeated, Kelly has grown used to her captor talking to himself. Or rather: conversing with the skull as he paces round the caravan. Their bickering might be weirdly entertaining if it wasn't so full-on creepy and downright terrifying.

As far as Kelly can tell, from what she's gleaned from their 'chats', now that she's moved out of full-on panic mode and actually started to listen, is this: the skull belonged to Joel, Liam's dead brother, and Liam had promised, or entered into some agreement, that he would kill a non grown-up, and she was one. She's also gleaned that her captor is, or believes himself to be, the Head Honcho, who she has certainly heard about, mostly from memes on Facebook – mainly photo-shopped, copycat signs that purported to be *amusing*. There really were some sick puppies out there. With all that in mind, her only hope now seems to rest on Liam being totally mad, rather than the actual serial killer. Kelly had heard the phrase *Between a rock and a hard place* in films, and though it understandably didn't spring to mind here, under these circumstances, the saying, albeit painfully insufficient, certainly applied in this case.

'Because it's difficult, Joel, alright?! I've got to know her. She's like – a pet,' explains Liam. 'Remember how we felt about Jasper.'

Yes; and what happened to Jasper? Uncle Gino shot him. Said he was lame.

'Jasper was our dog,' Liam tells Kelly.

Kelly nods, hoping to appear understanding; this has been her plan for a while now – an attempt to make Liam like her. So he wouldn't kill her. It had worked so far.

Just think of her as a lame dog.

'But she's not a lame dog! She's a kid!'
Look! We need her to hit one hundred.
'Argh!' Liam stalks the caravan clutching his head.
Kelly's wide eyes watch him closely.
And don't forget, encourages Joel, *I've promised to shut up about the whole killing-a-kid thing once it's done.*
Liam stares at the skull.
That was *the deal.*
'Right!' Liam snatches the hammer from the table. 'I'm sorry,' he splutters approaching Kelly, who squirms and contracts until there's a gentle knock at the door.
Christ, who the fuck is that?!
'How the hell do I know?'
'Hello?' calls a soft female voice.
'Who is it?'
'*Alison.* Come on, don't pretend you don't know.'
'Shit, it's her from over the way.'
Right, well, you're gonna have to open it.
'Why?'
She obviously knows you're in.
'How? The curtains are closed.'
Joel indicates the TV – though God knows how – a nature documentary: a piece on female insects eating their mates: black widow spider, praying mantis, redback spider . . .
And *you asked 'Who is it?' you daft—*
'Yoo-hoo, Liam!'
Another knock, a little louder now.
'Mumhfhh!' cries Kelly, triggered into action at last. 'Mumhfhh!'
For fuck's sake keep her quiet, hisses Joel's skull.
'Listen, you have to shut up or –'
Liam raises the hammer high above his shoulder.
Kelly nods frantically, already fallen silent.
'I know you're in there,' croons Alison.
Jesus, you couldn't make this shit up. Joel's skull seems to think a moment. *Right, you're gonna have to let her in.*
'What?!'
Well, obviously move this one first; unless you're planning on killing both of them. Hey! Joel's eyes would surely light up if he had any. *One hundred and one!*
'No, I'm not killing Alison; she's got two kids over there.'
'Come on, Liam,' knocks Alison. 'I know you want me.'
'Just a minute!'
Liam lowers the hammer and looks around.

192

Put her in the wardrobe! Joel urges.

Liam nods and finally springs into action. He picks up Kelly and carries her into the bedroom, his captive whimpering softly.

'Leee-am,' sings Alison. 'Let me in or I'll huff and I'll puff.'

A break in the rain and Joe has almost reached the east side of Finger Hill, where the path takes a decided downturn before zigzagging its way to the caravan park.

Good, good, getting the hang of it now you are.

'Oh thanks,' smiles Joe over a shoulder.

And it's here, distracted, just before the descent, that Joe comes a cropper. He'd been unsteady most of the way but now he actually falls off – and in doing so, scrapes his knee, bangs an elbow and muddies Yoda's face. Not so much a biking 'accident' as a simple lack of riding proficiency and taking your eye off the proverbial ball.

Never mind, only one fall have we suffered, encourages Yoda. *A lot worse could it have been.*

Yes, Joe's sure he'll pick it up soon enough; the wobbles and sudden inadvertent changes in direction had decreased greatly since he'd almost ridden into that fallen alder branch and nearly gone arse over tit.

To pushing the bike though, I suggest you return for the descent. Hmmmmm?

Hauling himself up, Joe sleeves the mud from his trousers then picks up the bike – and that's when he notices an object, illuminated by the moon, over on a low wall that edges one side of this part of the path.

Wheeling the bike closer Joe realises it's a small, dead robin. He leans the bike against the wall, gathers the bird, damp with rain, cups it in his hands and studies it.

Yoda nods. *Death is a natural part of life,* he advises. *Rejoice for those around you who transform into the Force.*

'I know but it's still sad,' sighs Joe stroking the bird's red chest gently with a fingertip.

Mourn them do not.

'Whoa, whoa.'

Miss them do not.

'Oh come on, I've got to stop you there.'

Attachment leads to jealousy.

'Does it, though?' contends Joe. 'I'm not sure I can agree with you there.'

The shadow of greed, that is.

'No, that's nonsense.'

Yoda pauses, thinks a moment. *Hmm, maybe you're right.*

'But what if we could . . .' Joe cups his hands around the robin and slowly raises the bird aloft, offers it to the heavens.

Yoda's eyes narrow. *Are you really trying to—?*

'Shush.' Joe is concentrating hard. He chants, low and quiet; intones what sounds like an incantation.

Believe this I do not, sighs Yoda disapprovingly. *Attempting to use the Force to—*

'I said, shut it!' barks Joe.

Hmm, crude the boy is.

Wasn't I just the same as a boy? asks Wilf's ethereal voice.

'Quiet, both of you – please!'

Yoda pulls a face. Wilf fails to speak again.

And now Joe chants a little louder, reciting voodoo-esque mumbo-jumbo as a witch-doctor or faith-healer might. Then he slowly opens his hands to reveal . . . a dead, wet robin.

There's a crack in the sky and here comes the rain again.

Saddened, Joe climbs over the wall and gently places the robin on a forked branch in a small tree. He stares sadly at the bird for a moment, disappointed and a not little angry. Then he scrambles back over the wall, remounts his bike, takes a deep breath and rides on, unevenly, to a backdrop of blackening sky and thunder that now sounds almost directly overhead.

After upping the television volume Liam opens the door to his visitor; who looks somehow different – perhaps it's the make-up and exceedingly tight jeans.

'Hi, sorry.' Liam leans against the door frame in a show of casual nonchalance. 'I didn't hear you the first time you knocked.'

'Then how do you know I did?' teases Alison.

'Huh?'

Fit but dim, that's fine, thinks Alison. 'Ignore me, I'm just teasing,' she winks. 'Sorry, do you have company?' She tries to peer around the obstruction that is Liam's considerable frame.

'No, it's just the telly. Sorry, it's a bit loud.'

'Well, that's why I came over; to complain about the noise.'

'Really?'

'No, silly,' smiles Alison. She pokes Liam's firm chest.

'Ah.' In the periphery of his lower vision, Liam catches sight of a raindrop rolling down Alison's cleavage. She's wearing a low-cut top that's starting to steam.

As Trevor pushes a bright green cigarette into the end of his cigarette-holder, he notices Becki and Chloe peering at him from their bedroom window. They're in their pyjamas, the closed curtains draped around their heads and shoulders.

The old man wiggles his fingers at them. One waves back, the other playfully sticks out her tongue.

Trevor holds up a long match and draws their attention to it. Then he closes his eyes and concentrates.

Becki and Chloe nudge each other.

Then the match ignites and the girls' mouths fall open.

'So . . . ?' prompts Liam, still blocking the doorway to his caravan.

'So, I came to ask you over for a drink,' blinks Alison. 'I'd let you invite me in there,' she grins, opening her umbrella as the rain suddenly increases, 'but the kids are in bed.' She sticks out her bottom lip playfully. 'And I can't leave them alone.'

'Actually,' he yawns, 'I was just about to hit the—'

The propositions and deferments are interrupted by a noise – a bump or thump – coming from the direction of the bedroom.

'What was that?' asks Alison.

'The TV, it does that sometimes. But on second thoughts, I'd love to come over for a drink. Let me just . . .' Liam briefly aims the remote at the TV then discards it and steps out onto the porch to join Alison.

'Silly, you turned it *up*, not *down*. It's louder now.'

'Make burglars think I'm in,' Liam tells her. He closes the door. 'You can never be too careful.'

'Oh, hun,' smiles Alison, 'there's no crime round here.'

She squeezes his arm as if to reassure him, an excuse to grope his considerable bicep.

'Come on,' urges Liam. He hooks an arm, leads the way.

'Ooo, masterful,' twinkles Alison. 'I like that.'

'We don't want to get soaked, do we?'

'Speak for yourself,' mutters Alison under her breath.

From up on Finger Hill, Don watches Alison (what he can see of her under the umbrella) and some bloke he doesn't recognise, scurrying hand in hand across the caravan park. The man had been leading the way but now *she* is, as if in fun, her back to the caravan, playfully dragging her catch.

The farmer snaps the telescope shut, curses a string of derogatory insults, and storms out of the Land Rover; he slams his door, which again fails to close properly, hurls the telescope into the back then rummages amongst the old tools, fence posts and rolls of wire.

Back inside, Jed continues to stare blankly through the rain-mottled windscreen; if it hadn't been for failing eyesight and cataracts the old dog might have spotted a boy on a bike, down amongst the caravans.

'What happened to you, Paul?' asks Sally, hands on hips. 'You used to play with Joe all the time. Now he's lucky if he gets a few minutes here and there.'

Paul is trying to watch a television documentary – a praying mantis enjoying a little one-way post-coital cannibalism with her now headless mate – but Sally is standing in the way.

'I've told you all this before but nothing changes, does it?' she persists. 'It goes in one ear and out the other.'

Paul throws her a scowl.

'Go on, lose your temper again.'

'I'm not going to lose my temper,' sighs Paul.

'Aren't you?'

'No!' Paul assures her. 'Have you finished?'

'No, I haven't, actually,' continues Sally. 'You knew he wanted a Mountain bike. What did you get him? A bloody Chopper.'

'That's a classic bike, that is.'

'It's not what Joe wanted,' fumes Sally. 'Same with the dog: you know he wants one but what do you do: buy a hamster. A fucking hamster! How's he meant to walk that?'

'I got a ball for it,' mutters Paul.

'What?' Sally frowns. 'Speak up.'

'I said, he doesn't have to – I got a ball for it.'

'But he *wants* to walk it,' rasps Sally.

Paul sighs.

'Jesus, you just don't get it, do you?'

Paul makes no reply.

'And what's with the so-called rugby training? You know he hates contact sports. Jesus, just kick a football around with him. He loves that. Or do you not remember?'

'Look—!'

'How do you think it makes poor Joe feel, eh?'

'Can I get a word in?'

'Sick of it, I am, sick of it. *He's your son, Paul!*'

'I'm sorry, okay? I'll sort it.'

'Don't tell *me*.'

Paul peers around Sally but she grabs the remote, turns the TV off, and then stares at him, silent and unblinking.

196

Jed stares wide-eyed at Don in the Land Rover. The farmer is back in his seat, holding a single-barrel shotgun under his chin, arm reaching down and finger on the trigger.

The dog cocks his head.

'Well, don't look then,' sniffs Don.

There's a long silence inside the vehicle; just rain beating on the outside as Don builds the courage to pull the trigger.

A flash of lightening and Jed barks.

'Hell's bells,' carps Don. 'Don't do that!'

Jed barks again.

'What?' huffs Don impatiently.

He lifts his chin off the barrel, takes his finger off the trigger. 'What is it?'

A peal of thunder rings out and Jed whimpers.

Don sighs; he knows it's not the tempestuous weather – the dog's seen countless storms.

'Want me to do you first, old fella?' asks Don.

Jed grumbles a throaty growl.

'Fine, so shut up, then.'

Don settles his chin back on the gun barrel then reaches down and positions his finger on the trigger. Time passes with Don frozen in place, Jed looking on, and the rain drumming incessantly on the Land Rover's bodywork and glass.

'Turn round,' orders Don. 'I can't do it if you're watching.'

Jed barks and barks again.

'Hell's teeth,' gripes Don.

But Jed is now scratching at the glove-box.

'Now what?' the farmer sighs.

Jed barks continuously – until Don catches on:

'Okay, okay, I'll call someone.'

Don leans the shotgun against his door, reaches into the glove-box, and pulls out the mobile phone. 'I don't even know how to use this stupid thing.' But after a moment he locates the button that turns on the phone and it jingles into life.

'So, who am I calling?'

Jed barks again.

'No, I'm not calling the family; they've enough to worry about.'

Jed whimpers.

'I said No,' huffs Don. 'Any other suggestions?'

Jed growls, low and gruff.

'Fine,' the farmer sighs. He prods tentatively at the screen, eyeballs the dog and asks: 'What's the number?'

197

The door to Trevor's caravan bursts open: Joe stands in the doorway, a cinematic curtain of slanting rain for a backdrop.

'My dad was right about you!' he announces to the drumbeat of rain pelting the roof.

'That's quite an entrance, Joe,' acknowledges Trevor.

Joe breathes hard, eyeliner-smudged eyes glaring intently, a mucky-faced Yoda glowering in unison over Joe's shoulder.

'And how did you get my photo album?' Joe demands to know after spotting the album on the table before Trevor.

'You left it behind. Don't worry, it's been quite safe.'

Left it behind, sniffs Yoda. *A likely story, that is, hmm?*

'Well, don't stand on ceremony, dear boy, come in, do.'

Joe has turned stony silent but he steps inside.

'Would you like to sit?'

Sit, do not, advises Yoda. *A trap it might be, hmm?*

Ignoring Trevor's offer, Joe swings his attention to the robot cabinet. This makes the old man smile to himself.

'You want to know why I don't just make him appear,' he suggests. 'And complete my collection – correct?'

Although Joe is surprised by this insight it doesn't appear to lighten his mood.

Trevor holds out a fist.

'What's that?'

'Come, and I'll show you,' smiles Trevor.

'What is it?' grunts Joe.

Careful now, cautions Yoda. *Watch him.*

Dubious, Joe edges over.

Trevor opens his hand: a silk handkerchief.

'Pfft,' puffs Joe. 'What's that for?'

'For your eyes,' indicates Trevor. 'Your make-up's run.'

Joe plucks away the hankie and wipes above his cheeks.

'Look, sit down,' requests Trevor gently. 'Tell me what happened, and I'll explain about the missing robot. Yes?'

Joe slings the backpack onto the seat opposite Trevor and slumps in beside it.

Keep yourself between Trevor and the door, you must, warns Yoda, eyes on the old man.

Trevor leans forward, arms on the table.

'Time to reveal all,' he smiles.

'Bit dramatic,' sniffs Joe.

'Says you,' retorts Trevor.

CHAPTER 16
Where Are We Now?

Don is on the phone. It's ringing.

'See, there's no one there,' he tells a staring Jed. 'Oh, wait.' The dog tilts his head to the left.

'Hello, and thanks for calling The Samaritans,' intones an overly-perky female voice; an automated attendant. 'I'm sorry but all our operators are busy at the moment.'

Don rolls his eyes.

'However, your call is important to us so please hold and one of our good Samaritans will be with you as soon as possible.'

'Unbelievable,' gripes Don.

Jed cocks his head to the right.

'In the meantime, please choose one of the following options. If you're just having a bad day, press One. If you're a depressed farmer—'

Don presses Two.

'At least that explains the eyeliner,' smiles Trevor.

Joe has finished dabbing his eyes with the handkerchief but if anything, he's made it worse.

'I thought you were going to *reveal all*,' he rasps, still agitated.

'And I will, I just need to gather myself first.'

'*Gather* yourself?' scoffs Joe breaking into a hacking cough.

'Let me fetch you a drink,' offers Trevor, rising.

'No, I'm fine,' splutters Joe. 'There's really no need.'

'Oh, but I insist,' contends Trevor. 'You are a guest.'

As Trevor fills a glass from the tap, Joe tells him:

'I think the rain or cold got into my chest a bit, that's all.'

'Yes, you should be careful.'

Trevor puts the glass before Joe and retakes his seat.

'Didn't you think to wear a coat?'

Joe coughs and drinks a sip of water.

'I told the milk story, to my sister and her friend.'

'Oh yes?'

'They thought it was silly.'

'And indeed it is.'

'Silly *bad*, not silly *good*.'

'I'm not sure I know the difference.'

'They weren't impressed.'

'Well, that's understandable; it is *my* story, after all. I doubt *anyone* could tell it in quite the same way I do.'

'But you said stories can improve on a retelling: people add new parts, drop a redundant bit, add a joke, bring in an extra—'

'Did I say that?'

'Pretty sure.'

Remember it well, I do, nods Yoda assuredly. *Yesssss.*

'Hmm, I might have done,' accepts Trevor. 'Sometimes I *do* contradict myself.'

Yoda sticks out an angry hand: on the table, the photo album begins to shake violently and rise an inch.

'I remember one time in *The Comedy of Errors*—'

Joe slams his hand down on the album.

'This is no time for levity!'

Yoda quickly retracts his hand and Trevor waits to see what Joe will say next. The boy clearly has something else on his mind.

The thing, prompts Yoda softly at last.

'And I couldn't do the thing,' scowls Joe.

'The thing?' asks Trevor. 'What thing?'

Joe's hands tighten into fists. '*The* thing: the trick!'

Trevor closes his eyes, shakes his head and sighs.

Into thin air make an object vanish? Do that, even I cannot.

'I tried with a snow-globe,' snarls Joe. 'But hey, guess what? I failed – big time.'

'But you *did* do it. You *have* done it. I saw you. Right here at this table. Mr Sparky, remember?'

Hmmm, muses Yoda suspiciously.

'It was probably just because you were upset,' suggests Trevor. 'Was anything bothering you at the time?'

Yoda's eyes narrow. *Probably* you *it was*, he accuses.

'Yes, of course,' blurts Joe. 'It *was* you. *You* did it.'

A mind-trick, points Yoda.

Trevor sits back, disappointed. He looks to the heavens.

'If powers divine behold our human actions, as they do, I doubt not then but innocence shall make false accusation blush—'

'Oh, stop with all this quoting Shakespeare crap!' demands Joe. 'Just admit it was you. I know it was you.'

Yes, certain are we, adds Yoda. *Hmmmm.*

'So, you believe I can do magic but you can't, is that right? You know you really should have more faith in yourself, Joe.'

'Magic,' scoffs Joe fuming. 'What was I thinking?'

Trevor pushes the glass nearer to Joe.

'Here, drink some water. No need to get all worked up.'

Joe, red in the face, takes a sip.

200

'It was you, though, wasn't it?' he growls, still looking hot and agitated. 'Just admit it!'

'Listen,' soothes Trevor, 'if you really believe I did it; if you are convinced that it was I who made Mr Sparky disappear; actually made him vanish – then you must believe in magic. You must.'

'No,' barks Joe. 'It's just uh, uh, a con – a cheap trick. You're a charlatan! Or worse! People talk you know.'

'I'm afraid they always will,' sighs Trevor. 'You really shouldn't listen to them. I'd hoped you had more faith.'

'Doesn't it bother you: the whole town talking about you?'

'Are they?'

Yoda nods. *Small place.*

'I thought you hated gossips,' coughs Trevor.

'They're saying terrible things.'

'What, and there's no smoke without fire?'

This comment strikes a chord with Joe. Even Yoda sees it. And now Trevor rises; he moves from window to window.

'Look, people believe what they want to believe. It's regrettable but you can't change their minds, and to try can actually make things worse. Such people are not worth losing sleep over.'

'Why are you closing the curtains?' asks Joe.

'Because it's getting dark.'

Joe appears apprehensive.

Trevor returns to the table and sits. He touches Joe's arm.

'I think it's time for me to show you something else; something big – something *really* big.'

'Right, that's it. I've had enough of this. I'm out of here.'

Joe stands, grabs his backpack and points at the water:

'And that's probably drugged.'

Nerys and Billy arrive at the police station at the same time, their shift about to start. Nerys approaches the counter.

'Anything happened?' she asks the other officers.

'Yeah, right,' scoffs Bevan removing his jacket from the back of a chair. The fifty-nine-year-old constable's only noteworthy features are a bushy seventies moustache, sideburns to match, and a Buddha belly he can only suck in for half a minute, tops.

'Not a dicky-bird,' Pippa, a pear-shaped bookish-type in her early twenties, informs Nerys.

Once the shift change is complete and the station personnel back down to its usual quota of two, Billy sits at the desk with the computer terminal and gets straight down to some serious business: checking his Facebook account followed by a few rounds of online war games.

'Okay, I'll be in the loo if you need me. Bit constipated.'

'Little more information than I needed, thank you,' mutters Billy as the sergeant disappears through a side door.

After five minutes or so, Billy had changed his status to *In a Relationship* to *It's Complicated* and back to *Single*, scratched his head at a meme that made no sense to him, and watched a video of a farmer's daughter pushing a wheelbarrow of manure up a muddy slope, only for her to slip and suffer said wheelbarrow tipping its crappy contents all over her own head! Billy loves 'epic fail' clips. He's about to click on another when the phone rings.

The PC searches for the handset, throwing papers left and right. He moves files and rummages under desks and counter.

Tring-tring.

Why is the base unit empty? Who would leave the handset anywhere other than its cradle? Why even *touch* the phone? It's not like it ever rings – except now of course!

Tring-tring.

Probably Bevan making personal calls again!

Tring-tring.

Finally, Billy locates the handset, in a desk drawer with Pippa's copy of *The Eyre Affair* (by Jasper Fforde) and her secret stash of marshmallows.

Tring-bloody-tring!

What the fuck is it doing in there? Billy wonders, but no time to worry about that now.

TRING-TRIN—

'Llanidloes Police Station, Constable Mills speaking,' puffs the PC. 'How can I help?'

'Who is it?' shrieks Nerys in the doorway. She's waddled in, still crouched in a semi-squat posture, toilet roll in hand, trousers and matronly knickers around her knees.

Billy holds out a palm: *I've got this.*

'What is it?' badgers Nerys. 'Tell me!'

'Really?' Billy asks the caller. 'And *where* exactly?'

Jed stares at Don, still on hold in the Land Rover. The phone plays The Smith's: 'I Know It's Over' – the *gloomiest* of bleak ballads, even by Morrissey's standards.

Suddenly, the song breaks for the return of the perkily voiced automated attendant: 'We're sorry,' she fawns, 'but all our operators are still busy. You wouldn't believe just how much doom and gloom there is out there.'

☆ ★ ☆

Neither has changed position since last we saw them; not even an inch: Paul persists, stubborn on the sofa, transfixed by the blank TV – which has remained off the whole time – and Sally clearly has no intention of switching it back on. She stands stock-still, statuesque, television remote in pocket, hands on hips and a face like thunder.

'I can stand here all night,' warns Sally.

A moment's delay then Paul, with great reluctance, finally scrambles. 'Right!' he whines heading for the stairs.

Back in the caravan, Trevor takes up a spot by the robot cabinet; moving into position as though he were stepping onto a small stage. Joe has retaken his seat at the table.

'Well, first of all, thanks for staying to hear me out, Joe.'

'Okay, okay, but could you quicken it up a smidgen, this is starting to feel a bit weird.'

'A smidgen – I haven't heard that word for a—'

'Whatever, let's just keep it moving, eh?'

'No problem,' agrees Trevor. 'And now, ladies and gentlemen, I think it's time.'

Joe appears sceptical and sulky, as if he's reverted to his old, disbelieving self. 'Time?' he sighs, arms folded. 'Time for what?'

'Time I explained; time we restored your belief – time to reveal the truth about the missing robot.'

'More drama,' huffs Joe.

Yoda narrows his eyes.

'I'm about to show you something incredible, Joe. Something more incredible than anything you've ever seen before – ever.'

To run, be ready, cautions Yoda in a low voice.

'But I have to warn you,' coughs Trevor, 'that what I'm about to do . . . could be extremely dangerous.'

'Yeah, right,' mutters Joe.

Paul enters Joe's bedroom to find his son missing; just the discarded steampunk hat and cane on the bed – and the robot snow-globe on the sill of the open window.

'Shit!' fumes Paul. Out with the mobile but his call goes straight to answer machine. 'Arrrrggghhh!' he rages.

Trevor, still standing by the robot case, concentrates hard, eyes closed, fingers massaging tiny circles into his temples.

'Watch the space,' he drones. 'Watch the space.'

'Fine,' Joe sighs. And he leans forward, the better to see, resting folded arms on the table.

Hmm, a waste of time this is, mutters Yoda.

But seconds later, in the cabinet, the robots either side of the empty space begin to vibrate gently.

'Yoda, look,' blurts Joe.

Then slowly, almost indiscernible at first, but ever so gradually, a small silver robot materialises in the gap.

'Oh, my God,' exclaims Joe. 'Trevor, you did it!'

'Quiet, please. I am analysing,' announces the talking robot from the top shelf.

Paul reverses the Range Rover out of the garage at speed, wheels spinning off the driveway and onto the cul-de-sac.

The tyres squeal and the vehicle races away.

Joe, now at the cabinet, studies the new robot; handling it, turning it over. 'It's real!' he tells Yoda ecstatically.

Hmm, not a mind-trick?

Joe tests the robot's weight on a palm.

'No, *definitely* real,' he gushes.

But, in turning back to Trevor, Joe's smile vanishes instantly, for the old man's appearance has suddenly turned a deeper shade of pale – almost deathly.

Joe quickly replaces the robot on the shelf and throws an arm around Trevor to support him as the wobbly actor's knees give way. Joe somehow manages to walk Trevor back to the table where he sits him down.

'Are you okay, Trevor?' asks Joe anxiously. 'Speak to me.' But the old man, now with bleeding nose, commences a slow lean to one side. 'No, Trevor, wake up,' pleads Joe. '*Please* wake up.'

Look, instructs Yoda, indicating the cabinet.

Joe swivels his head to the middle shelf and watches in silence as the small silver robot slowly fades away.

Paul takes a hard right and slides the 4x4 onto Mazy Lane, a winding, serpentine 'short-cut' that links the houses west of Finger Hill to the dual carriageway on its eastside. The routinely quiet lane is considerably quicker than taking the circuitous main road – as long as you don't meet anything coming the other way.

'There you go, ladies,' smiles the barmaid of The Mount Inn, 'two lemonades.'

Maxine is still in her Gothic Carnival outfit; Lucy has changed: she's now dressed head to foot in a long dark chador (a full-body cloak) and a full-face black niqab – only her eyes on show.

'Oh, and a couple of vodkas,' smiles Lucy under the veil.

The barmaid nods at the ARE YOU 18? sign hanging behind the bar and raises an eyebrow.

Lucy's covered head tilts; an unspoken: *Well, not far off.*

'Oh well, nice try, Lucy,' commends the barmaid.

The girls pay for their lemonades and transport them to a free table away from the bar. On the way, they pass Noah, sitting on the piano stool, staring at the piano keys. Some regulars are looking at him and shaking their heads; others are laughing openly. Lucy and Max have seen this kind of insensitive behaviour before and don't like it.

Meanwhile, back in the caravan, Trevor is still extremely groggy. Joe offers the glass of water.

'Here, Trevor, drink this.'

'You're a good boy, Joe,' smiles Trevor weakly.

At their little table, both girls take a swig of lemonade.

'Perhaps wearing this was a mistake,' complains Lucy after struggling to manoeuvre her glass under the niqab.

'Here, this might cheer you up.'

Max leans forward, conspiratorially, and opens her bag to show Lucy what's inside: a small bottle of vodka.

'Surprise,' she sings softly.

'Nice one,' laughs Lucy, shielding her friend as she pours a splash of alcohol into each glass.

'Hey, Noah,' quips a skinny dude in a baseball cap. 'Keep the noise down a bit, will you?'

This makes several regular drinkers cackle boisterously, but the remark annoys Lucy immensely; you can see it in her eyes. Max, too, is far from happy. Noah's only levitating his fingers over the piano keys; not actually playing – just looking as if he might.

'Yeah, we're trying to talk here!' barks a burly farmer-type with a square face and shovel jaw.

A large section of the pub's clientele whoops and hollers.

Angered by this, Lucy's eyes narrow and she breathes hard inside her niqab. If Joe were here, it would surely make him think of Darth Vader.

'Easy, Luce,' soothes, Max.

But Lucy isn't for quietening; she's already on her feet.

'Hey!' she bellows. 'Why don't you leave him alone? He's not doing any harm, is he?'

A sea of surprised mugs, some amused, others nettled, turns to face her.

'No, he isn't!' continues Lucy. 'But you're all giving it some, aren't you! Yes, that's right, I'm talking to *you*,' she points. '*And* you. All of you! Does anyone have a problem with that?'

'Sit down, Fatimha,' shouts a sixty-something with a beer gut and watery eyes.

Lucy rips off her niqab.

'Coz if they do, I'll fight you,' she bawls. 'I'll fight you, right here, right now. *Come on!*'

Paul's car, almost at a standstill, somewhere between the tip of Finger Hill and Tall Trees Trailer Park crawls its way through a large flock of sheep being shepherded in the opposite direction, along the narrow lane, towards the farm on Bryn Crow, presumably for a fleecing or a dip or whatever – so much for the so-called short-cut.

'For fuck's sake,' mutters Paul. 'Who the fuck moves sheep at this time of day?' he grumbles.

Once the last of the ewes and working dogs and farmer in his Land Rover and sons on quad bikes have passed, Paul floors the accelerator and is soon making a blur of hedgerows as he weaves past open fields.

'Nonsense,' retorts Trevor huskily, '*lots* of people have this gift; think about it – musicians, artists, writers, great singers, actors, poets, composers.'

'I think there's a difference,' insists Joe as he continues to comfort a colour-drained Trevor.

'No, no difference: they all make something wonderful appear from nowhere,' explains Trevor. 'One moment there's nothing, and then, as if by magic, beautiful music, great art, wonderful books, moving performances; things that speak to the heart and soul.' He coughs. 'Yes, all such people have a similar gift.'

'A gift?' wonders Joe with a frown. 'Not sure I can agree with you on that one.'

'And you have it too, Joe,' enthuses Trevor. 'I can feel it.'

'Aw, you're just saying that.'

'No, I honestly believe you have the makings of a wonderful storyteller.'

'Hmm, I still say there's a difference. You made a missing robot just . . . *appear!*'

'Yes, and a lot of good it did me,' sighs Trevor. 'He's not there now, is he? And as you see, it's so terribly draining. One can only maintain it for so long. Any longer and, you know, *boom!*'

'Boom?'

'Boom,' nods Trevor.

'Boom,' laughs Joe. He indicates that Trevor should have another drink of water and as Trevor obliges, Joe drags over the photo album and leafs through the pages.

Trevor observes the boy with a sparkle in his eye – as if he knows exactly what Joe will say and do next.

Joe turns to the last page, the one without Mr Wonky, then a knowing smile forms on Trevor's face as he watches Joe stroke the photo-less page with a finger.

'So . . . ?' poses Joe.

'Your missing photo?' asks Trevor.

Joe nods sadly and the old man muses:

'Hmm . . . I suppose I could – at least, for a moment.'

'Really?'

'If only I wasn't so tired,' wilts Trevor.

Joe isn't sure if Trevor's hamming it up or not.

'Yeah, I understand,' he sighs pushing the album away.

'But why don't *you* do it?' encourages Trevor.

'Me? No, I couldn't. Could I?'

'If you believe,' Trevor tells him.

Yoda nods wholeheartedly.

Yes, listen to Trevor, you must.

Trevor sits a little straighter; wincing as he does so.

'Think what you've already achieved. You *can* do it; you just have to make it so. But remember, you'd only have the photo a few seconds. Any longer and it could be dangerous.'

'Boom?'

'Boom,' nods Trevor.

'What do you think, Yoda?'

Hmm, strong is the Force. But ready, are you?

Joe considers the question. 'Yes,' he nods, 'I am.'

'Are you sure?' checks Trevor.

'Fear not, old man,' quips Joe. 'I'm Joe the lion, made of iron.'

Yes, the right spirit that is, urges Yoda.

Joe turns to Trevor and announces:

'Cover me, Sire, I'm going in.'

Joe's playful attempt to be all Shakespearean amuses Trevor; and now he waits, as Joe focuses, staring hard at the blank page, channelling his energy . . .

'Good,' encourages Trevor nodding.

But Joe grows red in the face.

'Don't forget to breathe,' advises Trevor.

Joe sucks in a deep breath and hurriedly lets it out then repeats – until he's almost panting, loud and raspy.

Calm, at peace, passive, guides Yoda softly.
'Nice and steady,' instructs Trevor.
Joe centres himself, brings his breathing under control.
A moment passes but behold: gradually, indiscernible at first, but then, bit by bit, a faint photograph, featuring the unmistakable form of a snowman manifests in the album.
Mr Wonky!
Joe gasps, excited, but this makes the picture fade.
'You must keep concentrating, Joe.'
Yes, focus, focus! Yoda directs.

Paul's vehicle barrels through the entrance to Tall Trees Trailer Park and turns sharply, wheels churning mud, the car sliding sideways through puddles as the tyres struggle to gain purchase in the wet.

'Can you feel it, Joe?' whispers Trevor. 'Can you?'
Joe nods feverishly.
'He's almost there,' Trevor tells him softly.
The scene in the caravan: dim gaslight, low voices, hands held across a table – appears as a séance would.
Joe's eyes narrow; he takes a deep breath, holds it and fixates on the thin, see-through photograph that is unquestionably re-emerging, by degrees, on the album's previously empty fifteenth page. The faded image crystallises and strengthens until is it truly solid, as substantial as Mr Frosty on page fourteen.
'Boom!' exclaims Joe.
Trevor smiles.
Yoda blinks and shakes his head as if he can't quite believe it.
Mysterious are the ways of the Force.
Finally letting out the breath he'd been holding in, Joe picks up the picture and smiles at it; then he holds it to his chest and looks skyward.
The old man nods. 'Well done, Joe.'
After a beat Joe proudly shows the picture to Yoda. He shows it to Trevor, too, but as he does, he suddenly becomes dizzy.
Trevor, moving slowly, changes seats: his turn to support Joe.
'Oh, this isn't good,' coughs Joe.
As he rests in Trevor's arms, the photo starts to fade.
'Is it over?' asks Joe. 'Has it gone?'
'Nearly, but you had it, Joe. You really had it.'
'But I couldn't keep it. I couldn't keep my photo.'
'I know, Joe – I know.'
'I've lost Mr Wonky – *again.*'

Headlights illuminate the curtains for a moment then a car pulls up sharply beyond the caravan's main window.

'Are you sure it wasn't you?' asks Joe feebly.

'Oh dear boy, I'd never even seen Mr Wonky. Not until now. There was no photo, remember?'

'True.'

Outside: the barely detectable scrape of metal on metal followed by the hard, airy thump of a tailgate door.

'Did it look like Mr Wonky?' asks Trevor.

'Exactly like him – it *was* him.'

'And if I had made the photo appear, would I really have been able to get every single detail just right, hmm?'

'I believe you,' sighs Joe, eyes closing.

Trevor seems improved now but Joe has become even groggier; he appears desperately weak, exhausted, burned out. Trevor holds Joe tight as his head drifts to one side.

'Poor, sweet boy,' whispers Trevor gently brushing hair from Joe's brow.

And that's when Paul bursts in, wheel brace in hand.

CHAPTER 17
Is it Nice in your Snowstorm?

The first thing Paul saw when he barged into the caravan was Trevor comforting Joe, and now he approaches them looking like he might explode at any second. Trevor, on the other hand, seems calm, unmoved, as if he had expected exactly this.

Joe sits up, groggily. 'Dad, hi. It's okay. I'm alright.'

'Has this nonce touched you?' fumes Paul. 'Has he?!'

'What? No,' replies Joe.

Paul glares at Trevor, who smiles back amiably.

'Don't lose it, Dad,' appeals Joe weakly.

Paul puffs and snorts but keeps it together – just about. 'Come on,' he orders. 'You're coming with me. Right now!'

'Mr Evans—' starts Trevor.

'And if you know what's good for you –' warns Paul.

Somewhat comically, Paul tries to look intimidating. He picks up a small robot, thinks about throwing it – but finally settles for dropping it into a full laundry basket by the toilet door. All this whilst brandishing the wheel brace.

'– You'll stay away from my son!'

Paul gathers Joe in his arms and carries him to the door where he has trouble squeezing Joe through the doorway.

'Dad, I can walk,' suggests Joe quietly. 'I think.'

Paul, softening a little, gently unloads his son. Joe glances back from the doorway. Trevor smiles and nods, then Paul ushers Joe outside.

As Paul shepherds Joe around the caravan, guiding him to the car, Trevor opens a window above their heads.

'It *is* a gift, Joe, it is,' smiles Trevor. 'And I hope you can accept it. Joe, listen to me: don't hesitate – take it quickly.'

'What's that?' barks Paul. 'What's he saying?'

Trevor appears oddly content as he closes the curtain.

'Trevor,' calls Joe tenderly. 'What do you mean?'

'He's crazy,' snorts Paul. 'Come on, let's go.'

But when they reach the car, and Paul opens the passenger door for Joe, out of nowhere, the air suddenly turns cold, *bitterly* cold. Paul looks around, as if for an explanation, misty breath hanging in the frosty air. And then it begins to snow; slow at first but soon falling fast and heavy. Snow like never seen before, immediately thick and dense; building a thirty centimetre layer before their very eyes. Unrelenting, it falls on everything in sight: caravans, porches, the Range Rover, the burger van, the Lambretta across the way – the whole trailer park covered in an instant blanket of glittering white; easily a good sixty centimetres deep in less than a minute.

'Wow!' gasps Joe. He seems to have regained his vigour.

Looking up to the dark grey sky strewn with billowy bright clouds, Joe feels as if he's been magically teleported into the centre of a giant mythical snow-globe.

And, if that were not special enough, all the surrounding trees now become a multitude of colours: reds, blues, yellows, greens; their branches illuminated with countless strings of industrial-sized fairy lights, the type you would expect to see adorning buildings and lining city streets at Christmas-time. The lights ring the entire site, highlighting the snow in a series of alternating magical colours and bestowing upon the place an enchanted grotto feel.

Joe wades over to what was the thoroughfare, now an unspoiled carpet of pristine snow, a covering that glimmers in every direction, and he turns circles, arms outstretched, face-up, flakes fluttering onto his hair and eyelashes.

'This is amazing!' sings Joe.

Paul, for once, is speechless.

Had you been flying low overhead, or watching from a drone on high, you would see that the whole caravan field is totally white, whilst the unlit, surrounding fields are darkest green and free from snowfall; the exact opposite of when Joe's garden was the only space without snow, after Owen and his cronies had destroyed Mr Wonky.

And speaking of Mr Wonky, back on the ground, Joe spots a large, one-eyed snowman with a conical hat.

'OMG!' shouts Joe. 'It's Mr Wonky!'

'Who?' Paul asks.

Joe ploughs through knee-high snow towards the snowman. 'Mr Wonky!' he calls back.

'It can't be,' mutters Paul, trying to make sense of it all.

Alison appears at her caravan door in a bath towel. She looks around, shocked by the snow, but not so shocked that she forgets to check if Liam has come out to witness the spectacle; her being the *main* attraction – how could he resist once he's seen her all damp-haired and wrapped in fluffy white Egyptian cotton; bare-shouldered and legs on display? (Shame he'd only stayed for a couple of minutes earlier, leaving his drink, and her, because he'd forgotten, he said, to take meat out of the freezer for tomorrow.

Promised to come right back but didn't.) But nope, Liam is again 'Missing in action'. Perhaps it's just as well, thinks Alison. She wouldn't want to needlessly hand other residents the chance to further gossip about her alleged 'slack' morals with men-friends. Maybe she'll head on over there when it's darker and the girls are fast asleep. Still, shame Liam's not on his porch; he's missing all this exquisite wonderfulness.

As Joe reaches Mr Wonky, the last of the fluttering snow stops falling, turned off as abruptly as it had started.

He pats the snowman on the shoulder and recalls Trevor's instruction: *Don't hesitate.*

What did he mean?

Joe hears the sound of giggling children: Becki and Chloe, dressed in winter coats, gloves and rubber boots have run outside, almost taking Mum's towel with them in their hurry to play.

'Hey!' shouts Alison fixing her towel. But the girls don't hear: they're already busy having fun making snow angels.

'Fine, but not too long; don't want you catching cold.'

Not too long? Catch cold? It already feels several degrees warmer—Yes, of course! *Not too long.* Joe now understands exactly what Trevor meant by 'Don't hesitate.'

He quickly searches pockets and comes up with his phone. 'Dad!' shouts Joe. 'I need you to take a picture of me with Wonky!'

But Paul is dashing for the safety of his car, retreating from Becki and Chloe as they target him with snowballs.

'Dad!'

Too late: Paul is in the car, sheltering from the girls' playful assault. As they giggle and pelt his window, he shakes a critical finger at them before checking just how spoiled his hair is in the rear-view mirror.

Joe wades over to Alison's porch.

'Mrs Thomas, can you take a photo for me?' There's a creeping desperation in his voice.

'Are you kidding?' snorts Alison, indicating that if he hasn't noticed, she happens to be in a towel.

Disappointed and deeply concerned, Joe looks around. Why are no other neighbours out on their porches to witness the sudden freak weather?

'Oh no,' he sighs, seeing his only option.

Nevertheless, he labours in her direction and calls out:

'Mrs Beal, can *you* take a picture for me?'

'What?'

Joe holds up his phone and points at Mr Wonky.

'Can you take a photo of me with the snowman?'

'Be right there,' she shouts. 'I'll just get my camera.'

'No, no, I have a phone!'

But Mrs Beal has vanished, back into her caravan.

'Mrs Beal!' screams Joe.

He scans the area for an alternative solution. Who knows how long this magical snowscape will last? But Becki and Chloe are too wrapped up in chasing each other around the Range Rover with snowballs (which rules out Paul) and there's still no-one else around; not a soul – just a few lights on here and there in various caravans. Should he knock at some? No, it would take too long.

'I can't find my camera!' bays Mrs Beal now returned.

'This is a camera!' hollers Joe, phone held high. 'See?'

Mrs Beal offers a thumbs-up, takes a step forward, then stops and regards her snow-covered porch steps.

'I'll just put my boots on!' she calls.

'Fuck's sake,' growls Joe; anguish warms his face as his eyes sweep the area. 'Oh, this is hopeless,' he tells himself.

But he needn't have worried, for after a mere forty-seven seconds – with Joe feeling every tick and every tock – Mrs Beal is back and soon descending her steps.

Joe turns to the snowman to make sure he's still there – he is – then he sets his phone to the camera app and twists to check how far Mrs Beal has got.

'Come on, Mrs Beal—!' Joe starts to call.

He doesn't finish because she's right in his face.

'Yes?' asks Mrs Beal.

'Jeez!' blurts Joe, startled. 'That was quick.'

'Oh, I can move when I want to,' agrees Mrs Beal.

'In the end,' mutters Joe.

'So, get on with it then,' urges Mrs Beal. 'I'm freezing my tits off out here.'

'Okay, you just press that button.'

'I know, I know,' protests Mrs Beal. 'Listen, me and Mr Beal used to take lots of photos of each other back in the day. I had this little black number he liked –'

'One second!' requests Joe drudging back to the snowman.

'No rush,' advises Mrs Beal. 'I was telling you about Alfie: Lord, he was a saucy devil; I remember one time—'

'Ready!' calls Joe posing with the snowman.

'Oh, okay. Which button was it again?'

'The white one! Just aim and press!'

As Joe stands there, waiting, he notices neighbours, finally out on their porches taking in the wondrous snowscape. He doesn't know who all of them are but there's Leon Blank (the guy with the

Lambretta scooter) and Jayne Angel his girlfriend; Mrs Kennedy the music teacher, Atrium Boldywang (a reclusive painter who hardly ever shows his face; each of his canvases a slightly different view of the interior of his trailer), Marta the Polish dental hygienist, and that overly tall bloke, who, if Joe isn't mistaken, is a line cook in The Cliché Café.

Now *you come out*, thinks Joe. *Where were you when—*

'I can't see a white button,' calls Mrs Beal. 'Wish I'd brought my specs!'

'*What!*'

'Just kidding,' she tells him. 'Settle down.'

'Come on, Mrs Beal! Please hurry!'

'Right, right, I've got it. Keep your hair on.'

'Just take it, Mrs Beal,' urges Joe. '*Please!*'

'Well, smile then.'

'I am smiling!' hisses Joe through a fixed grin. 'Just take the frickin—' A flash from the phone and Joe relaxes at last.

'Thanks, Mrs Beal,' he smiles.

Joe wades back, retrieves the camera and checks the photo. All is well. But then he notices Mrs Beal staring at Trevor's caravan.

'That's weird,' she observes.

Joe follows her gaze and yes, something strange *is* occurring: the caravan looks dull and out of focus.

'Are you seeing what I'm seeing?' squints Joe.

The caravan – is it glowing? – shifts from blurry to overly sharp and back again; like a weird pulsing heartbeat.

'It's like a weird pulsing heartbeat,' notes Joe.

'Well, I haven't got my specs but I'd say it was more of a—'

FLOOOOOOMPH! A sonic yet near silent explosion: the kind of sound you *feel* more than *hear* – a huge, translucent energy wave bursting outward from Trevor's caravan, bright, blue, awesome, and somehow seen in slow motion.

'Ttttrrrreeeevvvvvoooorrrr!' shouts Joe, hair blowing back as though in a gale-force wind.

For a split second the energy wave pulls Joe and Mrs Beal forward, leans them towards the blast, as if sucking the air from around them; then the old woman is lifted off her feet and blown backwards. She lands on her back in the snow a caravan length away. Joe too is plucked from the snow and carried through the air. He lands on Mrs Beal.

With our drone's eye view, we again see the trailer park from high above: witness how, from Trevor's caravan (the blast's epicentre) the huge concentric ring of energy expands out across the snow-covered space, and on, into the bordering green fields beyond, like an enormous bomb blast but with no actual physical destruction. Individual residents are bowled over, snow blown and piled high against the facing sides of trailers and vehicles, trees bent and shaken, and yet, surprisingly, there's zero damage to speak of; nothing serious or lasting, anyway.

From her kitchen window, Sally looks out to a strange luminous glow on the horizon, watches as it spreads across the night sky.
    After a moment, she feels a vibrant FLOOOOOOMPH!
    The energy wave rebounds off the hills and bounces all around, echoing through the valley.

Up on Finger Hill, Jed is peering through the Land Rover's mucky windscreen at Don's twitching boots when the wave hits. The force sends his master's feet swinging back and forth above the vehicle's hood. Then the dog sees the rocking scarecrow plucked from the earth and blasted against the windshield where it instantly disintegrates into fragments and dust. And here comes the flying, spinning scythe: it smashes through shattering glass – its rusty blade just missing his head.
    Seconds later, with the blue nylon rope still around his neck, the branch from which Don is hanging snaps with a loud crack and the farmer bounces off the vehicle's roof and onto the ground. This strange intervention is lucky not just for the farmer but for the girl he'd spotted whilst he was up there: the one in the caravan in the trailer park below – tiny hands waving at a window upon which she'd written HELP (in what Don took to be toothpaste or shaving foam) on the glass. He'd seen the message and the girl's distraught face when the lightning-bright flash had illuminated absolutely everywhere a split second before the blast happened.
    And now, after crawling into the Land Rover and fending off Jed's licks and attentions, Don retrieves his phone from the glove-box, dials 999 and then passes out.

Another observation, from our drone's highest perspective yet, reveals the translucent shock wave expand so far that it swallows the lights of not only Llanidloes but other nearby towns: Llandinam, Cwmbelan, Trefeglwys, Llangurig.

Lucy and Max flank Noah at the fruit machine. 'See, this is much more fun than sitting at a boring old piano,' Lucy tells him.
    Smiling, Noah hits the button.

As the symbols spin, the pub lights flicker, tables shudder, pictures rattle on the walls, the fruit machine judders and the barmaid attempts to steady clinking rows of hanging glasses. Some patrons grab their drinks to prevent spillage, everyone scanning in all directions – is it an earth tremor, a quake? (Back in 2007 Powys County had a quake; recorded at a 'mere' 2.9 on the Richter scale it was far too weak to feel. This shaking has all the hallmarks of a 5 or 6.)

And now, after the forerunner, the full energy wave races in, passing through for several seconds: unmanned glasses quiver across table tops and smash to the floor; several pictures tumble from walls; people bend at the knees to brace themselves, or, as one old couple do, dive to the floor. And three lucky star symbols line up in a row – Noah has hit the jackpot.

'Wow! What was that?' asks Maxine straightening up. 'Was it a quake – an earth tremor?'

'I've no idea,' replies Lucy. 'But it was amazing! A bit scary but yeah, awesome.'

Ignoring his big, noisy payout, Noah looks to the piano.

Back at the trailer park, the event has passed and there's no longer a trace of snow anywhere; the Christmas lights have all vanished, too – and the snowman.

'What the hell *was* that?' asks Paul under flattened hair.

Joe's worried face pokes out from Trevor's caravan door.

'Dad,' he squeals. 'Call an ambulance!'

In the aftermath, as the regulars discuss the weird events of the last few minutes, Noah, over at the piano, hovers his fingers over the keys for a moment – then plays a few notes.

Hearing the nascent sounds, Lucy and Max walk over.

The tune sounds odd at first, a little jarring even; no-one is sure if the melody is painfully terrible, or actually the precursor of something good. But regardless of anyone's expectations, the promise slowly develops and Noah's notes build, until he's playing a composition that nobody recognises but everyone acknowledges is instantly moving; a profound piece that is undeniably exquisite, hauntingly so, a tour de force.

And then he sings.

If Noah's piano-playing expertise was unexpected – which it most unquestionably was – his voice is even more astonishing; it's immediately clear that as well as enjoying the compositional skills of a classic composer, he has the voice of an absolute angel.

Think Thom Yorke's emotional sweep meets Wolfgang Amadeus Mozart's keyboard skills.

And now the music emanating from Noah's spider-like fingers rises into an arrangement even more passionate and exhilarating, swells into a grand performance of astounding beauty and magnificent chords then expands into lofty harmonics which are truly sublime.

It would be fair to say that the barmaid and regulars are dumbfounded and agog. For those who recall seeing Paul Potts' or Susan Boyle's first appearance on *Britain's Got Talent*, this is one of *those* types of moments. The kind of extraordinary episodes one *never* forgets.

Lost in the song, Lucy and Max sway to Noah's artistry.

'Are you okay, Trevor?' asks Joe. He turns to Paul: 'Dad, what's happening?'

Alison and Mrs Beal look on as Trevor, Joe holding his hand, is wheeled on a gurney steered by two paramedics toward a waiting ambulance. The Llani police car has turned up too. Nerys and Billy clamber out, the PC with a Cairn Terrier in his arms.

As the officers approach, the dog yaps excitedly.

'You've found Trevor's dog!' exclaims Joe.

'We have,' confirms the sergeant. 'Got him right here.'

'Dad, they've found Hamlet!'

Paul shrugs, nonplussed.

'I didn't know he had a dog,' Alison tells Mrs Beal.

'Can you hear me, Trevor?' asks Nerys. No response. 'Is he going to be alright?' she asks the ambulance crew.

The female paramedic makes a see-saw gesture with a hand.

'Don't worry, Hamlet's fine,' the sergeant informs Trevor. 'Mister de la Touche?'

'De la Touche?' snorts Paul. 'Bit of a poncy name.'

The cold comment draws black looks all round.

'So, he's got a dog, has he?' smiles Paul, hoping to sound more human. He strokes the dog and almost loses a finger.

'Cute little guy's been missing for ages but we found him,' Billy tells the onlookers.

Nerys pats Trevor's hand. 'See, I told you we would.'

Alison smiles but it's an affected one in keeping with the overall expression on her face. She'd never seen the dog before, this was news to her; and just because someone has a pet doesn't make them a nice person – even if the owner is about to be loaded into an ambulance. For Alison, questions remain, and she's yet to be convinced that the old man is anything other than a deviant.

'He turned up in Tylwch,' explains Nerys, 'travelling cross-country, about four miles out but heading this way.'

'A rambler called it in,' adds Billy. 'Said she spotted him on the other side of the Afon Dulas river. Could tell he wasn't a working dog and was concerned a farmer might shoot him if he started worrying any of their sheep.'

'How do you know he's his?' challenges Alison. 'They all look the same to me.'

'True; he doesn't have any distinguishing features and he's lost his collar,' concedes Nerys. 'But his microchip implant was a dead giveaway.'

'We had him scanned,' adds Billy. 'He's registered to Trevor.'

Alison is forced into begrudging silence.

'Poor thing could use a good meal,' observes Joe.

'Yes, but at least he's back now, eh?' Nerys tells Trevor.

Hamlet yaps.

'That's right, you're home now, boy,' adds Billy.

'Look, this is all very well but we really need to get the patient to hospital,' presses the male paramedic keen to load the gurney into the ambulance.

'Hey, Trevor!' barks Joe excitedly. 'Do you want me to look after him till you get better?'

'Now come on, son,' balks Paul.

'My hand!' squeals Joe. 'Dad, Trevor squeezed it! Do you think he's saying yes, he does want me to look after him?'

Paul can't find an excuse in time so the PC hands the terrier to Joe. As the crew move to lift Trevor into the ambulance, Joe transfers the dog to his reluctant dad then steps back to Trevor.

'Joe, what are you doing?' asks Paul.

'Giving him a kiss.'

'No, Joe,' Paul tells him. 'Absolutely not.'

Alison makes a face but Mrs Beal seems fine with it, which is just as well because Joe is adamant. He leans over and kisses Trevor's forehead.

'Don't worry, Trevor,' smiles Joe. 'I'll look after Hamlet.'

The dog yaps as Trevor is rolled into the ambulance.

'You'll take care of him, won't you?' Joe asks.

'We'll do our best, son,' replies the male paramedic climbing in to accompany Trevor. The female indicates that everyone should move back and she closes the doors.

As Joe waves at the departing ambulance, Hamlet licks Paul's face and he visibly softens.

'Yes, yes, good boy,' grimaces Paul.

As the ambulance exits the trailer park, lights flashing and siren wailing, Joe turns to his dad.

'Thanks, Dad,' smiles Joe. 'I mean it.'

Paul nods. 'You're welcome, Joe.'

And now Paul receives a massive bear hug from his son; a long, meaningful squeeze – the type that helps people to renew bonds and move on, even if it has started raining again.

Meanwhile, the two-way radio attached to Nerys' shoulder squawks into life:

'Nerys, are you there? Are you hearing me? Over.'

Nerys keys her radio.

'Go ahead, dispatch,' she replies evenly. 'Over.'

'We have a Code 2-0-7,' blurts Pippa's crackly, filtered voice.

'A 2-0-7!' she repeats excitedly. 'Over.'

Nerys discreetly pops in an earpiece and steps away. She nods at something she's told and scans the caravans as she drifts towards the police car. There, she discreetly checks her gun is loaded then beckons Billy over.

'What's up, Sarge?'

'We have a potential 2-0-7 in progress.'

'What's that?'

The sergeant sighs and shakes her head forlornly.

'Didn't they teach you anything in the academy? It's supposed to be one of the first things you learn; right after the phonetic alphabet and how to put your police trousers on.'

Billy has grabbed a waterproof combat-style poncho from the car boot and slipped it on.

'Oh, wait, I know,' he declares. 'Is it a Lewd Conduct?'

Nerys rolls her eyes. '2-0-7 is Possible Kidnapping.'

'Jesus,' barks Billy. 'Possible Kidnapping.'

'Check your Taser,' instructs Nerys. 'Make sure it's fully charged. You never know.'

'On it,' replies Billy eagerly.

Nerys places a finger on her earpiece: another update. Then, keying her radio, she confirms:

'All received. Which caravan; do we know? Over.'

CHAPTER 18

The Big Key

It's raining hard on the caravan roof. Kelly, still tied but no longer gagged and now back on the sofa, watches as her captor angrily rips the blank piece of cardboard he's been staring at for hours on end – over several days.

Couldn't think of anything, huh? taunts Joel's skull.

'No, okay! I'm done. Spent,' fumes Liam. 'I can't think of a single caption that's evenly remotely funny.'

Useless.

'And so . . . Kelly . . . I'm gonna let you go.'

Wait, what?

'Really?' checks Kelly.

'Yep,' nods Liam.

'Thank you,' sniffs Kelly. 'Thank you, thank you.'

You promised me a kid, Liam!

'No!' bellows Liam. 'Enough of that talk!'

Kelly gasps. She's seen her captor argue with the skull countless times but each episode is as terrifying as the first.

'Now shut up, you're scaring the girl.'

This is it, intones the skull. *You're about to make that big mistake; the mistake that gets us caught.*

'We're not going to get caught,' insists Liam.

We were lucky to get away with your last fuck up.

'Come again.'

When you let that other *girl go – the one in the woods.*

'Paige? I didn't let her go, Joel – she escaped.'

Useless.

'Hey, I was exhausted, okay! It was after a long night. I'd buried *your* body, the dad's, those two yappy dogs, and then that fella who came banging on the side of the van; the dick who wanted to know if everything was okay.'

Went after him with the spade, didn't you?

'Yeah, that's right. So excuse me if my back was turned for a minute – not even that.'

Enough time to chew through the tape and run off.

'Exactly: run *off* – I didn't let her go. But *again*: they didn't catch us.'

Fine, we got lucky, but now you're gonna let another *one go?*

'That's right, I am, and we still won't get caught.'

He turns to Kelly:

'Of course there is one problem: you've seen me a lot longer than Paige did. If you give the cops a description . . .'

'No, no, I won't,' pledges Kelly. 'I promise.'

Like you can take her word for it!

'Well, I don't suppose it'll matter,' concludes Liam. 'I'll be changing my appearance and torching the van. I'll steal a car; move somewhere far from here. Best I don't say where. Actually, I'm not sure yet. But somewhere with lots of old people; I've decided that's the best way to boost my numbers – beat Shipman.'

Our numbers. And you'll still have to do signs!

'Maybe, maybe not. Maybe there's an alternative to signs. I dunno, I'll think of something!'

Well, I've heard everything now.

'So, you *are* letting me go?' checks Kelly.

Liam shrugs. 'Sure. Why not?'

'Okay,' nods Kelly. 'Right away?'

Crazy. Absolutely fucking crazy.

Liam cuts Kelly's hands free.

'But first we'll have some ice cream, okay?'

Kelly rubs her wrists, made red by the duct tape.

'Uh – okay.'

'Ben and Jerry's Cookie Dough. How's that sound?'

'Uh – good.'

'And when we've finished,' he tells her, '*freedom.*'

Un-fucking-believable.

Liam takes ice-cream from the fridge's ice-box, scoops into two bowls and hands one to Kelly with a spoon and a smile. He then sits beside her.

Jesus, look at you, eating ice-cream like it's some kind of fucking birthday party! What a fucking idiot.

'Don't!' bellows Liam launching his bowl at the wall. 'Don't *ever* call me that!'

Kelly cowers as her captor angrily confronts the skull.

Why? Joel scoffs. What will you do?

'Smash your fucking skull in!'

Liam hears Joel laugh at him mockingly.

'Yes, fuck it, I'm gonna hammer your fucking cranium!'

Do it then!

'I will!' pants Liam, breathing rapidly through his nose. 'Should have done it ages ago!'

Well, go on!

'But first I'm having my fucking ice-cream!'

Liam grabs a replacement bowl, defiantly plonks it on the counter, opens the fridge, removes the carton of Ben & Jerry's and slams the fridge door shut.

What the fuck?

'Go on, Kelly, eat up,' instructs Liam.

Kelly nervously shovels in a spoonful of Cookie Dough.

Nerys creeps past the burger van, gun drawn. Billy backs her up, yellow Taser at the ready. Rain streams off their ponchos. After padding up the wet porch steps, Nerys stops and listens.

'All the curtains are closed,' observes Billy quietly.

Nerys nods that she's noticed that and places an ear against the rain-dappled caravan door.

After a brief pause, Billy asks:

'Is it open, or do you need the Big Key?'

(The Big Key: Llani Force's pet name for their battering ram.)

Ear now off the door, Nerys tries the handle: she pulls gently but the door is locked.

'Oh, crap,' she mutters under her breath.

'What?' Billy peers through the rain.

'He's threatening to smash her skull in – you ready?'

'Fuck yeah!'

'Right, quick, pass me the Key.'

'Oh shit,' hisses Billy.

'Well get it you, idiot,' orders Nerys. 'And fast.'

Back in The Mount Inn pub, Noah plays on beautifully, his phenomenal voice truly spellbinding.

Lots of regulars have crowded around.

Lucy and Max are dancing together, still oblivious to everything but the song.

Just seconds after the last of the Ben & Jerry's has been scooped, the caravan door bursts in and armed police officers storm through the splintered doorway, their weapons instantly trained on a startled Liam.

Shocked, Kelly screams and drops her bowl. She grabs her ankles and buries her face into her knees, too terrified to watch the shit-storm about to go down.

'Armed police officers!' yells Nerys. 'Drop the weapon or we will fire!'

'It's an ice cream scoop,' counters Liam.

'Drop it! Drop the scoop!'

Liam drops the ice-cream scoop.

'Now kick away the scoop,' orders Nerys.

'Or just step away from it,' offers Billy.

'No, *kick* it away,' overrides the sergeant. 'Do it now!'

'It's just a scoop,' repeats Liam. 'A regular—'

'*Kick it away!*'

He does.

'Now, hands behind your head and down on the ground! Do it now! Or we *will* shoot you!'

'Okay, okay, I'm co-operating.' Liam laces fingers behind his head. 'Please don't shoot.'

'Then lie down, motherfucker!'

'Billy!'

'Sorry.'

Liam drops to his knees.

Shoot him, he's trying to escape!

'Judas!' bellows Liam at the skull.

Shoot him in the face!

'What was that?' grills Billy. 'Did you say something?'

'No, nothing, but do *not* shoot me in the face.'

'Then lie down!'

'I *am* lying down.'

'Billy, calm down,' instructs Nerys. 'Just cuff him.'

'Okay, I got this,' barks Billy. 'Hands behind your back!'

Liam complies and Billy cuffs him.

Everything is abruptly quiet now, apart from the little girl sobbing – a sight which affects Nerys deeply.

'Put that scum in the car,' she tells Billy.

'Gotcha, I'll make this filth wish he'd—'

'No, no, just put him in the car,' orders the sergeant. 'I'll have no beatings on my watch.'

'But—'

'The car, PC Mills!' commands Nerys. 'I'll call it in.'

'Fine, agrees Billy. 'Come on, you.'

The prisoner is hauled to his feet; rough but effective.

'Easy, copper,' warns Liam. 'You know who I am, right?'

'Mr fucking nobody,' sneers Billy.

Liam laughs and looks the constable in the face.

'Wow, you really have no idea, do you?'

'Oh, I think *I* do,' states Nerys. 'Now, get him out of here.'

'My pleasure,' responds the constable.

As Billy drags Liam from the caravan Nerys comforts Kelly. Then the sergeant's two-way radio crackles into life.

'Dispatch.'

'Go ahead, dispatch.'

'Reports of a loud noise and raised voices at your 20. Over.'

'Yeah, it's okay, Pippa, it was probably us. And don't worry: everything's under control; we've found Kelly – she's safe and she's going to be okay. Over.'

'Oh, yay!' cheers Pippa's filtered voice. 'Over.'

'Can you send a car to take her home please? Over.'

'Sure, I'll come myself. Bevan can cover the desk. Over.'

Nerys stands under a large black umbrella, an arm around Kelly, who, despite herself, can't resist stealing glances at her captor, now in the back of the police car.

His head on the rainy window, Liam stares back blankly.

'Don't look at him, honey,' Nerys tells Kelly. 'A car will be here in a minute to take you home.' And with that the sergeant turns her back on Liam and pulls Kelly in close; well, as close as she can with her extended belly.

With one eye on the sergeant's back, Liam slowly leans over onto his side – then he rolls onto his face and attempts to work the cuffs around his backside.

'Now, are you sure you don't need to see a doctor?' Nerys asks.

'I'm sure,' sniffs Kelly.

'He didn't hurt you in any way, did he?'

'No. I just wanna go home.'

'Okay, honey, look, here's the car now.'

A Vauxhall Nova approaches, headlights illuminating the rain.

'Pippa will take you home.'

The car pulls up and policewoman Pippa steps out. She advances behind an understanding smile.

'Kelly, this is Pippa – she's going to take you home now.'

'Hi, sweetie,' smiles Pippa. 'You ready to go?'

Kelly's eyes swing back to Nerys.

'Go on, it's fine; Pippa will look after you.'

'Come on, angel,' encourages Pippa.

With Kelly safely secured on the back seat, Pippa is soon executing a three-point turn and driving for the exit.

Nerys waves goodbye even though Kelly isn't looking.

And here's Billy, back with what's left of a roll of POLICE LINE – DO NOT CROSS tape.

'One caravan successfully cordoned off,' reports the soaking wet constable.

'And you sealed the door?' checks Nerys.

'Oh, shit.'

'Jesus,' sighs the sergeant.

'Sorry – I'll uh, just go and do it.'

225

☆ ★ ☆

When Billy finally joins Nerys in the police car, the sergeant has a question: 'Off the record, Constable,' – Nerys swivels her head to face her colleague – 'how did he get that lump on his head?'

Billy turns and studies the prisoner in the back.

The constable shrugs.

'Must have done it himself, getting in the car.'

'You're supposed to—'

'It's okay,' Liam interrupts. 'After what I've done it's the least I deserve.'

'A little late for that now, mister,' sneers Billy. 'Kidnapping's a serious offence, you know.'

Liam's eyes meet Nerys' via the rear-view mirror.

'He really doesn't have a clue, does he?'

Nerys can't help but smile to herself.

'What's he talking about?' gruffs Billy.

'Will you tell him or can I?'

'Go ahead.'

'Okay, but first I wanna ask you a question.'

'Shoot,' sniffs Billy.

Liam raises his cuffed hands before him, points a finger at his window and asks:

'Did you lock this door?'

The police officers' faces react in the way you might expect at finding their prisoner is no longer cuffed behind his back. Thank goodness for the separation grill.

Meanwhile, Liam has tried the handle and discovered the door actually opens.

'Billy!' shrieks Nerys.

'What?! I thought these had auto-locks; no-one's ever—'

'Never mind that, get after him!'

So, Liam's running through the rain, feet slipping, but making progress in putting space between himself and the police car. He jinks right and heads between caravans.

Nerys and Billy, already out, pursue at speed, police boots squishing and splashing through muddy puddles.

As Liam throws a swerve to the left, around the back of a caravan, Mrs Beal appears from nowhere.

'Stay back, Mrs Beal!' bellows Nerys raising her gun.

If Mrs Beal hears the command she pays it no heed, for she is soon flying at the escaping prisoner and bringing him to the ground by way of a spectacular rugby tackle.

226

As soon as Liam hits the mud, though, he is already pushing off the old woman with his cuffed hands and scrambling back to his feet, eyes fixing to Finger Hill.

'Halt or I will shoot!' warns a crouched Nerys quickly on scene.

'Stay down, Mrs Beal!' orders Billy as he stalks the target, moving closer, the Taser aimed directly over the old woman's prostrate body.

'Final warning!' yells Nerys.

But Liam is not for halting. Swiftly up, he ducks behind the caravan, tacks yet another turn before Nerys or Billy can get him cleanly in their sights, and then he's back on the trailer park's main thoroughfare, running for the hill as fast as his legs will carry him. He's fit, fast and strong, and even with all this mud, he's soon leaving them behind.

But here's the police officers scrambling into view.

'Last chance, I mean it!' screams Nerys from a distance.

Bollocks, thinks Liam. He knows a British cop wouldn't shoot someone in the back; it wouldn't be sporting. No, if he can just reach the trailer park boundary without being body-slammed by another surprise pensioner or going arse over tit in all this mud, he should be fine. They won't catch him on foot, their patrol car can't follow up a hill, and he seriously doubts Powys County has a helicopter they can call for assistance anytime soon. Yes, he will run up this fast-looming hill, slip into the trees at the top and disappear into the night. It just needs one small hop over this rapidly approaching small wall and—

The percussive bang reaches Liam's ears a split-second after his jawbone, tongue and all his teeth have flown out in front of his face. He is still alive when he collapses into the mud just inside the perimeter of Tall Trees Trailer Park. Even has the wherewithal to know he's been shot in the back of the head.

Last warning? The bitch wasn't kidding.

The Head Honcho shot in the head; it was kind of ironic now he thought about it. He laughs, mostly from the throat, which is understandable given what's missing. As his blood puddles in the mud, he once again imagines Joel, now reunited with his head, sitting atop the low boundary wall.

I told you, you'd fuck it up.

'Oh, shut up,' Liam attempts to counter; though it comes out nothing more than a couple of wet grunts.

Still . . . ninety-nine, eh?

'Yeah, not bad,' agrees Liam, the words unrecognisable as he coughs up blood. 'By the way: Sorry I messed up.'

That's okay, bruv, I forgive you, smiles Joel. *It's not your fault you're an idiot.* And the image fades away, but Liam isn't quite dead – almost but not quite – he just has enough time to feel twelve-hundred volts shoot through his twitching body, before he finally kicks the bucket.

'Holy crap, what are you doing?' rasps Nerys.

'I've seen it in movies,' retorts Billy. 'Sometimes they play dead and when you get close –'

'I shot him.'

'Might just be wounded, faking, waiting for us to—'

'I shot him in the back of the head, Billy. Look, that's most of his face on the wall.'

The PC nods. 'I should probably stop Tasering now.'

'You think?' Nerys keys her radio. 'Dispatch, are you there?'

Billy pulls the prongs from the dead guy's back.

'Dammit, Bevan, if you're on another smoke break.'

'He might be on the bog.'

'Yeah, well, he better be back on the desk pronto. We need to get chummy here bagged and removed, and the dicks and SOCOs called in for the crime scene.'

'Wait, there won't be an internal investigation about, y'know, what happened here, will there?' checks Billy reattaching the Taser to his vest.

'Hardly,' scoffs Nerys. 'Who'd doubt this psycho didn't pose an immediate threat to life; the public's *and* ours.'

'Exactly,' agrees Billy, a little relieved.

Nerys turns to her constable.

'You do know who we've just killed, don't you?'

'You mean *you* killed.'

'Okay, *I* killed.'

'No, who?'

'The Head Honcho.'

'Yeah, right; and how would you know that?'

'The clues,' replies Nerys. 'The Mancunian accent – the skull – the cardboard –'

'The cardboard?' echoes Billy.

'For the signs.'

'Pfft, that could be a coincidence. And the girl: that's strange, isn't it? The Honcho's never killed a kid before.'

'And he didn't get to kill this one, thankfully.'

'And what's with the skull? It's normally *heads*.'

'True. I'm not sure what the deal with that is. Not yet.'

'Probably just another weirdo copycat. Not the real Honcho at all.'

'Oh, I'm pretty sure I'll be proved right, Billy boy; once the dicks have been in and checked everything. Besides, we've got the Honcho's DNA on file, remember.'

'Yeah, then we'll really know – one way or the other.'

'Yes, we will,' smiles Nerys. 'And once they've confirmed it *is* the Head Honcho – guess who brought him down? With her first ever live firing.'

Billy appears nettled. 'I Tasered him,' he grumbles.

'Yep, but the varmint was already down, pardner,' drawls Nerys in a Wild West cowboy accent.

The 'sheriff' shapes her hand into a gun, blows on it then spins and holsters it.

'Brung him down with a single shot,' she intones.

'But we get equal credit, right?' asks Billy.

'Dream on, Deputy.'

CHAPTER 19

Setting the Stage

Joe's been updating Trevor on the latest competition news for the past twenty minutes.

'And they've decided on *Lexington* rules,' he tells him. 'Just four words – no subs.'

Trevor, hooked up by tubes and wires to machines, monitors and drips, makes no reply; he's as quiet as his hospital room.

'When will he be conscious again?' Joe asks the nurse who pops in to check on the patient.

The nurse gestures a polite *Impossible to say*, offers a sympathetic smile then scribbles a note on a clipboard hanging on the end of Trevor's bed.

'Will you let me know if there's any change?' asks Joe.

'Sure, we'll keep you posted,' promises the nurse before disappearing into the hospital corridor.

Don's morning had got off to an unconventional start. Yes, he'd woken up on the ground next to his Land Rover before (with only the slightest memory of the previous night – akin to a weird dream he could barely recall) but coming to beside a length of noosed rope with a neck that burns like a ring of fire – that was something new.

And yet, despite the intense burning around his neck and pain in both legs, he'd felt strangely positive, somehow lifted, almost overwhelmingly so. And what had happened to his low spirits and dolefulness? They'd mysteriously disappeared; he didn't know how – but they had.

He's still feeling oddly confident now as he cheerfully drives the battered Land Rover up the bumpy rutted entrance to the farm and parks beside the barn.

And after jumping out, the driver door actually closes properly this time. So surprised is Don by this that he rounds the vehicle, opens the passenger door, and after Jed has climbed down, shuts that door; no attempts, no banging, it closes easily – first time.

From inside the barn Don hears whistling: an unmistakable tune only his wife ever whistles.

After he's flung the telescope and rusty scythe into the weed-infested junk pile beside the pig-sty, the farmer runs a finger around the collar of his overalls, stretches his hot neck then saunters into the barn.

Carol, seventy-two, has been a land-girl all her life, and it shows; she's stacking bales of hay that would trouble a non-farming type half her age, her broad shoulders, stout arms and bull thighs operating in tandem to make light work of the task.

Unseen by Carol, Don approaches quietly and playfully grabs his wife from behind. Shrieking as they fall into the hay, she smacks him in a jovial fashion and the pair are soon laughing and exchanging good-natured shoves.

'My goodness, Don Jenkins,' laughs Carol. 'Where have you been all this time?'

They push and pull, her tittering at the silliness of it all, Don kissing and squeezing her like he used to back in the day; until a few years ago – probably around the time of his 'retirement' when he slipped into his seventies.

But now she pushes him back abruptly and tugs open the collar of his overalls.

'What's this?' she grills.

Don gently rubs his neck.

'Don't worry about that, dear,' he soothes earnestly.

The farmer closes his collar, a sheepish look on his face.

'I've been a bit stupid, but I'm alright now.'

Carol studies him for a beat – deep eye-to-eye contact – two souls that know each other inside out; she sees that he means it, and then feels something prodding her leg.

'So you are, you cheeky scamp,' she laughs eyeing the bulge in his overalls.

'Come here, you,' slobbers the farmer impishly. He grabs Carol and lurches, an uncaged tongue aimed at her mouth.

'Down, boy, down!' she quips playfully, turning her face away. 'I think I preferred you depressed, you horny old goat. At least you left me alone.'

'You love it!' teases Don. He tickles her vigorously and she falls into fits of giggles.

Outside, Jed is being stalked by the other farm dogs – the ones that have to work for their grub – but a single wholehearted growl from the collie and they back off, leaving him alone to happily walk in circles chasing his tail; if one can call it 'chasing' at that speed – pedestrian. Not that it matters to Jed; he seems to have not a care in the world, as the other dogs look on, stupefied and suspicious.

Paul drops a heavy toolbox at his feet – it clunks loudly as it hits the grass – and he stares at the old, rickety, leaning shed. Wilf's Workshop looks about ready to collapse.

Creaking open the shaky door, Paul steps inside. And here he discovers a *family* shrine. Not just Wilf's photo, possessions and Storytell trophies but a picture of Paul, all his diving medals and swimming cups.

Paul smiles to himself and scans the dim interior: the *Trees of the UK* poster and furry yeti suit hung on the wall; a stack of Wilf's vintage paperbacks on the workbench, now covered with his travelling rug; and the snowman album, open to the page with Mr Frosty and a *new photo*, the one taken by Mrs Beal: Joe and Mr Wonky.

Visibly moved, Paul touches the photo. What had he been doing hiding in the car just to protect his hair? Now he thought about it, he couldn't believe he'd acted in such a pathetic manner. He'd be throwing out all his gels and sprays and putties – along with his pastes and gums and pomades – as well as the clays and foams and oils and balms – and by 'throwing out' he meant using them until they were empty and then not replacing them.

'Sorry, kids, but you'll just have to find something else to rib me about,' he remarks playfully. 'Bet Sally will be disappointed, though. I know she likes me to look good.'

'Yeah, right.' As if on cue, Sally slips inside with Emily in her arms. 'Talking to yourself again?' she quips.

Paul tickles her softly under the chin – the baby, not Sally – and when she gurgles – again, the baby, not Sally – he kisses her lightly on the forehead.

Paul looks into his wife's eyes and smiles.

'You soft bastard,' she jests gently.

'Not in front of the baby, please,' winks Paul.

He laughs and Sally shakes her head but they seem closer now.

'Aw look, he's pinned up your Trees poster,' smiles Sally.

'Yep,' nods Paul. 'I'm afraid it's all going to have come down, though,' he sighs.

'Oh, Paul,' replies Sally tenderly, 'I hope you know what you're doing.'

Joe rides into school on the Raleigh Chopper, steady but a little self-conscious.

'Nice ride, Joe,' enthuses Katie as Joe stows the bike in the bike-shed.

'Yeah?'

'*Yeah.*'

'Thanks,' he smiles; a pinch of pride, albeit downbeat.

'You're welcome,' replies Katie. 'So, how's he doing?'

'Oh, he's . . . the same.'

Katie nods and squeezes his shoulder.

Another girl appears: Nigela, a fellow finalist now that Lily has dropped out on account of a sudden bout of really vicious stomach cramps, which had absolutely nothing to do with the onset of stage-fright. Neither was it to do with having a bad hair day or not being able to find anything to wear, as some of her so-called friends had claimed.

'Today's the day, eh, Joe?' intones Nigela.

'Yep.'

Nigela racks her bike. 'You heard what's happening?'

'Yeah, no subs,' sighs Joe.

'No, I mean about the television.'

'Television?'

Katie points to a Newyddion Teledu Cymru (Television News Wales) van parked beside the school hall. A small team, one female and two males, are setting up, lifting equipment from the side of the van: camera, microphone, lights, that kind of thing.

'They're streaming us live on Twitch and YouTube,' claps Nigela eagerly. 'And they're putting us on ITV Wales; again in *real-time*. We're probably going to be seen by tens of thousands of people! Exciting, huh?'

Joe doesn't look so sure.

'*Hundreds* of thousands if the Internet's got anything to do with it,' offers Katie.

Joe throws her a look.

'Just saying,' responds Katie.

'*Millions* if something weird or funny happens and it goes viral,' adds Clifford dismounting his bike. 'I don't know about you guys but I'm shitting myself.'

Joe peers in through the school hall's main doors.

The stage is being set for the competition: helpers putting chairs in place; the camera crew moving cables and lights; television presenter Gail Thursday checking sound:

'One-two, one-two,' tests Gail. 'We're here today for the final of this year's Llanidloes High School Storytell. How's that for level, Andy?'

Meanwhile, in another part of the school, two boys have sneaked into Mr Schneider's classroom:

Owen is deftly marking the top edge of a word card with a minuscule ink spot on the top edge (left-hand side). Gary checks the box, clearly searching for other particular words.

'That's *three* for the semi,' cackles Owen.

As he slides the marked card back into the box, Melvin, passing in the corridor, spies his mates and quickly enters.

'What are you two up to?' he wants to know.

'Shut the door!' barks Gary.

Melvin complies and approaches.

'Come on, let me in on it.'

'Let's just say,' grins Owen, 'my story's already sorted – I'm just making sure some key words come up. Mwhahaha.'

'Mwhahaha,' parrots Gary.

'You've . . . already got your story?' frowns Melvin.

'From the library,' brags Gary.

'As per usual.'

'Wait . . . you mean . . . you cheat?'

'Boom!' Gary has found a word he's happy with.

He shows the card to Owen.

The word is BALLET.

'Yeah, perfect,' sings Owen. 'That's *all four* for the final.'

Gary hands the card to Owen who carefully marks it microscopically with his pen, this time on the right-hand side top edge, as Melvin looks on with a furrowed brow.

Joe appears apprehensive as he stares at all the empty seats set up for the audience; even more so when a huge LLANIDLOES HIGH SCHOOL ANNUAL STORYTELL COMPETITION banner rises over the stage. The memories of last year's fiasco fill the hall: the mocking laughter, the hoots of derision, the walk of shame—

Joe snaps back to reality when Mr Schneider interrupts:

'Hello, Joe. All set?'

'I guess,' replies Joe hesitantly.

'And you're okay with the rule changes?'

'Sure, Lexington, why not; only four words and no subs – what could possibly go wrong?'

'No, not that; I'm talking about the time limit change.'

Joe looks shocked.

'Sorry, Joe, I thought I'd told everyone. Ja, thinking time's been reduced to fifteen seconds.'

'Fifteen!'

'Uh-huh. The TV guys thought it would make things snappier. The same reason they wanted Lexington.'

'But *fifteen*? That doesn't seem like any time at all.'

'I'm sure you'll be fine.'

Mr Schneider turns away and addresses a group of kids hovering near the stage: 'Could some of you collect the card box und easel from my room, please?'

When only Hugh offers to help, the teacher claps his hands energetically. 'Come on, people. Not long to go now.'

After marking another card, Owen slips it back into the word box. As he does, a boy with a haughty air and the nostrils to go with it enters the room. He stops in the doorway and takes half a step back when Gary barks: 'Who are you?'

'Hugh,' states Hugh a little hesitantly. Then, composing himself, he asks: 'What are you lot doing?'

'Getting the cards; what does it look like?'

'But Mr Schneider asked me to get them, personally.'

'*And?*'

'And he said we need them on stage now.'

'So, take them then.'

Owen and Gary move toward Hugh, push him aside and exit.

After a short beat and a shake of the head, Melvin also heads for the door, leaving Hugh with the tricky task of transporting both word box and easel singlehandedly.

Joe has withdrawn to the relative safety of a cubicle in the boys' toilets. Sitting on the cistern, feet on the seat, he stares at the back of the door. Joe may have sought sanctuary in a small, closed space, but the personal insults are not helping.

At the top of the door some wag has scrawled:

JOE EVANS SUCKS COCKS

Horrible to see a blatant lie about oneself written down – especially in caps – but Joe laughs it off as best he can.

Under this defacement, another wit's hand has written, in a different pen: FOR FREE!

The graffiti continues:

FOR FUN TIMES CALL JOE NOW ON – and here Joe is disturbed to see his *actual* mobile number displayed for the whole world to see; well, the school, anyway – the male half.

After his number, yet another hand has scribbled:

DRIFTERS AND WASHED-UP OLD ACTORS A FORTY

'That's *forté*, you idiot,' sniffs Joe.

On the wall someone has scratched:

JOE EVANS SLEEPS WITH HOBOS

'*Hobos*,' scoffs Joe. 'Same as *drifters*, really. And who says *hobos*? – Probably that snotty American kid with the entitlement issues. Next.'

JOE EVANS PICKS HIS NOSE.

'Bit random; who doesn't? Nice to see a full stop, though; good punctuation costs nothing.'

I ♥ JOE EVANS – SIGNED KATIE GRIFFIN
'Fake news but at least it's upbeat.'
And they keep coming . . .
LUCY EVANS IS A RUG MUNCHER
'Pretty sure that's not true but even if it is.'
REALLY, JOE – SNOWMEN AT YOUR AGE? . . . WILF –
WHAT KIND OF A NAME IS THAT! . . . JOE'S DAD COULDN'T
GET WOOD IF IT FELL ON HIM.
What is this, the anti-Evans cubicle? Joe wonders. *Or are* all
the stalls like this!
CHOKE-ARTIST!!!
'Might not be me.'
OOH, I'M JOE AND I'VE READ THE DICTIONARY – CHECK
ME OUT
'I've never said Ooh *or* Check me out.'
THIS JUST IN: JOE FINGER-BLASTED MRS BEAL!
'Oh that's just wrong on so many levels.' Inevitably, with each
dig, Joe grows a little more exasperated, until finally:
JOE EVANS WEARS HIS SISTERS KNICKERS.
'What?!' barks Joe.
Even without it's glaringly absent apostrophe Joe is visibly
shaken by this final, damnable lie.
'It was one time,' he fumes. 'And only for a laugh!'
Joe growls and rocks; offended, outraged, resentful – and
though uninvited, Mr Schneider appears as a spiteful wraith:
'Fifteen seconds, fifteen seconds only,' he taunts before laughing
like the proverbial hyena.
The teacher is quickly followed by Owen mugging a scornful
grin. 'No subs, none at all?' he scoffs. 'Piece of piss for me but I
don't know about choke-artist Joe.'
And here comes Gregor Chikatilo, Russian PE teacher and
part-time sadist, joining in the imagined persecution: 'Millions
vatching,' he sneers in a heavy accent. 'Let's hope you don't lose
your knickers.' He too laughs hysterically.
The cruel dig registers and Joe's mind jumps back to an
embarrassing moment suffered during an afternoon diving
session in Llanidloes Sports Centre's swimming pool.
(The centre is on school grounds. In agreement with the local
council, the school has free access to the pool for all kinds of
water-based activities: swimming, diving, kayak lessons, etc.)
Joe climbs out of the deep end, the dark blue water still
rippling from his best ever dive. He nailed it for once. Pure luck
perhaps but it still counts. He turns to bow to the sea of faces
lining the pool, many of them classmates, but not a single person,

despite his perfect tuck-pike-and-reversed-half-roll, is clapping; indeed, everyone's laughing – and several are not just laughing, but pointing as well.

And then Joe spots Mr Chikatilo using a pole to fish out . . . from the water . . . yes, his swimming shorts!

Suddenly feeling an airiness about his personage – a kind of overly cool freshness – Joe realises he's naked and cups his tackle, at which point the laughter increases.

'Aw, don't laugh,' hollers Gary. 'The water must be cold!'

'It can't be that cold, surely!' yells Owen.

Joe, his mind now snapping back to the cubicle, covers his eyes as if to block out the memory, only for his senses to pick up on something else unpleasant:

The presence of others beyond the stalls and then the unmistakable sound of boys pissing in urinals – and even before they speak, Joe just *knows* it's the Beastie Boys lined up out there.

'It's genius,' laughs Gary. 'We can't lose.'

'That saddo won't know what's hit him when he hears my *latest* story,' brags Owen.

'But it's not really *your* story, is it?' laments Melvin.

Gary hawks into the trough. 'Oh, shut the fuck up, Melvin, and stop acting like a bitch.'

'Jesus, he's starting to sound like gutless Joe,' mocks Owen. 'Spineless *and* useless.'

'But it's cheating,' grumbles Melvin. 'A story from the library, marked cards—'

'Keep your fucking voice down, you prick!' warns Gary.

'Yeah, shut it, Melvin,' adds Owen. 'What the fuck is wrong with you?'

'I'm just saying,' replies Melvin.

'Yeah, well don't,' snaps Owen. 'Now come on, it's nearly time – let's go fuck shit up.'

Joe, frozen by the revelation of Storytell skulduggery, listens as the Beastie Boys pass the cubicle.

'Hey, snap out of it, Melvin,' cautions Owen. 'And don't even think about squealing.'

'Yeah, snitches get stitches, mate,' threatens Gary.

No sound, barring echoey footsteps, then Melvin asks:

'Are we not washing our hands?'

'Jesus, what's he like?' mocks Owen.

Joe, angry and intense, tightens his fists.

The Ice Cave looms large, protective and welcoming, but Joe musters a steely resolve and refuses to enter.

☆ ★ ☆

The stage is set: in the middle but back a way, Hugh is behind a podium topped with the boxed word cards, next to Katie, also behind a podium, this one bearing the countdown clock; the easel is to the left as we see it; and on the right: four chairs featuring, from left to right:

Joe, Owen, Clifford and Nigela.

Mr Schneider is our host.

'Okay,' he hails into a microphone, 'just a quick recap of the rules: very simple; each contestant will choose four random word cards – no subs.' He pauses for dramatic effect. 'Und after the words have been revealed they will have an energising *fifteen* seconds thinking time.'

Mumbles from the audience. *Energising?*

'Yes, that's right. Not the usual *thirty* but fifteen electrifying seconds in which to *create* und then – after the buzzer sounds – *narrate* a short story which must include *all four words*. Failure to include all four words is an automatic elimination. The merit of each of our opponent's stories will ultimately be decided by you, the audience –'

'Jesus, get on with it!' calls a voice in the crowd.

'See me afterwards, Gary Price,' counters the teacher. 'I know your squawky voice when I hear it. Okay, where was I? Oh yes, so the draw has been made, und in our first semi-final, *Joe Evans* –'

Paul, Sally, Lucy and Max cheer wholeheartedly over the top of a ripple of polite applause that rattles out from the full house.

'Go, Joe!' bellows Max much to Katie's annoyance.

'– Will be battling against . . . *Nigela Lewis*.'

Nigela nods to friendly applause and a standing ovation from Mrs Lewis, a middle-aged version and near doppelganger of her daughter.

'Sadly,' explains Mr Schneider,' Lily Morgan dropped out at the last minute with a poorly tummy.'

'Shame!' yells Owen.

'Probably nerves.' Mr Schneider chuckles. 'Even I've got butterflies und I am only the MC.'

No-one laughs.

'But anyway: our thanks to substitute Nigela for stepping into the breach at the last minute.'

'*Shame*,' Owen explains to Joe, 'because she'd have wiped the floor with you.'

'Trash talk,' notes Joe. 'Good one.'

'Still, at least that means I can piss on you in the final. Assuming you get past Nigela.'

They both regard Nigela on the end. She is a studious looking girl with braided hair, large eyeglasses and an unsightly mole on the tip of her chin.

'Which leaves our second semi-final. Clifford Griffiths –'

More courteous but lightweight applause.

'– who will face . . . Owen Roberts.'

Perhaps clapping fatigue has set in, for the response, though still civil, is audibly fading. Not that Owen cares. He's sure they'll be cheering him champion by the end of proceedings.

'Gonna wipe the floor with you, posh twat,' Owen tells Clifford.

'I'm not posh,' gripes Clifford. 'Hugh's the posh one.'

'Whatever,' Owen retorts.

'Yes, it should be an exciting battle of wits up here,' rejoins Mr Schneider. 'They're all good storytellers so it should be quite the *thrilling* final.'

'Jesus, could he overwork it anymore?' Joe asks Owen.

'Pucker up, buttercup,' he replies, 'you're going down.'

'Okay, let's get this show on the road!' bellows the MC.

Re-energised, the crowd find a second wind of applause, this time laced with whistles and cheers from relatives.

'Alright, here we go! Oh, and for the record, Hugh is in charge of shuffling the cards so as to make sure there's no skulduggery, und Katie here, as ever, will be our resident timekeeper. Thank you, Katie und Hugh.'

One person, Katie's friend Aretha, applauds.

'Talk about an anti-climax,' sighs Joe. 'Build it up and then –'

'Okay, so just to recap—' Feedback blares from the speakers and the teacher is forced to wait a moment. 'Sorry about that,' he continues. 'Ja, so Nigela will play Joe und Clifford will play Owen; the two winners of each semi-final to face off in a win or lose grand final!'

'I can't believe he's still milking it,' mumbles Joe.

'What's up, Joe?' sneers Owen. 'Impatient to be exposed for the useless little shit you are?'

'Und so, without any further ado . . . *LET'S STORYTELL!*'

A smattering of tired applause.

'I call Joe Evans to the stage.'

Joe sighs, stands and shuffles over.

'Have you mixed the cards, Hugh?' asks Mr Schneider.

Hugh presents a thumbs-up.

'Excellent, if you'd like to choose your words, Joe.'

Joe moves to the box.

'Remember: no peeking; blind choices only – und once you pull up a card, it's yours.'

Joe's hands hover over the box for several seconds but sensing an awkward, embarrassed puzzlement from the audience, he abandons this technique in favour of simply pulling out cards indiscriminately.

After picking the fourth he moves to select a fifth.

'No subs, Joe,' reminds Mr Schneider. 'Not this time.'

'What a dickhead,' scoffs Owen to Clifford.

Clifford nods. He's never liked Joe either.

'Okay, now pass your cards to Hugh – that's right, face down – und, Hugh, if you will kindly place the cards on the easel, backs-out of course.'

Hugh positions the cards as requested.

'Und now please step forward und stand on the cross.'

Another shout of encouragement from Max has Mr Schneider back on the mic:

'Please! I must to ask for absolute silence at this juncture. Our contestants must be allowed time to think.'

'On the X please, Joe.'

Front and centre, Joe looks down. 'I am on the X.'

Mr Schneider turns to Katie.

'Fifteen seconds ready on the clock, Katie?'

Katie nods.

'Ready, Joe?'

'As ready as I'll ever—'

'Okay, reveal the cards, Hugh!' intones Mr Schneider emphatically and Hugh quickly turns the cards, resetting them face-out on the easel.

DISFIGUREMENT. FOGGY. BARNACLE. HINGE.

Though clearly visible under a spotlight, Mr Schneider reads them out.

'Pfft, piece of piss,' mutters Owen to Clifford, who frowns – he's not so sure.

'Alles klar?' asks Mr Schneider. 'I mean, alright, Joe?'

Joe nods glumly.

Mr Schneider announces: *'Then start the clock!'*

Katie thumps the timer and the countdown begins:

[00:15] . . . [00:14] . . . [00:13] . . .

Joe stares at the words.

[00:12] . . . [00:11] . . . [00:10] . . .

You could hear the axiomatic pin drop.

[00:09] . . . [00:08] . . . [00:07] . . .

'Oh, you'll need this,' barks Mr Schneider.

And he creeps forward, crouching so as to make himself less of an intrusion.

'Sorry,' whispers the teacher. He passes Joe the microphone and backs off, hands raised apologetically.

[00:06] . . . [00:05] . . . [00:04] . . .

Joe stares at his words and lifts the microphone to his face where it picks up his breathing, amplifies each gruff breath, and transmits them around the hall.

[00:03] . . . [00:02] . . . [00:01] . . .

The timer hits zero.

BZZZZZZZ!

CHAPTER 20

Let's Storytell!

Joe's story had not gone well: some strange nonsense about a disfigured old woman who went to buy a replacement hinge for the door to her fish shop, only to become lost in a fog. And Joe *knew* it was drivel: weak, humourless, rambling tripe. The folks in the audience weren't even sure he'd finished so ambiguously poor was his denouement.

They applauded eventually, after a long, awkward silence. Oh, he *has* finished. But it was a low, pitiful smattering at best, despite his family's best efforts to forcefully raise the volume.

Joe had handed the microphone back to Mr Schneider with a heavy heart, traipsed over the stage under the darkest of clouds, and suffering an overwhelming sensation of actual physical shrinkage under the intense scrutiny of his peers, the entire school population and the no doubt huge number of live YouTube, Twitch and ITV viewers, he'd retaken his seat beside Owen, who could hardly contain his glee.

'Wow, you stunk,' Owen told him.

'Thanks,' replied Joe.

Even staunch supporter Katie had felt moved to ask:

'What's wrong with you? That was awful.'

'Yep.' Joe couldn't disagree. 'Any comments on YouTube?'

'You don't want to know,' warned Katie, offing her mobile.

And now, after selecting her cards and moving to the cross, Nigela has the mic. Her selected words are: FLAG. KITTEN. HOAX. CLASSIC. Much better than the previous words, *his* words, reckons Joe; he believes he could easily make a short story from this sweet little lot. Oh, but look at that! *Nigela has frozen.*

Mrs Lewis looks around, angry with the audience, as if it's somehow *their* fault her daughter is floundering. And the crowd grows yet more uncomfortable and fidgety, their whispers and mumbled observations spreading like bad news or a foul stink throughout the hall.

'Shit, she's choking,' complains Owen.

'Flag, kitten, hoax,' Nigela rambles softly to herself, the microphone by her side. 'Kitten in a flag? A classic hoax? . . .'

'Go on, you can do it,' pushes Clifford under his breath.

'You lucky bastard,' Owen hisses at Joe. 'I don't believe this, you're gonna get a fucking bye.'

Joe can only shrug.

☆ ★ ☆

At twenty seconds after the clock expired Nigela is still to say anything into the microphone beyond: 'Er, Um,' and 'So . . .' – Surely she won't be allowed much longer in which to actually make a proper start. Disqualification looms . . .

Nigela nods nervously but she's not speaking words anymore; not a single one – her only action is to swing her blinking, startled gaze from easel to crowd and back again.

'Yeah, so, there's this kitten,' she finally starts.

'Go on, Nigela!' yells Mrs Lewis. 'You got this, honey!'

But Nigela adds nothing else; it was just another false dawn. And so, after a full fifty seconds of hesitation, wishful beginnings and no real substance, Mr Schneider can put it off no longer and he steps in to save the contestant any further embarrassment.

'Nice try, Nigela, never mind,' soothes the teacher commandeering the microphone. 'Come on, give her some applause, guys – it's not easy up here.'

Blushing pink, Nigela seeks the sanctuary of her chair to a ripple of pity applause.

'Through by default,' rasps Owen at Joe.

'They haven't voted yet,' Joe reminds him.

'What's that you're saying, Hugh?' asks Mr Schneider.

'The vote,' mouths Hugh.

'Oh ja, the vote,' clicks the MC. 'I'm such a dummkopf.'

Mr Schneider beckons Nigela and Joe back to the stage, places himself between them and addresses the audience:

'Okay, ladies first: who thinks *Nigela* did enough to win that round?' And with that, the teacher levitates his free hand over Nigela's head. There's a chorus of cheers from Owen, Gary, Clifford and Mrs Lewis, over a soupcon of sympathy applause from elsewhere. 'Come on, make some noise if you want Nigela to go through to the final,' encourages Mr Schneider.

But there is no extra noise to speak of.

'Alright, alright, und who thinks *Joe* won the first battle?' Mr Schneider's hand hovers above Joe's head.

Though somewhat muted in many sections of the audience, the clapping for Joe is undeniably a touch louder and ever so slightly more enthusiastic than it was for Nigela – this despite a series of boos and jeers from Owen, Gary, Clifford and a greatly agitated Mrs Lewis.

'Okay, it's unanimous,' announces Mr Schneider.

'What?' carps Owen. 'No way!'

'*Joe* goes through to the final,' confirms the teacher.

'Fix! Fix!' yells Clifford as Nigela slopes off the stage.

'But who will he go up against?' asks Mr Schneider impishly.

'*Time for our* second *Battle Royale!*' booms the teacher's voice through the PA system. '*Let's Storytell!*'

The nurse noticed the mad activity on Trevor's monitor just seconds before the patient's eyes blinked open to the brightly lit hospital room.

'Mr de la Touche,' effuses the nurse. 'Welcome back.'

'What day is it?' coughs Trevor. 'What time!' he adds more urgently upon being told.

'Let me fetch the doctor,' soothes the nurse edging away.

'In a minute,' insists Trevor. 'But please, could I trouble you to first turn on the television, Nurse?'

The nurse frowns but locates the remote and brings the television set out of sleep mode.

'Great, thanks.' Trevor clears his throat. 'And pass me the remote?' he smiles.

The nurse hands Trevor the device and the old man's thumb is immediately flipping channels.

Owen retakes his seat to the sound of resounding applause.

'Beat that, dickhead,' he challenges Clifford.

Clifford rises and walks, a tad apprehensively, towards the word box.

Owen's words were: FIRE, ALIEN, WIND, and BAT.

He told a story about a creature named Ziggy, who arrived on Earth in a flying saucer. He brought knowledge that explained how wars could be prevented and how cancer could be cured. He brought this information from Jango, a planet where the natives conversed by means of farts and whistles and tap dancing.

Ziggy landed at night in Arizona. He'd no sooner landed than he saw a house on fire. He rushed into the house and farted and whistled and danced, warning the family inside about the terrible danger they were in. But the head of the house brained Ziggy with a baseball bat and that was that.

Short but sweet.

Owen bowed and there rose a raucous ovation.

Joe thought this story about a misunderstood, dancing messenger sounded familiar but his troubled mind just couldn't place it; his musings on the matter not helped by loud applause and the sickening sight of Owen milking the adulation, smugly peacocking to the left and to the right – and then there was Gary, inviting those around him to stand, as he had done.

245

With 'Beat that, dickhead,' still playing on his mind, Clifford selects his words.

'I'm sure I've heard that story before,' mutters Joe.

Remember, Joe, there are no new stories, not really; only variations of old ones.

Mr Schneider passes Clifford the microphone, Hugh turns the cards and Katie starts the clock.

[00:15] . . . [00:14] . . . [00:12] . . .

Clifford considers his selected words as the precious seconds of thinking time tick away.

CURE. SLAVE. COUNT. ASYLUM.

[00:08] . . . [00:07] . . . [00:06] . . .

'Cure, Slave, Count, Asylum,' he recites.

[00:03] . . . [00:02] . . . [00:01] . . .

Buzzzzzzzzz! The timer's ring makes Clifford jump.

Was that really fifteen seconds?

He raises the microphone to his lips and swallows hard.

'He's choking too,' laughs Owen.

But Clifford isn't choking; he's framing an idea.

'Yeah, so my story,' begins Clifford, 'is about an extremely rare, little known medical condition: Sleep-Skip Syndrome; in which sufferers jump – in time and place – whenever they fall asleep.'

'What the fuck is he talking about?' huffs Owen.

'Wait, you've never heard of Sleep-Skipping?' baits Joe.

Owen shakes his head.

'Seriously? Sometimes known as Dream-Dive Disorder. No? You're kidding me. What about Bed-Bucking?'

'Balls.'

'Sack-Jacking,' ribs Joe. 'Latin name: Tempus Somnum Ferventis. We covered it in Year 2 Science. Still no? Oh, come on it's basic primary school stuff. Don't you ever—?'

'Fuck off,' snorts Owen.

'Alex Fisher,' Clifford continues, 'was one of those poor unfortunates who suffered from this debilitating syndrome. Indeed, Alex had an extremely *severe* case of Sleep Skipping – or *Dream Dancing* as some people refer to it.'

'Yep, that's another name for it,' Joe tells Owen.

'So much so, that Alex didn't just skip a handful of times – most sufferers only skip a few times per lifetime – Alex skipped *every* time he – *or* she – slept. One day he'd be a bellboy at a 1960s hotel, and the next, on waking, she'd be a Victorian harlot. Each 'rebirth' – because that's kind of what a Sleep-Slip is – was someone entirely different, in a whole new location; in a different year – randomly jumping backwards or forwards in time.'

Clever, thinks Joe. *Very clever indeed.*

'Take the time Alex was 'Edith' – a suffragette in 1913. Along with her good friend Emily Davison, she agreed – on May 30th – to throw herself in front of King George's horse at Epsom Racecourse on the following day. But the next morning she woke on the high seas of 1781 as 'Dembe' – an African male, human chattel, on the British slave ship: Zong. Woken rudely too, for he was to be thrown overboard, along with scores of others, in order to preserve water for the crew. You see, the ship had been overloaded with slaves at the expense of proper provisions; and once they hit 'the Doldrums' in mid-Atlantic, a space with little or no wind, they ran into chronic water shortages; disease and malnutrition was rife.'

'You can tell Clifford's studying History, can't you?'

'*Zong?*' frowns Owen.

Joe rolls his eyes. Clearly Owen *never* listens in class.

'The solution: reduce the number of slaves by jettisoning 132 of them – chained wrist to wrist to wrist – into the flat, cold sea.' Clifford shrugs nonchalantly. 'The human cargo was insured, after all. But as Alex-Dembe was dragged on deck he hit his head so hard on a wooden beam that he immediately fell unconscious.'

'He's got them eating out of the palm of his hand,' mutters Joe noting the faces of the audience.

'Bollocks,' hisses Owen in denial.

'He awoke a few days later as William Plunkett-Nugent, the Earl of Carnarvon; quite the step up. And boy did he make the most of it. For as long as he could stay awake, anyway. A lavish party was thrown at Highcastle Manor, his stately home, with expensive food and fine wines; a naked orchestra and erotic dancers – bodies cavorting and gyrating all over the place.'

The MC takes a hesitant step toward Clifford; clearly wondering if he should intervene. Where is Clifford going with his potentially bawdy tale? This is a family audience and Storytell narratives need to be sensitive to that fact.

'So much depravity and pleasure to be had that Earl Fisher, or *Count* Fisher as he might be referred to beyond the United Kingdom, snorted copious quantities of mysterious powders – shipped in from the far East – to fend off sleep.'

'I know the feeling,' sighs Owen. 'Talk about boring.'

'I think it's good,' counters Joe.

'But no-one, male or female, can stay awake for more than a few days,' continues Clifford. 'And eventually the Earl, lying betwixt two shapely courtesans, after a whole week of partying, inevitably succumbed to slumber.'

He pauses, takes a breath.

'So, was that it?' sneers Owen.

'Clearly not,' replies Joe. 'A slumber from which Alex awoke as 'Eliza' – a razor-thin, shaven-headed American female in a 1930s mental asylum: The Clinton Psychiatric Hospital, Pennsylvania; from Count to cuckoo – what a bummer. But here in the lunatic asylum, Alex-Eliza, draped in drab, grey uniform, took the opportunity to discuss her strange condition with the doctors. And why not; what difference would it make? Whether they believed her or not, thought her mad or sane, harmless or harebrained, Alex would be free upon her next awakening.'

'Jesus, it's going on a bit, isn't it; when will it be over?'

'He's about to wrap up,' advises Joe assuredly.

'But after the doctors had listened, heard all of Alex-Eliza's deranged ramblings, they approved her continued confinement, certified the patient as crazy, and set about administering a course of treatment; a course that consisted of dunkings in freezing cold water, electro-convulsive shock therapy and a full-scale lobotomy. And in a way the treatment worked – for after waking from the operation, Alex Fisher found that she was still Eliza, and completely *cured* of the Sleep-Skipping.'

Clifford bows then offers the microphone to Mr Schneider.

'Yo, yo, check it out!' booms the teacher. 'Let's hear it for Clifford! A great little short there,' he crows.

Under the applause Owen has a grievance:

'It says *Cure* not *Cured*.'

Joe rolls his eyes.

'Clifford in da house! That's what I'm talking about.' Mr Schneider pats Clifford on the shoulder. 'Nice one, bro, that was dope; the bomb – a really wunderbar story.'

Owen frowns; such praise sounds dangerously like favouritism to him. Joe frowns as well; reckons the teacher's been watching too much 8 Mile.

'Alright, guys und girls, time to vote!' booms the teacher.

He beckons Owen back to the stage.

Standing between the pair, Mr Schneider again addresses the audience: 'Okay, okay, the boys blew the roof off but who do you think did enough to win the battle? Who do you want in the final? Let's hear it; make some noise! First for Clifford!'

The teacher's hand hovers over Clifford's head.

A lot of noise; a very popular choice it seems.

'Alright, und now who wants to see Owen go through to the final? Who thinks *he* won the battle? Come on, let's hear you!'

Mr Schneider levitates a hand over Owen's head.

A chorus of cheers from Gary and plenty of others; another popular choice – they clearly enjoyed the farting alien story. It's really close. So close that Gary feels compelled to stomp his feet then bang his chair on the floor to give the volume an extra boost.

'Oh, it's neck und neck,' notes Mr Schneider.

Joe agrees; reckons the noise level *is* about the same as it was for Clifford – he just hopes Mr Schneider won't be fooled by the addition of the blaring megaphone Gary's suddenly produced from nowhere. No doubt snuck in inside Melvin's big stupid coat.

'Owen, Owen, Owen!' chants Gary through the megaphone. He elbows Melvin but Melvin refuses to blast the air-horn he's holding close to his side.

'It's very close,' teases Mr Schneider. 'Very close indeed.'

A long, sharp blast of air-horn pierces everyone's ears.

'Mr Smallwood's office right now, Gary!' barks Mr Schneider. 'Und take your toys with you.'

Gary shoves Melvin, though with little effect.

'*You* were supposed to be on the air-horn,' gripes Gary before shuffling off for the headmaster's office.

'But notwithstanding the childish nonsense from Mr Price, it's decided,' confirms the teacher. '*Owen* will play Joe in the final.'

'Of course,' sighs Joe.

Surprisingly, Owen sticks out a charitable hand. But when Clifford moves to shake it, Owen shoots the hand to his face, thumbs his nose, wiggles his fingers and sticks out his tongue.

'That's mature,' mutters Joe.

Clifford, to his credit, congratulates Owen like a grown-up, smiles magnanimously, and then leaves the stage – yelling 'Fix!' over a shoulder as he departs.

'Okay, everybody, time for a short break,' announces the MC. 'Cakes und refreshments are available in the canteen; kindly provided by Talerdigg Bakery of Long Bridge Street. Please meet back here in thirty minutes for the final of –'

The teacher raises the excitement level in his voice:

'– Llani High School *Storytell Final 2013!*'

Trevor is still tapping the television remote: annoying Kids channels, one after another . . . banal quiz programmes . . . a string of blaring music stations . . .

'Didn't have this many channels in my day,' he grumbles. 'Come on, where are you?'

249

'Okay, sorry about that,' advises the nurse returning. 'The doctor will be here shortly; she's just got a bit of an emergency: Mrs Harris has taken a turn for the worse.'

'Found it!' barks Trevor.

'Is it *worse* or *worst*? Anyway, I really don't think the poor dear has long to—'

'That's great,' interrupts Trevor not really listening. 'Now, would you mind passing me my coat?'

'Your coat?' asks the nurse.

'Yes, on the chair. I need something from the pocket.'

'What's up with you?' Katie grills Joe in the corridor.

'What do you mean?'

'*What do I mean?* You've got a face on you like a slapped arse. What's wrong?'

Joe looks around. 'We can't talk here.' He's referring to the number of people milling about.

Katie grabs his hand and drags him into the girls' toilets.

'I can't be in here,' protests Joe.

'Course you can,' insists Katie. And once they are installed in a booth, she asks again: 'Now, what is it? What's up? Your story – it was like you weren't even trying.'

Joe makes a face.

'Come on. Spit it out.'

'It's Owen, okay,' blurts Joe. 'He's cheating.'

'What? How?'

'He's been copying his stories from the library or something.'

'Stories from the library?' echoes Katie. 'But even if he'd read every book in there, how would he—?'

'– Make sure he gets key words?'

Katie nods.

'He's marked the cards.'

'The little shit,' hisses Katie. 'But when? How?'

'I don't know but he has. I overheard them talking just before we went on stage.'

'You know, I thought that alien story sounded familiar.'

'Yeah, me too.'

'In fact, it reminded me of your princess in the well, story.'

Joe gives her a look.

'A little bit,' appeases Katie.

'Remember, there are no new stories, Katie; not really – only variations of old ones.'

'Oh, yeah,' agrees Katie vehemently. 'I'm not saying that *you*—'

'No, no, of course not,' smiles Joe.

'Hmm,' ponders Katie. 'Preselected keywords; marked cards – I can see how it might work.'

'Exactly; and how is anyone supposed to compete with subterfuge like that? It's like knowing the answers to the questions before you take the test.'

'We tell the teachers,' shrugs Katie. 'I'm sure once Mr Schneider and—'

'No, we can't.'

'Why not?'

'Because we can't prove it.'

'But the cards – if they're marked.'

'They'll be too hard to spot. He's too clever for that.'

'Pfft, he's not clever.'

'Okay, no, but he is street-smart.'

'I'm not sure he's that either,' scoffs Katie.

'Seriously, how can I compete? I'm all *improvised freestyling*; but *him* – he's got his story all worked out ahead of time.'

'And it's not even *his* story.'

After a long pause, it's Joe who speaks:

'So, what are we going to do?'

'Not a clue,' sighs Katie. 'If you don't want to snitch on the rat.'

'We can't. If I accuse him and then they can't find the marks I'd just look like a bad loser.'

'Er hello, you haven't lost yet,' Katie reminds him.

'No, but if I get another set of crappy words in the final.'

'They weren't that bad.'

'Oh, thanks.'

'Anyway, it's probably just because you were flustered after hearing what they'd been up to.'

'Yeah, and now I have to go and do it all again,' groans Joe. 'Storytelling isn't easy, y'know.'

'I thought Clifford's sleep-skipping story was excellent.'

'Right, well that's not helping.'

'A bit long-winded but—'

'So,' Joe interrupts. 'Any final advice?'

Katie shrugs, puffs her cheeks and shakes her head.

'Oh, cheers for that, Katie.'

'The only thing you *can* do, I suppose.'

Joe raises an eyebrow. *Which is?*

'Do it for Trevor and Wilf.'

'Good advice, thanks. I'll just go out there and—'

'Yep, win it for them – they'd love that.'

'Right, so no pressure then.'

'And for *you*, of course. You know – if you can.'

'If I can?'

'Well, let's face it: you never were much good at storytelling. Not really. But hey, there must be other things you're good at.'

Joe glares at Katie, who, after a beat, breaks into a smile.

'Oh, I see. This is all part of your Behaviourism course, isn't it? *Reverse Psychology.*'

'No, I've said it before. You're not very good.'

'Well, thanks, Katie.'

'Jeez, it's not the end of the world, Joe. Don't you think you're taking it all a bit too seriously? It's just a silly school competition at the end of the day.'

'I know,' snaps Joe. 'But I want to beat Owen. That little mofo's been getting under my skin for years.'

'Then go out there and destroy him!'

Katie prods Joe in the chest.

'I will – I bloody will.'

Joe fills his lungs as if preparing to dive from high cliffs into breaking waves. Katie squeezes his shoulders. 'You ready?'

Joe nods and growls, playfully, like a big cat. 'Ready,' he replies. 'Joe the lion, made of iron – that's me.'

And he certainly appears ready; prepared, primed – somehow wired for action.

'Good,' nods Katie. 'Now give me your hand.'

'What?'

'Your hand, give it to me.' Katie takes a pen from her shoulder bag and writes on Joe's extended palm.

'Quite long, isn't it?' notes Joe after a while.

'Shush,' chides Katie, and once done, she smiles, closes his hand, turns him around and playfully smacks his bum.

'Now, go get 'em, tiger,' she urges.

'*Lion.*'

'Whatever.'

Joe exits the booth, ignores three startled girls gawking at him in the mirrors behind the sinks, and marches out.

As Joe exits, Katie leans round the door and calls:

'Remember, Joe: Gut that motherfucker!'

The girls regard Katie with wide eyes and dropped jaws.

'Not *literally*, obviously,' Katie tells the girls.

'Do you think he can do it?' asks Aretha, her head appearing from the end stall.

Katie thinks for a moment.

'I think he's about to be destroyed – and humiliated.'

'Who?' asks Aretha. 'Owen or Joe?'

'You figure it out,' replies Katie.

252

CHAPTER 21
The Final: Owen's Story

Trevor's hand, trailing a tube, reaches into a coat pocket and pulls out a small robot.

'What's that, a lucky charm?' asks the nurse.

'No, this is Mr Signal,' smiles Trevor. 'He's more of a go-between; a messenger; see his semaphore flags and Morse code lamp – the flare gun on his belt?'

'Oh yes, very nice.'

'I collect them – robots.'

'I have a growing collection of spam emails,' quips the nurse. 'A few million more and I think I'll have them all.'

Trevor coughs harshly; long and loud.

The nurse grabs a jug of water from the bedside unit and pours. He offers a half-filled glass to Trevor.

'Water doesn't agree with me,' whispers Trevor, his voice throaty. 'Could I trouble you for— sorry; I don't know your name.'

'Nikolai.'

'Could I trouble you for an orange juice, please, Nikolai?'

The nurse checks inside the bedside unit then turns back to Trevor empty-handed.

'I don't have any,' grins the patient.

'No problem,' laughs Nikolai. 'I think we have juice in the nurses' station.'

After the nurse leaves, Trevor sits up, cups the robot in his hands and sets to squeezing.

Joe, his face a mixture of determination, apprehension and uncertainty, is back on stage, watching the audience file back into the hall; many are already in their seats.

'Ready to be destroyed, loser?' challenges Owen.

Joe covertly checks a sweaty hand, opens it like a tiny book, and studies the words of encouragement Katie wrote across his palm. The message reads: RELAX, BREATHE, FOCUS – AND GUT THAT MOTHERFUCKER!

Joe nods to himself and recalls their conversation in the toilets but the message seems to warp before his eyes; as if a heat haze were blurring the ink – and now something totally strange and entirely unexpected happens:

A tiny robot appears in his hand.

Mr Signal.

Joe catches his breath and smiles, and as he realises with absolute certainty that Trevor is okay, a single tear rolls down his cheek. Joe lifts up his eyes, to the balcony at the back of the hall, and stares intently into a TV camera aimed his way, or at least, pointed at the stage.

Joe appears in a television close-up; gazing out from the set as if he were seeing right into Trevor's room.

Trevor had seen Joe's reaction to the robot materialising in his hand; as the smile, albeit a weak one, on Trevor's face will testify.

On the screen, Joe nods in acknowledgement.

Trevor smiles weakly then closes his eyes, tired now. But Nikolai returns with a doctor, a face on her like a sour pudding despite an affected smile.

'So, how are we feeling today, Mr Touche?' drones Dr Cronk.

'He prefers to be called Trevor,' advises the nurse.

'Can you hear me?' asks the doctor.

'Yes,' sighs Trevor softly. He rubs a temple.

'I asked how you feel,' repeats Cronk in a manner consistent with the holy trinity of self-important doctors everywhere: succinctness, detachment and a degree of haughtiness. 'Hmm?'

'The show must go on,' manages Trevor.

'Well, I'm glad you're awake, anyway.' The doctor stoops to shove a thermometer unceremoniously into Trevor's ear.

'Tickles,' smiles Trevor feebly after a few raspy breaths.

'What's that?' replies Dr Cronk. 'Speak up if you can, Mr de la Touche. I can hardly hear you.'

'I said it tickles,' repeats Trevor faintly.

'All the hairs in your ear, I dare say,' smiles the doctor; a smile as cold as a fish. (Trevor's and Nikolai's eyes meet; an unspoken understanding between them.) 'And what's that you've got there?' asks Cronk in a tone one might expect a kindergarten teacher to address a child.

Trevor smiles but doesn't speak.

He unfurls his fist to reveal Mr Signal.

'Got your little robot, have you?' drones the doctor.

The patient's nod is almost imperceptible.

'Keep your head still, please,' sniffs Dr Cronk.

Nikolai mimes strangling his senior from behind which makes Trevor want to laugh. He's too weak to express amusement properly but manages a lopsided grin – from a corner of which, a length of dribble drools onto the neck of his pyjamas.

'Any mention of dementia on the notes?' asks the doctor without lowering her voice. 'Mental illness or anything?'

'Er, no, I don't think so,' replies Nikolai unhooking the notes from the end of Trevor's bed.

The doctor removes the thermometer and checks the read out. 'No recorded diagnosis of neurosis, mania or psychosis?' She leans over the bed and shines a pen-torch in the patient's eyes.

'No, no mention of anything like that, Doctor.'

After straightening up, the doctor again regards the robot gripped in Trevor's hand.

'You like that, don't you?' she asks as if speaking to a baby.

Trevor nods and half-expects Cronk to waggle his cheek.

'Okay, you seem fine for the moment, Mr Touche,' decides Dr Cronk. 'I'll look in on you again later, alright?'

And with that she is gone.

As Mr Schneider thanks all those who have returned for the final, Katie leans over from the countdown timer and slyly scrutinises the tops of the word cards. Hugh, manning the box as if his life depended on it, spots the intrusion.

'Back off,' he warns quietly. '*I'm* Words – you're *Clock*.'

Katie curls a lip at him and resumes her position.

'What have you got in there?' sneers Owen noticing Joe's cupped hand. 'Another one of your toys?'

'Nope,' shrugs Joe. 'I got nothing – just like you.'

'*Funny*,' scowls Owen. 'Just so long as you're not cheating.'

Joe opens his hand to confirm its emptiness. Nothing beyond a few tiny sweat-smudged ink stains.

'See,' he retorts pointedly, 'big fat zero.'

'Cocky to the end, eh, loser?' smirks Owen. 'I guarantee you won't be so cocky in a minute.'

'Okay, everyone's back in the house!' booms the MC as the last few individuals traipse back into the hall. 'Let's get this Storytell party started!' He's almost levitating with anticipation. 'I hope you're ready for the final!'

Joe's eyes roll; Heinrich's taking this far too seriously.

'Now, we gotta do the coin toss – und seeing as Owen is the defending champion, he gets to choose.'

Mrs Kennedy appears from the wings and passes a microphone to Owen. Seems they've finally found a second.

'What you wanna do, Owen?' intones Mr Schneider. 'Is it heads or tails?'

'Heads,' calls Owen and the coin is flipped.

'Heads it is. Okay, Owen, who goes first?'

'I'll go,' showboats Owen rising to his feet. 'Give the choke-artist a bit more thinking time.'

This comment incenses parts of the audience and draws jeers and hisses from Lucy and Max.

'It's okay, it's okay, just a bit of good-humoured Storytell trash talk,' Mr Schneider tells the crowd as Owen swaggers to the word box. 'Come on, give him a hand.'

Polite applause, an over-egged cheer from Gary (who's been allowed to return after a lecture on fair-play from Mr Smallwood), and from the back, a shout of: 'Clifford was robbed! Fix! Fix!'

'No shouting now, Clifford, thank you,' chides the MC.

'Yeah, sit down, loser!' Owen hands his chosen cards to Hugh.

'Alright, here we go,' booms Mr Schneider. 'I don't know what's gonna happen!'

Owen struts centre-stage as Hugh sets the cards on the easel.

'Okay, Owen, fifteen seconds thinking time.'

'I don't really need it but okay.'

'You ready, Katie?'

Katie nods.

'Then, Hugh – turn those cards!'

Hugh turns the cards and the MC announces the words. There's a low mumbling in the audience. What would they do with Bottle, Ashes, Ballet and Gas? Could they come up with something? Anything? In just fifteen seconds?

'Okay, Owen, your time starts . . . NOW!' booms Mr Schneider. 'Katie, hit that clock!'

[00:15] . . . [00:14] . . . [00:13] . . .

Owen pretends to consider his cards, give the words a little thought. BOTTLE. ASHES. BALLET. GAS. And the clock counts down. When it reaches [00:05] Owen winks confidently at Max.

Max isn't impressed; she blows a raspberry and issues two thumbs-down.

'Quiet please,' requests the teacher. 'Let the teller tell.'

BZZZZZZZ! the clock blares and Mr Schneider indicates Owen should start, which he immediately does:

'My story is about a sad, lonely little boy called Mo. One day he bumped into Travis, a creepy old down-and-out alcoholic who claimed to be a poet.'

Katie, quickly realising what Owen's game is, narrows her eyes and shakes her head. She looks to Joe who's nodding along to the story as if to show he isn't fazed.

'More than anything in the world,' continues Owen, 'little Mo wanted to be a ballet dancer. The old man said he could help and invited Mo back to his grubby bedsit on the far side of town.'

'Remarkably similar to your own recent experiences,' whispers Hugh insidiously into Joe's ear.

'Pfft,' retorts Joe trying hard not to appear concerned.

'Hey,' Katie snarls at Hugh, 'back to your station.'

'Well, Mo agreed,' Owen tells the hushed audience. 'And so the old drunk escorted Mo back to his squalid, cramped room, a place full of dust and empty wine bottles.'

Picture a grubby bedsit at night: a dark, cramped, filthy room laid out like a theatre set and weakly lit by streetlight beyond a grimy window. A young boy enters followed by an ageing drunkard. The old wino closes the door with his back and locks it.

'It's very dark in here,' stutters the boy.

The staggering boozer searches a pocket for a match. Once lit, the candle's flickering light investigates stained, damp walls marked with mould under peeling flock wallpaper.

Travis, the wino, bears an uncanny resemblance to Trevor. Mo, the nervy young boy, is a dead-ringer for Joe.

'There,' slurs Travis eyeballing the boy. 'Now we can see what we're looking at,' he slobbers.

Mo scans the bedsit: Victorian in appearance; camp thespian portraits on the walls; cobwebs and signs of unsightly spillage on bare floorboards; a bed with an iron-railing headboard and blood red covers.

'Why don't you dance; show me how good you are,' suggests Travis. 'You'll find a leotard and tights behind the screen.'

Mo hesitates.

'Here, let me light the lamp.'

Travis moves behind the changing screen to a small, thin-legged dressing table, ignites an old oil lamp there with the flame from his candle, and turns up an eerie glow. Returning, he presses against Mo and sets the candle on the mantelpiece of a cold empty fireplace.

Travis licks his crabby lips. 'Go on,' he urges.

As Mo strips down and pulls on the leotard and tights, Travis watches the boy's silhouette cast upon the screen. He grabs a half full brandy bottle from a wonky table and takes a long swig.

'Mo was a proper little show off,' Owen's disembodied voice tells us. 'And so he danced. He danced all around the room; Pirouettes and Jetés, Passés and Arabesques.'

As Mo performs these Pirouettes, Jetés, Passés and Arabesques, a drooling Travis watches with a sly, creepy look upon his face and knocks back more booze.

'But don't feel sorry or concerned for Mo,' Owen's narration continues, 'for Mo wasn't as sweet as he made out. He had ideas to steal the old soak's booze money – what little there was of it.'

Mo dances; prancing around like a tiny Rudolf Nureyev. He spins and jumps, leaps and turns, dances and keeps on dancing until Travis finally shows signs of passing out. Then Mo stops. And once Travis has staggered to the bed, taking the bottle with him, and plonked down his sorry arse, Mo moves to the kitchen; ha! *kitchen* – it's basically a tiny, curtained area with a greasy cooker, sink, draining board and a single drawer. But in this open drawer there's a knife. Mo had spotted it whilst dancing. And now he grabs it. Then he pads over to the bed where Travis has laid back, neck exposed.

'Listen to me, you filthy tosspot,' hisses Mo. 'I'm taking your beer money; all of it. Do you hear me?'

The whole scene is starting to look and sound like a badly acted play but perhaps that's the point.

'That's what you think,' slurs Travis. 'I'm going to have you for my supper – with some baked beans and a nice—'

He holds up the bottle to check the label but it slips from his grasp, rolls off the bed and clunks onto the floorboards.

Mo jumps onto Travis and a struggle ensues as he tries to stab the old man in the throat.

'You little shit!' rasps Travis.

The feverish fight continues and in the melee the knife ends up flying across the room: it knocks over the candle, dousing the flame, and lands on the floor by the hearth of the fireplace. Mo is also now thrown from the bed. He lands on his back by the wall but immediately springs to his feet. After running over and picking up the knife, he turns back towards the bed – and Travis, who is labouring to become vertical.

'Time to die!' yells Mo. '*Time to die!*'

But the old barfly is up and moving, and just in time. They meet in the middle of the room and Mo swings the knife, missing Travis' neck by inches. With the boy slightly off-balance, Travis kicks him in a shin. Mo squeals and hops around.

'You lily-livered swine!' blasts Travis.

Having hopped to the other side of the room, Mo now sprints, screaming like a banshee; he jumps onto the bed, uses it like a trampoline, and lands both feet squarely in Travis' chest. The blow sends the old man flying into the changing screen and dressing table, where his stumbling body knocks the oil lamp onto the floor. Flames immediately shoot up the threadbare curtains and set fire to Travis' trousers.

Jumping up, pants still aflame, Travis grabs Mo and hurls him across the room, where he slams into the ancient, greasy cooker with such an almighty thud that the crusty gas pipe it is connected to cracks in two and now the pipe is hissing out lethal fumes.

Travis, meanwhile, has deliberately fallen onto the bed, and after a desperate battle, he successfully manages to smother his burning trousers with the bedclothes.

In the school hall the audience is captivated; not a soul moving – other than Joe shaking his head.

'And as the room filled with lethal gas,' continues Owen, 'Joe – I mean, Mo – moved back to the fireplace. He picked up the matches and again approached the bed.'

Owen stalks the stage as Mo surely stalked the bedsit.

' "Stay away from me, you little shit," rasped Travis unable to move his burnt, jelly legs.'

Owen's hand reaches down for an invisible prop.

'Mo picked up the bottle from the floor and splashed the remaining brandy all over Travis' chest, groin, arms, legs, and matted hair.'

Owen mimes the splashing of brandy, and amongst the mainly open-mouthed audience, someone actually gasps.

Back in the bedsit, Travis pleads: 'Don't do it.'

But Mo smashes the bottle on the old wino's head and knocks him out cold. Then he takes a match from the matchbox and bends to Travis' brandy-soaked body. In slow motion, he drags the sparking match along the side of the box.

Mo sniffs the air. 'What's that?' he asks no-one in particular.

'Gas,' Owen tells us.

Yes, Mo smells gas; but too late – the match bursts into flame and a bright orange explosion obscures everything.

'Boom!' exclaims Owen's voice-over as Mo is blown through the window accompanied by pieces of flying debris and the sound of breaking glass. 'The massive, violent explosion could be seen for miles,' he narrates.

'And like that,' Owen tells the riveted audience, 'the seedy old alcoholic was gone; never seen again from that day forward. Never found; simply lost with the ashes. And Mo?'

By the simple power of storytelling we are now transported to The Royal Opera House where a young male ballet dancer is performing Swan Lake on stage.

'Many years later, he went on to join the Royal Ballet,' Owen's voice informs us.

The young male dancer is amazing. The audience love him. See how the female dancer rises in steady hands.

'No, not as a dancer,' clarifies the narrator. 'He was taken on as the janitor.'

And now we see Mo, grown into a middle-aged man – a chubby little loser in soiled, caretaker overalls; he's standing on badly bowed legs, leaning on a broom, watching the ballet from the wings. Behind him, a figure in a suit, unmistakably the theatre manager, approaches at speed looking none too happy.

'Mo,' he barks, 'we need more bog-roll in the Gents' khazi.'

The janitor turns unsteadily.

'And we've got another blocked one in the Ladies' – sort it out,' orders the manager. 'Now.'

Mo tips his cap and hobbles away on mangled legs, limping and bobbing as he goes.

'See, he could never dance again,' explains Owen's voice. 'Because of his legs: so badly mangled in the explosion.'

Shuffling and clumping away, Mo looks back to the stage as the dancers take their curtain calls to flowers and rapturous applause.

The school hall audience clap and cheer, Gary leading the way with a piercing fingers-in-mouth whistle. Melvin's not so keen but the crowd are sold; just about every head nodding approvingly in unison.

But Gail, the television reporter, appears troubled. Frowning, she grabs her bag and pulls out a paperback.

As Owen bows, acknowledging the applause with fake humility, Joe looks on, blank, frozen, and frankly, beaten.

'Very good, very good,' booms Mr Schneider.

Owen holds out his microphone as if to do a mic-drop.

'No, no, let me get that.'

Mr Schneider relieves Owen of his microphone.

'Thank you, Owen – quite a disturbing story there. Okay, Joe, you're up.'

'Beat that, little man,' winks Owen to Joe as they pass on stage.

CHAPTER 22
The Final: Joe's Story

'Okay, now let's see what our final contestant can do,' announces Mr Schneider. 'Ja, ja, give him a hand.'

Joe vaguely hears the applause as the MC directs him to the word box where Hugh is randomly reinserting ASHES and GAS.

Although somewhat deflated by Owen's undeniably impressive story, albeit an obvious dig at his and Trevor's relationship (Mo and Travis indeed!) Joe recalls some of the advice he's collected in recent times.

Breathe slowly and keep calm, reminds Wilf.

Yes, relax, agrees Yoda. *Let your mind be at peace.*

And take your time, advises Trevor. *Pace yourself. Don't rush the delivery.*

But most importantly, adds Katie, *gut that mother-fucker!*

And seemingly without thinking about his selection, Joe's hands have already selected four cards. Wait, are these the right four? Has he picked intuitively or poorly? No matter, he would look like a complete dork if he answered 'No' to the question now emanating from the speakers: 'Okay, are you happy with your choice, Joe?'

By way of answering the teacher, Joe hands his cards to Hugh who sets them on the easel.

'Right, so please take your place front and centre.'

Joe walks forward and accepts the secondary microphone offered by Mr Schneider.

'Good luck, Joe,' the teacher asides off-mic. 'Ready, Katie?'

Katie offers a thumbs-up.

'Ready, Joe?'

Joe nods.

'Okay, Hugh, spin those cards! *Let's storytell!*'

Hugh turns the cards, resetting each one on the easel.

Mr Schneider announces the words for those who can't see them clearly: those at the back of the hall, those with poor vision, and those on their phones.

'*Unicorn*,' he booms. '*Forest . . . Yeti . . .* und *Snow.*'

'Lucky mofo,' carps Owen. 'Talk about bloody easy!'

'Quiet please,' demands the MC.

'Okay, Joe, you have fifteen seconds.'

Joe is smiling if he did but know it.

'Und your thinking time – starts now.'

There is absolute hush in the hall.

In the silence, Joe spots his dad filming with his phone. Paul waves and offers Joe the fist of solidarity. Sally puts her hands to her mouth. Lucy and Max hug each other. Up in the balcony, the eye of the camera stares down, and nearby, Gail shows her book to a crew member.

You can do this, advises Wilf's voice from the ether.

Fallen in your favour the cards have, hm? Yoda notes.

Your audience awaits, Joe, prompts Trevor.

'This is it,' reminds Katie in a voice just loud enough for Joe to hear, 'your big chance.'

All faces are locked on Joe.

UNICORN.

FOREST.

YETI.

SNOW.

Then *BZZZZZZ!* The clock shrieks as time expires.

There follows a thick noiselessness.

'He's choking,' observes Owen keenly.

Believe in yourself, encourages Wilf.

Yes, listen to your grandfather, you must, urges Yoda.

It's Showtime! sings Trevor.

Now eviscerate that cocksucker! orders Katie's voice.

'He *is*, he's choking,' snorts Owen.

Joe is quiet, yes – but *choking*? He's nodding along to a silent rhythm as if feeling the story beats.

'Haha – choke artist,' intones Owen gleefully.

'Allow me to set the scene,' begins Joe suddenly moving. 'It was Christmas morning and overnight had seen: heavy snowfall, crisp and white and clean. Lookie, an elderly man – he's leading his young grandson – towards the centre of a large forest where they'll enter – and wade through deep snow on a big adventure—'

'No, no, lose the rap!' cautions Katie from the back.

Joe swivels his head questioningly.

Katie gestures for him to stop. 'It's not a rap battle,' she frowns. 'And you're not Eminem. Just tell the frickin story.'

Mr Schneider signals that Katie should hush now.

There's muttering in the audience.

Owen makes a derisive snort.

Mr Schneider warns him not to.

'Okay, I'm going to start over,' Joe advises.

'Useless!' barks Gary.

'Perfectly within the rules,' Mr Schneider points out.

'Speak from the heart,' encourages Katie in a low voice, a hand on her chest. 'Good luck,' she adds in a whisper.

'Katie, please,' cautions the MC.

She raises hands and retreats behind her podium.

Joe takes a moment to reset, and after pacing the stage, he rediscovers his rhythm and restarts, not in rap, but in earnest: 'Allow me to set the scene for you,' he relates softly. 'It was Christmas morning and overnight had seen a heavy snowfall. Now picture, if you will, an elderly man: he's leading his young grandson through the deep snow towards a large forest. They're on a big adventure.'

He glances at Katie who nods favourably.

'The grandfather,' continues Joe, 'had told the boy he'd found something amazing and wanted to show him.' He sticks out a hand, painting the scene. 'So the pair pushed on through the thick carpet of fresh, crisp snow.'

Far below us, the ground is an ocean of sparkling white powder. Making tracks, a tall figure leads a shorter figure towards a rounded embankment beyond which lies a dense bank of snow-laden trees – the forest's edge.

And now, as we float down, nearer to the only souls around; we can better make out an elderly man in a checked cap and scarf: he's talking incessantly to a young boy. Clearly excited to show him something, the old man gesticulates, as if he's acting out, perhaps, the movements of some huge creature. Whatever he's relaying is obviously captivating the boy; the lad appears not just royally entertained but riveted.

'The morning air was still and quiet; their breath, misty before them,' the narrator tells us: Joe's voice. 'Hardly a sound could be heard, just the cold crunch underfoot, echoing gently against the approaching forest trees.'

But now two crows caw loudly, flap from their snowy perches and fly off over the interlopers' heads.

Raising a hand to his chest, the elderly man stops abruptly. The young boy, still holding his grandfather's hand, looks up and asks: 'Are you alright, Grandpa?'

'I'm fine,' the elderly man assures him.

'Too much Christmas dinner?'

'Probably,' laughs the old timer.

And so, they push on until, almost at the trees, the old man stops and points to the ground. A trail of huge footprints leads into the heart of the forest.

'Yeti?' asks the boy wide-eyed.

'Maybe,' nods the old man. 'Should we go on?'

'Might he be dangerous, Grandpa?'

'No, luckily for us Yetis are known to never attack old men or young boys.'

'That's lucky,' puffs the boy.

'So, we follow?'

Excited, the boy nods and the duo advance. They wade through a last bank of thick snow, break through the tree line and drift deeper into the forest; then they weave between tall pines to the gentle soundtrack of a calling wood pigeon and the unmistakable tap-tap-tap-tap-tap of a distant woodpecker.

The grandfather points out a Barn Owl high in a fir. The boy admires the bird's snowy plumage, intense black, marble eyes, and white heart-shaped face.

'Beautiful,' whispers the boy.

'Indeed.'

Moments later, the boy spots a flame-red fox peeking out hesitantly from behind a snow-covered fallen silver birch. He pulls quietly on his granddad's sleeve but the moment is lost as a hacking cough from the old man cracks the chilly air and the fox simply vanishes. Both the woodpecker and wood pigeon fall silent and now the owl beats a retreat: a silent course navigated effortlessly between branches until the boy loses sight of it.

'Never mind,' puffs the old man, a hankie at his mouth.

'Never mind,' parrots the boy, wide eyes on Granddad.

'The boy didn't know it,' Joe's narration continues, 'but his grandfather was very sick. Far beyond stomach pains, a bad cough and losing his hair. At the grandfather's wish, the boy hadn't been told of the seriousness of his ill health. "Stay in, stay warm," they'd said but the kind old man knew how special this time of year was to his grandson, and he was determined to give him yet another wonderful Christmas, another set of happy memories he would one day be able to share with his own grandchildren.'

'Do you think we'll get more snow, Grandpa?' asks the boy, scooping up a handful. The snow isn't exactly deep between the trees – not like outside – but it's still plentiful.

'Would you *like* more snow?' checks Granddad. 'Yes?' The old man laughs. 'Well, if you want more snow, if you *really* want more snow, what do you have to do?'

'Believe it will snow.'

'*Really*—'

'*Really* believe it will snow.'

'Yes, because if we believe, *truly* believe –'

'Everything is possible.'

'Exactly that,' agrees the boy's granddad. 'Everything *is* possible – and *anything* can happen.'

'Anything *can* happen,' agrees the child.

'Everything is possible and anything can happen,' narrates Joe's voice. 'This was something the old man had told the boy since he was but a babe in arms – a miracle who had survived a birth so premature (twenty-two weeks) that he had been given only a two percent chance of survival; indeed, the family was told it would require something approaching a miracle.'

A sparrowhawk swoops in silently and catches a much smaller bird on the wing; so fast that the intrepid pair hardly catch a glimpse.

'And yet here he was with his beloved grandpa,' continues Joe's disembodied voice, 'the boy had made it. Perhaps all those days and nights the old man had spent at the hospital whispering words of encouragement beside the incubator as the machine kept the infant warm and maintained his breathing had indeed brought about that miracle. The granddad thought so, anyway. He'd never doubted the boy would make it, and perhaps, by whispering softly to his tiny grandson day after day, night after night, he had made the child feel the love, take in the reassurance, sense that belief; maybe even believe it himself. Who knows? But what we do know is that despite the massive odds stacked against him the boy *did* survive. And is it any wonder then, that the two have always been so close?'

'Is it starting to get dark, Grandpa?' asks the boy looking around. 'Will we be okay?'

'Oh, we've plenty of time yet,' smiles the granddad.

The old man appears to be waiting for the boy to notice something he's already seen, and after a few more steps the boy stops and points.

'Look, Grandpa!'

'Oh yes, would you look at that.'

Ahead, in a sunken clearing ringed by small lanterns hanging on branches, there stands a large, furry Yeti – an ape-like creature with thick, pale fur.

Amazed, the boy glances up to his granddad.

Then, unseen, they move forward, crouch behind a thick bramble bush, and watch the Yeti as it comically scratches its back against the bark of a tree.

'See, I told you we'd find him,' whispers the old man.

'Is that definitely him, Grandpa? Is that the abominable snowman? Is that Bigfoot?'

'Sure looks like him to me.'

The boy scratches his head. 'But I though you said they lived in Tibet – and that's far, far away.'

'Maybe he's on holiday.'

'In winter, Grandpa?' frowns the boy.

'Maybe he's like you. Maybe he loves snow, too.'

Again, the boy's brow furrows.

'Don't they have snow in Tibet?'

'Okay, let's stop talking now and move closer,' proposes the old man. 'You'd like a better view, wouldn't you?'

'Can we?' asks the boy excitedly.

'Of course,' smiles the old man. 'Everything is possible and anything can happen,' he reminds the boy. 'Come on.'

And with that the pair move slowly around the thick bramble bush, nearer to the lip of the clearing – only metres from where the Yeti is now singing softly. He sounds much like Chewbacca – who'd have thought it.

'Everything is possible and anything can happen,' repeats the narrator. 'The boy didn't really understand at the time – not fully. He thought his grandfather was talking about magic and wishes, about fantasy stories, hopes and dreams, that kind of thing. And in a way he was. Because what he meant, what he surely meant – as the young boy would learn later – was that if you truly believe in *yourself*, if you can do that, then you can make anything happen.'

Creeping to the very edge of the crater, the boy's eyes light up, because there, in the clearing, is not just the Yeti but a snow queen in an elegant white robe and resplendent headdress. Incidentally, the snow queen bears a striking resemblance to Joe's mum, Sally. And the surprises don't end there, for next to the snow queen, sitting upon a magnificent white unicorn, is a small, winged fairy in a silver mask. Oddly, despite the mask, the fairy is a dead-ringer for Lucy when she was younger. As for the Yeti, he's now gently stroking the neck of the unicorn; a proud creature if ever there was one.

The scene is truly beautiful, a magical fantasy to touch all the senses. The boy's face is a picture, full of wonder and fascination and joy.

And then it starts to snow.

'That kind old man was my grandfather,' Joe tells the hushed school hall audience. 'His name was Wilf. He died last Christmas. And I miss him.'

266

Paul, deeply touched, smiles wistfully. The audience are also moved; everyone listening intently, hanging on every word: Sally, Lucy, Katie, Max, Katie, Hugh, Mr Schneider, *everyone* – everyone that is except Owen and Gary.

Gary makes a loud 'Pfft' noise and Owen yawns theatrically: 'Boring,' he intones. But those nearest to them clearly disagree and scold them with intense glares.

The old man and the boy exit the trees and plod back through the tracks they'd left in the snow on their approach, Joe gesticulating excitedly to Granddad Wilf as he, Joe, continues to relate what he witnessed in the forest.

And as they head away, our view drifts back to the forest clearing, to the Yeti and snow queen, fairy and unicorn.

'And the Yeti,' rejoins Joe's narrator voice, 'that big, soft, gentle, crazy, lovely Yeti . . . that was the boy's dad. *My* dad.'

The Yeti removes its head and it is indeed Paul (in the furry outfit you may recall seeing in Wilf's Workshop). He removes the 'horn' from the white horse, looks to where Joe had been crouched, up on the ledge, close to the bramble bush, and smiles.

'You can take your mask off now, Lucy,' Yeti Paul tells his daughter. 'He's gone.'

'No, I'm keeping it on,' grins little Lucy. 'I love it.'

'Yeah, and I just might start wearing this around the house,' jokes Sally the snow queen.

From his hospital bed, Trevor watches Joe's face slowly fill the TV screen as the camera zooms in.

'His name was Wilf. He died last Christmas. And I miss him.' Joe's watery eyes glisten under the stage lights. 'And that may sound kind of sad,' he continues from the television, 'but you know what else is sad? That young boy never realised the *wonderful* creature, the Yeti, that *special individual*, was his dad. Not then. It was only years later . . .'

'When he grew up – *I* grew up,' clarifies Joe in the school hall, 'and discovered the Yeti suit, which Dad had kept in the shed with all *his* dad's special things. That's when it first started to dawn on me. I knew how sad I'd been, how sad I'd felt losing my grandfather, but I never stopped to think how tough it must have been for my dad, too – losing *his* dad. But I do now.'

Joe looks out to where his family are sitting; they're smiling sadly – Sally is filling up.

'I have lots of fantastic, incredible memories,' sighs Joe wrapping up. 'But I'm not going to waste the opportunity to collect even more.'

A big 'Aw' from the audience and spontaneous applause.

Clearly moved; Paul nods and smiles.

Teary, Sally hugs him.

And Joe, painting a smile upon his face, bows like Trevor surely would. He even throws in a playful curtsey.

Proud, Paul joins in the clapping.

Max blows a kiss and Lucy asks:

'Was that us he added in there?'

'I know!' sniffs Sally, applauding. 'Clever boy.'

'I loved your outfit, Luce,' effuses Max.

'Me too,' smiles Lucy.

She whistles approval and points at Joe who waves.

'What a load of crap!' barks Owen.

'Oh, come on now, Owen,' soothes Mr Schneider. 'Und mind your language please.'

'Mine was way better!'

'Oh yeah?' challenges Joe. He's not having that; he's buzzing now – hopping around the stage as if suddenly filled with adrenaline, perhaps from the ongoing applause and shouts of 'Bravo! Bravo!'

'Get off the stage!' yells Gary. 'What a load of bollocks!'

Beside him, Melvin dabs his eyes with a tissue.

'No – bollocks to *you*, mate!' retorts Joe.

'This is such horse-shit!' fumes Owen.

'Now, now, come on, boys,' appeases Mr Schneider. There has never been a commotion like this before. Not during Storytell. Not since *he* became MC.

'Yo, yo, check this out,' chants Joe into the microphone.

'Jesus, is he trying to rap again?' whines Owen to the teacher. 'Don't make me laugh.'

'Take it off him!' yells Gary. 'Shut him down. Enough already.'

But Joe retains the microphone, keeps on moving and keeps on rapping, his free hand marking the distinct beat he's feeling in his mind.

'For your information, Owen,' raps Joe, 'mine wasn't sourced from someone else's books. Stealing story ideas from a library? They're meant for readers not plot crooks.'

'Sir, is this Storytell or a rap battle? Because if—'

'No, but if this *were* a battle, I'd beat you there too,' insists Joe. 'Coz I know something about you.'

Owen over eggs a frown and shakes his head like this is news to him. *Denial.* 'This is such bullshit!' he complains.

'You're the bullshitter, mate.'

'What did you say?' hisses Owen.

'You heard!' shouts Katie.

Owen jumps up and moves toward Joe. Mr Schneider intervenes and has him sit back down.

'Look, look, hear me out,' intones Joe upstaging.

'Seriously, what the fuck is he doing?' bleats Owen.

'Language!' the teacher warns.

'Why aren't you stopping him?' barks Gary.

But no-one's for stopping Joe – this is clearly going to play out and Owen and Gary are stuck with it – he raps:

'Thought that short about the alien sounded familiar? Oh, yeah, now I remember, it's Kurt Vonnegut Junior!'

'Shut him down!' pleads Owen. 'What the fuck?'

'Okay, dunno about the bedsit story, I'll admit. I doubt it's bona fide but it could be legit. But Ziggy from Jango? Sorry, even if you did change a name; that's still a steal just the same. My supporters, your supporters, this might cause a schism. But passing off a Vonnegut as a Roberts' – that's plagiarism. See, he wants be a hero but he had a big fat zero; poor boy dried up like a drought. But, hey, he found an out: Storytell rules? They're only the school's – go flout.' Joe shrugs dramatically. 'So why not hit 'em with The Dancing Fool by Kilgore Trout?'

'Wicked rhymes!' exclaims Max.

'But back to the bedsit with Travis and Mo? Or wait, should I say Trevor and Joe? Yes, the old man is my friend, I say it proudly; I'll even cheer it loudly. Owen can make his nasty jokes, he's not funny, just a cowardly bully. I do like globe-shakers and snowmen and yeah, I've read the dictionary. If that makes me a loser or saddo then sod it – here, have a raspberry.'

'Oh!' shouts Lucy approvingly.

'And I do have a Yoda backpack made by my sister; so what? I can style it out; hell, I'll use a tongue-twister: It's sleek, sharp, slick, smart and classy. And if you thought that was tricky, how about smart, chic, snazzy, jazzy and sassy? No good at computer games! Yeah, okay, I die every mission. But throw me a word and I'll hit a definition. One word, two words, three words, four; synonyms, antonyms, metonyms – want more?'

'Yeah!' shouts Melvin approvingly.

'No, don't jeer; see, Owen's never actually read a book ever. Not even a bestseller. Forget picture books, I'm talking fiction: novel, novella. Not one paperback but he gives *me* flack, this crackerjack who thinks he's so clever. So think about that before you dis me or Trevor.'

'In your face, Owen!' bellows Katie.

'Oh, and those rumours about yours truly and Katie Pratt: How's this? I kissed her. Guess you musta missed that. And yeah, I did lose my hero last Christmas, I know. I'm still standing here screaming: "Let it snow!" And "who has a name like Wilf?" I'll tell you who: an honest and decent man, Granddad Evans, who was nothing like you!'

The MC finally steps close to Joe and asks for the microphone.

'And yeah, yeah, I'll wrap it up, what the hell. Coz, I really don't care, first place or runner-up, I'm done with "Let's Storytell!" ' Joe holds out a hand and drops the mic.

Mr Schneider leaps forward and catches it.

'Okay, okay, I have no idea what's going on,' he puffs, 'but we still need to take the vote. Come und join us, Owen.'

Owen isn't happy but eventually makes a move to join Mr Schneider, he on one side, Joe on the other. He makes a face at Joe as the teacher addresses the audience:

'So, we have Owen with his bedsit und ballet story on this side, und we have Joe und his Yeti in the forest on this side. First, let's hear it for Owen.'

Mr Schneider holds a hand over Owen's head; totally unnecessary but he seems to like the ritual – and there comes back a goodly amount of applause: it was an excellent story, after all. Funny, dark, just what people like.

'Okay – und now Joe.'

The teacher levitates a hand above Joe's head.

Gary defiantly folds his arms but Joe's classmates and family applaud then increase and sustain it. Owen shakes his head. This is not going how he'd planned.

'Alright, alright,' announces Mr Schneider, 'I think—Wait, what's this?'

TV reporter Gail has interrupted the vote with breaking news. Up the steps and across the stage, she whispers her urgent information into the teacher's ear.

He nods and makes a face that chimes: *Really?*

Gail hands him a paperback and the microphone picks up a snippet of what she has to say, something about an old play; no baked beans in the original but basically the same. Owen appears troubled, crestfallen – that look people have when they know they've been rumbled and everyone's about to learn all about it.

'Well, in that case,' sighs the MC.

As Gail steps back, shaking her head at Owen, the teacher again addresses the audience:

'News just in: it has come to my attention that Owen's story is exactly the same as a play – a little known play, it seems – "*The Boy With The Bowed Legs*".'

And he raises the book as proof. Not that anyone needs proof; they can see it written all over Owen's crimson face.

'A play,' continues the teacher, 'which apparently toured the country many years ago.'

He turns to Gail and she nods.

'With the once famous actor . . . Trevor de la Touche?'

Again Gail confirms.

'And let's not forget *The Dancing Fool* by Kurt Vonnegut's Kilgore Trout,' Joe tells Mr Schneider.

'Well, I haven't checked that one out yet but regardless, this seems proof enough.'

The teacher returns Gail's paperback.

'Shame on you, Owen,' he tells Owen off-mic.

'Yeah, shame on you, Owen,' sneers Joe.

'So, Owen is disqualified,' announces the MC. Over boos and jeers, all aimed at Owen, he adds: 'I'm not sure how he picked his cards to aide und abet this despicable travesty –'

But here's Hugh with a magnifying glass and several of Owen's selected word cards to share his discovery of microscopic marks.

The audience show their increasing disgust and contempt and Gary slinks away as Melvin joins the chorus of catcalls and hisses.

'But it actually made no difference, I think,' Mr Schneider announces, 'because clearly the popular vote of you, our wonderful audience, went – for a moving, heartfelt und totally *original* story – to *Joe Evans*. Well done, Joe!'

The loud applause continues to ring out as Katie runs over with the trophy which, after a kiss on the cheek, she awards to Joe. Cameras flash all over the place and here's the official school events photographer to record the moment for posterity.

Clifford is trying to make himself heard at the side of the hall. Some appeal about him deserving a second chance seeing as he lost out to the cheat in the *semi-final*!

Had Joe heard Clifford he might have said:

'Yeah, let Clifford have it; his story was probably the best anyway. Besides, I'm not really interested in trophies and praise – not anymore. I just like to tell stories because they're fun. I realise that now.'

But even if Joe had heard Clifford, and he *had* said that, no-one's interested, for the whole Evans family is now on stage, congratulating Joe wholeheartedly with smiles and excitement all round. And last, but by no means least, Paul, after hanging back a second, now steps up and embraces Joe in a tight, loving, meaningful hug.

'Well played, Joe,' Paul tells his son. 'I'm really proud of you. And here's to no more wasted opportunities.'

He sticks out a hand . . .

'Deal?'

Joe shakes hands with his dad then they hug once more.

'And again, well played, son.'

'Thanks,' replies Joe. *I thought Clifford's was easily the best but fine,* he decides. *I'll keep the trophy – sorry, Clifford – but only because it's a happy reminder of this moment and not because I'm enjoying the adulation and applause.*

Yeah right, Joe.

Back in the hospital, Trevor's nurse, Nikolai, returns to discover the television on but his patient missing.

CHAPTER 23
Out With the Old

In the car, on the way back to the house, Joe manages to stop Hamlet from licking his face long enough to look to the top of Finger Hill and catch a fleeting glimpse of the scarecrow, rebuilt by the farmer after the explosion or blast or burst or whatever the hell it had been on the trailer park that day: a total mystery to everyone, except perhaps Trevor and Joe, of course – and neither of them would be telling their story in full anytime soon. Even if they understood all the ins and outs of the events, the bigger picture, the true nature of the incomprehensible and the unearthly workings of the metaphysical – which they assuredly did not – who would believe them?

The glimpsed scarecrow no longer appeared scary; he seemed friendly and more sympathetic, somehow. Joe might well have employed a little alliteration to describe him: affable, approachable – affectionate, even. Perhaps it was his new oversized, brightly-coloured head with large eyes and painted-on grin. (What was that, papier-mâché?) Maybe it was the goofy cap, petrol-green overalls and whimsical rubber boots; lack of a rusty sickle and ripped, red cagoule; or being perpendicular rather than leaning at a spooky, unnatural angle. Or maybe it was just because Joe had grown up a lot lately.

'What are you going to do with your trophy, Joe?' asks Sally filling the kettle in the kitchen.

'Put it in the shed,' smiles Joe as if the answer should have been obvious.

Paul and Sally exchange a look.

'Yeah, I need to speak to you about that,' begins Paul.

Joe turns sharply and stares.

Sally slyly pushes Paul's toolbox under the kitchen table with a foot. Joe hears the scrape and quickly becomes red about the face.

'I had to,' explains Paul. 'It was nearly falling down.'

'No,' barks Joe. 'You didn't!'

'Joe—' starts Sally.

'How could you?' rasps Joe at Paul. 'After all we've said!'

'Sorry, Joe, but I couldn't just leave it as it was.'

'You . . . you . . . cocksucker!'

'Joe!' exclaims Sally.

'Bit strong,' mutters Lucy.

'Joe, let me explain,' tries Paul, but Joe is already out through the back door.

'I thought you were going to move that,' complains Sally. 'What if I'd tripped over it carrying Emily?'

'Sorry, I'd meant to,' replies Paul. 'I'll move it now.'

In the back garden Paul approaches Joe, who's standing near where the old shed used to be, Storytell trophy in hand.

Stopping beside his son, Paul drops the toolbox; it clunks loudly as it hits the grass.

'It was about to collapse,' explains Paul after a moment.

'I know,' sighs Joe.

'You're not mad?'

'No, I love what you've done.'

'Really?'

'Yeah, it looks awesome.'

Hamlet runs over and is picked up by Joe. 'Wilf's *New* Workshop,' he reads stroking the dog's head.

'Yep, I had it altered.'

The old WILF'S WORKSHOP plaque, now polished to a lustrous shine, has a Y-shaped insertion symbol between WILF'S and WORKSHOP with *NEW* etched above it.

'Seemed only right to have a new sign for a new shed.'

'It's amazing. Look, Hamlet.'

'Wait till he sees the inside,' exults Paul.

Paul opens the door to Wilf's new wooden workshop (alpine ski-lodge style). The door opens smoothly, silently, with neither squeak nor shake, and Joe steps inside. Paul smiles to himself then follows.

'It hasn't changed a bit,' observes Joe evenly.

'Exactly,' smiles Paul.

Joe looks around, double checking everything: the *family* shrine of candle-lit photos, possessions and trophies on top of the old trunk; the workbench still covered with Wilf's travelling rug; the snowman album; the furry Yeti suit hanging on the wall beside Paul's old *Trees of the UK* poster. The only thing missing is Joe's Raleigh Chopper bike – that lives in the garage now, for quick and easy access, seeing as he uses it so much.

'Thanks for this, Dad.'

'Well, I hadn't been in here for a while – too long really – but after seeing what you'd done with the place, I thought you and Wilf deserved a rebuild.'

They stand and stare and nudge each other playfully.

'So, are you going to add your trophy to the others?' asks Paul at last.

'Yeah,' nods Joe. And he adds his Storytell trophy to Wilf's Storytell trophies and Paul's diving medals and swimming cups.

Paul puts a fatherly arm around Joe's shoulder.

'Well done, son, I'm proud of you. And I know Grandpa Wilf's proud of you, too.'

Joe smiles to himself and Hamlet licks his face, then Joe swivels his head to look out of the window.

'Think it'll snow this Christmas, Dad?'

'Maybe,' Paul muses.

A silent beat passes.

'I checked the long range weather forecast,' advises Sally from the doorway; the way she's leaning against the door frame suggests she's been there a while. She makes a sad face. 'Forecast says: No – sorry, Joe.'

'Sally,' scolds Paul, squeezing Joe's shoulder.

'What?' Sally replies. 'I was just saying.'

'What was it Grandpa always said?' prompts Paul cheerily.

'If we think about it hard enough,' begins Joe.

'If we think about it hard enough,' Paul takes over, 'we can make anything happen.'

CHAPTER 24

Strangers When We Meet

'Out, out, brief candle!' performs Trevor. 'Life's but a walking shadow, a poor player that struts and frets his hour upon the stage and then is heard no more.'

There's a moment of silence then the small, elderly audience applauds and Trevor takes his bows.

'Bravo!' shouts an old woman. Up on her feet in not much time at all, she dashes towards Trevor, if a woman with a cane can be said to dash. 'Bravo!' she repeats.

'Why, thank you,' smiles Trevor. He seems much improved since last we saw him in his hospital bed, but in truth, not yet *fully* recovered – not quite his old self.

The old woman lurches forward and bear hugs Trevor as the captive audience continues to applaud.

'What a splendid crowd,' he wheezes. 'And appreciative of The Bard to boot. I think I'm going to like it here.'

The old woman, still locked in a backslapping embrace, eyes Trevor with a twinkle in her eye and whispers:

'Oh, it can be an exciting place alright. I'm in Room 6.'

'Room 6, duly noted,' blinks Trevor a tad apprehensive.

'I think you're lovely,' winks the old woman.

'Come on now, Mrs Lavender, let the gentleman breathe,' cautions a carer. 'He's hardly had time to unpack.'

'Room 6,' repeats Mrs Lavender.

'Time for your bath, Enid,' informs a second carer. 'Come on, this way, sweetheart.'

As Mrs Lavender is prised free and escorted away, across the retirement home's lounge, her slippers and cane hardly touching the patterned carpet thanks to the carers' hands locked in under her armpits, Trevor notices, at the back of the dining area, a cleaner: a dumpy, agitated woman with a thatch of straw-coloured hair, firmly telling a young girl, about nine or so, to sit and wait.

The girl slumps onto a chair, plonks her drawing book and elbows on the table and returns to a half-finished sketch of the pot plant in the corner of the room.

'That's Amber,' sighs an old man appearing at Trevor's shoulder. 'Poor thing has to wait while her mum works shifts.'

The cleaner glances at the girl's incomplete drawing, sighs and shakes her head then marches impatiently away, presumably to start dusting or vacuuming or something.

'The kid loves to draw,' explains the old man, 'but it can't be much fun sitting there all day.'

'Why isn't she in school?' asks Trevor.

'Home-schooled,' snorts the man. 'Can you believe it?'

'Well, she's in a home,' quips Trevor. 'So, I suppose it's half right.'

The old man rolls his eyes. 'Polish,' he sighs.

'Is that so?'

The man nods. 'They come over here, taking our jobs—'

'How old are you?' Trevor interrupts, looking the old racist up and down.

'Eighty-eight. Why?'

'No reason,' smiles Trevor. 'You're looking *fantastic* on it. I wouldn't have put you a day over sixty-five.' He was being kind, for in truth the man appeared at least *a hundred and eight*. 'Will you excuse me?'

'Free country,' shrugs the octogenarian. 'At least, it was the last time I checked.' But he's speaking to himself: Trevor is already entering the dining area.

'Hello, Amber.'

Amber frowns suspiciously.

'How do you know my name?'

No accent that Trevor can detect.

'You just look like an Amber,' he smiles. 'May I sit down? I'd like to watch you draw.'

Amber hides the drawing pad. 'I'm not very good.'

'Alright if I have a look?' asks Trevor softly.

Amber shrugs then plonks the pad in front of Trevor.

He leafs through the pages: her drawings are mostly of trees, plants, bees, ladybirds and a few of faces; *old* faces – portrait sketches. They are naturally somewhat childlike and rudimentary but show great promise.

'Is that Mr Cooper?' laughs Trevor.

Amber shrugs.

Trevor tilts his head. 'Why, it most certainly is. You've even captured the hairs growing out of his ears. And nose.'

After browsing through more drawings Trevor decides:

'These are lovely – really nice.'

'Thanks,' sniffs Amber.

Trevor senses that no-one has ever given the girl much encouragement; she appears totally unaware of her budding, natural gift.

'No, I mean it, they're wonderful,' froths Trevor pushing Amber's pad back. 'Oh, my name's Trevor, by the way.'

As Amber returns to quietly drawing the plant he studies her. She has amazing potential if she did but know it.

'Do you enjoy sketching plants?' Trevor asks.

'Yes, but mostly insects. Beetles . . . bugs . . . flies.'

'I have known many illustrators in my time, Amber,' beams Trevor. 'Have you heard of Raymond Briggs; Beatrix Potter – Ernest Howard Shephard? I knew them all,' he boasts. '*Personally*, I mean.'

If Amber is impressed she doesn't let on. Besides, she's busy shading a section of leaf shadow.

'Ernest drew all those marvellous toy and animal characters in *Winnie the Pooh* and *Wind in the Willows*,' continues Trevor imperiously. 'I'm sure you've seen them. And you might not believe this but he once asked me for my notes on Mr Toad's wardrobe – *Me*, Trevor de la Touche. Well, I told him: "Ernest, old chap—" '

'I'm sorry,' smiles Amber. 'Can you please stop talking?' she asks politely. 'I like it quiet when I'm drawing.'

'Absolutely, dear girl,' agrees Trevor. 'Mum's the word.'

A carer appears in the doorway.

'Like me to run a bath for you, Trevor?' she asks.

'My dear, I am a RADA-trained actor and artiste, and as such, more than capable of filling my own tub, thank you. You may not know it but I have performed at Her Majesty's Theatre Haymarket, the Theatre Royal Drury Lane, *and* the Queen's Theatre Shaftsbury Avenue.'

'Oh, we'll have to introduce you to Martin in Room 9,' smiles the carer. 'He thinks he's the king of Scotland.'

CHAPTER 25

Beginning to look a Lot like Christmas

Night-time; a night much like any other – this one happens to be in December.

Paul and Joe are back in the shed, the space illuminated by a handful of flickering candles and a small fir tree laced with fairy lights; the playful illuminations constantly fading in and out on a loop of changing colour. Joe, sitting cross-legged under a crisscross of festive decorations strung across the ceiling, observes his dad as he tries to tell a story.

There are the words on the easel:

SIDESHOW. OWL. FLOOD. SHERIFF.

'So, anyway, the deputy drives the wagon, the horses at a gallop, back towards Windy Creek, with Annie, the bearded lady riding shotgun –'

'Why are you wearing the suit again?' interrupts Joe.

'Because it's warm, okay?' Paul rubs his hands up and down the chest of the Yeti suit. 'Snuggly. May I continue?'

'Fine.'

'But when they get into town, the sheriff is nowhere to be seen, so they head for the saloon –'

'Want me to turn the heater up?'

'No, I'd like you to be quiet,' replies Paul calmly. 'You know what *quiet* means, right?'

Joe shrugs. 'Could be a number of things: *no* sound; *a little* sound; hushed; peaceful; muted; silent – and they're just a few *adjectives*. For *nouns* and *verbs* we could—'

'Let's just go with *silent*,' interrupts Paul with a smile.

'Okay.'

Neither speaks for a moment.

'You do know it's annoying when you do that whole dictionary thesaurus thing, right?' checks Paul.

Joe nods. 'Sorry.'

'Good, so are you listening or what?'

'Go.'

'So, now they're in the Silver Dollar saloon,' continues Paul, 'but guess who they find in there, non-other than—'

'Willy "Sly-Eye" Wyoming?'

Paul widens his eyes and stares.

'Also annoying?' inquires Joe.

'Exactly. Now, who's telling this story, you or me?'

Joe raises a mittened hand of submission.

'Proceed, sir,' quips Joe in his best cowboy accent.

Paul raises an eyebrow.

Joe gestures that he's zipping his mouth.

'Great,' adds Paul sedately. 'Then I'll continue.'

Paul waits to see if Joe has anything else to say.

He doesn't.

'Now, where was I?' frowns Paul.

'Willy "Sly-Eye" Wyoming?'

'That's right,' agrees Paul. 'Thank you.'

'No problem.'

'So, anyway, Sly-Eye Willy says (and here, Paul adopts *his* best Old West accent): *"You lookin' for me, Deputy?"* But the bearded lady, raising her Winchester double-barrel shotgun, steps in front and says, "No, but *I* am." "Who the hell are you?" spits Willy. "What's up, Wyoming, don't you recognise me?" smiles Annie. "No, I surely don't," laughs Willy, "must be the beard!" And all the cowpokes in there are whoopin' and a hollerin' . . . *until Annie pulls the trigger. BANG!* Then silence. Nobody runs, nobody walks; they just stare wide-eyed at Annie and her smoking gun with its second cartridge unspent. One brave ranch-hand stutters, "G-g-g-good shot," but other than that, no-one speaks. Then Annie says, "Now, does anyone else – besides poor dead Willy here – wanna say somethin' amusin' 'bout my Vandyke goatee?" '

Paul pauses – then he grins and spreads his hands.

'Is that the end?' checks Joe.

'Yep,' acknowledges Paul. 'What do you think?'

Joe nods several times before finally saying: 'Good.'

'See,' laughs Paul. 'And you didn't think I could do it, did you? Come on, be honest.'

'Well . . .'

'Now, let's go and grab us some supper, partner,' smiles Paul reprising his cowboy accent. 'I'm starving.'

On leaving the shed, Joe remarks:

'You know you didn't mention the owl, right?'

'Oh, shut up,' teases Paul.

'Just saying.'

'You always have to be right, don't you?' prods Paul playfully.

'Says you!' kids Joe.

The retirement home living-room is also strewn with Christmas decorations, and a large white tree that takes up the whole corner of the day room.

'Good morning, Amber.'

'Morning,' smiles Amber, sketching in the alcove of the room's bay window.

Trevor holds out a small, wrapped gift.

'And Merry Christmas.'

Amber studies the present then glances to where her mum, huffing and puffing, is mopping the floor of the sun lounge.

'I'm not supposed to accept presents from strangers.'

'I think you're safe in here, don't you?' smiles Trevor. 'And besides, we're hardly strangers now.'

'What is it?' asks Amber.

'Open it and see.'

Again Amber looks to her mother who's now complaining to a carer that Mr Wellman should be in pads. This is his second accident in as many days, apparently.

As the carer explains that Mr Wellman *is* in pads but keeps taking them off when no-one's looking, Amber unwraps her gift: a small wooden box; and in that box, a polished teardrop of golden amber.

'Wow!' intones Amber.

'Like it?'

'Are you kidding? Do you know what this is?'

'Well, if I'm not mistaken – and I don't believe I am – what we have here is a glass rock.'

'Not just *glass*.'

'No?'

'No, silly, it's called *amber* – the same as me.'

Playacting surprise, Trevor asks:

'The rock's called Amber?'

'Yep.'

'Huh, you don't say.' Trevor scratches his chin. 'What are the chances?'

Amber holds the fossilised resin up to the window.

'Look, there's a dragonfly inside,' she points out.

'Oh, yes,' nods Trevor. 'But how did he get in there?'

Amber rolls her eyes.

'He must have got stuck in a tree, silly,' she advises. 'Millions of years ago, probably.'

'Fascinating. You obviously know a lot.'

Amber places her dragonfly-in-amber on the coffee table and takes the sketchpad and an orange pencil from her bag.

'I'm going to draw him,' she beams.

'How exciting,' froths Trevor.

☆ ★ ☆

'I don't see why we had to go to church on Christmas morning,' complains Joe to his mother from the backseat of the car. 'We've never done that before.'

'I told you: because I wanted to say a little prayer for Wilf,' explains Sally.

'Oh, yeah,' sighs Joe.

'You didn't mind, did you?'

'No,' replies Joe, his face slumping against the window.

Lucy, riding shotgun, exchanges a look with Sally then turns to face Joe: 'Come on, little bro, try and cheer up. We all miss him you know.'

'It's not that,' retorts Joe. 'Well, it's not *just* that.'

'So what is it, then?' asks Sally. 'It's a lovely sunny day and—'

'Exactly,' Joe interrupts.

'What's wrong with a lovely sunny day?' asks Sally swapping a knowing look with Lucy.

'Beats me,' shrugs Lucy playfully.

Joe, absentmindedly stroking Hamlet, stares outside, at a bright, crisp, sun-filled day.

'Nice church outfit by the way, Lucy,' comments Sally on her daughter's cotton thawb (an ankle-length, long-sleeved kaftan robe tied with a fancy sash).

'Oh thanks. It was either this or the Hussar-style braided jacket and short skirt over black leggings.'

'Well, I think you chose wisely.'

They continue a flat, inane conversation about Lucy's latest fashion projects but we get the sense this is all a playful tease aimed at Joe for some reason.

'It didn't snow,' he mutters at last.

'What's that, Joe?' asks Sally.

'Speak up, bro,' teases Lucy.

'So much for *if you believe*,' mumbles Joe mockingly, 'if you *truly* believe, anything is—'

The car pulls onto the drive and Sally kills the engine.

'Why has he stopped talking, Lucy?' asks Sally, adding as an aside: 'As if I didn't know.'

'I think he's seen something,' replies Lucy.

And Joe *has* seen something: a large white truck parked at the kerb and Paul at the front door shaking the hand of a man in white overalls. Joe watches the man walk past the car and climb into the truck; it has SNOW BUSINESS written in big letters on the side. He jumps out of the car, watches the truck drive away, and then approaches his dad.

'What's that?' Joe asks indicating the large noisy machine beyond the open gate at the side of the house; its motor rattling and rumbling, the long, thick, blue pipe that runs from it, shivering and quivering.

'Follow me,' winks Paul mysteriously.

Paul and Joe follow the blue pipe along the side of the garage and around the corner of the house – where Joe, his dad hanging back, discovers the back garden – all covered in snow. *Completely* covered, and over a foot thick!

'Foam?' asks Joe in a noncommittal tone.

'Better than that,' froths Paul. 'According to the brochure, this is *real* snow, not pretend *foam* snow.'

He reads from a pamphlet produced from a rear pocket:

'With its *ice crystal nucleus*, our machine-generated snow is much denser than natural snow, and as such, this "super snow" will withstand more warm days and rain events before it disappears than boring old non-man-made snow ever would.'

Lucy and Sally appear in the kitchen doorway, smiles upon their faces.

'Did you hear that, Joe?' checks Paul. 'About the snow? It says here that the air-to-water ratio—'

'Paul,' heckles Sally.

'What?'

'He's not interested in the air-to-water ratio.'

And it's true; Joe stopped listening a while back: he's currently running around in the snow being chased by a yapping, bouncing Hamlet. Lucy joins them.

'I thought he liked details,' sniffs Paul pocketing the folded brochure.

'*Air-to-water ratio*,' mocks Sally playfully. 'Get in there!' she urges.

'Right,' laughs Paul, 'who's for a game of—'

And that's when the snowball explodes on Paul's forehead, splattering over his face and into his hair.

'Lucy!' blasts Joe theatrically.

'What?' Lucy protests. 'Don't listen, Dad; that was Joe!'

Paul laughs, wipes the snow from his face and joins in.

A family snowball fight ensues with a highly-amused Sally retreating a little into the kitchen whenever a stray snowball splatters near the doorway.

285

'Excellent,' enthuses Trevor critiquing Amber's dragonfly drawing. 'That's absolutely marvellous.'

It's *not* absolutely marvellous to be fair – but, as was noted before, it *does* show promise.

'Thanks,' responds Amber rather imperiously.

'I think with a little more practice and guidance from your truly,' starts Trevor.

'I'm going to draw you next,' announces Amber.

'You are?'

Amber stands. 'Yes, come on.'

'Like to see some magic first?' asks Trevor.

'Nah.'

'Really?' Trevor frowns. 'Why not?'

Amber folds her arms and makes a face. 'My uncle was a conjurer. I've seen every trick there is.'

'Bet you've never seen magic like this before,' challenges Trevor. 'I'll have you know that I once inadvertently performed one of my mystifying illusions during a performance of The Winter's Tale at the Royal Variety in front of Her Majesty.'

Amber rolls her eyes. 'Is it a card trick?' she sighs.

'No, I'm going to use the dragonfly.'

Amber folds her arms and pouts as Trevor flamboyantly slides the amber stone (resting on the wooden box) from Amber's side of the coffee table to his. Then he leans over the stone, places both hands on it, and raises an eyebrow at Amber.

She tilts a sceptical head. *Go on, then, if you have to* glowers her cynical expression.

Trevor takes a long, deep breath, closes his eyes, concentrates hard, turns slightly pink, lets the breath out through his nose, and then, with a showman's flourish, pulls his hands away, spreading them wide.

'Ta da!'

Amber stares at the box – or rather at the space on the lid, where the stone was until a moment ago.

'Impressed?' asks Trevor.

'Hmm, a little bit,' admits Amber hesitantly.

'Okay, well, that's a good start,' Trevor enthuses. 'And do you accept that it's *not* a trick,' he asks. 'That the amber really *has* vanished?'

'No, silly, you probably palmed it. Now come on, we're going to the sun lounge, the light's better in there.'

And with that, Amber helps Trevor to his feet; hoists him right up – stronger than she looks.

'Are you alright?' asks Amber looking the old man over.

Trevor rubs his temples.

'Have you got a headache?'

'No, no, I'm just a bit dizzy, is all.'

'You probably stood up too quick,' advises Amber. 'I see that happen a lot in here.'

'Think I just had too much ice cream at lunch,' suggests Trevor shakily.

'Wow, you *are* groggy. Come sit down in the sun lounge and I'll get you a glass of water.'

'Oh, that's very kind. Don't suppose you'd want your model passing out on you.'

'Nah, I could still draw you,' decides the artist.

'Yes, I suppose you could,' laughs Trevor trailing Amber somewhat unsteadily in the direction of the conservatory. 'So, tell me: what *could* I do to make you believe in magic again, young lady?' he asks. 'I mean, *truly* believe.'

Amber stops. 'We'll need my sketchpad and pencils,' she reminds Trevor, pointing at the coffee table.

'Pad and pencils, of course,' blinks Trevor heading back.

'I can see this one's going to be a real challenge,' he mutters to himself collecting Amber's stuff.

Then, as Amber exits the lounge with Trevor following behind, the golden stone and its inadvertent passenger, unnoticed by residents and staff, slowly fade back in and reappear on the small wooden box.

EPILOGUE
After All

The Evans family have built a huge faux-snow snowman, the biggest yet: Mr Zenith.

(If you asked Joe about the name, he'd probably vaunt: 'Zenith; Noun,' then mention, at the very least, Apogee, Acme, and Apex.)

The snowman stands looking thoughtful but jolly in the middle of the imitation-snow-covered garden. Trevor's old cigarette-holder, complete with fake spliff made by Sally, is stuck in his line-of-jellybeans smile and he's proudly sporting Wilf's cap and scarf, as all around him, the animated Evans' are enjoying sack loads of energetic Christmas fun: Lucy and Sally are lying on their backs making snow angels, and Paul and Joe dive into the icy whiteness and pretend to swim – everyone laughing as Hamlet bounces around them, ever-circling, yapping in the snow.

'So, that was my story,' the old actor's voice tells us, wrapping up, 'or rather, *Joe's* story. For the main adventure – the one that *really* mattered – was always about Joe; he had the leading role, not I. Yours truly was a mere support actor – *Joe*, the *real* star.'

A noisy, friendly snowball fight plays out now around Mr Zenith, with much kicking of snow at each other and Hamlet running to chase errant snowballs.

'Aw, Joe the lion, made of iron,' reminisces Trevor fondly. 'He'd found peace and fortitude after the loss of his beloved grandfather Wilf; rediscovered and rekindled the love and kinship within the rest of his family. The young man had learned about loyalty, belief and perseverance – and, of course, the nature of a good yarn. Plus, he had his dog, Hamlet, a loyal companion to remember me by; not that I think for a minute Joseph Edward Evans would ever forget the time he met the magnificent Trevor de la Touche.'

And now, as we drift away, climb drone-like, up to where winter clouds drift lazily like so many ghosts, and gaze down upon the Evans' garden, the only snow-laden area, you continue to watch – hopefully, smiling – as Joe, Paul, Hamlet, Sally and Lucy, kick and chase a football around in the ersatz snow.

And here, if this were a film rather than a story in a book, another moving, powerful, Noah piano masterpiece would surely play; and perhaps, after a moment, as the credits rolled, there

289

would be a picture-in-picture insert: a final glimpse of Trevor teaching Amber, his new project; offering her advice, instruction and encouragement as she draws her latest sitter, Mrs Lavender — and then everything fades to black, a blackness upon which someone, we know not who, would almost certainly superimpose the caption:

"Magic is believing in yourself.
If you can do that, you can make anything happen."

- Johann Wolfgang von Goethe.

ADRIAN BALDWIN IS

a Mancunian now living and working in Wales. Back in the Nineties, he wrote for various TV shows/personalities: Hale & Pace, Clive Anderson, Brian Conley, Paul McKenna, Smith & Jones, Rory Bremner (and a few others). Wooo, get him.

Since then, he has written three screenplays, one of which received generous financial backing from the Film Agency for Wales. Then along came the global recession to kick the UK Film industry in the nuts. What a bummer!

Not to be outdone, he turned to novel writing – which had always been his *real* dream – and, in particular, a genre he feels is often overlooked; a genre he has always been a fan of: *Dark Comedy*.

The Snowman and the Scarecrow (another dark comedy for grown-ups) is the author's third novel.

For more information, check out: **adrianbaldwin.info**

The author invites readers to contact him at:

adrian@adrianbaldwin.info
Twitter @AdrianBaldwin
facebook.com/AdrianBaldwinAuthor

Printed in Poland
by Amazon Fulfillment
Poland Sp. z o.o., Wrocław

89738843R00170